# Where's The Line?

## Howard Wayne Kemp, Jr.

This book is a work of fiction. Names, characters, places and incidents either are products of the author's imagination or are used fictitiously. Any resemblance to actual events, locales or persons, living or dead, is entirely coincidental.

# DEDICATION

This is for my Granny, Laomi Clampet. Her unconditional love and support will always dwell in a corner of my heart.

# ACKNOWLEDGMENTS

There are a bunch of people I would like to thank.

First, must be my wife. She has been tolerant during the entire process. Without her loving encouragement and support not only would this book be just a cockamamie idea but the last decade plus might have been a giant waste of life. Thank you, Ann for not permitting me to waste life. It's one of the reasons why I love you.

And this book sat as a pile of unedited papers for nearly six years. Lisa Hall, who has never read the book by the way, was a persistent voice whispering loudly, "Get that damn book done." She was constantly making suggestions trying to motivate my procrastination. Some might have called it nagging but I thank her for being a voice that cared.

I also want to thank everyone I have ever met in my life. I have borrowed a piece of every one of you to create characters and scenes in this book, which are fictional I am compelled to add. I do not intend to give you any credit but I sincerely acknowledge your importance. Nor will I mention any of you by name so that you can live happily without the guilt by association with me.

# 1

Captain Bluebeard's Bar stands across the street on the south side of the campus. It is a popular spot to take a break from the rigors of class, studying, tests, and maturity. Students are liberated at twenty-one and they are anxious to wield their new sword. They stand near the barstools in a herd. Perhaps, the young pirates want to be as close as possible to the source of the grog but most stood there because the spotlight is much stronger at center stage. The college experience has always been about more than the mastery of the three R's.

Having evolved through rites of passage years ago, three professors of Psychology were sitting at a table in the middle of the room having drinks. Jim and Natalie shared a pitcher of beer, while Powers drank white wine. The conversation at the table was about the departmental budget. Powers was listening, or so his body language suggested but his tongue was coiled and eager to change the subject at first glimpse of an opening.

"Alumni donations are down."

Powers nodded as though he were interested. He wasn't. He looked past Natalie's shoulder at his car glimmering in the setting sunlight. The restored Thunderbird convertible devoured a year's salary. Powers dropped weight during the lean diet of that year. His reward has been a thinner body and a "global warming nightmare," according to his colleagues. His eco-friendly colleagues delighted in toting a backpack and peddling to class.

"Why not help the environment and exercise simultaneously?" They said. Powers had seen many of them caressing the sleek fender of his baby blue pride and joy.

"I heard the new Music Studies building would end up costing twice as much as proposed," Jim said.

Powers broke his gaze and traded smiles with Natalie as Jim continued his tirade about the budget. Powers was counseling Natalie's niece, Theresa. As he studied Natalie's face, he thought it remarkable that they looked so much alike. That's where the similarities ended. Natalie's niece was a pleasant and gracious teen with an inferiority complex. Theresa was not attractive, not particularly bright, and not athletic. All might be overcome if Powers could unearth a speck of ambition; he had not. She deserves an inferiority complex, Powers thought.

"Poor recruiting is the reason the football program is not generating enough income," Jim uttered over the lip of his glass.

Powers had vowed to stay out of the counseling business, yet here he was with three patients. He needed the money; Powers lived beyond his means. Everyone knew. More importantly, he needed material for a book. The book was important for two reasons. He could halt the charade of trying to help people and Dean Harrington would stop preaching. "Publish or perish." Powers was sick of the cliché and tired of the admonishment.

So, his friends sent referrals. Rex Latham, Powers first referral, came to Powers asking to be cured of too much sex drive. Rex was in the midst of his seventh affair in six years of marriage. Every time Powers dispelled a myth of infidelity causation, Rex adopted a new one. Rex has no interest in monogamy; he merely wants to tell someone. Rex could not be a book; the library is full of Rexs'.

Arthur Paulson visited on Mondays. Arthur wants to believe the world distrusts him because his intelligence compels him to be blunt and practical. He has never been in a relationship and he has no friends. Arthur finds it hard to talk with people.

"They will only disappoint me," he says.

Arthur's loneliness would be better treated by a dermatologist. Remove the massive mole and clump of hair from his chin and more people would be likely to engage him in conversation.

*Arthur would not make a good term paper, certainly not a book. And timid Theresa will not be a book either.*

Natalie said, "Down. Enrollment is down? That's news to me."

Powers drank his wine, still looking for the change in the conversation.

*I'm expected to produce a book about healing.*

Psychologists are supposed to help people heal.

*Most people do not want to be healed bad enough to be healed.*

That was the credo he developed early in his professional career as a social worker for a State agency. His cases were all domestic issues involving custody of children. Employed for a mere six months, he lost his desire to help. The caseload was heavy and did not allow enough time to help and certainly not to heal. Powers concluded that it did not matter. The people did not want help. The law bound two people together who did not want to be bound to each other. They were not interested in the psychology of the break up or the future feelings that might emerge. They merely wanted to be unbound. His job was to produce paperwork to justify a reasonable arrangement to feed and house the children. The system was just going through the motions; Powers learned to do the same. The calluses of his real world experience have disappeared but the charade of real world healing left a scar.

Movement from across the table caught Powers' eye and snapped his pity party. Natalie and Jim were holding their glasses in the air.

*Toasting? Toasting what?*

Powers held his glass up and waited to hear what they were honoring.

"To budget cuts," said Jim.

"Yes, to fewer conferences and seminars," Natalie chimed and produced a pronounced frown.

"To higher tuitions and larger salaries," Powers added.

They shook their heads in disapproval. They honored his toast despite his ego centered nature. Jim slammed his glass to the table. Powers expected him to wipe his mouth with a sleeve.

Jim used his open hand to clear the foam and asked, "Powers, have you ever met Harm, the owner of this bar?" He said, pointing at the man behind the herd at center stage.

"No," Powers answered, and then asked, "Harm?"

"It's short for Harmon, Harmon Evans. He's an interesting fellow. I know him from high school. He was a hell-of-a ballplayer. He surprised everyone, when he didn't go on to college."

He leaned into the table a little and added, "They wanted him here."

"Didn't have the grades?" Natalie asked.

"His grades were fine. He joined the Marines," Jim said.

"Wanted to prove he was a tough guy?" Powers insinuated.

"Harm was a tough guy and still is. He loved playing basketball but school couldn't hold his interest," Jim said as he glanced at Harmon.

"College is an infinite learning experience. He couldn't find something that interested him?" Natalie said as she turned to get a better look.

"He wanted to work, be his own boss, and make money," Jim responded.

"That's what he told you?" Powers asked. "No one makes money in the service. The newspapers are full of stories about how our soldiers, sailors, and marines are living below the poverty line. You have a PhD in Psychology, Jim. You think maybe he's masking some real issues."

"He became an officer in the Corps, did two tours and saved enough money to buy this bar when he got out. He's doing alright."

"He spends a lot of time here. Is he married?" Natalie asked.

"He's not married and Harm enjoys what he does. He enjoys being here." Jim defended Harmon.

"I suspect he is here because he has to be. That's one less employee he has to pay. He has sacrificed his freedom to be his own boss," Powers offered his off the cuff analysis.

"So, you would rather stay under Harrington's thumb than live Harm's lifestyle?" Jim asked.

Powers gloated, "Oh, absolutely. I have an above average salary and I work about five hours a day and take the whole summer off."

"Harm has no debt and over a half a million dollars invested in a variety of options including coastal property. He's not worrying about recessions or budget cuts," Jim said.

"Really!" Natalie chimed in.

"That's it; I am leaving the analysis game and getting into booze," Powers quipped.

Jim and Natalie laughed and Powers laughed with them as he stole a glance at Harmon Evans, the success story. Powers did not have five hundred dollars in the bank. He hoped his envy was not exposed to the group.

"I'm going to introduce you two," Jim said.

"Me?" Powers asked while pointing to himself. "Why?"

"He wants someone to help a student. He wants to pay for the counseling," Jim said as he poured more beer in Natalie's glass, and then filled his own.

"Introduce him to someone else. I do not want to fill all my spare time in analysis. You do it, or go to our revered leader."

"I can't do it. I know the kid and Harrington doesn't practice. Don't be sarcastic. Can't you take a few minutes to talk to him? It's not a commitment to counsel the kid," Jim said.

Powers straightened his tie and sat little taller and said, "He should go off campus. There are dozens of shrinks in this city."

"He's testing us," Jim said with raised eyebrows.

"Testing us?" Natalie asked, "What does that mean?"

"I suggested some of my friends in private practice. Harmon said, "So, it's true, those who can do and those who can't teach?"

"Every time I hear that I get angry," Powers said.

"Yeah, but it's a hard point to counter," Natalie responded.

"Really?" Powers asked. "What about, if everyone practiced, there would be no one to teach. I would argue that an expert has a gift and they perform tasks naturally. Most of them are utterly incapable of explaining how they accomplish what they do. Furthermore, I like to teach. It is a job. Everyone should have a job. Why am I to be respected less because I like to teach? If everybody did, as he suggests, who would teach?"

Powers paused briefly and leaned further across the table and added, "And I also would assert, that most of his experts have been to class and have learned. Would that not mean that we are expert at teaching?" Powers leaned back and crossed his arms across his chest.

"Those who can teach, do – period. Tell him that."

The three of them sat in silence. Jim's eyes cut away from Powers. Natalie raised her gaze from the beer glass to look at Powers.

"That's a mighty sturdy soap box, Mr. Meade," Jim said.

"You sound a little defensive, Powers. Want to talk about it?" Natalie said and smiled.

Powers looked at her, not wanting to smile but he did. He was being defensive and selfish. He used the levity to ease back into their good graces.

"Of course, I will talk to this kid. I cannot allow him go around with a negative opinion of our department," Powers said as he thrust his chin upward, assuming the noblest of poses. Then he asked, "By the way, who is the student?"

"Eddie Dreyer," Jim said and waited for them to react.

"Isn't he on one of the athletic teams?" Natalie asked.

It resonated like an uncertain guess, not unlike the sheepish responses each of them hear from poorly prepared students every day. Jim breathed an exaggerated sigh of disbelief and looked at Powers, who shrugged ignorantly.

"Basketball? He is the premier guard in our conference. He's an all-star." Jim asked Powers. "Do you not attend any of the games?"

"No," Powers said flatly.

"Don't you read The Observer?" Jim asked.

"Not the back section," Powers responded.

"You are truly an academic elitist," Jim muttered into his glass of beer.

Powers shrugged his shoulders as if to suggest the slur were a compliment he was proud to accept.

Jim continued, "Eddie Dreyer is a very good basketball player."

He spoke in a slow and syncopated style as though he needed to communicate to a foreigner. Jim pretended to shoot a basketball.

"How very clever," Powers responded. "So, I'm supposed to help some jock who only gained admittance on his athletic prowess?"

"Eddie Dreyer scored thirty-three on the ACT. I won't embarrass you by asking your score."

"Ok. We've got it. An All-American boy has some problems and because these problems could spill over onto the basketball court, his friends are concerned because he might start playing poorly." Powers paused to sip wine. "Where's the outrage when an Engineering student has problems."

"Powers, you can be so callous," Natalie said without a smile.

"Engineering students don't fill the seats at the arena," Jim said.

"Then we would have even greater budget cuts," Natalie added.

"Will you two lighten up? This is a bar, for God's sake. I am just trying to have some fun," said Powers.

"I'll have Harm call you but you have to promise to behave," Jim cautioned.

"Callous, I may be," he said looking at Natalie. "And irreverent," said Powers, turning his attention to Jim. "But stupid, I am not. I can look at the size of that man and guarantee you I will not anger him. I will treat his concerns with commensurate respect."

"Fair enough," Jim responded.

Powers smiled and held his glass of wine as if he was toasting the agreement. His honest emotions were masked. Powers was not ready to voice his doubts about the actual healing process to his friends. He was not helping Rex or Arthur, and it was becoming apparent, his guidance was unlikely to change Theresa's life.

*How am I to help a star basketball player?*

Doubt flowed like lava down a mountain destroying all belief in the practical application of psychological principles. Powers pondered how his associates would react, if he told them, "I am incapable of healing anyone." How would the head of the department respond, when Powers told him, "My book will be about the psychology of a man who teaches psychology but has no faith in the healing process?"

11

Powers looked deeply into the last swallow of his wine and finished it. He turned his head ever so slightly and stole another glance of Harmon Evans.

*Those who can't, teach.*

The tattoo of a love gone wrong would have been easier to remove than to erase the denial clouding Powers reasoning.

# 2

Powers heard the door close followed by a click.

"Patty, please leave the door open. It gets too stuffy in here," he bellowed, while continuing to read the stack of papers on his desk.

Powers heard a clicking noise. He looked up.

A tall student filled the doorframe to his office.

"I closed the door when I came in. There's no one else out there," he said as he tilted his head toward the outer office space.

"You are not a student of mine, are you?" The professor asked while closing a file in front of him.

"No," he answered. "I'm Eddie Dreyer. Mr. Evans said you would talk to me."

"Eddie." Powers stood. "Yes, he and I spoke this morning and I did agree to counsel with you."

Powers reached to shake Eddie's hand. Eddie towered over him. Powers was stunned by the size of the large hand but it was Eddie's eyes that captured his attention. They were pale blue and set deep in high cheekbones in stark contrast to his brown complexion. His face was smooth, clean shaven, and unblemished except for a tiny crescent shaped scar on his left cheekbone. His hair was cropped close to this scalp. His intriguing pale eyes pulled at Powers like a whirlpool yet in the very next blink the eyes were the blue of flame daring anyone to enter. Powers shook his head a little to break his gaze.

"First," Powers said releasing his grip. "We need to set an appointment. You can call Patty tomorrow. She will find a date and time that fits both our schedules."

"I'd rather not involve any other people. I don't want anyone to know I'm here. We aren't going to meet on campus, are we?"

"Oh I see. That would explain the click. You locked the door." Powers said and watched as Eddie nodded his head.

"No Eddie; the sessions will be in an office at my home. Have a seat."

Eddie answered back quickly, "I'd rather not. I want to spend as little time in here as is necessary. If someone recognizes me, rumors could get started."

"Students and professors talk in offices all over the campus, every day. No one will jump to conclusions because you are sitting down," Powers explained.

Powers looked at the computer screen and scrolled through the days of the week. Eddie continued to stand.

"Okay, how about Monday evening at five thirty?" Powers asked.

"That won't work. I have practice every afternoon, plus, I'm in a hurry. Could we get together this evening?"

"Eddie, I have commitments this evening," Powers answered.

"What about early tomorrow morning? I want to get started. If you can help me, help me now," Eddie stated rather powerfully.

Eddie's insinuation tripped a switch. Powers removed his reading glasses and wondered about the remark.

*Is he displaying doubt about psychological treatment? Is he questioning my skill?*

Powers tapped his chin with his reading glasses and watched Eddie's eyes dart around the room like a tiger protecting his cornered prey from thieving hyenas. Powers concluded Eddie was merely aggressive. He had entered the office with one objective. Eddie wanted an immediate appointment. He intended to get it. The aggressiveness of his tactics suggested control issues. Star athletes are accustomed to preferential treatment; however Powers could not allow Eddie to be in control. This was not the Athletic Department and Powers was not required to babysit Mr. Dreyer.

"Eddie, can you help yourself?" Powers asked with a slow pace and he tried to convey genuine sincerity.

"What do you mean?"

"Do you need help?" Powers re-phrased the question.

"Some people seem to think so," he said establishing intense eye contact.

"I am only interested in what you think."

"So, you want me to admit that I need help," Eddie said and continued, "Fine. I think my mental game is off and if you can help me get back on track, then I want some help."

"I will help you explore events and thoughts. I will help you search for a source of this derailed feeling but it is not logical to guarantee results."

"Fair enough," Eddie replied.

14

Powers put his reading glasses on his nose and returned his attention to the calendar. Eddie admitted to needing help so Powers compromised his schedule.

"Can you come to my house tomorrow morning at eight?" Powers asked.

"Absolutely."

"Please be on time. I have a ten o'clock class. We will have one hour to talk," Powers explained as he scribbled on a business card.

"I'm never late," he heard Eddie say.

Powers reached across the desk to hand the business card to Eddie.

"Do you know Sherwood Drive?" He asked.

"Yes," Eddie answered.

Eddie did not take the card. He turned and left without another word or signal.

He could hear Eddie's footsteps disappearing down the tiled hall. Such a contrast to Theresa, he thought. Eddie Dreyer was more than a challenge; he was pure confrontation. It reminded him of high school circles. The Eddie's of the world were always in a different circle from Powers. Eddie is not the bully who beats you up. In truth, not many kids get beat up; they get frightened. Eddie is the bully who frightens; it is generally sufficient. Powers stood and watched through the window as Eddie's athletic frame glided across the courtyard.

Powers walked to a closet door and opened it exposing a full-length mirror. Powers tried not to measure himself against other men. Too often, comparisons only lead to envying the unobtainable. All of his friends were average people.

More often than not, wives would say, "Why can't you dress more like Powers?"

"Powers, how do you keep the weight off?"

"Can you help me get Al to shave?"

"My God, I wish Reggie were half as tidy as you, Powers."

"I'm surprised some woman hasn't snatched you up already."

Powers pulled his shoulders back and tugged on the bottom and side of his vest as though it were a little tight. He looked himself up and down. Every detail was in order; there were no improvements to be made. Yet, he stood in front of the magic mirror envying Eddie's size, strength and youth. Powers turned his head from right to left as though he might discover ink stains, food crumbs, or a pimple. Nothing there. He leaned forward. His brown pupils appeared dull and shopworn from grading the stack of papers. He leaned back and

15

wished he had not worn the green shirt; it dragged his brown eyes and brown hair into a dull drab leafless forest. Powers reached up to his chin and tried to mold his jaw line tighter and squarer. He dropped his hand. Powers had been trying to re-shape his narrow face for forty years. It did not work today either. He closed the mirrored door. Unobtainable.

Like most kids in the academic circle, Powers took comfort in being smarter than jocks. He sat in the background through high school watching the jocks bask in popular glory and believed his turn would come in the real world. The real world was not any different. There will always be an athlete of imposing size, enviable attractiveness, a GPA of three-point-eight and an aggressive nature. The circles do not end with high school graduation. Everyone must play with cards dealt to them. Natalie's niece was looking at five cards; none of them match. Powers was holding three nines but Eddie Dreyer was holding the full house, aces over kings. Powers turned out the lights and locked the office door. In the silence of the hallway, Powers could have sworn he heard the dealer snickering like a spitball assassin in the back of the classroom. He brushed the back of his neck as he walked from the building.

# 3

The doorbell chimed at seven fifty. Powers opened the door and Eddie Dreyer walked in without being invited. Powers did not see a car parked in the driveway or on the street. He closed the door.

"Eddie, where is your car?" He asked.

"It's parked down the block," he said without bothering to explain.

Powers led him to an office and invited him to sit. With a minimum of prompting, Eddie began telling his story. His Dad was a basketball coach; his Mom played basketball in college and now worked as a personal trainer. Powers listened as Eddie succinctly profiled his life. He described a life of pressure to out-perform his peers.

Powers was captivated by his total recall and his ability to live up to all the expectations. Everything was going according to plan for Eddie until two weeks ago. Eddie described himself as being 'in the zone' in a game against the Bucs. He said it was like everyone else was moving in slow motion and the basket was four foot wide. He recalled every play from the first five minutes of the game. Eddie had scored six straight baskets and stolen two passes. He said he was unstoppable.

Then he heard a shouting voice. He said it was familiar and it disturbed his concentration. Then he realized the voice was inside his head.

"It's unfair. Ya' gotta' play fair," the voice said.

Eddie explained that the slow motion world vaporized and he had the ball stolen from him and went on to describe a series of plays untypical of his skills.

"Professor, I made errors that cost us the game and I've played poorly in the last two games."

"Eddie, am I to believe, that these are the first errors you have ever made in any basketball game?"

"No. I take bad shots, make bad passes, and get sloppy with ball handling. Everyone does," Eddie remarked.

"Then why do these errors have special significance?"

"Because I heard a voice," Eddie said as his teeth gnawed at his lower lip.

"Telling you to play fair?" Powers hoped for more details.

"Yeah. That's what it said." Eddie said with a slight hesitancy.

"Eddie, is it a voice you recognize?" Powers asked as he scribbled notes.

"It's my brother's voice," Eddie blurted out. "He used to say that all the time, when we played."

"You did not mention a brother. Tell me about him?"

"There's nothing to tell. He's dead; he died from a brain tumor four years ago."

"Were you close?" Powers asked.

"Okay. Let me bring you up to speed, so we can move on. We were brothers, just like everyone else, except he had a tumor and no basketball skills. Was it easy to wake up and find out that the brother I treated badly was going to die? No. Was there anything I could do about it? No. I've had plenty of lectures about grieving. I know the stages. I'm not in denial. I saw the body. I saw them put it in the ground. I know he's not coming back. Anger. Hell yeah. I was mad."

Powers watched as the boy unloaded; he did not have time to ask questions. Eddie was running through the standard grieving list faster than Powers could ask. He noted Eddie's pitch was higher, his aggression was louder, and Powers could see Eddie's chest heaving with every beat of his pounding heart. Powers did not interrupt him.

"I made promises to treat everyone nice, to see them as equals. The problem was as soon as I started thinking about fairness I also started playing basketball poorly. My Dad was mad; my Mom was disappointed; my Coach was questioning my heart. I couldn't win."

Eddie's chin fell to his chest but he snapped it back up, as though someone had reminded him that only losers look down. His blue eyes flared into an intense fixed stare.

He continued. "Literally, I couldn't win. It was my senior year. Coach pulled me aside during our fourth game.

He pointed to some men in the stands and said, "Those are college scouts. Which Eddie Dreyer are they going to see this evening? Will it be the best basketball player in the state or the stranger who has been wearing Eddie Dreyer's uniform for the past few weeks?"

"Your dad said that to you?" Powers asked slightly stunned.

"No, Coach Gorman said it. My father was not my high school coach. When he got the head job at Central High, we did not move. He didn't want to coach me and my mother did not want to move, so we didn't. My school and Central High were not in the same district. I never played against a team coached by my father."

"Well, what happened after Coach Gorman admonished you?"

"At the tip off, I shoved my defender. It cleared a path to the ball and an easy basket. Within minutes, I used a subtle elbow to clear space for another open shot. I stepped on the foot of a player trying to make a move, allowing me to steal the ball. I had a huge game. I continued to have huge games until I started hearing his voice," Eddie said as he lowered his head slightly and began to work on the lower lip again.

"His voice? What was your brother's name?" Powers asked.

"Griff. Uh, Griffin." Eddie said softly.

Powers sat quietly watching him. He looked like a boxer sitting in the corner between rounds befuddled by a losing strategy. Eddie looked weary but rather than console him, Powers rang the bell for another round of questions.

"It seems you are experiencing guilt because you did not accept Griffin as an equal," Powers suggested.

"That's the decision I reached over three years ago," Eddie said as he raised his head to answer the bell.

"What decision?" Powers asked.

"I just told you."

"No. No you didn't," Powers stated.

"Oh, I get it; this is another control mechanism. You want to hear me say that I feel guilt because I treated my brother like crap even though I knew he was going to die. Is that what you want to hear?" Eddie's voice was growing confrontational.

Powers studied Eddie. His body was motionless, his hands gripped the arms of the chair, but his head was turned to confront his inquisitor without fear. This was not a sinner weeping at the pulpit begging forgiveness and guidance; this was a man searching for an earthly solution.

"Eddie, listen to me. Guilt is not a feeling; it is a condition. The guilt you feel is not abnormal. It does not take a psychologist to surmise that you are a perfectionist. You judge everything by the right choice and the wrong choice. You made an error and normally you put an error behind you easily, yet this one will not go away." Powers paused. "I do not believe that Griffin is the source of your conflict."

"Then what is the source?" He asked, as though he immediately agreed.

"Eddie, whose standards are you trying to live up to?"

19

"Standards?" Eddie repeated. "Everyone's. My standards are a culmination of what my dad preached, what my mom expects, and how a coach plans to use me. That's what we all do, isn't it? We try to measure up."

Powers was scribbling notes. He peeked over Eddie's shoulder at the clock.

"Eddie, that's all the time we have for today. We both have classes to attend. Why don't we set Thursday's as our regular session time? Eight o'clock?" Powers suggested.

Eddie stood up, put both hands on the corner of the desk, and leaned forward. Powers was uncomfortable; Eddie was inches away from his face.

"Professor Meade, can't we speed this up. I have a game Saturday. The team cannot afford for me to have another melt down. I need this out of my head. I need it out now."

"This is your conscious and subconscious mind. It will take time," Powers said.

"All I need to do is confront the source of my conflict. You think I'm trying to live up to somebody else's standards rather than my own. Isn't that right?" He asked.

"I think it could be but we do not have time to pursue it now." Powers sensed his impatience was being reflected in his answers.

"Then how about tonight?" Eddie asked.

"I have plans."

"How about tomorrow morning?" Eddie persisted.

"Eddie, I must get to class."

"Can we meet again on Saturday morning?" Eddie re-asked.

Powers was disturbed by the relentless way Eddie pushed him and he was intimidated by Eddie's reigning presence over his desk. Powers pushed his chair back and stood up. He stepped around to the end of the desk and walked to the doorway. He hoped Eddie would recognize the action as an indication that the conversation was over.

Eddie released his grasp of the desk. He turned around, sat on the edge of the desk, and held both palms skyward. He raised his eyebrows.

"Tomorrow morning, then?" He asked.

"I will see you tomorrow morning at eight. However, Eddie, in the future, I will not be badgered into commitments. Do you understand?" Powers said.

"I understand what you said," Eddie responded.

Eddie rose from the desk. Powers escorted Eddie to the front door and opened it for him. Eddie put one of his large hands on the door, halting the swing.

"Maybe you could hypnotize me and make my problem go away," he said with a smile.

Powers stared in silence. 'Is Eddie using levity to re-connect? Is he serious? Am I supposed to laugh,' Powers thought? Eddie released his hand from the door.

"See ya' tomorrow, Doc," Eddie said as he walked down the sidewalk.

Powers closed the door without responding. He clung to the doorknob and watched as Eddie strolled down the sidewalk toward a car, undoubtedly stashed around the corner. Powers felt a cold shower of disappointment overtake his mood. He should not have agreed to meet with Eddie. Powers felt a fear that suggested he would never control the treatment of this star athlete. Powers could see Eddie's aggressive nature drove him to push everyone until he got what he wanted. Regret continued to dominate his thoughts.

Powers walked back to his office, made a few notes, grabbed his briefcase, and left for class. He was looking forward to getting back to the safety of the flock, back to theory and all things hypothetical.

As he drove, he could not stop thinking about Eddie Dreyer. And his comments about Hypnosis. It was like a bell ringing in his head. He had not hypnotized anyone in five years and he had only been successful on two of ten attempts.

*Will this be a good idea for Eddie Dreyer?*

He arrived on the campus and parked the car. As he walked to the classroom, Powers wondered if he could speed up the process for Eddie Dreyer. He had a compelling reason to do so; he did not like Eddie Dreyer. The sooner he could be free of his impudence the better. He entered the classroom, greeted the students, and began his lecture.

# 4

Powers read the note, "Drop by my office before you leave today." He considered ignoring Harrington's request as he crumpled the note and threw it into the waste can. Harrington did not send email or leave voice mail. He sent someone to hand deliver the note. This was not how Powers wanted to start the weekend. He could not however, ignore a request from the head of the department. Powers walked upstairs to Harrington's office.

"Go right in, Powers. He's not with anyone," said the secretary.

"Thanks. Hey, how's that burn coming along?" He asked her.

"It's fine but at fifty five, I've finally learned; never pick up a pan on the stove without a hot pad," then she smiled while shaking her head in embarrassment.

Powers returned the smile and tapped on the doorframe of Harrington's office.

"Come in, Powers. Close the door, would you?" Harrington said as he looked over the top of his tiny rimless circular eyeglasses.

Donald Harrington collected his PhD at Berkley just after the flowers were being scattered all over San Francisco. He jumped on board the peace train, adopted a John Lennon look, and came east to spread enlightenment. It was more like the Crusades. Time modernized his appearance, but not his message. Birkenstocks and Doc Martens replaced the tire-tread sandals. Sport coats lent fashion to his t-shirts; his favorite was Power To The People. Those who found themselves unable to agree with him generally moved on to somewhere less enlightened than this campus. Powers Meade was a weed in Donald Harrington's flower garden.

"You know, it still feels like being called to the Principal's office," Powers said as he closed the door and walked toward the desk. "Is this about next semester's lesson plans?"

"No. It's about tenure. Yours comes up for review next spring," Harrington said.

"Yeah, I've been looking forward to it," Powers said.

"I'm not going to recommend you for tenure," Harrington's statement landed like a thump to the forehead of a daydreamer.

"What?" Powers said hoping he had misheard the Dean.

"I want to bring in another professor, a published one. I can't do that if my budget is obligated to support you," the Dean said with a coldness that left Powers staggered.

"I am working on a book concept about __." Powers was saying when Harrington interrupted him.

"It's too late, Powers. I've made up my mind on tenure but I am not firing you," he said.

*This is impossible*

Powers could not process this revelation.

*Is my mouth hanging wide open in astonishment?*

*Do I look as dumbfounded as I feel?*

Powers straightened his spine, closed his mouth and tried to seem composed.

"No, but you are telling me that when you find a better man, you will replace me," Powers accused.

"Or woman," Harrington added to highlight his open-minded wisdom.

Powers knew any argument would be futile; and he would not beg for another chance. He rose and walked across the room prepared to weather the sucker punch quietly. But he stopped; stoicism fit him oddly.

He paused his walk to the door, looked over his shoulder and said, "You've concluded that I'm not doing my job adequately; that's fine, but what about you? Your job is to improve the prestige of the department. Given that mandate, how do you justify your position Harrington? It seems you might have forgotten honesty is a cornerstone of all psychoanalysis, especially self-analysis. Were it not for tenure, would you still be here?"

Powers raised his chin and reached for the door knob. He had one last shot to take at Donald Harrington.

"Oh, and the juvenile book, you wrote, hasn't been checked out of the library in seven years. There, I feel better, don't you?"

He left before Harrington had an opportunity to respond. He snapped the door closed but stopped short of slamming it. He turned to see Wanda peering at him with a look of concern.

"Don't stop baking, Wanda. Your cookies are the best in town." He said with a smile and left the building.

23

He placed his briefcase in the passenger's seat and slid in behind the wheel. The sound of leather adjusting to the weight and motion of the human body seemed amplified. He started the Thunderbird; noise quieted his rumbling thoughts. But Harrington's voice kept ringing in his ears.

*No Tenure.*

Powers knew his weaknesses. He never lied to himself. He did not want to counsel people. He enjoyed the teaching. Psychology works sometimes but sometimes it does not. Powers marveled when psychological principles were applied successfully but he also exposed failures. Powers believed his method of teaching psychology was honest and the best way to train students for a real world, a world where success does not just happen. Most of the time, a clear-cut answer was cloaked in a coat of heavy resistance. It's a world, where wooden stakes, magic bullets, and happy endings disappear like Brigadoon just when you need a lifesaver.

*No Tenure.*

Perhaps, "Progress Despite Failure" should be the title of a book he would write. A book.

*Why didn't I write a damn book?*

Now he would be forced to move to another town or state. Private practice remained an option but Powers knew he would be a failure because he did not want to do it. He wanted to stay wrapped up in the world he had created.

He arrived home without remembering the short drive. The Thunderbird engine went silent. Powers went straight to his liquor cabinet and poured a glass half full of gin. He topped it off with cold tonic water. He took several large swallows; sipping did not fit the occasion. Powers eased into his leather chair. It fit like a glove and at this moment it felt like a large protective womb. Powers took another gulp.

Honesty was taking hold as the anger dissipated. Powers accepted blame for an uncertain future. He called Dean Harrington an "asshole communist," out loud on his way back to the liquor cabinet for another gin. Powers Meade would spend the immediate future in an altered state of mind, far, far away, from the aura of Harrington's groovy sixties.

"Damn it, No Tenure," he said to the walls.

# 5

Powers heard the loud ringing noise but could not place it in reality. His eyes blinked open; the throbbing headache forced them closed again. He rolled over hoping the headache would go away. It did not and neither did the ringing. He sat up; he was wearing yesterday's clothes. A second dose of reality, the ringing was his doorbell. Powers willed his wobbly legs to carry him down the stairs. He peaked out the window; Eddie Dreyer stood on the porch.

"Fuck," he muttered as he checked the time on his wristwatch and waved his hand through the air to dissipate his foul juniper marinated breath.

Powers looked in the mirror. The man staring back at him looked tired, unshaven, and disheveled. He looked like a half-awake drunk. He grabbed a baseball cap from the coat rack. He covered his bed head and opened the door. Once again, Eddie stepped in without invitation.

"Geez, Doc. It's a miracle I wasn't spotted out there," he said as he closed the door.

"Eddie, don't call me Doc," Powers stated.

"Sorry. Can we get started?" Eddie asked.

"You're pushy. I'm not comfortable with that either," Powers said.

"If this is gonna' be Kick-Eddie-Day, I'm gonna' split."

"That choice is yours to make," Powers said flatly and opened the door.

Eddie appeared shaken. His confidence lacked the ferocity exhibited yesterday. He seemed uncertain of his next move. Powers had the upper hand for the time being. He used it.

"Splitting or staying?" Powers asked mindful of his own splitting headache.

"Staying,"

"Have a seat over there, I'll be right back," Powers instructed and pointed to a sofa in the parlor.

Powers went to the kitchen and started a pot of coffee. As it brewed, he splashed water on his face and tried to catch up with reality. His office looked more like a schoolroom during a teacher's absence than a chamber to aid the mentally unhealthy. Wads of yellow paper dotted the floor. Last night's food and drink still lay on the tables. Powers gathered the litter and put them in the waste can. He picked up the yellow pad and reviewed the ramblings. Amongst doodles, crude drawings of Harrington, and curse words Powers had scrawled, "Use Dreyer. Specialize in Sports Confidence." Powers re-read it. He had invested hours in thought about his future and this was the best conclusion, to specialize in helping other impertinent egomaniac athletes like Eddie Dreyer. He could not believe he had arrived at such an unpleasant conclusion.

Powers grabbed the gin bottle and placed it back in the liquor cabinet. He gave the door an extra little push as though he wanted to be sure the gin could not escape and fill his head with absurd ideas or throbbing pain again.

He walked back to the parlor and motioned Eddie to follow him to the office. Eddie sat in the chair opposite the desk as Powers placed his leather bound notepad and his favorite pen on the desk. He adjusted a desk lamp but did not sit down.

"I am going to get a cup of coffee; can I get you a cup?" Powers asked.

"No. I'm not the one with a hangover," Eddie said as he crossed his legs and peered into Powers' eyes.

*He is still measuring me.*

Eddie might have lost a battle at the door but that was history. Once again, Powers felt control being wrestled from him. He knew there would be no progress if Eddie controlled the sessions. Powers could not dispute the truth; he had a hangover. He continued to challenge Eddie's quick tongue.

"No, all you have is little voices in your head," Powers said.

Eddie snapped to his feet and moved closer to the desk.

"Are you making fun of me?" He asked through a tightened jaw.

"Do you hear voices?" Powers asked, trying not to look as frightened as he felt.

"Yeah, I hear my brother's voice. I'm not making it up." Eddie said in a very defensive tone.

"Then I'm just stating a fact, aren't I?" Powers said, standing his ground. "Now would you like to discuss your voices or my alcohol consumption?"

"I don't give a shit whether you are an alcoholic or not. I just want to get rid of the voice." Eddie said as he sat back down in the chair.

Powers could hear the deep rhythmical breathing as he walked past Eddie on his way to the kitchen. Moments later, Powers returned with a full carafe of hot caffeine. He settled into his chair, poured a small portion and sipped at it, allowing the swirls of steam to warm his face. Powers could see Eddie's patience crumbling but he continued to float the caffeine through his body. Powers lowered the cup enough to ask a question.

"Eddie, do you really like basketball?"

"Would I spend every damn day doing it, if I didn't?" He questioned back.

"You are being confrontational; it is unnecessary and unhelpful. Now, do you really like basketball?" Powers asked again.

"I love basketball more than anything else."

"What other hobbies do you have?"

"None; and basketball is not a hobby. It's my job," Eddie stated. "It's why I am here."

"What about your education? Isn't that important to you?" Powers asked.

"Nope. I'm not learning anything of value in the classes I attend."

Powers probed. "Nothing?"

"Do you think I'm lying to you? I've answered the question," Eddie continued, "May I ask you a question?"

"If you must," Powers said as he brought the cup up to his lips. Powers prepared for Eddie's attack. Whatever Eddie asked, Powers hoped the cup would help hide his reaction.

"You said guilt is a condition not a feeling. If we deal with the condition, we can make the guilt fade away; you want to help me set goals based on my expectations, not those of parents or peers. Isn't that where we are headed?"

Eddie's insight surprised Powers, but he hid his facial expressions behind the cup. He sat the cup down, refilled it, and scribbled a note on his pad. Eddie continued before Powers could respond.

"Professor Meade, what I really want to do is play basketball. It gives me everything. I get joy, pain, victory, defeat, control, competitiveness and friendship. The standards I have set are high and they have become mine. I do not believe my problems run any deeper than my mistreatment of my brother. I think since I've admitted it, I am on the road to recovery." Eddie presented his analysis and awaited his compliment.

"Eddie, I know you think you have this all figured out, but if you do, why are you here this morning?" Powers asked in a sympathetic tone.

"I want you to hypnotize me. Plant a non-guilt guard or something. I feel bad; I'll get over it in time so why not take the short cut?"

Again, Eddie caught Powers off guard.

"It's not that simple," Powers answered.

"It's got to be. My uncle went to a hypnotist and he quit smoking. He hasn't had a _ _," Powers cut him off.

"Hypnotherapy has shown mixed results at best."

"I'll take the chance. What's the harm in trying?"

"Eddie, listen to me. Hypnosis is a broad term. It means different things to different people." Powers felt like an amateur as he tossed canned responses to an experienced manipulator.

"I understand that, Doc - Sorry, Professor," Eddie said as he flashed both hands up in the air to prove he was apologetic. "I already practice a little self-hypnotism. I relax and talk to myself; I pre-play a game in my mind and post suggestions."

Curiosity drove Powers to disregard his professional image. He rose from the desk and sat in the chair next to Eddie. "Does that work?"

"Oh yeah, it's not foolproof but I know it helps. I study my opponent on videotape. When I get the chance, I close my eyes and imagine him defending me. I create moves to counter his natural tendencies. I am the leading scorer in the conference. I know I have talent but I work hard at this game, harder than anyone."

"And you go to all this trouble because it's your job not your passion," Powers asked.

Eddie quickly rebutted, "What's the difference?"

Eddie paused, and then pointed his finger at Powers.

"Have you seen the guy who walks around campus with a laptop computer literally hanging around his neck?"

28

Powers nodded and decided to return to his desk. Everyone had seen the boy Eddie referred to. He could be seen sitting anywhere, pecking away at his keyboard. The kid was in Jim's Psych 101 last semester. Jim gave him a D.

"The dude's name is Randy Dix. He's a chemistry major and a frickin' genius. From the time he wakes until he goes to sleep, all he thinks about is chemical compositions. One of our assistant coaches teaches Grad classes in chemistry. He says Randy already knows more than any professor on this campus. Randy wants to unlock mysteries that you and I cannot understand. Is he passionate about chemistry or is it his job?" Eddie said with an admiration for the rumpled geeky Randy Dix.

"I understand your point, Eddie. Basketball is both your passion and your job. Please try to understand mine. Hypnosis is not dealing with your issues in reality," Powers explained.

"Reality? Reality rolls around at eight o'clock tonight," Eddie said as he stood. "Reality is this evening; I have a game this evening."

"The time frame is too short for a cure or even a patch, Eddie. I have had some success with subconscious suggestions but it requires a carefully worded script, and a susceptible patient," Powers said.

Right then, is when it donned on Powers; he had opened the door. He should have condemned hypnosis as an option.

*Am I subconsciously hoping to attempt hypnotherapy?*

Eddie did not give him a second chance to slam the door closed.

"Great, let's do that; let's whip up a script." Eddie said excitedly.

Powers lifted the coffee to his mouth and took a few more swallows. Again he hoped the cup would cover any fear and the pause would curb Eddie's pressure.

"Eddie, slow down. We have made some headway. You can see a path to healing. I think it would be a good idea to let this process settle in your mind." Powers could see Eddie was about to protest but Powers continued, "I will write a script and we can fine tune it during the next___"

A loud metallic crash interrupted Powers. It was at the door.

"Goddamn it, that little shit," Powers bellowed.

He had spilled coffee on his lap when the noise startled him. Powers wiped at the wet spot as he walked to the door. Eddie followed him. Powers opened the door and stared down the street. He bent over and picked up his metal door clapper. It had fallen off when the paperboy's aim sent the morning newspaper directly onto the door. He set the ornate metal on a table and picked up the paper. He turned to find Eddie immediately behind him. Powers closed the door.

"Aren't you going to make him pay for the repair of your door?" Eddie asked an added, "Do you want me to chase his ass down?"

"No, and I apologize for the outburst. He did not break it. The clapper was loose. It needs a new bolt. I have been meaning to repair it. I suppose my hangover was reacting to his good aim. Any other day, I would be grateful the paper was at the door rather than in the wet grass," Powers explained as he walked back into his office.

The walk was long enough for Eddie to regain the offensive.

"Professor Meade, I don't want to wait for another session." He reached for the newspaper and said, "May I show you something?" Eddie pointed to the wrapped newspaper.

Powers shrugged his shoulders and said, "Sure."

Eddie removed the paper from the plastic sleeve, pulled out the Sports section, and pointed to the lead article. Powers looked at it.

It read, "Cougars Look To Take Conference Lead Over Terriers."

*Why would any school choose a Terrier as a mascot? And why is a mascot necessary, anyway?*

Eddie interrupted his thought, "If you look at the latest line, you'll see that we are favored to win by fifteen," Eddie said and pointed at the newsprint. "They are the worst team in the conference. I have to play well."

Powers said, "But Eddie, if the Terriers are the worst team in the conference and the Cougars are the best, victory can be assured with less effort."

Powers thought the logic to be simple.

"I am tired Eddie. Give yourself a pep talk; you will win. Let's meet again on Monday."

"My pep talks are about the technical aspects of the game. I don't know how to make voices go away. Let's meet again today at four. I have to be at the arena at seven," Eddie said.

"Eddie, I have explained to you that you are too confrontational. I will not be bullied into__"

"Please. I'm scared. I've spent most of my life doing just as everybody expects me to, as I expect me to do. The prospect of failing again, like I did the other night, is terrifying. If someone beats me, hey I can deal with that but I can't live with beating myself and letting my team down. Can we meet again at four? Can we please try this

30

hypnotherapy?" Eddie asked in a tone that sounded sincere.

*No. I will not.*

He should have said the words out loud. But Powers felt excited by the chance to try again; but the prospect of failure scared him as well. Torn and tired, Powers would not prevail against the determined Eddie Dreyer.

"I'll see you at four but think about this and I mean really spend some time thinking. I do not think you will be susceptible to hypnotic suggestion. I think you are a control freak. I do not think you trust people, which is crucial to hypnotherapy. I think your resistance will doom hypnosis. You think about that, Eddie. Think about adding that to your mind's agenda. That's more failure. Let me say it again, I do not believe you will be able to relax, trust me, and allow your subconscious to receive the helpful suggestion. Think about it. If you are not here at four, I will understand and I will expect you on Monday."

He turned his back on Eddie and opened the door.

"Don't say anything, just go and think about what I said."

Eddie did not say a word. Powers closed the door and walked straight to his bed. He closed his eyes and wondered if the challenge would bring him back or convince him to wait.

Powers opened his eyes.

*He'll be back.*

Powers reached over to set the alarm. "It's a sure fire winner; he will be back," Powers said as he closed his eyes, again.

# 6

Powers shut off the alarm and sat up in bed. His eyes were open; the Tiffany lamp sat on the bureau, and the Voisson painting hung on the wall, where it had for nine years. The magnolia brushed against the window screen. The scraping sound reminded him that it needed to be trimmed, as it had for several years. It would grow higher than the window; the scraping would eventually stop. All were clear signs; he was sitting in his own bed. Yet Powers felt disconnected.

The clock read one, yet his body screamed go back to sleep. He wanted his Saturday routine back. He could not remember the last time his Saturday started with a hangover rather than coffee and croissants. He exhaled, cleared his throat with a lazy cough, and stood on the hardwood floor.

With every blink of his eyes, awareness replaced disorientation. He covered a bagel with cream cheese as he waited on a fresh pot of coffee. He ambled down the hall to his office and picked up the notepad from Eddie's last session. He sprawled out on the leather sofa, chewing the bagel and drinking the hot coffee.

He blinked a few more times, rubbed his eyes and stared at the notes. Eddie would arrive soon. A competitive nature consumed Eddie and he would navigate any course to achieve his goals. Eddie said he would be back at four; but Powers knew he would be early. Powers glanced at the clock. He took a bite of the bagel and began to write a script to remove the ghost from Eddie's head. He labored with the wording; basketball ignorance interrupted his progress. He sipped his coffee; additional caffeine would not improve his understanding of the game.

Powers went to the computer and logged on to the Internet. He typed in espn.com, clicked on college basketball, and found information about the Cougars. He discovered Eddie Dreyer mentioned everywhere. Powers scanned articles, reviewed box scores, and wrote notes on terminology and strategy. He clicked on a banner. It lead him to a statistical breakdown of the past thirteen games. It surprised Powers, to find a gambling line among the statistics. Why would a team's ability to cover the betting line have been recorded as a legitimate statistic? A dollar sign denoted success. Powers counted nine dollar signs in the thirteen games. Powers checked his notes. Eddie knew the betting line on the game with the Terriers.

"Why is Eddie interested in the line?" Powers wrote on his pad.

He clicked on a banner that took him to a betting website. Within minutes, he learned that a ten-dollar bet paid nine dollars and ten cents. Ten times out of thirteen, the Cougars would have paid a good return. He wondered if Eddie might be wagering on his own games. What other reason would he have to be concerned with the betting line? He circled his question about betting. Powers knew wagering on Cougar games would carry a ton of guilt. Add that to his brother and Eddie's psyche could be under constant attack.

He logged off, showered, and shaved. He emerged from the steam-blurred bathroom refreshed. Powers made a sandwich and went back to his office. Powers did not like Eddie and never could but Eddie's predicament intrigued him and the possibility of hypnosis as a treatment excited him. Psychologists empathize, or sympathize, in an unprofessional moment; but Powers felt neither. He felt joy. Eddie had proven to be impudent, combative, and one-dimensional but the challenge brought pure joy to Powers.

Hypnosis would draw immediate criticism from his peers; they would chastise him for employing parlor tricks, especially so early in the process. Yet, Powers did not care what they would think. He would return Eddie to normal. He rationalized that he would be performing as the patient requested. He finished a rough draft of his script for Eddie's session and set it aside.

Powers stepped outside to fill his lungs with fresh air. He had not given this kind of commitment to anything in years. A small flame of pride sparked inside. He checked his watch and walked back in the house. He knew Eddie would be early; Powers guessed he would arrive in the next forty-five minutes. Powers entered his office, sat at the desk, and polished his script. He read it and deemed it appropriate.

He revisited the ESPN website. He needed to know the names of the teams remaining on the schedule. He wrote them down. A pop-up advertisement from a betting site had appeared. He closed it and heard the doorbell. Powers checked his watch. Eddie was ten minutes early.

As with previous visits, Eddie looked nervous standing on the porch. He did not want to be seen at a psychology professor's house. Powers opened the door.

"May I come in?" Eddie asked.

Powers recognized the conciliation, yet the show of respect gave him and uneasy feeling.

"Of course," Powers responded and stepped aside to allow Eddie to pass.

"Professor Meade, I did what you told me; I thought about it. I can do this."

Powers closed the door and turned to see Eddie standing like a soldier volunteering for a dangerous mission. Without commenting on Eddie's decision, Powers walked to his office; Eddie followed. Powers motioned him to sit in a leather chair.

"No couch?" Eddie quipped.

Powers should not have been dispirited by the return of Eddie's insolence. This Eddie, the one with the mischievous grin, is real. The polite one at the door that was a decoy.

*Eddie Dreyer is still a jerk.*

Powers hoped his facial expression and body language were broadcasting indifference. Powers did not respond to the comment. Something captured Eddie's attention; it was the computer screen.

Eddie stood up, leaned over the desk and said, "I see you have an interest in gambling; where's the line? Has it changed? Is it still fifteen?"

"Eddie, please sit down. I have been doing some research on basketball and gambling to prepare the script for this session."

"So, you knew I would come back." Eddie asked.

"I suspected you would not back down from a challenge."

"I'm not doing it because you used reverse psychology or because you challenged me. I want to do this because it will help my game."

"I understand that. I have lost interest in arguing with you about hypnosis. I am prepared to use hypnotherapy to help you. However, I need to know why you are so interested in the betting lines," Powers asked.

"Because, someone is judging me. Someone somewhere has decided what I am capable of doing. If some cigar smoking fat guy in Vegas has decided that I'm fifteen points better than the Terriers, I want to prove him wrong. I can do that in three ways. I can win by more than fifteen, I can win by less than fifteen, or I can lose. I don't lose very often."

"It motivates you?" Powers asked hoping for confirmation.

Eddie nodded yes.

"But you do not bet on the games?" Powers was still looking for the proper motivation.

"Hell, no. I can't think of a quicker way to lose respect with the team plus I would be crucified by the press. And I would be drummed out of school by this university, hell, any university."

"Eddie, team is important to you?" Powers asked.

"Absolutely. They are number one with me."

"But you take the point spread so seriously, as if it is totally your responsibility to cover the points?" Powers probed.

"It's just my thing; it motivates me. Reporters and students ask me about the lines every day. I tell everyone the same thing. If you bet against me you're gambling." Eddie said without a smile.

Powers let the words bounce around in his head as he peered into Eddie's eyes as though he could read Eddie's mind. Powers wanted to see the truth, any truth. He could feel his eyes scrunching into a squint. Clearly, clairvoyance would not provide the answer. Powers relaxed his face. It would be easier to unwind a golf ball than to unveil the truth inside Eddie Dreyer. Powers cleared his thoughts and dismissed his conscience.

"Ok. Let's get started with this script. It is imperative that you do exactly as I tell you to do. You must lose your cockiness, lose your sense of humor, and lowers your defenses. Are you prepared to do this?" Powers asked.

"Would I be here if I wasn't?" Eddie said dismissively.

Powers stared at him. He was prepared to remain silent for as long as necessary. He would not speak until Eddie realized that the comment did not reflect willingness to lower defenses. The silence amplified the ticking clock and the weight adjustments in the leather chairs. Powers could hear Eddie's breathing.

"You're waiting on me to apologize for the last comment, aren't you?" Eddie asked.

Powers did not respond nor change his facial expression.

"I am ready; that's just my style. It slipped out. You're in control," Eddie said.

"No, you are in control," Powers said. "I am here to guide you but you must be willing to listen and hear. You cannot do that if you are busy preparing your next sarcastic comment."

"Okay, okay, I get it." He took a deep breath and blinked a new expression on his face. "I am listening; I will hear."

"Close your eyes, Eddie. Gently. Do not scrunch them tight. Use a five, five, eight count. Breathe in for five, hold for five, and slowly breathe out for the eight count," Powers instructed.

Eddie began following the instructions without hesitation. Powers watched as Eddie breathed rhythmically.

"Eddie, rest your forearms on the arms of the chair with the palms of your hands facing up and allow your fingers to relax. Continue breathing rhythmically." Powers said slowly and methodically.

Eddie continued to follow instructions precisely. Powers paused to allow him to slip further into his breathing. Eddie was relaxing. Powers could see it in his face.

"Picture a staircase with handrails barely visible in the darkness. Look up the stairs. You see a light at the top. Nod yes when this picture is vividly clear to you, Eddie." Powers asked.

Powers sat quietly and waited. Eddie's head nodded yes Eddie was cooperating and seemed highly susceptible to coaching. Powers could only rely on Eddie's actions. The years Eddie had spent visualizing sport scenarios must have made the process easy for him.

"Eddie, there is noise at the top of the steps. It is a faint noise. It is a mixture of voices, squeaking, grunting and cheering. Do you hear it?" Powers asked concentrating to keep his fear of failure hidden.

Eddie's head tilted a little then he nodded yes.

"Hold the rails and when I say 'begin', you will climb the five steps to the top. When you reach the lights at the top you will step onto a basketball court. Everyone is dressed to play except you. On the far side of the court is a door with a sign that reads, "Eddie's Control Room." You will walk toward the room to get ready for the game.

At the door stands your brother.

Say to him, "Griff, I was wrong to make you feel less special."

He will say, "Thank you Eddie. I forgive you. Now play up to your expectations."

You will step into Eddie's Control Room. You will dress for the game. When you walk back out on the court, there will be no voices piercing your concentration. The game will precede and you will be in total control. The buzzer will sound the end of the game. You will be victorious. You will celebrate your accomplishments. Nod yes if you understand."

Eddie nodded.

"Are you ready to begin the climb up the stairs?" Powers asked.

Eddie nodded yes.

"Begin. Step one. Step two. Three. Four. Five. Loud noise. Do you see your brother by the control room?"

Eddie nodded yes. Powers could feel his own heartbeat increasing. Eddie Dreyer is not the kind of person that would play along just to be polite. The relaxed state had to be working. Powers continued to guide him.

"Walk to him. Repeat these words. "Griff, I was wrong to make you feel less special."

"Griff, I was wrong to make you feel less special." Eddie's verbal response caught Powers totally off guard. He had not expected Eddie to talk out loud. Eddie was deep in a trance. Powers felt excitement but he also felt apprehension. He continued with his walk through Eddie's trance, like a teen walking through a haunted house.

"What did he say to you?" Powers asked.

"Thank you; I forgive you, Eddie. Now play up to your expectations."

Powers gave the next instruction, "Go into the Control Room. Change for the game. Go back onto the court. Is the noise bothering you?"

"No."

"Is Griff asking you to play fair?" Powers asked.

"No."

"Do you hear anyone critical of your game?" Powers quizzed.

"No," Eddie said as he cocked his head from side to side listening for criticism.

"When I say 'begin' walk back across the court to the stairs. Climb down the steps. When you reach the bottom, you will open your eyes. You will be refreshed, free of voices that disturb your concentration on the basketball court and unaware that you have been in hypnotherapy. Do you understand?"

"Yes," Eddie said without hesitation.

"Begin. Walk across the court. Walk down the steps. Slowly. Step five. Step four. Step three. Two and one," Powers coached.

Powers studied Eddie's facial expression. He feared that, in the next moment, Eddie would open his mouth with a cocky comment. He worried that it did not really work. He was prepared for Eddie to roar into laughter. Eddie opened his eyes with several quick blinks. He shrugged his shoulders to loosen up. He rubbed his hands together to regenerate blood flow.

"What do you remember?" Powers asked.

"You were telling me to breathe in a rhythmical pattern," Eddie answered.

"I offered you the opportunity to encounter your brother. You did it and tonight you will play without interference," Powers stated.

"Just like that?" Eddie asked in disbelief.

"Just like that," Powers replied, even though he wanted to add, "I hope."

He did not want to discuss the particulars with Eddie. Powers ushered him to the door.

Eddie paused before walking away and said, "Are you sure?"

"When you start clucking like a chicken, it will be apparent I was successful," Powers said with a smile.

"Funny, Doc," Eddie said with a forced smile, as though his mother stood behind him, pinching him, demanding politeness in public.

Eddie left. Powers closed the door and with a sigh leaned against it. Powers took a deep breath and let it out slowly as he walked back into his office. He sat down at his desk and began typing notes into his computer as fast as his fingers would comply. It seemed he could not type fast enough. When the last thought had emptied from his head, he sat back and watched the blinking cursor. He decided he had captured the experience. Powers closed the window. Behind it was the pop-up ad for the betting website he had seen earlier that day. It was flashing at him; it blinked "Sign Up Now!"

He stared at the flashing box.

*How confident am I that I helped Eddie? Would I bet on it?*

He had never bet on anything. He heard Eddie's voice saying, "Betting against me is gambling." He clicked on the "Sign UP Now" button. Ten minutes later, Powers Meade had placed his first bet. He wagered twenty-five dollars on the Cougars to beat the Terriers by fifteen. Powers believed he was wagering on his own handiwork. He helped Eddie Dreyer and Eddie would prove it this evening.

Powers walked down the hall. He stopped to straighten a photo of his mother on the wall.

"Mother, you would not believe the day I've had."

He continued walking. Powers was euphoric. He pulled a bottle of wine from the rack.

Some angelic voice whispered, "Agonizing headache, remember?"

He remembered; but he also recalled unobtainable tenure, an insolent student patient, and a visit to the shady side of his profession. His day had seen one too many valleys and one too many peaks. Powers wanted to level the path to the end of the day. He stood the bottle on the counter and pulled the cork. He poured and toasted his success. Powers continued to this office. He sat at the computer and entered a synopsis of the day's events. He pushed back from the computer and poured another glass.

*What a day indeed.*

# 7

Much of the Sunday morning sun rose in the sky as Powers slept. It was eleven before he walked outside to replace his doorknocker and pick up the newspaper. He abandoned his routine and pulled the Sports section from the bulky Sunday paper. Normally, the Sports section was cast aside with the other unnecessary weight of the newspaper. Powers did not have to search for information on the game. In a town without professional teams, college teams are the lead story.

A six-by-six inch photo of Eddie Dreyer shooting the basketball monopolized the front page.

The headline read, "Dreyer Scores 37 in a Rout."

Powers located the final score as eighty-eight to sixty. He read the entire article. The essence of the column reported Eddie Dreyer had put his recent mishaps behind him and played brilliantly. Powers was pleased that Eddie had played well but he was more impressed with his own accomplishment. He had helped someone; furthermore, his wager had paid forty-seven dollars and seventy-five cents.

Powers used his Sunday to put together a plan to help other athletes. Monday morning, Powers sat at his desk vitalized. He believed he could begin a successful career helping other athletes. The phone rang and Patty picked it up.

A few seconds later she called out, "It's Harmon Evans, Professor Meade."

Powers picked up the receiver and twirled his chair toward a view of the campus.

"Good morning, Mr. Evans. How's business?" Powers asked.

"It's eight-thirty in the morning; it's kinda' dead right now but in general, it's steady," Harmon said.

Powers chuckled: Harmon continued. "I spoke to Eddie last night. He's a different kid. I must congratulate you; how much do I owe you."

"Nothing, Mr. Evans, absolutely nothing. Working with Eddie lit a fire under my butt and rekindled my desire for private practice," Powers claimed.

"I would feel better if you would charge me something."

"Fair enough. You owe me a glass of the best whisky in your bar," Powers said.

"That sounds like a bargain. Are you sure?" Harmon asked.

"Well, I don't want to sound cheap, so make it your best scotch whisky." Powers said.

"Now it's a high price. I can make more money but Macallan can't make more whisky from 1987. Are you sure I can't pay you in money," Harmon asked.

Powers laughed at the dry humor levied by Harmon Evans.

"Sorry. I insist on the whisky, especially now that I know its twenty five years old."

"It's a deal. Look me up the next time you are in Bluebeards," Harmon said.

"I think it will be soon. I feel like celebrating."

"Whenever, and thank you again."

"Have a great day, Mr. Evans."

He called Natalie and Jim; they were in class. He left messages for both of them to meet him for drinks at Captain Bluebeards at six. He wanted to get the word out about his new endeavor. Powers taught his three classes and returned to his office. He reviewed his outline for the new consulting business. He was satisfied that the points were well conceived. He printed copies the document for Jim and Natalie. At five forty five, he began his walk to the bar.

As Powers reached the midway point of his walk, he saw Eddie Dreyer walking toward him with two students of similar height. The distance between them closed quickly.

Powers slowed his pace, nodded, and said, "Hi Eddie."

Eddie did not respond; the group kept walking. Powers could hear their conversation as they passed.

"Dude, who's that?" The student on Eddie's left asked.

"I don't know. Another somebody who wants a brush with fame," Eddie said.

"They all want a piece of us when we win," bragged the other student.

"Hey the dude may be queer for your gear, Eddie," one of them said, then laughed at the remark.

"Cool it, Troy. He might hear you," Eddie replied.

41

Powers could no longer hear their conversation but he could hear them continue to laugh. He understood why Eddie did not want people to know he had been talking to a psychologist but Powers was irritated by the cruelty of the snub.

He continued his walk to Captain Bluebeards. His enthusiasm had diminished. He dealt with a reality that every athlete might be a jerk with egos the size of their libidos.

Powers tightened his grip on the briefcase. It reminded him that he needed a source of income.

*Still, it's a good plan.*

Powers stood at the entrance of Bluebeard's with his ego still throwing a tantrum. He opened the door to Captain Bluebeard's and spotted the friendly wave of his colleagues. He put on a smile, waved, and sent his ego to the corner to pout. Powers took a seat at the table and saw Harmon Evans walking toward the group. Harmon set a very healthy serving of Macallan whisky in front of Powers.

"As promised, Professor Meade," Harmon said.

"I don't deserve it but I'm keeping it," Powers said with a laugh as he reached to shake Harm's hand.

Powers lifted the glass of whisky to his nose, allowed his eyes to close briefly, and sipped.

"Thank you," Powers said as he saluted Harmon with the glass.

"You are wrong; you do deserve it. Enjoy it," Harmon replied as he walked away.

"What was that about?" asked Natalie.

"I've been so busy trashing Harrington for forcing me out that I forgot to tell you about Eddie Dreyer," Powers said.

"May I try that whisky?" Jim asked.

"Only a little, your palate isn't sophisticated enough to appreciate it," Powers joked.

Natalie and Powers watched as Jim took a drink. Jim sat the glass back in front of Powers.

"That's smooth but it's still not my cup of tea," Jim said.

Natalie and Powers turned to look at Jim with raised eyebrows.

"What? The metaphor? Gimme' a break. No one else in here would have given it a second thought," he said.

"Just because we frequent a bar full of lazy youth devoid of proper grammar, does not mean we must be dumbed down," Powers said.

"Dumbed? It's too late," said Natalie with an unsuppressed laugh.

"Jim is not a whisky man; what about you Natalie? Would you like to try a twenty five year old whisky?"

"No." She feigned a shiver. "Tell me about Eddie Dreyer."

"Eddie was in my office for three sessions last week and based on his performance, I pronounce him healed," Powers proclaimed.

He closed his eyes, smelled his whisky and sipped it.

"Please!" Natalie exclaimed. "One does not heal mental disorders in a week. Psychology does not work that way."

"No, but hypnotherapy does." Powers had not intended to blurt it out but there it was hovering in the air like smog.

"Powers, you hypnotized that boy?" Jim asked in a whisper.

"Yes." He leaned across the table and whispered, "Have I committed a crime? Should we speak in code?" Powers said as he leaned back upright.

Both of his colleagues disregarded the sarcasm.

"This is very interesting. How much can you share with us?" Natalie asked.

"I've already said too much. But I will say this; it could not have been simpler. You would not believe his susceptibility level." Powers sipped and continued. "He's hypersensitive about seeing a therapist. I just passed him crossing campus and the ungrateful Judas snubbed me and denied he knew me to his friends. I believe I heard him belittle me."

"Don't begrudge the youth, especially the males. Maturity comes slower for boys," said Natalie.

"Must one be fully mature to be courteous?" Powers shook his head and expelled air in exasperation. "Regardless, I am confident, neither of you will tell a sole about the hypnosis nor tell anyone he has sought help," Powers said.

He was asking psychologists, trained to be inquisitive to dam up the flood of questions. Like punished children deprived of dessert, they both nodded agreement with disappointed faces.

Powers accepted their nods as commitments and said, "This brings me to my next revelation. I want to specialize in this kind of client. I can help any athlete with a mental block in their game."

"Mental blocks in their game?" Jim repeated and raised his hands in disbelief. "A week ago you didn't know a thing about the game."

"What does that mean, Powers?" Natalie asked.

"Athletes reach plateaus. They want to get better. They want to make fewer mistakes. They want to run faster, jump higher, or get

43

stronger. I am going to help them do that." Powers beamed over the top of his rapidly diminishing whisky.

"Powers, you don't know anything about athletics. I've never seen you at a game or a meet. You didn't play in school, did you?" Jim asked.

"No. Does that matter? Why are the two of you so negative? I am a teacher. I learn stuff and then regurgitate it to other people who want to know about it. Natalie does not have Alzheimer's but she teaches students about it," Powers preached. "I can learn about sports. I was able to help Eddie Dreyer; I can help others." He unlatched his briefcase and gave each of them a bound set of papers.

"I want you to read this. I need you to help promote me," Powers said.

"I'll read it," Jim said as he thumbed through the pages.

"Me too," Natalie said. She read the cover page. "Powers Meade: Specializing in Performance Plateaus." "Perhaps, I should read it twice."

"That's all I ask. So, how about another round?" Powers said. He raised his hand to catch the attention of the server. "That's a damn fine whisky."

# 8

Powers stood on the back patio trying to decide if the storm clouds would pass. He wanted to grill his stuffed pork chop. He checked his watch, stepped inside the house, and turned on the television. The local weather forecast would be airing in a few minutes. He poured a glass of wine and prepped his green beans. The weatherman appeared and stated with some assurance that the clouds would not produce rain.

Powers reached for the remote when the newscaster said, "Next, we will go live to Fleming Gymnasium. We will get Eddie Dreyer's perspective on the game between the Cougars and the Spartans. Stay tuned."

He left the television on and went out onto the patio to light the grill. Powers had not spoken with Eddie in five days; he was anxious to examine his demeanor on the television. Powers wondered what the odds were of Eddie saying, "Well, Joel, I'll tell you; if it weren't for the brilliant psychologist, Powers Meade, I would never have been able to turn it around."

The thought brought a smile to his face. He knew praise was not forthcoming but Powers was curious to see Eddie handle questions about the game. He walked back into the house.

Powers watched as the cameraman widened the shot to include Eddie's upper torso. The reporter talked with Eddie about the standings and the match-ups for the evening. The reporter asked Eddie about his recent inconsistent play.

"Eddie, your last game was sensational. Have you put that disaster against the Bucs behind you?"

"Oh yeah. No one is perfect. I had a couple of bad games. You can't allow stuff to get inside your head. Basketball is as much mental as it is physical. I've trained myself to be mentally tough. Mind over matter, you know." Eddie smiled into the camera.

Powers grimaced and gave the television a thumbs-down gesture.

"Yeah if you believe hypnotherapy is mind over matter," Powers sniped.

"The Spartans play a similar defense. Do you expect the Cougar offense to explode again this evening?" The reporter asked as he pushed the microphone closer to Eddie's face.

The cameraman tightened his shot.

"I always expect our offense to explode. We have great athletes," Eddie replied.

"Their box-one zone defense is tailor made for your pull-up jumper," the reporter said with a smile and waited for Eddie to elaborate.

"Their defense doubles-up real well but we have a solid game plan," Eddie answered.

Powers noted that Eddie would not boast of his own abilities nor would he criticize the opponent. Yet, Powers knew Eddie would do both once the game began. The interviewer knew it as well. He changed the line of questioning.

"This place is a little special to you, isn't it Eddie? You fine-tuned that jumper right here in this arena. You could say, you grew up here; isn't that right?" He asked.

"Yeah. As a matter of fact, my parents live about a mile from this gym," Eddie said flashing a smile.

"Go on, tell the folks about your dad," the reporter urged.

"He's the basketball coach at Central High."

"He used to bring you down to this very gym to work on your game," the reporter said, showing he had been digging up facts. "He wanted you to feel the presence and pressure of the larger venue, right?"

The camera shifted back to Eddie. Powers watched as Eddie's expression seemed strained. He looked uncomfortable. The camera shifted back to the reporter and he motioned to someone off camera. The camera shot widened to accommodate another person.

"Eddie, recognize this guy?" The reporter asked with a beaming smile.

A fit man with a near bald head, polo shirt, and whistle around his neck joined Eddie and the reporter on camera.

"Hey dad," Eddie said and half smiled.

"Welcome Coach Dreyer, it looks like you came straight from practice," the reporter said as he motioned toward the whistle.

"Yeah – it seems like there is always one of these things around my neck. My wife says it stays there so I can choke myself when I say

46

something stupid," he said as he fiddled with the silver instrument.

The reporter laughed; Eddie smirked while Coach Dreyer looked at the whistle.

"This is one heck of a shooter you raised," said the reporter pushing the mike back in front of Coach Dreyer.

"He has a ton of natural talent but the hard work is what makes him special," Coach Dreyer responded.

"You worked Eddie here under the big lights. It certainly helped him. You should have brought your team down here. Maybe Central would have given Eddie a run for his money," the reporter joked.

"There are rules against that but I had more freedom with my own family. His family is the toughest defense he ever faced. His mother played college ball. She, Eddie's brother and I would gang up on him. Sometimes, it would be three on one. He really had to work to get his shot off," Coach Dreyer said. "Yep, he's got talent but his work ethic and determination make him special."

"A brother?" The reporter said with surprise. "So, we can expect another Dreyer in a Cougar uniform in the near future."

The speechless seconds seemed interminable. Eddie's eyes cut to look at his father. Coach Dreyer's eyes blinked.

"Eddie's brother is no longer with us," Coach Dreyer said as he fidgeted with the whistle hanging on his yellow shirt.

The interviewer had done his job. He did the research. He found the father and learned about the training. But unexpectedly, a tombstone crashed onto the hardwood court and crushed his plans for a feel-good reunion with backslaps and good wishes. The reporter turned and faced Eddie and said the only thought that came into his head.

"Good luck tonight, Eddie."

They shook hands and he turned to Coach Dreyer,

"Thank you for joining us this evening, Coach"

"It was a pleasure," the coach replied and walked out of the camera frame.

"Ladies and gentlemen, Coach David Dreyer of Central High and father of Cougar star Eddie Dreyer. And I'm Joel Pattinger, live from Fleming Gymnasium."

The cameraman locked on the reporter but Powers could see that Eddie had jogged off court without waiting to exchange pleasantries with his father. Powers clicked off the television and took his pork chop to the grill.

Powers sat on the patio and listened to the pork chop sizzle. He drank his wine and analyzed what he had just witnessed. That reunion screamed an absence of love. Powers began to wonder if he shouldn't approach Eddie about this family tension. Isn't a psychologist obligated to explore the deeper issues? Powers began to regret the hypnotherapy decision. Eddie Dreyer would never be healthy without confronting the issue with his father. Powers consoled himself by remembering he helped Eddie get what he wanted.

Powers went to the grill and turned the pork chop over.

"The client does not want to be healed," he said as he poked at the pork chop.

*It is no different than the State Agency. I gave the customer what he wanted. The patient asked one issue to be resolved. I resolved one issue.*

Powers preferred his reality cold; he shoved his scarred conscience back into the closet.

# 9

Later that evening, Eddie brought the ball up the court. He glanced at the scoreboard. The Cougars had a six-point lead with two-ten to play. It had been a tough game and everyone was tiring. He knew he could take his man to the hole but the zone defense would collapse on him, they would foul, and the clock would stop while he shot the free throws. Eddie did not want the clock to stop; he wanted to get this one over. They should be winning by a dozen but Eddie had turned the ball over a few too many times.

Without the ball, he would not be tempted to drive to the hoop or shoot an open jumper too soon. He would let the rest of his teammates move the ball around and chew up the clock. He passed the ball to Kenny but Kenny was not expecting it. The ball bounced off his hip; it was rolling on the floor. Eddie was closer to it than the Spartan defending Kenny. They both sprinted toward the loose ball, arriving almost simultaneously. Eddie reached out ready to push the Spartan putting him at a disadvantage, when he heard his brother.

"Not fair, Dad! Why do you let him push me? That's cheating."

Eddie pulled up; the Spartan retrieved the ball, sprinted the length of the court and slammed a dunk home, cutting the lead to four.

Eddie rushed to the other end to run the in-bounds play. One fifty-five remaining. No one in the arena knew why he had frozen. They saw the Spartan beat him to the ball, but Eddie knew differently. He could have controlled the dribble and ticked forty-five seconds off the clock. But he did not; now the score was too close.

Eddie broke free and took the inbounds pass. He dribbled the ball up the court under constant harassment from the Spartan defender. Eddie ate up ten seconds and passed the ball to Donnell. Donnell immediately passed to Kenny, who passed back to Eddie. Just the way they practiced it. But Eddie did not want the ball. He feared he would commit an error. Without the ball, Eddie thought the voice would remain silent.

He dribbled right and passed to Steve, who passed to Kenny, who passed back to Eddie. One-thirty remaining. Eddie passed to

Donnell; Donnell had an open look at the basket but passed the ball back to Eddie. Eddie was frustrated. Donnell should have taken that open shot but he did not. He did not take it because Eddie always took charge at the end of the game. They were trained to put the ball in Eddie's hands when the game was on the line.

Eddie dribbled left; the voice returned. "Throw it to me, Eddie; I'm open." It was thunderous, like a unified chant from the fans, except every voiced sounded like Griff.

Eddie checked the clock; he had eight seconds to get off a shot. He dribbled toward Kenny, used the screen, and put up a seventeen-foot jumper.

"You, ball hog," he heard Griffin say just before he released the ball.

The words detonated in his head, sending memory shrapnel into every nerve of his control. Eddie's shot bounced hard off the iron rim. Big Donnell fought hard for the rebound and came up with the ball. The Spartans fouled him. The clock stopped with just over a minute in the game. Donnell was the worst free throw shooter on the team. He missed the first shot but made the second. The Cougars had a five-point lead.

The Spartans brought the ball up quickly and put up a three point shot that missed. Donnell pulled down the rebound and threw it the length of the court to Steve. He was wide open and scored the easy two. The Cougars were up by seven. The Spartans managed another two points but time expired and the Cougars won by five.

Everyone left the court but no one left faster than Eddie Dreyer. He quickly showered, dressed, and got on the bus. He was the first one there. As he sat at the back, he knew the coach would scold him for avoiding the media but Eddie knew the media did not need him to write their stories. They would report about the Cougars' mental toughness. They would write about the team's ability to handle the pressure at the end. But Eddie Dreyer knew it was luck and he had been trained to never leave a game to chance. Luck is a demon with a mandate to cheat everyone, equally. Eddie had no desire to be equal. The team began to trickle onto the bus. They were exuberant and grateful to have won. Eddie felt neither.

# 10

The coffee scented kitchen was unusual for Saturday morning. Powers Meade sat at the breakfast table finishing an English muffin with Strawberry jam rather than his normal trip out to Manny's Bistro.

*Two Saturdays in a row, Manny will think I've died.*

He drank his coffee and waited. He knew Eddie Dreyer would call; and he knew the call would come early. Powers set the alarm and awakened early in anticipation of the call. The paper had been read and neatly stacked on the corner of the breakfast table and the Sports section sat on top. It verified that the most important part of the newspaper had been reserved to enjoy last, like dessert. A large photo captured the Cougar's center, JayJay Donnell, muscling down a rebound. An accompanying column questioned Eddie's leadership and mental health.

"Am I the only one, who saw Dreyer freeze up at the end of the game? If it were anyone else, I would suggest that he be tested for drugs, because he looked lost on the court," the reporter wrote.

As Powers re-read the quote, he mumbled aloud, "Eddie Dreyer does not have a drug problem; he has a father problem." Powers was certain the issue would continue to disrupt Eddie's focus until Eddie came out of denial.

As expected, at seven o'clock, the phone rang and Eddie demanded to come over. Despite his tone, Powers agreed to let him come by.

Powers was accustomed to the routine. He opened the door as soon as he saw Eddie striding up the walkway and quickly closed the door behind him. Eddie did not speak right away. Powers motioned to enter the office; Eddie entered. Powers sat in his chair and waited for Eddie to sit down.

Eddie paced near the shelf studying various objects. He seemed to be looking for something specific but Powers knew Eddie would not find it on the wall. The silence had an edge to it as though it would cut the first sound. Powers was determined that Eddie must initiate the conversation so he sat silent, waiting.

"Professor Meade, I'm worse off for talking to you," Eddie said as he continued to stare through the items on the shelf. "You didn't make things better." He turned around. "You made them worse."

He had fired a salvo across the bow. Eddie fixed a threatening glare. Powers knew he was waiting to gauge its effect. Powers did not respond, despite the anger he was feeling, He wanted to reprimand Eddie for an illogical allegation but one angry person in the room was plenty.

"My brother is still in my head; so you didn't help me at all. It was better when I was the only person who knew about this. And who knows where you have blabbed since then," Eddie blurted out.

"You came to me for hypnotism not help. Also, if it did not help, how do explain your previous game? Hypnotism is a tool, that's all," Powers said.

"Whatever." Eddie said and turned his back to Powers.

"Is that it? You've said your piece, now you want to leave," Powers said. "Did you have to come to my house to say that? Why didn't you just send me email?"

Eddie snapped his head around and glared at the professor. He walked around the desk and stood within a foot of Powers chair. Powers tried to disguise a dry throat swallow as Eddie's threatening presence towered over him.

"I'm here because Harmon Evans told me to come. I don't want to talk to you. The truth is I'd like to bust you in the face," Eddie snarled.

Powers pulse quickened and fear commanded reason. His glib tongue was dry and quiet.

"But I know I can't do that. The school would suspend me; maybe even expel me. I can't let that happen," Eddie said and straightened up.

Powers was thankful to have some of his space back. He summoned all his courage and stood. Even though Eddie said he could not hit him, Powers remained unconvinced.

"Eddie, your problems are deeper than your brother and me. I saw the interview with your father. I saw your discomfort. I do not know all the details but I know you are trying to live up to his standards. That is what is haunting you."

"Doc, I'm not listening to you. I can fix myself."

"Eddie, the hypnotism worked." Powers said.

"No, it didn't. I had one game free from him. It was my positive pre-game talk. But my brother's voice came back. I didn't

52

think I needed to talk to myself about it every game but I guess I do."

"No, Eddie, the voice came back because your dad triggered something the hypnotherapy did not cover."

"Leave my dad out of this," Eddie snapped back,

"I cannot leave him out and neither can you," Powers counseled. "I can help you."

"You're a quack; you can't understand real athletes," Eddie said.

Something inside Powers snapped. The years of being bullied had finally chased him to the cliff's edge. He could turn and stand his ground or he could stand there and wait to be pushed over the edge.

*I will not allow this boy will not abuse me.*

"You know what, I may be a quack but I am going to sleep tonight. You are not," Powers said as he walked around Eddie. "You are going to go home and listen to imaginary voices. Your evening will be restless. You have no idea how to control this and for a control freak, like you, that's borderline insanity. I do not have to dribble a basketball to understand father-son relationships." Powers continued his path to the door. "And another thing son, winners conquer obstacles; losers deny their existence."

Powers stood at the door with his hand on the handle. Eddie took a few steps toward the middle of the room but stopped short of the door. Then suddenly he began laughing..

"No, Doc. A loser is someone who can't control his temper. You think you can provoke me. I face players trying to get inside my head every damn day. You're a fuckin' amateur at head games," Eddie said as he inched toward Powers with the grin of a madman.

Powers tried to steel himself. Eddie's grin grew larger. Powers imagined Eddie's verbal assault was building behind that scary grin.

"First, if I'm a loser, how come no one's interviewing you on television?" Eddie asked and re-pasted the grin. His second comment was coming. "And if I'm the loser, how come I never see your picture in the paper?" Eddie asked. "And do not call me son again. You're not my father. My father is a man, not a pansy-ass shrink."

Once again, Eddie stood within inches of Powers. Eddie made a quick slash through the air with his hand and snapped his fingers. Powers blinked; Eddie laughed.

"You seem speechless, Doc. Is this a professional tactic? Are we in session now? Because, if we are, I think I can help you," Eddie said as he walked to Powers chair and sat down. "I've noticed you aren't hooked up with a woman. Would you like to talk about that?"

Powers watched as Eddie threw his leg up on the desk.

"Eddie, you suspect I am afraid of you and I am. So you are not accomplishing anything by trying to ridicule me. The fact remains; no one is expecting me to beat the Wildcats on Thursday night. I'm not under that pressure; you are," Powers said slowly to conceal his nervousness but his hand tightened on the door handle.

He found himself hoping it could be turned either way to open the door. At this moment, he could not remember; he just wanted to get out if necessary.

"We'll take care of the Wildcats," Eddie said.

"No you won't," Powers said softly "Normally, you can control your universe and when you do, the Cougars have a chance to win the close games. But you are not in control. You want to work on your mental game against Carlos Robinson not ghosts. You do not know how to fight ghosts. That is why you are angry. That is why you are here. It has nothing to do with me."

"I'm not angry," Eddie denied.

"You are angry and you are masking it behind this "trash talking macho thing." Powers made quotation marks with his hands. "To claim different is merely more evidence of denial."

Eddie pulled his leg off the desk he put both elbows on the arms of the chair, brought his hands together, and rested his chin upon the knuckled perch. The body language suggested a pensive state. Powers made a peace offering.

"Eddie, I apologize for calling you a loser. I lashed out because you insulted me. I was unprofessional. I know you are not a loser. You are a skilled tactician whose performance is being hindered by conflicting expectations."

Powers peered at the top of Eddie's bowed head. He wished he were a mind reader instead of psychologist. He gambled that Eddie would listen. Powers dragged a chair near Eddie and sat next to him. Eddie responded by straightening his posture and holding his head high.

"I'm gonna' leave," Eddie said as he slapped his hands against his thighs.

"Do you want to go home and face this issue alone?" Powers asked.

"I can handle it." Eddie said with all the confidence he could muster.

"No you can't, Eddie." Powers said almost begging for belief.

"There's nothing you can do. You've given it your best shot. Maybe, this kind of problem requires a real doctor, a psychiatrist. You're just a college teacher." Eddie said as he reached a hand behind his neck and began to massage.

If Eddie had turned to look at Powers, maybe he would have sensed the anger Powers was masking and maybe he could have motivated Powers to try again, to give it the old college try. But he did not. He sat there rubbing his neck on his throne decreeing absolutes on a whim.

Powers was not accustomed to relentless attacks. His emotions went up and down like a basketball that Eddie mindlessly dribbled. Powers wondered, why bother? Let him walk away? Powers did not care if the Cougars won a basketball game. And a familiar truth surfaced. Powers did not care if Eddie conquered his conflicts. Powers was satisfied; he had determined the real issue. That was all the success he needed. This would be just one more person he could not help.

*I cannot help someone who does not want help. Screw this kid. I have bigger items on my to-do list.*

He mentally pictured the list and Harrington was at the top. Powers needed a new source of income. He did not have time for this ungrateful self-centered jock. Eddie interrupted his thought process.

"When you tried to hypnotize me__," Eddie began.

"I did hypnotize you," Powers interrupted.

"How do you know that?" Eddie asked turning to look at Powers. "I don't know it."

Powers wondered why he bothered to defend his action. He did not want to explain it to Eddie. Powers took a deep breath and pushed aside the anger and resentment one last time. He rested his elbows on the desk and leaned forward.

"Eddie, you were in a trance. It was important for the experience to be a mystery to you. The script I employed created a safe environment for you to face your brother."

"But I heard his voice again. Do you expect me to see you before every game? Are you trying to make me dependent on you or just trying to get as much money as you possibly can?" Eddie asked with a tone that would slice through the thickest skin.

Powers knew he should not have tried to explain. He will always torment me. Powers stormed to the door and opened it.

"Here's the bottom line, Eddie. I see no reason to lie to you. I do not like you. I do not like people like you. You think you get a free pass to insult people, walk on them, and use them. Most people do not see the real you. They see a basketball star. What I have seen is not only a bully but also an asshole. Now get out." Powers said without yelling, though he wanted to scream.

"So, that's the bottom line?" Eddie asked, as he remained seated.

"Yup, that's it. I am just a college teacher and Monday I will go teach my classes. No guilt. No pressure. No voices. How is your Monday shaping up?" Powers quipped.

"You're a dick." Eddie said.

"Is that your best shot, Eddie?" Powers asked as he swung the door open wider.

"What kind of doctor are you?" Eddie's voice screamed. "You aren't supposed to treat people this way."

Powers recognized the opportunity to re-connect the doctor patient relationship but did not. He was tired of Eddie's competitiveness. Powers knew that as soon as he softened his attack, Eddie would ridicule him again.

"Doctor? No Eddie, I am a quack who teaches college classes."

No rebuttal. Silence hung thick like the prelude to a tornado.

"What would it take for you to help me?" Eddie asked.

Again, Powers felt like this was a moment for reconciliation but he could not embrace it. The distance from the doorway to the chair gave Powers a feeling of safety. He did not let loose of the door handle and Eddie did not rise.

"I knew you would ask, Eddie," Powers said. "I knew because I have known people like you all my life. You will say or do anything to get what you want. You are willing to deal with the consequences later. You are the kind of person, who makes a deal with the devil, because later is later, now is all that matters."

Truth cuts without emotion or remorse. It should have been be the perfect weapon for Powers Mead. But his rapier clanged against impenetrable metal.

"Believe whatever you want to believe. I'm okay with that. Now, will you help me?" Eddie asked.

Powers realized he could not win; he could not hurt Eddie nor could he get even. It is just another basketball game to Eddie. Powers had the ball and Eddie needed it back. The diagnosis was accurate; Eddie willingly took this little slap of truth to get to help. He is an addict looking for a fix. Tomorrow is not today's problem.

Powers continued to stare. The truth of reality was suddenly inescapable; Eddie had been trained to win at all cost.

*At ALL COST.*

The words washed over his training. The relationship was changing as they stared at each other. Eddie would allow Powers to insult him, undergo hypnosis, play his game, and go right back to treating Powers as a quack who teaches college classes.

Powers closed the door and walked across the room. Eddie vacated the chair to permit Powers to sit in the throne. Powers straightened the things Eddie had moved. He pushed the computer mouse pad back into place. The screensaver disappeared. The betting website ad popped up again. He closed the ad and returned his attention to Eddie.

"Eddie, I cannot win. You do not care if I insult you. You do not care if my insults are true or false. You just want the voices to go away. Am I right?" Powers asked.

"Are you really looking for the truth here?" Eddie asked.

Powers nodded yes.

"Nothing but net Professor Meade. A voice in my head during a game is unacceptable but a college professor despises me," Eddie shrugged indifference. "I could care less. Whatever it takes, to make the voice disappear, I will do."

"Why not try another psychologist or psychiatrist?"

"Nope. You are the only person who knows and I want to keep it that way," Eddie replied.

Powers said, "Ok, Eddie, I'm going to hypnotize you but there will be a condition."

"What?"

"In my script, I'm going to plant a suggestion that you leave me alone, that you never come see me again. Can you live with that stipulation?" Powers asked.

"Perfect. I don't want to come here," Eddie answered and added, "While we are being honest, I don't like you either."

Powers had become immune to Eddie's barbs.

"I need a few minutes to prepare. Read a book; you can read, can't you?" Powers toyed with him.

"You do date women, right?" Eddie fired back.

Eddie walked over to the bookshelf and examined the titles. Powers ignored him and began typing on his laptop. He kept the original script but new ideas were popping into his brain.

Powers piled all the ideas onto the page and began arranging and editing the directions logically. He quickly read through the script. He finished typing and hit the print button. He closed the cover to the laptop. He dimmed the lights, took the printed pages from the printer and reviewed them one more time. He was ready.

"Eddie, sit down. Rid yourself of the animosity that you feel toward this process and me. Start the breathing exercises. Control your heartbeat. As you feel yourself settle down, close your eyes and continue the rhythmic breathing. I will be right back. I will be in the hall practicing the script. Do you understand?"

"Yeah, I've got it."

Powers walked into the hall. He held two scripts; one in each hand as though he might get the two confused. He read each to himself. He paced the short hall shifting his attention from one script to the other. He crumpled the left one into a tight ball and dropped it into the can. He read the chosen script one more time, took ten long breaths, and returned to the office.

Eddie's ability to get lost in the rhythm of breathing amazed Powers. He studied Eddie's face; Eddie seemed tranquil and immune to danger. Powers took another breath and settled into his chair as quietly as he could.

"Eddie, I am ready; are you?"

Eddie replied, "Yes."

"Eddie, every time you begin a pre-game meditation session, you will conclude with this routine. Do you understand?"

"Yes."

"You are standing in total blackness. A light comes on and you can see the staircase with handrails. Look up the stairs. You see a bright light at the top. Nod yes when this picture is vividly clear to you."

Within seconds, Eddie nodded yes.

"Eddie, there is noise at the top of the steps. It is a faint noise. It is a mixture of voices, squeaking, and pounding. Nod yes, if you hear it?" Powers requested.

Eddie nodded yes.

"Hold the rails and climb the five steps to the top. When you reach the light at the top you will step onto a basketball court. Everyone is dressed to play except you. On the far side of the court is a door with a sign that reads: "Eddie's Control Room." Walk toward the room. At the door stands your brother. Say to him,

"Griff, I was wrong to make you feel less special." Powers instructed.

"Griff, I was wrong to make you feel less special," echoed Eddie.

Griffin says to you, "Thank you, Eddie; I forgive you. Now play up to your expectations."

"Do you hear him say it to you Eddie?"

"Yes."

Walk across the court, go into the control room, and dress for the game. Walk back out on the court. Is your brother there?" Powers asked.

"Yes."

"He's smiling at you, isn't he?" Powers suggested.

"Yes," Eddie said and smiled.

"Eddie, Look to your right; your father is standing there. Do you see him?" Powers asked.

"Yes," Eddie said. His smile disappeared.

Powers paused to swallow and wet his lips. He tried to compose himself but he could feel his body tensing up. He continued.

"Your father says no one is more talented than you. Forget your team mates; take charge of the game." Can you hear him Eddie?" Powers asked.

"Yes."

"Your brother says, 'No Eddie. Do the right thing. Involve your teammates.' Do you hear him, Eddie?"

Eddie nodded. His head turned from side to side. It was barely noticeable. Powers imagined Eddie struggling with what to do.

"Eddie, listen to Griff. Your father's voice will fade into the darkness; it is gone. Repeat these words, I will involve my teammates at critical points in the game," Powers instructed.

"I will involve my teammates at critical points in the game."

Powers listened as Eddie continued to breathe with precision.

*Am I going to get away with this?*

Fear sizzled through his body like a jolt of electricity.

"You must play fair. Carlos deserves to win. Who deserves to win, Eddie?" Powers asked as he stretched his professionalism to an unrecognizable point.

"Carlos," Eddie recited.

"Now, the crowd is chanting: Meade–Meade-Meade. Can you hear them?"

Eddie's face seemed confused. His head turned as if to listen harder. Powers worried. 'I've gone too far.'

"Yes," Eddie finally responded.

"They are reminding you to ask Professor Meade for help with the next game. You cannot win the next game without the help of

59

Professor Powers Meade," Powers stated.

"Walk to the stairs. Climb down the steps. When you reach the bottom, you will be refreshed, your plan for the basketball game will be clear. You will be unaware that you have been in hypnotherapy. Do you understand?"

"Yes," Eddie answered.

"Begin. Step five. Step four. Step three, two and one."

Powers waited. He analyzed Eddie's facial expression. The Exhilaration was mesmerizing as he waited but his fear felt like deafening claps of thunder in his chest.

Eddie opened his eyes with several quick blinks. He shrugged his shoulders to loosen up and rubbed his hands together to regenerate blood flow.

"What do you remember?" Powers asked.

"You were telling me to breath in a rhythmical pattern."

"I introduced a script to your subconscious to deal with Griff, your father and to leave me out of your future. You seemed highly susceptible. Your next game will be played without voices," Powers explained.

"We're done?" Eddie asked in a controlled tone.

"It's done," Powers replied as he walked toward the door and let Eddie Dreyer out.

# 11

Powers examined his ticket and took the maroon plastic chair labeled twelve; Jim sat in thirteen.

"Never?" Jim asked.

"Nope," Powers responded as he opened the program booklet given to him by the student at the door.

"It's hard to believe you have never been to a basketball game."

Powers shrugged his shoulders slightly and continued to turn the pages.

"Well you picked a good one for your first," Jim said as he clapped his hands together and rubbed as if he were warming them up on a cold day.

"I suppose that's because of the matchup between Eddie Dreyer and Carlos Robinson," Powers said while leaving his eyes trained into the program.

"How in the hell do you know about Carlos Robinson?" Jim exclaimed. "Oh, Eddie Dreyer must have mentioned him during the session, right?"

"Client privilege," he said with a stop sign hand. "I did my homework."

"I'm impressed. But don't you worry about Carlos. The Cougars set picks relentlessly. Eddie will pop open all over the court," Jim said as he mimicked Eddie shooting a shot. "Nothing but net."

Powers chose not to request an explanation. The game tipped off and Powers watched Eddie. He did not care where the ball went, he just watched Eddie. The lead went back and forth; the Cougars had a three-point lead at the intermission. They started play in the second half and immediately Carlos stole the ball from Eddie and scored. The game continued to seesaw. With three minutes to play the Wildcats held a two-point lead.

Eddie broke free on a pick and stopped. He was open ten feet from the basket but did not shoot. He forced a pass to a teammate. The teammate was not looking for the pass; he was expecting Eddie to shoot. The Wildcats claimed the loose ball and on the breakaway, Eddie fouled the man in the act of shooting. A collective groan erupted from the Cougar frenzied crowd. One free throw went awry and one went in. The Wildcats had a three-point lead.

Eddie brought the ball up court and was fouled in the act of shooting. He missed the first; the crowd groaned again. The crowd noise reminded Powers of an orchestral performance without a conductor.

*How did they know exactly when to crescendo without sheet music?*

Eddie missed the second shot.

"What the hell?" Jim screamed.

The Wildcats dribbled to Powers right. A Cougar player intercepted a pass and ran the length of the court, to dunk the ball. Many spectators leapt to their feet causing vibration under Powers feet.

"Yessssss!" Jim yelled as he high fived the man in seat fourteen.

The Cougars trailed by one with twenty-seven seconds remaining. After a time out, the Wildcats' inbound pass was tipped and a scramble for the ball ensued.

"Tie ball. Tie ball!" Jim yelled.

Powers heard others advising the referees. The referee whistled; action stopped and tie ball was indeed called. Jim leaned over to explain the arrow pointed in the Cougars favor. Powers shook his head as though he understood.

The Cougars threw the ball inbounds and immediately passed the ball to Eddie. The stage was set.

"Now, we got 'em!" Jim said. He grabbed Powers by the shoulder and shook him. "Watch this."

Eddie searched for a path to an open shot as time clicked off the clock. He slid off a pick, pulled up to shoot from twenty-five feet, and shot it twenty-three. The air ball was rebounded by the Wildcats, time expired, and the jubilant Wildcats began a hug fest. Jim threw his mangled program to the floor.

"Man, talk about ugly," he said to no one in particular.

They joined the herd of disappointed fans exiting the arena. Powers followed Jim up the aisle and out into the night air.

"I've never seen Eddie play worse," Jim said.

"I thought it was an exciting contest," Powers responded.

"A contest is an event held by the Piggly Wiggly to see which kid can color the best Easter bunny. This was a game, Powers; it was a battle and Eddie Dreyer is the principle reason for the loss," Jim said louder than he intended. He offered an apologetic grimace.

"You people put tremendous pressure on him," Powers said.

Jim said, "Yes, Powers. Yes we do. That's why he is here. Eddie Dreyer is here to win basketball games."

"You mean to play basketball games. I counted four other players on the court with him at all times," Powers said.

"No. Eddie is here to win. If we just wanted people to represent the school in good spirited fun, we would not give him a free ride," Jim explained. "He's expected to win."

"What do we expect from the academic scholarship holders? Do we not have Engineer Scholarships?" Powers asked.

"No one wants to buy a ticket to watch Engineers Build or a Physics Problem Solved," Jim said. "Don't be a dope."

"A dope? How colorful your language becomes when you talk sports. Anyway, we are a peculiar lot. We give athletes scholarships, bathe them in adoration, baby them, award them degrees, then call them dummies behind closed doors, and have the temerity to complain when they lose," Powers said as he gazed at the stars with one hand on his chin and the other behind his back.

"No shit, Freud or should I say Sherlock?" Jim said as he made fun of Powers' Sherlock Holmes pose.

The two men reached Jim's car. Powers waved bye and started toward his car.

"You know Eddie is normally cool and in control. He's the best player in this conference. You didn't see him at his best." Jim's adoration had returned.

"I know his performance did not reflect the historical record." Powers agreed.

"No it didn't. I guess you still have a job because he needs help. Chase away whatever is bothering him, Powers. He's fun to watch, when he's on his game."

"Now, I have a better understanding of the game. I can see the enormous pressure he faces. But, I believe, he inflicts more pressure upon himself than any of you could ever generate."

"Any of you? Jim asked.

"Yes, any of you fanatics."

"It was a good game. If it didn't make you a fan, you'll never be one," Jim said.

Powers said, "I'll never be one. I see no difference between Eddie Dreyer and the lion performing in the center ring except that the whip cannot be heard nor seen."

Jim shook his head in exasperation. They both waved goodbye. Alone, Powers felt free to acknowledge his accomplishment. He had manipulated the manipulator. He drove home and rushed into the house. He bound up the stairs, logged on to the Internet, and checked his mail. The only email in his inbox was from his betting website. Powers read the brief message; his five hundred dollar wager on the Wildcats had paid nine hundred and fifty five dollars. Powers had profited nicely from Eddie's performance.

Powers would not have wanted to choose which feeling thrilled him the most. He was electrified with excitement about the money and he was elated to have orchestrated vengeance. Eddie Dreyer, the cocky intimidating manipulator, was but a circus lion performing as Powers directed. A geeky professor held the whip no one could see.

He powered up his iPod and dialed up Charlie Parker; jazz filled the room as Powers filled a glass with Syrah. Tomorrow, Eddie may break down the door and beat Powers to death for ruining his game but tonight Powers would wallow in his vindictive and profitable victory.

# 12

The phone rang for the fourth time, Patty had stepped out of the office, and Powers answered it.

"May I speak with Professor Meade?" The voice requested.

"This is he."

"This Eddie Dreyer, you quack. You told me I would play up to my expectations. I sucked. I cost the team a win. You're a liar. I don't want your help anymore, ever, you queer quack."

"Then start by not calling me." Powers abruptly hung up the phone.

Powers turned to look out the window. He wondered how Eddie would react to the sudden termination of the telephone conversation. Eddie's subconscious was following orders.

"You cannot win the next game without Powers Meade's help," were his instructions.

He was calling for help but anger drove his emotions. Eddie's rage frightened Powers. Nothing in the hypnotherapy suggested Powers was safe from retribution. He turned back to stare at the phone; he expected it to ring. It did not.

Powers continued his work with fractured concentration. His eyes were constantly monitoring the window and the door as though Eddie might suddenly appear. At four, he packed his briefcase walked cautiously to his car. He relaxed a little during the drive home. He walked upstairs to his office and saw the blinking light indicating a message. He dialed his voice mail. The message was from Eddie; it was short.

"Fuck you, quack. I'll call whenever I please."

Powers erased the message. In twenty-four hours, Eddie had to be ready to play another game. Basketball is a dictator, and Eddie its foot soldier. His marching orders never changed. He will need confidence in his game. He has nowhere else to turn. Powers was convinced Eddie would come for help.

The cell phone buzzed and rang. Powers answered it.

"I'm gonna' whip your ass, Doc. I don't care if they expel me," Eddie said.

"Do not threaten me. How did you get my cell phone number?" Powers said with as much calm as he could muster.

"It's not a threat; it's a promise," said Eddie in a growl.

"Your basketball career will be over," Powers countered.

"Yeah but hearing your bones break and seeing you bleed will be worth it."

"I will call the police and you will lose your scholarship," Powers said in an attempt to bring Eddie back to reality.

"So, I'll sit a semester and go somewhere else or maybe I'll turn pro."

"Not if they believe you are disturbed and that you have been in therapy for weeks. I will tell them you have a mental disorder. I will tell them you are unbalanced and capable of violence. No one will offer you sanctuary," Powers said as he walked to the window to peek out the blinds.

*Where is he? Across the street? In the backyard?*

Eddie continued, "That's a lie. I'm not sick. They won't believe you."

The phone went dead. Eddie had hung up. Powers stared at the cell phone and tossed it on the desk. He went downstairs, peeked out the slatted window and locked the front door. The sun disappeared behind trees, houses, and horizon. The darkness illuminated his fear. Powers wondered if Eddie's anger could override the hypnotherapy. Could he have discovered the negative suggestions? Powers flipped the light switch; the room went dark. He took another look outside; seeing nothing, he left the room.

He searched for a weapon. He determined his best choice would be an antique walking cane. It felt solid in his hands. He waved it through the air menacingly. He imagined hitting Eddie but logic told him that Eddie would take it away; and would beat Powers to death with it. He put it back in the hall tree stand.

Powers heard the cell phone ringing again. He picked it up and answered.

"I'm coming over," Eddie said with absolute calm.

"Then I am calling the police," Powers answered.

"It won't be necessary. I need answers and you are the only one who might be able to give them to me."

The anger was absent from Eddie's voice but Powers kept his guard up.

"I don't think so. This isn't working out. You are dangerous," Powers stated.

"I am angry but I am not dangerous. I blame you and I lashed out but all I want to do is play basketball and win. Can't you help me win?"

"I do not want to. I do not want this kind of confrontation in my life," Powers answered.

"What about my life? Have you done what Harmon Evans hired you to do? Have you cured me? Have you removed the demons that are fucking up my game?"

"You do not want help, Eddie. You are not willing to face the issues that conflict you."

Powers could not seem to control his thoughts. A relationship with Eddie represented an exciting experiment for a professor about to be unemployed. However, Powers felt inept handling Eddie in reality butaz feared his own greed in hypnotherapy. Eddie could be a source of income.

Using Eddie to make money from betting was a temptation Powers found difficult to resist. He argued against himself. Who in their right mind would consider wagering on college basketball as a source of income? Eddie is too volatile and wagering is too much of a gamble. The only reasonable course was to get Eddie out of his life. The knock at the door startled Powers and snapped the ping-pong of thoughts like the pop of a towel on an unsuspecting ass.

"Let me in; I won't hurt you," Powers heard Eddie say.

Powers moved closer to the door and put his hand on the deadbolt to be reassured it was locked.

"No, I think it would be better if you found someone else to talk to."

"Professor Meade, I don't want to start all over. I don't want to tell some other shrink about my family and the voices. I promise to be cooperative."

"Eddie, you will say anything to get ready for the next game."

"Yes and I will do anything to get ready for the next game. I want to play and I want to win. Period. Why is that so hard to understand? Why is that wrong? Let me in," Eddie pleaded.

"It is a game, Eddie. I do not believe you are as driven to win as you say you are. Even if the drive to win is innate, you cannot succeed because you are a victim of the expectations forced on you by your father and mother," Powers said with his right ear pressed close to the door.

"That's where you are wrong. They laid a foundation and they pushed hard. They preached relentlessly about more work, more study, and longer practice but I have chosen to win at all costs. I love the contact, the smell, and cheating without getting caught. I love taking advantage of my opponent's weaknesses. I want to demoralize him, leaving no doubt that I am the better player. This is my psyche; it is my commitment to winning."

"Then you are sick, Eddie."

"Why? Because I want to win, I'm sick; because I am willing to pay the price?"

There was a pause. Powers worried he was looking for another entrance. He heard Eddie's feet shuffle.

"I'm right, professor," Eddie continued. "You don't understand. You've never wanted to be the best. You've never been willing to pay the price. You're happy in mediocrity. In my world, you're sick. I can't understand why you want to live such an insignificant life. But that's okay Doc. We need mediocre people giving mediocre effort. It's the mediocre people, we winners roll over on our way to victory. Does that make sense to you?"

Powers did not respond. Neither of them spoke. With the exception of a few crickets, silence dominated the moment.

"Hey that's not an insult," Eddie said. "I'm just stating facts from my perspective?"

Powers was hurt by Eddie's comments but found them difficult to attack. Eddie should be allowed to pursue excellence. Powers knew he had no right to sit in judgment.

*Why do I live in mediocrity?*

Powers reached for the deadbolt and with more curiosity than fear opened the door. He was prepared for a ruse; he would not have been surprised if Eddie had pushed through the door and blasted him in the face. Powers could picture Eddie standing over his bleeding body laughing and yelling, "Sucker. Chump. Queer. Quack. Loser."

Eddie walked in. He walked past Powers and stood reticent at the doorway to Powers office.

"Thank you for letting me in."

"Now what?" Powers asked.

"You're the doctor; you tell me." Eddie said softly.

"No, I am not your doctor. I am a college psychology professor who tried to help a bar owner help a student. For the most part, I have failed. You tell me specifically what you want," Powers said still anticipating Eddie's physical assault.

68

"I think your hypnotic suggestions are working. Voices did not bother me last night but new problems have risen. We need to deal with them."

"What new problems?" Powers asked. Powers knew; he hoped Eddie did not.

"I did things to allow Carlos Robinson to win the game. I don't know why but I did. I gave up the ball at a crucial moment in the game. I don't do that. Something inside my head is over-riding my training. It must be my brother and the idea that I must be fair. This script of yours must have a flaw, a loophole."

"I said specifically. Specifically, what do you want?" Powers scolding tone seemed to alarm Eddie.

"I want no interference from this "play fair" voice and I want to strengthen my resolve to win at all cost," Eddie said without hesitation. "Specific enough?"

"I can do that," Powers stated. "But, when I have finished, will you leave me alone? Forever?"

"I thought you fixed that in the last session."

"Evidently, I have a flaw in my script," Powers replied. "I will do this but not this evening. I want a flawless script."

"I play tomorrow night, so when will we meet?"

"Tomorrow morning at eight," Powers said.

"Fine," Eddie responded.

Eddie walked to the door and let himself out without exchanging another word.

Powers went to the kitchen and took hot tea upstairs to his bedroom. He sat in bed, fully clothed, wide awake, and sober; he opened the laptop and started writing. Eddie Dreyer is a better analyst than he knew. Powers agreed with him. Eddie's win at any cost strategy is not a variation of his parent's propaganda; he wanted it for himself. Powers was convinced Eddie set his own expectations.

Powers began to list all the commands he wanted to include in the script.

His script would be effective but he could not stop feeling manipulated. Twenty year-old Eddie Dreyer told him what to do and Powers did it. Powers stared at the list. Suddenly a new set of objectives occurred to him. He typed,

"Punish the bully"

"Use his ass"

"Protect yourself"

Within seconds, his training and a modicum of civility coerced him to type counter points,

"Help him"

"Do the right thing"

"Undo the effects of your anger"

Powers looked at the clock; midnight approached. He had thought away four hours. He stood to walk around for a few minutes. He paused at the liquor cabinet but opted for another cup of tea. Eddie would be back in eight hours and Powers was torn between the two sets of commands.

He settled back onto the bed. He slurped at the tea.

Then he typed, "Please everyone."

As a strategy, he knew it never worked.

He deleted the thought and typed, "Please me."

He stared at the words. The goal called to him. It was selfish, maybe even shallow, but comfortable. Eddie became a secondary objective.

This had become about Powers' future, not Eddie's.

He typed: "What do I want?"

From there ideas flowed easily. When he stopped typing, he looked at the list and couldn't take his eyes off of one particular thought. Money. Money had never been a goal for Powers. He lived comfortably but spent all he earned. However, with the loss of his position at the university, money would become imperative. He did not want to leave his cozy life.

Harrington, Eddie, the town, Harmon Evans, Jim, Natalie, everyone was getting what they wanted except Powers.

"Winners need mediocre people to roll over," Eddie had said.

Eddie was right. Most people are not the winners. Most people get rolled at some point. The masses get used to it. Shit happens. But the gene pool lottery winners, the physically gifted, and the ruthless they are different. They do not let shit happen to them. The masses walk mindless on a path and are surprised when they step in the shit. They continue walking and continue to step in it. So the masses develop faster ways to clean their shoes. They never consider walking a different path. Winners choose paths. They decide what steps to take and if necessary they re-direct the steps of losers.

*Shit happens.*

Powers admitted to himself he had always taken the path of least resistance.

"I am not a winner; I must be a loser." Powers reasoned out loud. "I am definitely a shoe cleaner."

Powers was surrounded by new age philosophers. They preached incessantly. Life is not a competition between individuals; it is a competition with oneself. No one loses; he merely lacks the specific knowledge, has inadequate strength, possesses insufficient speed, or ran out of time. The explanations for failure were infinite. To many thinkers were trying to breed consequence out of failure. He knew his world was insulated. He knew it was naïve but he had not realized how incompatible his world was with reality. Winners fight for what they want. It took little time for Powers to review his life. He never fought. He never wanted anything bad enough to fight for it.

He reached for his cup; it was empty and cold to the touch. Another hour had passed. In seven hours, Eddie would return.

*Eddie is sound asleep.*

He would not be wide-awake thinking and re-thinking. He would not be worried about his profession or about earning money. No, Eddie's to-do list was simple.

"Convince Professor Mead to fix my head." Check.

"Get some sleep." Check.

"Go pick up the new head." Check.

"Win a basketball game." Check.

"Be arrogant." Check.

"Build a path over another loser." Check.

The picture of Eddie sleeping had a life changing effect on Powers Meade. In that moment, he decided money would be his only goal. Money changed everything. He would not need Harrington or the college. He looked at his new list and began deleting everything but Money.

He typed, "I will acquire a million dollars."

He knew goals had to be specific.

*A million dollars is specific.*

Powers began the process of updating his script to accommodate his new goal.

# 13

Powers heard the footsteps coming up the sidewalk. He sat up. He had managed to sleep for three hours. Powers peeked through the slat-covered window. Eddie's head turned left and right as his eyes scanned the neighborhood hoping his admiring fans would not see him. Powers opened the door before Eddie could knock. They walked into the office. With the desk lamp dimmed, Powers was eager and prepared.

"Sit down Eddie. I am anxious to get started."

"You seem awful excited. Normally you are subdued and grumpy," Eddie said.

"Your comments sent me into a tailspin last night. I did a lot of soul-searching. You opened my eyes. I have a game plan for my life. And actually, I have you to thank for that," Powers said with a broad smile.

"Okay," Eddie said. His face expressed confusion.

"Eddie, please begin relaxing and start your breathing routine. Control your heartbeat. As you feel yourself settle down, close your eyes and continue the rhythmic breathing," Powers said.

Powers could hear his own breathing. He had to concentrate to avoid joining Eddie's perfectly controlled breathing pattern. As with each session, Eddie continued to follow instructions precisely.

"Eddie, your pre-game pep talks will take place at your apartment not the gym. You will include this visualization in your pep talk, every time. Do you understand?" Powers asked.

"Yes,"

"Picture a staircase with handrails barely visible in the darkness. Look up the stairs. You see a light at the top. Nod yes when this picture is vividly clear to you."

Powers lead Eddie to the Control Room, as he had on the two previous sessions.

"At the door stands your brother, father, and mother. Say to your brother, "I was wrong to make you feel less special, Griff."

"I was wrong to make you feel less special Griff," Eddie echoed.

Say to your parents, "I am my own man; your expectations are no longer necessary. I will play my game, the way I expect to play."

"I am my own man; your expectations are no longer necessary. I will play my game, the way I expect to play," Eddie repeated.

They say to you, "You are in control. No one can stop you. And Griff says I forgive you, Eddie."

"Did you hear them say it?" Powers asked.

"Yes,"

You will go into the Control Room. In the Control Room, you see your computer. You will log onto the Internet and you will go to surefirewinners.com. Your password is E G O. You will examine the list of games and you will select a game that you believe is a winner. You will place a fifty-dollar bet on this game. The selection of this game is a test of your ability. You know winners and you must select a winner. After selecting a winner, you will exit the Control Room dressed and ready to go on the basketball court. There will be no voices piercing your concentration. You will be in total control. The buzzer will sound the end of the game. You will have played better than anyone else on the court. Nod yes if you understand."

Eddie nodded.

"Begin walking back down the steps. Five. Four. Three. Two. Stop. This routine will give you full concentration. You are unstoppable, if you follow this routine. Do you understand?" Powers asked.

"Yes."

"Two things are necessary in this routine: Address your family before entering the Control Room and show your basketball superiority by placing the bet," Powers repeated the instructions.

"Where must you place the basketball bet?" Powers quizzed.

"surefirewinners.com" Eddie recited.

"Repeat these words, to be relaxed and prepared to be a winner, I must bet on basketball winners."

"To be a winner, I must bet on basketball winners," Eddie repeated.

"Repeat these words; I will never call Professor Mead. I only met him once to pick up an article for Coach Barkley."

"I will never call Professor Mead. I only met him once to pick up an article for Coach Barkley," Eddie repeated.

"Repeat these words. I am not open to hypnosis."

"I am not open to hypnosis," Eddie said.

"You are about to take the last step. When you reach the bottom you will be refreshed, free of voices that disturb your concentration on the basketball court and unaware that you have been in hypnotherapy. You will take the Article for Coach Barkley and say 'Thank You, Professor Meade.' Do you understand?" Powers asked.

"Yes," Eddie said calmly.

"Step down," Powers commanded.

Powers stood and extended a folder across the arm of the chair. He waited while Eddie's breathing lost volume and became normal. Eddie's eyes opened.

"This is what you came for," Powers said as he pushed the folder closer to Eddie.

Eddie took the folder.

"Thank you, Professor Meade," Eddie said.

"I hope Coach Barkley finds it helpful," Powers said with a smile.

Powers stood and walked to the door. Eddie followed.

"I hope the Cougars win to tonight," Powers said as Eddie walked away.

"We will," Eddie said back over his shoulder.

Powers watched as Eddie thumbed through the folder. Eddie paused at the end of the walkway, as though he could not understand why his car was parked a block away. He tucked the folder under his arm and walked down the block.

Powers went back to his computer. The adrenalin flow tingled in his veins. He logged on to his new website surefirewinners.com. He had downloaded an elementary web design program and had uploaded the point spread for every game he could find.

Next, Powers chatted with web site designer over the Internet. When the conversation was over, Powers was assured the site would be completely interactive within two days. Powers instructed him to build a site that would bar access to everyone who did not have password. Powers was not interested in bets from anyone but Eddie Dreyer. Eddie's bets would always reach Powers by email.

Eddie would not think about the pre-game pep talk until late in the afternoon.

*Will this really happen?*

He reviewed all his instructions in his mind until fatigue overtook him. He set an alarm for three o'clock and let his body crash on the bed. The adrenalin began to fade and though his nerves were

74

needling through his body, Powers drifted into sleep.

# 14

The campus was quiet. Everyone vacates the college between semesters. Students and professors go off to re-charge as though fifteen weeks of classes drains one to the point of exhaustion. Roofers, police officers, soldiers, or waitresses might giggle at such adversity, as might the athletes. Basketball players do not receive the re-energizing break; games continue to be played and practices continue to be held.

Powers had not spoken to, nor seen Eddie for two months, yet Powers received a minimum of five bets a week from Eddie. He did not know why Eddie placed bets so frequently when he only played two games per week. Despite Eddie's expertise, he did not pick a winner every time. At first, it concerned Powers because he did not know when to bet on Eddie's picks but after conducting research on the Internet, Powers learned that winning sixty percent could be considered outstanding. Eddie won seventy-two percent of the time. Powers realized, he need not choose. Seventy two percent was providing a very nice return.

Powers was still troubled by the frequency of the wagers. Powers took a trip to the campus in an attempt to unravel the mystery. He walked into the athletic offices, greeted the assistant cordially, and asked to see Coach Barkley. She called the Coach and he appeared at the door almost instantly. He rushed through the door with his hand extended.

"Professor Meade, How are you? Come on in." His welcome was energetic.

"It's good to meet you Coach Barkley."

The coach motioned him into the office with one arm the other arm was patting Powers on the back. Powers entered ahead of the Coach, who pointed to a maroon and white leather chair. Powers sat. He glanced around the office, noting the dozens of awards and Cougar paraphernalia covering the walls and shelves. The office was neat and orderly. Coach Barkley closed the door. He sat down behind his large desk, laced his hands together, and rested his elbows on the desk.

"So, you want to talk to Eddie Dreyer about his mental preparation for games?"

Powers had expected small talk or basketball banter before the actual discussion. The coach was friendly, full of positive energy, but apparently preferred to get right to business. Powers should have assumed the coach would be aggressive; all successful athletes are aggressive, even old ones.

"Yes. As a psychologist, I am intrigued by methods athletes employ to strengthen their psyches. I am researching a possible book on the subject," Powers answered.

"Really," said the coach.

Powers found it impossible to determine if the Coach's reaction was genuine interest or veiled disbelief.

"Professor, I read the paper you wrote on motivation, the one Eddie brought to me. What made you send that to me?"

"I thought it might be helpful since you spend most of your days motivating teenage boys to perform in a manner befitting your strategies," Powers explained.

"Boy, I sure do," chuckled Coach Barkley. "Well I certainly don't have a problem with you asking Eddie a few questions. As long as you don't do some shrink-voodoo thing on him," he quipped with a big smile. "Hope you don't take offense to that. I'm just having a little fun with you."

"Not at all; I promise not to mess with his head."

"Well that's good because he's pretty darn important to the Cougars," the Coach said.

"Yes, I know. I have a friend who is a huge basketball fan and loves to watch Eddie play," Powers said.

"We all like to watch him play. Sometimes I catch our own players watching him play when they should be involved in helping him play."

Again, he laughed at his own insight. It was infectious; Powers laughed with him.

"Well, Eddie is the first guy at practice. He should be there in about thirty minutes. I told him you would be there to ask him a few questions. Will that work for you?"

"I'm sure that will be sufficient." Powers rose and the coach rushed to get the door.

"I want to thank you again for arranging this meeting," Powers said.

"Hey, I want to thank you for asking me, first. There are way too many people sneaking around trying to get to Eddie," he said and clapped Powers on the back.

Powers left the office and walked over to the gymnasium. He took a seat on the sideline and waited for Eddie. The coach was right; Eddie was the first person on the court. Eddie looked directly at Powers. Powers shivered momentarily as he waited to see if Eddie had any recognition of their real history. Eddie tossed a bag toward a chair, took a ball, and began dribbling methodically. There was no apparent recognition.

As the ball slammed to the court, Powers waited for his courage to catch up to his curiosity. Eddie knew a professor was coming to ask him a few questions, he also knew a stranger was sitting on a bench, yet Eddie did not initiate conversation. Powers stood and walked across the court and called to Eddie.

"Remember me? I'm Professor Powers Meade from the Psychology department."

"Yes sir, I remember. You want to ask me some questions?"

"I understand you go through a pre-game visualization process," Powers said.

"Who told you that?" Eddie asked.

"Kyle Leggett," Powers nearly shouted to be heard over the bouncing ball and cavernous facility.

"I don't know Kyle Leggett," he said as he stopped bouncing the ball.

"Kyle's girlfriend is the sister of Barry Drummond," Powers stated.

"Ahhh, so, my ex-roommate complained about my routine to his sister, who blabbed to this Kyle dude and he must be a psychology major who opens up to professors. Part of that sharing thing you guys do" Eddie said as he began dribbling the ball again.

"Something like that," Powers lied.

Eddie had delivered his dialog with purposeful intent. He had immediately surmised that the professor could not help him control a basketball game, thus he mocked the profession. He had begun the process of intimidation and taking control.

Do you visualize before every game?" Powers began the questioning.

"Yep"

"Do you do it to relax, to reduce stress?" Powers asked.

"Nope; I do it to prepare for the future. I live it in advance. I do it to take advantage of my opponent. He has weaknesses. I close my eyes, see them, and I visualize beating him," Eddie said.

He passed the ball from hand to hand, without mishap, even though his eyes were fixed on Powers.

"It must work. I understand you are the best player in the conference," Powers said.

"Some people say that," Eddie said feigning modesty.

"When did you start using this technique?"

"In the tenth grade. I read about self hypnosis in a book."

"You utilized self talk visualization for basketball at the age of sixteen?" Powers said; he hoped his amazement did not show on his face.

"Fifteen and I first used it for a geography test. I got an A."

"I can't imagine many teenage boys going to that extreme," Powers said.

"I never intended to be like other teenage boys nor do I intend to be like other men," Eddie boasted.

"Do you still use it for tests?" Powers inquired.

"I use it for everything. I want to win at everything so I use every tool I can get my hands on."

"Winning is your only goal?" Powers strayed from the subject but Eddie had opened the door.

"If the goal isn't to win, then why play?" Eddie replied.

"What about the competition, the exercise, the camaraderie?"

Eddie stopped dribbling.

"Are you here to analyze me or ask questions about my pre-game prep work?" Eddie asked as he tucked the ball under his arm.

"I apologize. Professional curiosity, that's all. So, you prep for everything; even a basketball practice, like this?" Powers asked.

"Practice is important. It's where the fundamentals are learned. It's the place where a team learns how to win. I want to win in practice too," Eddie stated without hesitation.

"Have you taught this technique to any of your team mates?"

"Nope."

"Have any of them asked you to show them this technique?"

"Sure, most of them. I tell them the name of the book. If they really want to work on their mental game they'll go buy it."

"And they don't?" Powers said with disbelief.

"I can't say for sure. But I doubt it; most people don't have enough concentration." Eddie pulled the ball from under his arm and

79

began to twirl it in his hand. "I need to get back to work. Are we done?" Eddie asked but it was implied they were through.

"Yes and thank you," Powers said.

"No worries." Eddie said and returned to his ritual.

Powers turned and walked away to the squeaking of Eddie's shoes and the bouncing ball echoing through the empty gymnasium. He also walked away with the answer he sought. Eddie wanted to win so badly he was visualizing almost every day and consequently, Powers received picks almost daily. A grin covered his face; he knew a pick was waiting for him at home. He hurried. Eddie had his goal and Powers had one of his own.

# 15

Eddie Dreyer was playing well. He was second in the conference in scoring, fifth in assists, fourth in steals, and tenth in rebounding. He was the favorite to win MVP. Two games remained in the season; with two wins, the Cougars would be the number one seed in the conference tournament. Six hours from game time, Eddie scrolled through his iPod. Music was part of his pre-game ritual. He did not choose soothing sounds to relax or angry music to lather his psyche into a rage. Eddie sought discord and his new favorite was Instrumental Chaos.

He pushed Play and closed his eyes and began to think about the game. Eddie recalled streams of coach-speak about strategy, teamwork and hitting the open man to theorize through his mind like one long sentence, uncluttered by grammar. Shoes squeaked on the hardwood floors as five players ran to where the coach assigned them to go, while five defenders moan and squeak in the chase. The ball bounced on the floor in a syncopated drum beat. The orchestration has one objective: get a player open to shoot the basketball.

Five players want to shoot at the beginning of a season but errant shots weigh heavily on confidence; and indecision cripples coaching. In the midst of chaos, most people want to be told what to do. Eddie embraced chaos and discord; knowing disorder was in the next moment prepared Eddie to take advantage of a court crowded with players following orders.

Eddie was uncomfortable. He opened his eyes, half stood and found his car keys under his butt. Eddie tossed them on the desk and noticed a small pop-up ad at the top of his laptop.

Eddie moved the mouse to close it. Slightly off target, the mouse opened the history tab; something repetitive and unusual caught his eye. He leaned in to examine the list. Eddie found over two-dozen visits to surefirewinners.com. He could not remember ever visiting the website.

He clicked the link. It was an internet betting service and the username read, EddieD. The account holder had a balance of over thirty-eight hundred dollars. He clicked on the statement tab and found that someone had made forty-one fifty-dollar bets including every Cougar game. Eddie stared at the screen with his eyes blinking. He could not settle on a single thought.

"What the fuck is this?" He said to the monitor.

He shut the computer down, hoping it was some kind of eerie glitch. He waited impatiently for it to cycle through its processes. There were millions of Eddies on the planet; it had to be someone else. It was too unbelievable for him to consider someone had wagered in his name. Eddie knew the consequences of betting. His college career would be over. Even if everyone who knew Eddie vouched for his credibility, this kind of evidence would doom him.

The computer finished cycling through. Eddie logged onto the Internet and typed in the address for surefirewinners.com. His machine was patched straight through; the password was locked in and the balance was still there.

"Goddamn it!" Eddie exclaimed. "Someone is trying to frame me."

Eddie got up and walked around the room for a few minutes. He needed to think more clearly. It did not help. He picked up a basketball and began to dribble it on the carpet. Eddie heard three loud knocks on the floor. The girls in the downstairs apartment were banging on the ceiling. It was a standard message to remind Eddie that he may live alone but he did not live in a vacuum. Eddie dropped the ball and sat back down. His eyes were glued to the thirty-eight hundred dollars.

"It's gotta' be a prank," Eddie said. "Who would do this? Troy. That bastard." He shook his head and forced out a smile. "He did this to me. Let's see how funny he thinks it is, when I take his money."

Eddie clicked on the link to withdraw funds. He chose close account and typed in a mailing address.

Eddie shut the computer down, re-started his music, and re-focused on his pre-game ritual. He sat quietly amid the chaotic noise. He closed his eyes and began to relax. He was breathing rhythmically. His mental images were clear. He saw the steps and heard the crowd. He walked up the steps to the court. He talked with his family, went into the control room, and just as he had been ordered, he logged onto surefirewinners.com and picked the Cougars to beat the Raiders by eleven. Eddie began to envision a perfect game. A game where he dominated his opponent. A game where he left the court victorious. Eddie walked back down the trance-induced steps and back into reality.

His breathing slowed, his eyes opened, and Eddie Dreyer was locked into his zone.

# 16

Powers Meade was in the kitchen when heard the familiar ding of incoming email. It never failed to excite him because this time of the day, it was usually a bet from Eddie. There were two emails from Eddie. Powers had two hours to place his bet. He continued shredding lettuce and cutting vegetables for his salad. He tossed it together in large bowl, poured the vinaigrette over it, poured a glass of wine, and took both upstairs to his desk.

He began eating an opened the first email. The first item was a request for withdrawal of funds; it was from Eddie. A fork full of salad hung half way between the bowl and his mouth. Powers was confused. Eddie had placed bets while in a trance. He should not be aware of an account balance. Surefirewinners.com should only exist in his subconscious mind. Powers dropped the fork back into the bowl and opened the request. Eddie requested to withdraw thirty-eight hundred dollars.

Powers opened the second email. Eddie was betting on the Cougars minus eleven. Powers took a large gulp of his wine and started placing bets. He visited six websites betting two thousand dollars at each website.

Powers closed the betting lines on surefirewinners.com. With zero promotion, the site still attracted betters looking to wager. Powers was not interested in developing the site as a business. He only wanted one customer but right now that one customer had him worried.

Having placed his bets, Powers began to pick at his salad. As he ate, Eddie's request continued to bother him. Was it Eddie making the request or had someone stumbled upon Eddie's username and password? Did something snap the trance while Eddie was making his selection?

Powers pushed the salad aside and opted to finish the wine. He came to two conclusions. Eddie was too volatile to covertly request his balance over the Internet. Secondly, Eddie would never jeopardize his career by being associated with gambling. He decided to disregard the request. Powers requested the Webmaster to unlock the password. The hypnotic suggestion gave Eddie a password. Eddie would enter it every time he placed a bet. Outside the trance, Eddie would not know the password. He hoped the problem would be solved.

Powers looked at his wristwatch, grabbed his bowl and glass and walked downstairs. Powers had agreed to meet friends at the campus auditorium to see the collegiate thespians perform "Fiddler On The Roof."

As always, Powers refused to be late.

# 17

It was a blowout; the Cougars beat the Raiders by twenty-two and the locker room was rowdy. Eddie scored a season high thirty-nine points but he was not contributing to the locker room merriment. He was still concerned about the betting site with the account balance. He needed answers; he tied his shoe and walked over to Troy's locker.

"Forget the mail. I'll take the thirty-eight hundred in cash," Eddie said as he looked around to be sure no one else had heard him ask.

"Dude, what are you talking about?" Troy said as he pulled a sweater over his head.

"Come on, Troy. I know you dummied up a website to play a joke on me." He gave Troy a slap on the shoulder and a 'caught-ya' wink.

"I did what?" Troy asked.

"Come on Troy. Give it up."

"Eddie, I don't know what you are talking about. What are you talking about?"

Eddie looked around at the emptying locker room. He leaned in close to Troy and whispered, "surefirewinners.com. Ring a bell?"

"No," Troy shot back. "Should it?"

"Ok, you're not shittin' me?" Eddie lost his friendly smile and said. "Cause if you are__,"

Troy cut him off, "Eddie, I'm in the dark here. Tell me what's going on?"

Eddie scanned the room; no one was nearby.

"I found a website for betting on games. I think someone has been betting in my name. I don't know what else it could be," Eddie said in a whisper.

"Man, that's messed up. They'll ban you from collegiate sports," Eddie whispered.

Troy closed the locker and stepped closer to Eddie.

"I know that Troy. I thought you were playing a joke on me. Hell, I was hoping you were fuckin' with me. Now, I have no idea what to think or do about it. You think I should tell coach," Eddie asked.

"Uh, hell no. Are you insane? If you involve him, he will have to tell the Dean. And you know what they are going to do. Say goodbye to the final game and the tournament," Troy said.

"That's what I thought. It's got to be a mistake. Someone is using an identical screen name to mine. That's the only answer," Eddie said as he searched Troy's eyes for agreement.

"Gotta' be. You should clear your history and delete all cookies. That stuff could still be misinterpreted. And make sure your bank records are in order. You haven't made any large deposits lately, have you?" Troy asked.

"No. Yeah, I'll clean it up. But it's weird," Eddie turned to leave, and said, "Catchya' later."

"Yeah. Talk to you tomorrow," Troy said.

"Hey Troy. Keep it to yourself, right?"

"I've always got your back Eddie," Troy said. "You know that." Their hands slapped together in brotherhood.

Eddie left the locker room. He heard the metal door slam against the frame behind him. It hung in the night air longer than the car engines and normal student revelry. He rushed home. He was ready to clear the history file and put this behind him. The one thing he could not explain away is why his computer has a history.

Someone had to visit the website from his computer to create a history; it didn't take a geek to figure that out. Eddie was careless about his stuff; friends and teammates were in and out of his place all the time. He toted the laptop around all day.

Eddie had a plan and was anxious to implement it. He would clear the history, delete the cookies, and initiate a password to protect his computer against unauthorized use.

He walked in the door, tossed his bag onto a chair and sat down at the computer. He rustled the mouse, the screen saver dissipated and Eddie logged onto the Internet. He resisted the temptation to check the website one last time. He deleted every temporary Internet file and shut the machine down. He was not wholly satisfied that his reputation would be safe but he had done all he could do for the time being.

He pushed the chair back and went to his bedroom. Eddie watched television until the local sports came on. He turned it off. The game was over. It was played as he expected it to be played; he did not need to see the highlights on television.

A textbook lay on the second pillow. Eddie opened it and began to read. His normal comprehension was missing. He allowed the book to rest on his chest while he stared at the ceiling.

Eddie thought about the gambling service. No one could prove Eddied had gambled. He had not deposit money with any betting service.

*Fear and worry are weights for the weak. I am not guilty of betting on college basketball. I will not worry.*

He lifted the book and began to read again but still his attention was divided despite the brave words.

# 18

The audience continued to applaud the curtain calls, the student playing Tevya entered the stage bowing and accepting his accolades. The performance was not powerful enough to hold Powers' attention. His mind wandered much of the evening. He stood clapping alongside his friends. Powers studied the young Tevya.

*Is this star as manipulative and ruthless as Eddie Dreyer?*

Powers would be suspect of talent forever after meeting Eddie Dreyer. All the ponds would forever be the same and the big fish would always eat the little fish.

Powers was among the first to stop clapping. The actors, like kids forced to come home for dinner, exited the stage and the crowd drifted from the auditorium to mingle in the Grand Hall.

The group drifted outside the building. Powers heard Jim suggest a round of drinks at Captain Bluebeards.

Some said, "Yes."

Others seemed unwilling.

Powers was thinking about the game; he wanted to know the score. Powers had pulled his phone from his pocket and was looking for the score and nearly bumped into a passing student.

He said, "Sorry. Excuse me but do you know if the Cougars won tonight?"

The boy said, "We won by over twenty."

"Thank you," Powers said.

A smile covered Powers' face; he turned to the group. They were still deciding who was going to Bluebeard's and who was not. Powers added incentive.

"The first round's on me. Now who wants to go?" He said with a sweeping right arm inviting the small group to the path.

"Count me in."

"What's better than free booze?"

"I'll have vodka."

"To Tradition!" some clever bass voice sang.

The group laughed and several of them began singing "Tradition" as they moved in the direction of the bar.

Powers felt euphoric. He had made nearly twelve thousand dollars this evening while he watched amateurs perform "Fiddler on The Roof." His grand total over the last few weeks was over forty-two thousand dollars.

He caught up with Jim, slapped him on the back.

"You know, I might buy two rounds," Powers offered.

Jim put his arm around Powers' shoulder and said, "Well, it's a great day to be your best friend!"

# 19

The Cougar lead was thirteen. Eddie looked at the clock; seven minutes remained in the game. He dribbled right up in Peterson's face and turned his back to him. He could feel Peterson on his hip; the stout but shorter guard had been banging on Eddie all night. Peterson had drawn four fouls trying to cover Eddie.

At this very moment, Eddie knew he could take Peterson. He could turn, show Peterson the ball, and wait for him to reach in. Eddie knew Peterson could not resist the idea of stealing the ball from the best player in the conference. Eddie also knew if he moved forward, just as Peterson reached in, the referee would see heavy contact initiated by Peterson. The referee would call a foul and Peterson's night would be over. Eddie could get the banging little bastard off the court.

But Eddie chose a different plan. He turned to face him, leaned in as close as he could get, and started up for a shot. As Eddie went up, he pulled his right elbow in and slammed it under the chin of Gary Peterson. Eddie felt the thud and watched Peterson fall backwards as Eddie continued up for a jump shot. The whistle blew as Eddie's shot scored. The referee rushed in and declared no basket. He called a foul on Eddie. It was his first. Peterson's mouth was bloodied. He toweled off at the sideline but stayed in the game. Eddie had tested his manhood; Peterson would not come off the court.

Peterson took the inbounds pass and started toward the Eagles' basket. Eddie met him at half court. He harassed Peterson's every dribble and move. Eddie saw an opening and reached for the ball. He knocked it away; they scrambled for it. Eddie batted it to a teammate. In the process, his knee caught Gary Peterson's tender chin. As Peterson groaned and grabbed at his chin, Troy slammed the ball home. The Cougars were up by fifteen. Peterson was bleeding again. He stood and gave Eddie a shove. Eddie did not shove back; he leaned back into his opponent's face.

"You got a problem?" Eddie snarled.

"You're a fuckin' punk," Peterson said.

"Hey, you get what you give, you lightweight," Eddie rebutted.

Players from both teams gathered around the two quarreling players. Both players were being restrained as the referees arrived on the scene.

"Fuck you, big-shot. I'm just playing the game," Peterson snarled.

"Then stay on the court, bitch. I got four more fouls to give you," Eddie shouted.

The referees positioned themselves between the two groups and tried to restore order. Coach Barkley called a time out. On the sideline, they huddled; the coach began yelling.

"What the hell are you doing Eddie? We have this game wrapped up. There's only four minutes to go. You should be concentrating on chewing up the clock, not engaging in petty crap. Leave the little bastard alone."

No one said anything.

Coach Barkley continued. "Show some class. Drop back in two three zone. Now, get back out there and play smart."

Peterson brought the ball up court. Eddie backed off but Peterson was sloppy with the ball. Jayson intercepted a pass and threw it to Eddie streaking down court. He had the ball and an advantage on Gary Peterson. Eddie slowed down to wait for him.

"School time, little man," Eddie yelled to him.

Peterson flew by as Eddie pulled up for a short jump shot. It was nothing but net. The crowd roared; the cheers were for Eddie; the roars of laughter were at Gary Peterson. The laughter seemed louder than the cheers. Peterson must have known the laughter was meant for his ears. Eddie ran next to Peterson, to press him all the way down the court.

"Was that your best D, little man?" Eddie screamed as Peterson struggled with the dribble.

"Get off me before I knock you out," Peterson yelled.

"Get back on defense, Eddie." Coach Barkley's orders cut through the noise.

"How's your mouth, little man," Eddie said to Peterson. "I feel another foul coming, can you?"

Eddie continued to harass him. Gary Peterson passed the ball but Eddie continued to tail him all over the court. The Eagles put up a shot; it missed. Donnell pulled down the rebound and passed the ball out to Eddie. He used his off hand to invite Peterson to come cover him. The crowd enjoyed Eddie's mockery of Gary Peterson. Peterson dutifully ran to cover him. Eddie evaded his defense easily; he toyed with Peterson as if it were a Globetrotter show.

Coach Barkley was livid. He was walking to mid-court to call a timeout. The Coach was going to take Eddie out of the game. At the same moment, on the court, an Eagle ran to assist Gary Peterson. Eddie saw the open lane and broke for it. Eddie was going to dunk the ball, send the crowd into frenzy, and put a nail in the coffin of Gary Peterson's pride.

Peterson trailed Eddie down the lane. When Eddie went up, so did Gary. The shorter Gary Peterson could not reach the ball. Eddie jammed it home but Gary lost his balance and rode Eddie's back to the court. They landed hard and Eddie's shoulder was twisted and took the bulk of Peterson weight upon impact. Tangled feet caused three more bodies to crash down. Another player's weight fell on Eddie at the bottom of the pile. One by one, players unknotted themselves from the pile. Four stood; one lay still.

The sight of Eddie Dreyer's white jerseyed body lying in the maroon painted lane silenced the crowd. Eddie could see Troy leaning over him. He saw the Coach and trainers rushing at him. Eddie heard advice coming from every direction. With Troy's help, he stood up and walked off the court. The trainer held Eddie's arm stable.

The crowd applauded as Eddie was escorted into the dressing room. The team doctor ordered Eddie into the ambulance. It sped away. Two minutes later, the game clock horn blared through the arena. The Cougars won the game by seventeen points.

# 20

Powers overslept. He awoke groggy. The wisdom of popping over-the-counter sinus medicine pills on top of the alcohol from Bluebeards was suspect in hindsight. Powers wanted coffee but time would not permit it. He would have to settle for the coffee at the school. The liquid had a vile taste; perhaps it was appropriate punishment for his behavior.

He had never been late; and Harrington would not have the satisfaction of thinking Powers had become apathetic without tenure. With briefcase in hand, he jumped in the car and rushed to campus. He walked in the door with four minutes to spare. He grabbed a Styrofoam cup, filled it with coffee. He was grateful he could not smell through his clogged sinuses. The combination of cheap coffee, Geraldine's wretched perfume, and Dan's midlife crisis cologne was almost more than the monster in his stomach could handle this morning. Powers preferred the scotch-medicated monster remain undisturbed, if at all possible. He felt a slap on his back; the coffee hit the rim but did not spill. Jeremy Whiting's cigarette scorched breath pierced Powers clogged sinuses and nudged the ogre in his stomach.

"I hope you left some for me, buddy. We all need morning caffeine," said Whiting. He stood there as though Powers would automatically agree with him.

"Take this cup. I think I will have the fake orange juice in lieu of counterfeit coffee," Powers answered as he handed the cup to Jeremy.

"Just doctor it up with cream and sugar. It's the caffeine we're after, right?" Jeremy suggested.

"Were that true, I could pop a NoDoz," Powers replied and added, "Excuse me Jeremy?"

Powers took his orange juice and walked toward Jim.

"Good morning, Mr. Meade," said Jim.

"I'm glad it is for you. My sinuses are swollen tight. I overslept. I have not had coffee," Powers said. After a brief pause, he added, "Good morning."

94

Jim watched as Powers sipped his juice and grimaced not from the discomfort of his stomach but because the Juice was not to his liking.

"You really are a snob, Powers."

"Guilty," Powers said with the shrug of his shoulders. "So, what's new?"

"Well, with the exception of the intellectual elitists in this room, everyone in town is talking about Eddie Dreyer."

"Let me guess; he had a big night and the Cougars clinched top seed in the tournament" Powers said with a smug smile. He expected his knowledge to impress Jim.

"That's true, but that's not the news. You haven't seen the newspaper, have you?" Jim asked.

"No, I did not have time."

"Eddie Dreyer is in the hospital. His season is over," Jim reported. "Hell, his career might be over."

"What?" Powers wanted to believe he had misheard. "What happened?"

Harrington stood at the podium asking everyone to take a seat. Jim sat down; Powers took a chair next to him.

"Well?" Powers asked expecting clarification.

"I'll give you the details when Harrington is through. I have to work with him. I don't want to piss him off unnecessarily," Jim said and focused his attention forward.

Powers sat through the forty-five minutes without making a note. Everyone began to rise; Powers had been staring out the window and did not realize the meeting had ended until Jim tapped his shoulder. Powers stood and mingled his way toward the door. He and Jim walked out of the building. Several people had already created a haze of smoke on the other side of the exit door. Whiting was the first person on the porch establishing a cloud of cigarette smoke for everyone to exit through. Both Jim and Powers waved their arms vigorously as they walked through.

"Alright, now fill me in on Eddie Dreyer," Powers demanded.

"You are awfully interested for a sports hater, Jim claimed.

"I am not a sports hater" Powers declared. "I have a professional interest; I worked with Eddie. Remember?"

"His clavicle is broken on the right side in two places, his left hand has multiple fractures, and his neck muscles are strained."

"How did that happen?" Powers asked.

95

"Toward the end of the game, Eddie went up to dunk. Several people fell at one time; Eddie was on the bottom," Jim said as they walked toward the Psych Building.

"Damn. He is such a big kid; it's hard to imagine that a fall could do so much damage." Powers said.

"They are all big. It was just bad luck. Well, bad luck and immaturity."

"Immaturity?" Powers asked.

"Inexplicably, Eddie took a dislike to the kid defending him. He fouled him a couple of times, did some showboating, and hounded him. They were both jawing at each other. Eddie wanted to make the kid look bad on the dunk. His cockiness must have pissed off the entire Eagles team. That's why so many bodies were at the rim when he got there. They all wanted a piece of his ass," Jim explained.

"What could have incited him to behave so strangely?"

"It's not strange for Eddie to talk trash or make an opponent look bad. It's part of his game. He needs to intimidate; he wants his opponent to feel inferior. What's different here is the lack of subtlety. He wanted everyone to see this kid get schooled."

"Schooled? Jim, must you infect our conversations with athletic slang?" Powers preached.

"You understood, didn't you?" Jim replied.

Powers nodded agreement as he opened the doors to the Psych Building. They went separate directions. Powers entered the classroom and went through the routine required to teach his class but his mind was on Eddie Dreyer. He went through the motions on two other classes and held office hours from three-thirty to four-thirty. He packed up and drove home.

Once again, Powers was faced with an uncertain future. He sat on the leather couch by the window. Across the room, his computer cycled through the screen saver. Every night, for weeks, he rushed home to find the basketball selection. It had been exhilarating. Tonight, the laptop monitor was not the source of potential fortunes; it was just an oversized night light in a dark room. Powers walked over and moved the mouse; the screen saver dissipated.

He typed surefirewinners.com and watched it load. Powers had been told his betting site could be made fully operational. He had always dismissed the idea. But today, Powers let the idea bounce around inside his head.

*I would have to leave the country to set up a real betting service and compete with a gazillion people who know what they are doing.*

96

The idea stopped bouncing.

Powers realized he would have to consider legitimate options. He went to the bathroom and picked up the sinus medication. Just as he was about to take the medication, he looked in the mirror; he saw the reflection of the whisky bottle on the bedside table. He tossed the pills on the counter and opted to uncork the whisky instead.

Powers poured a glass half full. He felt the whisky burn going down his throat. He returned to his laptop. Once again, it was time to re-write the future and whisky would be far more creative than sinus medication or sobriety.

# 21

Eddie Dreyer was released from the hospital and greeted by reporters at the front door. The reporters were respectful but questions were being asked. Coach Barkley stood at Eddie's side.

Coach Barkley spoke, "Here's the deal. Eddie is tired, sore, and disappointed. He wants to go home and rest. We will hold an official press conference Monday morning. He promises to answer all your questions at the press conference."

The coach pushed the wheelchair to the curb and assisted Eddie into the van. Barkley settled in behind the wheel and drove away from the reporters. The radio was tuned to a sports talk show; the commentators were hammering the Jaguars football team. Coach Barkley, suddenly fearful of hearing criticism of Eddie's antics, switched to music. It was a short drive and neither of them spoke during the trip.

Coach Barkley stopped the van and raced around to help Eddie out.

Eddie waved him off and said, "It's alright Coach. My legs aren't injured. I can make it inside."

"Well, if you're sure," Coach re-entered the van and said, "Be sure and call if you need anything; you hear me?"

Eddie nodded his head but did not turn around. His left hand was in a cast. Four fingers were exposed; the cast protected the broken wrist bone and thumb. His broken clavicle would heal but it would take a minimum of two months. A figure eight brace harnessed his back to aid healing. He would be able to remove it in three weeks. Until then, he had been instructed to limit his movement. The insertion of pins would leave everything sore for quite awhile.

He climbed the stairs, stopped at his door and fumbled with his door key. He understood the instructions clearly. The slightest movement caused sharp pain to shoot through his shoulder. Eddie grimaced as he unlocked the door and went inside. He slowly lowered himself into the oversized recliner and winced as he settled back. He dropped his prescription bottle on the table and stared around the room.

A tornado of thoughts began to spin, spinning too fast for Eddie to focus on just one. But the reoccurring thought of the end of his career frightened him the most. No one thinks of twenty as old age. But Eddie had been putting heart and soul into this job since the age of nine. Very few people can lay claim to that kind of longevity at the age of twenty.

*No. Not gonna' happen.*

Eddie Dreyer was not willing to allow thoughts about the end of his career.

He wanted to review messages from his voice mail. He struggled through the pain to remove the phone from his pocket. He had eight voice messages. He pushed play. Three were from Troy, two from other teammates, one from Harmon Evans, one from his father, and one from Gary Peterson. All the messages wished him speedy recovery, except his father. Coach Dreyer's message was critical. The highlights were "idiotic", "immature", and "unprofessional."

Eddie erased his father's message and saved the rest.

# 22

The most animated man in town did not hold the steering wheel with more than one hand. At stoplights, both hands were busy. He grabbed his head as if trying to prevent it from exploding. A southern evangelist on a Sunday morning had less expressive mannerisms. Coach Barkley's raw emotion was normally detonated on the basketball court sidelines with very few injuries but the minivan was too small for his explosive reaction to the loss of Eddie Dreyer from the team. His frustration, however, could not be contained. Coach Barkley did not require an audience to speak his mind.

"The best damn basketball team I'm ever gonna' coach," he screamed. "Now it's fucked. A twenty-five and five record, the number one seed in the conference tournament, and we're fucked."

The light turns green. One hand finds the wheel; the other slams the dash. He turned the corner and saw the three reporters gathered at his office door. His maroon and white painted minivan emblazoned with the Cougar mascot would not slip past them in anonymity. He parked and walked up to the porch where they stood.

"If you guys are waiting to see Coach Beckworth, you're early. Spring football starts in four weeks," he joked, rather than say, 'Go the hell away.'

"Come on Coach, just a few questions. The sports fans in this town want to know something," asked a face in a white polo shirt.

"This town packed the arena for Eddie Dreyer. Can't he give them a little something," asked a different face with a different microphone.

"Give them something? Eddie Dreyer gave them a hundred and ten percent every night," the Coach replied.

"Yeah, it's the extra ten percent everyone wants to talk about," quipped a third face hiding behind a beard and a third microphone.

Coach Barkley turned rapidly to face the bearded reporter. His intent was to flog the man until he promised to be respectful but wisdom prevailed.

"Tell your readers that we have eleven other guys on this team. Tell them that Verdell Avery is going to start at Guard. Tell them he's talented and the team will pull together. Tell them Eddie is special but it takes more than one player to make a team," Coach Barkley dramatized the words.

*But he wanted to say, We're fucked. We just lost over one third of our offense and Verdell Avery isn't ready. Now, go the hell away.*

"Do you really expect us to believe that Verdell can replace Eddie?" Asked the face in the white polo shirt.

"Dawson, I need to prepare for a difficult game. So, time is important to me and you guys are chewing that time up. So, type 'em up. I'm Mr. Cliché man today. That's all you're gonna' get. You know 'em; so just print 'em. Write about this team and what it needs to do to win." Barkley turned to walk away.

"You're doing your job, Coach. I would not be doing mine, if I ignored the Dreyer story." Dawson responded.

"Well Eddie Dreyer is not here. I assume that means you are here for a social call. Are you here on a social call, Dawson?" The coach asked Dawson but looked at all three of them.

No one answered him.

"I hope I am not being rude. Do any of you have a specific question about my strategy for the upcoming game?" The coach asked.

"Ok. Eddie will have a press conference Monday. You and your readers can find out what he has to say at that time. So I hope you will excuse me, I have work to do."

Coach Barkley glared into the eyes of each of them again before he turned. He walked past his assistant without comment, closed the door, and began talking to himself.

"The Dreyer story. The readers want to know the truth. If you want to know the truth, why in the hell, are you questioning a coach?" He said as he opened a drawer.

"We can't tell the truth. We have to believe our teams can win, even when they can't. Every time there is a game, someone loses. Do they think somewhere an honest coach has called the boys into a circle and said, "Boys, I'm not gonna' lie to you. You aren't as good as the fellas we are playing this evening. But let's do our best and see how close we can keep it." The coach screamed as he slammed the drawer closed. "Fuckin' Morons!"

"No! No, we lie, and we keep on lying until we believe it. Then we design plays that won't work with inferior talent. But we keep lying. We tell those players to run the plays and they will win. More lies."

101

Coach Barkley sat down in his leather chair and scanned the room for something to believe in. He saw the poster of the basketball schedule. Twenty-five and five. The five losses seemed insignificant because the Cougars were the number one seed. Win the conference tournament and the Cougars were headed for the big dance.

"Someone loses every game," he said as he clasped his hands behind his head. "And it is usually the team with the least amount of talent. We won twenty-five games because we had Eddie Dreyer and the other team didn't. Case fuckin' closed."

Coach Barkley twirled his chair around and looked out the window. Nothing on the horizon was going to change Eddie's broken bones. No superstar unknown player was walking toward his office. There was no salvation on the other side of the glass.

"Goddamn it Eddie," he mumbled softly. "What am I supposed to do? I'm just a coach. How am I supposed to convince these boys they can win? Hell, how do I convince myself?"

The assistant sitting outside his office could hear the grumbling, pacing, and pounding behind the walls. Meredith could not distinguish the words, nor was it necessary to understand. She had heard this routine before; it was normal behavior from the most animated man in town. She smiled and thought to herself.

When people asked her about Coach Barkley, Meredith always said, "He's a great coach. He's the most optimistic person I have ever met. I would bet he's working on a plan to win at this very moment."

# 23

On the first day, Eddie sat in his chair in the silent dark room and drank beer until he threw up. The second day he answered the phone; it was his father.

"Do you have any idea how embarrassing that was? Your Uncle Steve took Ben, so that he could watch his cousin Eddie play ball. What he saw was an idiot."

Eddie hung-up on him as soon as he recognized the call would be critical of his actions on the court.

*Why should I expect a father now? He's a coach and has always been a coach.*

Eddie wished Ben had not been there. He liked Ben, because Ben had no interest in athletics. He was a cool kid filled with imagination. Eddie was glad his uncle was a very different father from his own. Eddie started drinking beer again.

The phone rang a few more times; there were two knocks at the door. He answered neither. Eddie threw a pill in his mouth and washed it down with Gatorade. He went back to his recliner and eased down. He picked up the remote and clicked through the television channels.

His conscience rioted like a mob. The hoard paraded menacingly, back and forth, like protesters with picket signs.

"Eddie is a bad sport"

"Eddie makes bad decisions"

"Eddie is a bully"

"Eddie deserves to be injured"

"Cheaters never prosper"

"Eddie was wrong"

They were not creative but they were loud and relentless.

Eddie changed channels on the television but his mind remained tuned to the critical channel. He never considered his actions wrong. Every action he took was calculated. He intended to be the best player on the court. Size, speed, skill, and desire were enough most of the time. When additional aggression was needed, he applied it. If physical abuse weakened his opponent, he beat on them. His goal was domination. Wrong did not exist. Wrong is for the players at the end of the bench. The protesting conscience was wasting time; at best, Eddie was annoyed.

He continued clicking through channels. He stopped to watch a cheetah chase down a gazelle. In the two days he had been mired in his recliner watching television, it was cats four and gazelles one.

*The antelope team needed a better off-season training regimen.*

He crammed four Cheetos in his mouth, drank some Gatorade, and continued changing channels. Nudity in movies and the occasional cheetah victory provided momentary respite from his annoying conscience.

Monday arrived and Eddie was weary of the pity party. He had neither showered nor shaved for the three days. Shaving would be difficult but he would not face the reporters looking like a beaten loser. He knew he would have to look confident. Before a single question was posed, Eddie ran through his responses.

"Hard fouls are part of the game. Gary Peterson should not be criticized."

"I'm very competitive and sometimes my adrenalin gets the best of me."

"I want to focus on my rehabilitation and the future. I can't help this team win, if I'm injured."

"There is a lot of talent on this team. They will pull together."

They could write the story without him. Eddie wished he could tell them how he truly felt.

*The only thing I did wrong was fall without thinking.*

In the future, Eddie vowed to hold the rim much longer and spread his legs more forcefully. If he were to fall, he planned to fall on other people not on the hardwood floor and definitely not first.

"Learn from history," Eddie Dreyer said to the face in the mirror.

Eddie dressed and went outside and stood at the curb. Coach Barkley pulled up within a few minutes. Eddie reached down to pull on the door handle just as the coach was getting out to help him. Eddie felt sharp pain shoot up his neck and in his shoulder as he bowed his head to enter the van. Coach Barkley got back in the van, buckled up, and restarted the vehicle.

"I should have known you wouldn't accept help," the coach said.

"If I needed help, I would accept help," Eddie said.

"Well, how are you feeling? You know I came by yesterday. I knocked on the door; there was no answer. I assumed you were asleep."

"Probably. I slept a lot." Eddie lied. "I'm feeling better."

Eddie could feel the coach look at him as though he were trying to assess the mental state of his player. Eddie could feel his nervousness.

"There's no need for the lecture, coach. I will not embarrass the university at the press conference and I will not give them any quotes to inflame the situation," Eddie said.

Eddie struggled to turn and to look at the coach, since he did not reply to his last comment. He could see that the coach was shaking his head yes but he knew the coach wanted to say more, but he did not. The charade began early.

The van came to a stop; Eddie and Coach Barkley walked into the Athletic Building and down a hall to the waiting reporters. Eddie sat on edge of a table. His body ached, more so than over the weekend. He was sober, clean, and ready to talk with the reporters. Eddie was fortunate to be playing in a small town; four men and one woman were carrying recorders, cameras, and video cams.

"Eddie, how long will you be out?"

"Eddie, is Avery ready to start?"

"Hey Eddie, can the Cougars win without you?"

Eddie sat calmly, cracking one-liners and cranking out clichés as efficiently as Henry Ford rolled black cars off the assembly line. Finally, someone asked about the circumstances from the game with the Eagles.

"Eddie what provoked you to treat Gary Peterson the way you did?"

"In the heat of competition things happen. What Gary did is between Gary and me. I really don't hold any grudges. I don't want to live in the past. I'm going to focus on my rehabilitation and the future," Eddie answered.

"So, you are saying he provoked you," the woman asked.

"I'm saying it's over and I'm ready to move on," Eddie reiterated.

"Eddie, it looked as though you wanted to totally embarrass Gary Peterson," said the man with the video camera.

Coach Barkley had been quiet to this point. The press conference was going smoothly. He wanted to keep it that way. He walked between Eddie and the reporters.

"Eddie has answered that question. I think you guys have plenty of quotes," the coach said as he swung both arms in a motion that signified enough.

"One more question, Coach. Eddie, do you think what you did was wrong?"

"I said we are through. Eddie has work to do and I have a team to coach. Let's break this thing up, alright?" Coach Barkley responded as he continued to conduct the small orchestra of reporters.

"What about it Eddie, was it wrong? Do you want to apologize for hurting the team, for effectively ending their season?" Asked the bearded reporter.

"Since you won't leave, we will. Come on Eddie," Coach Barkley said as he turned and placed his hand on Eddie's tender shoulder. The questions continued as they walked. Eddie could feel the anger welling inside. He resented these questions from men who cannot play the game. The Coach was standing behind him and gently guiding Eddie down the hallway.

"Stop pushing me!" Eddie said and came to a halt. He turned around.

"Keep walking Eddie," Coach Barkley ordered him.

"Don't tell me what to do," Eddie snapped back while staring down the hall at the reporters standing outside the door.

Coach Barkley leaned forward. He whispered. The reporters could not hear his words but they were loud and clear to Eddie.

"I get paid to tell you what to do. They want the truth. The truth is you were wrong, immature, and you ruined our season, goddamn it. That's the truth. I know it and they know. If you don't know it, then you are really fucked up, son. I'm going to my office. You can follow me or you can talk to them and ruin what remains of your career."

Coach Barkley bumped Eddie as he walked by. Sharp pain shot through his body from the bump but Eddie continued to stare down the hallway. He could hear them calling his name.

"I'm not fucked up and I am not immature," he mumbled as he turned to follow the coach. "And I was not wrong," he muttered as he opened the office door.

Eddie did not follow Coach Barkley into his private office; instead, he took a seat facing Meredith, the coach's assistant. She peeked around the monitor and waved to Eddie.

"Hi," she said. "I think he expects you to go in his office."

106

Eddie was not ready to talk to anyone. The coach had criticized Eddie, he felt deprived of his status as star player, and his confidence was shaken. He looked at Meredith's smiling face and knew that she was trying to be helpful and should not be a target of his anger.

"Yeah, I know but I'm not ready," Eddie answered.

"Okay. If you want me to buzz him; let me know," she told him.

"I'm going to get some water," Eddie said as he stood and opened the door.

Meredith just nodded.

Eddie walked out and did not go back. He wanted to go home. He wanted to spend more time thinking. He wanted to get busy with recovery. He wanted to get back to normal. The ten-minute walk took twenty and Eddie would have sworn on a Bible that it took an hour.

He went inside and went straight to his computer. He sat and it seemed that every part of his body hurt. He pulled a pill from his pocket and washed it down with the Gatorade left from the night before. He was sick of the brace but he left it in place. He logged onto the Internet to do research on his injuries. An hour later, he had printed sixteen pages of information on the rehabilitation of injuries similar to his.

Eddie labored and groaned as he reached for the sixteen pages stacked in the printer. As he recovered from the shooting pains, he looked at the clock. It had been seventy minutes since he took the last pill. He decided to take another. He leaned back in his chair and started to breathe deeply. Soon Eddie's eyes were closed. His breathing pattern was sending him into a deep trance.

Eddie thought about the next game the Cougars would play. Automatically the steps appeared to him. He walked up; nothing had changed. His family stood waiting for him. He followed his normal routine. Eddie saw the game being played. He saw the young Raiders team play inspired basketball while Cougars struggled without their star player. The Cougars win a close game. Eddie uses the time to envision remarkable muscle recovery and solid bone healing. He walks down the steps and remembers, to win he must place a bet. Eddie logged on to surefirewinners.com and selects the Raiders plus nine.

# 24

Powers began his drive home. The long weekend sheltered away on the coast had been unproductive. He had hoped to start work on a book. All he had was a title, "The Rest Of Us." He knew he wanted to write about coping with mediocrity but none of the specifics were in place. The iPad was lying on the console. Dictation had been the plan. Ideas came to him but none of them made it into the machine.

Powers intended to make a case that most people deal with a life full of unrealistic expectations. He would assert that parents with bigger plans for their children plant and cultivate this unrealistic perspective. Powers would lay blame at the feet of an American culture that over-praises achievers. And lastly, he would draw upon his knowledge of Eddie to express the difference between excellence and mediocrity. He would conclude that people like Eddie Dreyer skew reality. Millions crash into a bar set unreasonably high.

Powers toyed with the idea of generating a fictional story to make his case, followed by an addendum of sound psychology to deal with realistic expectations. Powers was becoming quite excited by his concept. Yet nothing transferred from the mind to the machine.

One book and tenure might be back in the picture. Powers was uncertain that he believed everything he was planning to author. However, he was becoming passionate about doing it because he believed it was a means to an end. Powers was convinced it was his only choice. He would begin writing immediately, this evening.

Powers parked the car and unpacked his bags. He went to the computer and opened a Word Document. He typed an opening statement. He read it. He changed a word and rearranged the verb. He typed a second sentence. Powers decided the second sentence should be the open. He switched the two. His fingers fidgeted the keys as he waited for the next sentence to construct in his mind.

His mind was wandering; two sentences and he was having trouble remaining devoted. He saw the blinking envelope on his task bar indicating email had come in; he tried to ignore it and concentrate on the opening paragraph of his book. He could not. He clicked on the envelope to see the email. He found two messages. The first was from the TA; he was sucking up and thanking Powers for the opportunity to instruct. The second email was from Eddie Dreyer. Powers opened it. It was a bet. Eddie had picked the Raiders plus nine against his Cougar teammates.

Powers thought it had to be an old game that got lost in cyberspace. He went to ESPN to check schedules. The first round of the conference tournament was beginning. The experts predicted the Cougars would easily win the game.

Raiders plus nine. Eddie did not believe the Cougars could beat the Raiders by more than nine. Why? The Raiders had won only six games all year. The Cougars had beaten them by twenty, a few weeks ago.

Powers checked the clock. He had a little over an hour to place a bet.

*Do I really want to?*

This might be the last chance to use Eddie's selection. He could delete the email and go back to writing or he could place a bet and create a nice safety cushion, should the book fail to capture tenure.

*A safety net is a smart idea.*

Powers logged onto a betting service and bet five thousand dollars. He opened another and bet another five thousand dollars. Powers continued to place five thousand dollar bets until thirty-five thousand dollars were wagered on the Raiders plus nine. The wagers cut his nest egg in half but a win would add nearly seventy thousand dollars into his future. He printed the receipts and hoped Eddie was not overestimating his absence from the lineup.

With a glass of beer in one hand and a dish of mixed nuts in the other, powers returned from the kitchen. He sat the refreshments down and tuned in the game on the radio. He had abandoned the idea of staying calm. It would be impossible; he was risking thirty-five thousand dollars on the outcome of game played by excitable young boys.

He settled into his chair in front of the computer and typed a few more lines for the opening of the book. Powers paused to toss a few nuts into his mouth and wash them down. The game started; after five minutes of play, the Cougars were ahead by three. With only seven minutes elapsed, the nuts were nearly gone, the beer glass was empty, the Cougar lead was seven and the book was unchanged. His nine points seemed truly insufficient. Nervous energy devoured the last few nuts as the radio went to commercial. Powers sped into the kitchen and returned with three beer bottles, an opener, and the remainder of an open tin of nuts.

Powers focused on the Word document. He entered a few words, paused, and listened to the radio announcer. He continued the routine for the remainder of the first half.

He heard the voice in the box declare, "At halftime it's the Cougars forty-one and the Raiders thirty-five."

The radio chattered with interviews, recaps, commercials, and band noise. Powers tuned it out and managed to complete his opening premise. He read the twenty-six lines out loud, just before the second half started. A quick score by the Raiders prevented him from finishing. Four minutes later, the Cougar lead was reduced to four.

Powers used the remote to mute the radio while he read the paragraph out loud. It seemed good to him. Powers turned the sound back on the radio. The Cougars scored.

"Damn," he shouted as though the Cougars would go scoreless for the remaining fifteen minutes.

Powers rapidly typed an outline that he thought would serve as a table of contents. Less than ten minutes remained in the game and the Cougar clung to a six-point lead. He could not concentrate on the book. He took one last look at the monitor, then walked to a chair near the radio and stared at the speaker. He knew there was nothing to see; but he had thirty-five thousand reasons to listen to the game; anxiety dictated his attention. He opened the third beer and did not bother to pour it into the glass.

The Cougars were leading by two with three minutes to play. Powers could feel his heart racing as the game worked its way in his favor. The Cougars committed a costly turnover and the Raiders took possession of the ball.

The announcer expressed his personal opinion on the game.

"The Cougars undoubtedly miss Eddie Dreyer. Verdell Avery is going to be a fine player in time but tonight, the Cougars needed experienced leadership; they do not have it. They need someone who knows how to protect the basketball and score as the clock winds down."

The Raiders intercepted another pass and went the length of the court to score.

"The Raiders have tied this game with one-thirty to play," Powers heard.

His eyes were riveted to the radio. The Cougars passed the ball around and time continued to disappear. Avery put up a shot but missed. The Raiders grabbed the rebound. Three passes later the center for the Raiders dunked the ball to the disbelief of Troy Folger.

"The Raiders lead by two with only twelve seconds remaining," the radio voice sourly announced.

Powers began to smile and said out loud, "Up by two plus I get nine points. I'm up by eleven; I can't lose."

He suddenly wanted to experience the outcome. He was ready to count down the final ten seconds.

The announcer said, "The Cougars will have one chance to tie this game and send it into overtime. Maybe, in overtime Coach Barkley will be able to get these boys back on track."

"Overtime?" Powers practically screamed

"Overtime? How does that work?" Powers said to the announcer.

As though the radio voice had heard Powers, he explained.

"Folks if the Cougars can just score a two point basket, we can get into overtime. The scorekeeper will put five more minutes on the clock. Who knows, with five more minutes maybe the Cougars can pull away and win this game?"

The jubilant smile Powers had worn moments ago morphed into clenched lips confused by the unknown.

The Cougars brought the ball up the court and put it in the hands of Eddie's replacement. Verdell Avery drove hard to the basket, stopped, and pulled up for a short ten-foot jumper. His defender got a hand on the ball and it fell short. The Raiders won. The smile returned to Powers face.

"Folks this will be a very disappointing finale for a Cougar team that won twenty-five games this year," the radio announcer's words had all the sadness of a eulogy.

Powers could not take his eyes off the radio. He held receipts for a seventy thousand dollar payout. He made thirty-five thousand dollars in one evening. Eddie needed a pep talk and Powers received a selection. Powers had no way of knowing why Eddie had initiated a pep talk. What he did know was that the end of Eddie's season did not mean the end of Powers' money pipeline.

Powers turned the radio off and finished his beer. He walked over to the computer, clicked the save button, and closed the rough draft of his book. The book, that a few hours ago seemed all important, was closed; and in its place stood an Internet betting service.

111

Powers wanted to see his winning bet credit his account. He wanted to watch the balance change. He refreshed the screen every few minutes for nearly thirty minutes, watching the balances change.

"Four thousand five hundred and fifty dollars times seven," Powers said out loud. "Keep your tenure, Harrington; I found a better job."

# 25

By April, college basketball was over. The NCAA tournament pushed Powers' earnings to near three hundred thousand dollars. Eddie was rehabilitating and continuing to give himself pep talks. Powers worried that Eddie's pep talks would be confusing without the college games to choose from. Powers instructed the web master to list all the professional games. Eddie's selections trickled in two or three times a week.

Powers lost thousands of dollars posting Eddie's selections on professional games. Eddie's insight rarely produced winners. Powers stopped wagering and dreamed in anticipation of November, when the college season would begin.

On the twenty-first of May, an official letter arrived from the Office of Donald Harrington; Powers knew it was not an offer of tenure. The letter announced the addition of Morris Ecklund to the Department of Psychology. Powers did not bother to read the description of his achievements. He turned to page two which succinctly addressed his dismissal. It arrived on a Saturday.

Sunday morning, while many worshiped their god and others slept off hangovers, the campus office of professor Powers Meade was emptied. Jim and Powers took everything. Through the years, Powers replaced the desk, chairs, cabinets, and light fixtures. The curmudgeon look of Goodbye Mr. Chips never suited Powers style. Perhaps it had been the start of the rift with Harrington.

The outgoing educator left the office stripped to its bare soul. A clean slate awaited the new man. Powers imagined that soon the office would be cluttered with rickety departmental file cabinets, functional steel desks, and bulky cumbersome lamps. Hundreds of books; some, no doubt, authored by Mr. Ecklund, would fill the bookshelves, where Powers displayed vinyl albums, model cars, and travel photos. Diplomas, certificates, and ideological posters will replace the five numbered prints, which adorned the walls with imaginative interpretations and beauty captured in a moment.

Powers tossed the keys on the floor and closed the door. Jim drove his fully loaded pickup back to Powers house. They unloaded all his possessions into the garage, had a few beers, had a few laughs at Harrington's expense, and then called it a day.

In mid June, Powers faced another hurdle with Eddie Dreyer. The Mavericks won the NBA championship and professional basketball was over. Although Powers was not placing bets, every time Eddie orchestrated a pep talk, he was required to make a selection. Powers needed another solution. Powers could not control when Eddie would need to make a pick. Powers could not be certain how Eddie would react, if he could not find games to pick while in his trance. Destabilization of the hypnotherapy was Powers greatest fear. He considered posting the European League but the championship would be determined by mid September. The lack of familiarity could cause disastrous problems. Powers wanted something that would keep Eddie occupied until November. He stumbled upon the answer.

In the trance, the people and facts are real but everything else is imagined. Powers ordered the Webmaster to post the previous basketball season on the web site. Powers gambled that Eddie would review a list, see an easy choice, and make a pick. Three days later, Eddie made a selection. He picked his own Cougars to lose a game they had already won. Powers was pleased.

*It's a shame I cannot share my genius with someone.*

# 26

September ended; football players captured the attention of the campus paper as well as the local newspaper. But Eddie Dreyer's focus was on round ball. The Cougar basketball team would be organizing, practicing, and kicking off the season the first week in November. The last six months of rehabilitation frustrated Eddie. The process was slow and the improvements were unacceptable to him. He experienced set backs on a monthly basis; most of them occurred when Eddie pushed harder than he had been instructed. Eddie considered the possibility that his therapy was inept. That's why he was laying on an examination table seeking a second opinion.

"You may sit up," the doctor told him.

Eddie sat up and listened carefully as the doctor went over the x-rays. He referred to the latest pictures taken and compared them to the x-rays taken immediately following the fall. The medical terminology seemed unnecessary to Eddie; it clouded the explanation. His impatience caused him to interrupt the doctor.

"The cast has been off for nearly four months and I have been in physical therapy for six months," Eddie said in an attempt to direct the conversation.

"Yes I know and your progress is remarkable," the doctor replied.

"Remarkable? Then why don't I have a full range of motion in this shoulder and how come my hand hurts every time it is hit? And when will my strength return?" Eddie asked.

"Your shoulder and hand may not be the way they were before the injuries but they are much better than this," he said as he tapped his pointer on the old x-rays.

"Maybe I can simplify the question and you can simplify your answer. The hand is stiff and it aches. My shoulder limits my range of motion and hurts. What do I need to do to make it better?" Eddie asked.

"I can't say, Eddie. Hasn't anyone told you that the shoulder may never function as it did before the fractures and ligament damage?" He asked.

"But if it can, I'm the guy who can make it happen. I need you to tell me how to speed up healing. That's why I am here."

"No Mr. Dreyer, you came here seeking a second opinion on the status of your recovery. I have given it to you. The pressure put on your wrist, hand, and shoulder was significant. Bones were snapped; cartilage and ligaments were stretched, torn, and damaged. To whatever degree they heal, will take time."

"How long before they perform properly?" Eddie persisted.

"Mr. Dreyer, you are not hearing me. They perform properly now. Do they perform like the supple, athletic, and genetically gifted mechanisms that they were before several two hundred pound bodies smashed them into a hardwood floor?" The doctor asked. "No. No they don't. And I would be amazed it they ever will. You will have to learn to play with limitations."

"No, I don't. You think it's all about physiological shit," Eddie said as he leaped off the examining table "Well, it's not. You're not accounting for desire, Doc. You're advising me as though I were an average Joe who is not willing to pay the price to achieve perfection."

Eddie pulled his shirt off the rack and began buttoning it up.

"I'm not average anything. I'll work harder at it than anyone and my healing will exceed your predictions," Eddie said as he looked intently into the doctor's eyes.

"Eddie," the doctor said with a sympathetic tone. "Your shoulder hurts after every exercise period. Look at the x-ray. The bone is healed but you are jeopardizing the joint and ligaments by over training. If you overwork that hand, if will only get tired and sore, not stronger and better. My suggestion to you is to listen to your physical therapist; take a year off from basketball and allow everything to mend at a reasonable rate."

"Whatever," Eddie said as he brushed past the doctor on his way to the door. "I thought, as a sports medicine specialist, you would understand. But you don't. Maybe only former athletes should call themselves Sports Medicine Specialists."

Eddie slammed the door as he exited.

"Punk." The doctor mumbled as he pulled the x-rays from the light. "A delusional punk, at that."

Eddie went back to his apartment. He began a pep talk session by controlling his breathing. He was beginning to drift. His concentration was broken by the sound of his phone. Eddie blinked and turned his head to watch the phone dance across the desk. The phone rang again. He picked it up and pressed the button.

"Yeah, this is Eddie," he answered.

A trance had been broken. Eddie looked at the laptop as he listened for the voice on the other end of the line.

*Why am I at this gambling web site?*

"It's on," Troy said. "We're going to scrimmage with some guys who play for the Pirates."

"What time?" Eddie asked.

His eyes still focused on the web site.

"Two," Troy answered.

"Alright, see you there."

"Are you sure you wanna' ball. Is your shoulder better?"

"I said I'd be there, Troy," Eddie snapped.

"Chill man. I'm just asking, alright."

"Yeah, later," Eddie said and tossed the phone on the chair.

He continued to look at the screen. On several occasions, Eddie would walk into the room and find this site as the last place he had visited. His mind filled with questions. Why would it be on this screen, if he had not been at the site? Was it possible some cookie was hidden in his files? Could it direct this pop-up?

A password was required for entry. Eddie tried his normal password; it did not work. He attempted a few variations without success. He was denied entry. Unlike the previous time he discovered this website, there was not an automatic log in and there was no account balance. The other discovery must have been some electronic fluke.

*Some geek with a new pop-up technology.*

He did not have time to unravel the mystery of surefirewinners.com. Eddie cleared everything from his temporary Internet files. He left no history and deleted all cookies from his machine. He shut the machine down.

He left the desk and tied his shoes. He should be stress free, confident, jazzed, and in the zone. He was not.

*Why didn't I do a pep talk?*

He remembered starting his visualization; he could not remember finishing.

"Damn, Troy's phone call disrupted my routine," Eddie snarled.

Eddie was out of time. He had twenty minutes to be at the gym, loose, and ready to play. He shook his head, grabbed his bag, and left the apartment.

As he jogged across the campus, Eddie fought the memories of the last few scrimmages. His once dominant presence was missing. He missed shots, blew passes and reluctantly chased loose balls and rebounds. No one was critical of his play but they knew he was vulnerable.

Eddie wished he had tried another pep talk. He needed his mental advantage. He opened the door and walked out on the court. The noise of basketballs, shoes, swishing nets, and clunking iron always triggered a rush for Eddie Dreyer.

Once he was oblivious to defeat in this place. Eddie eased onto the court like a shark patrolling waters; he need not be hungry to eat. But lately, it seemed everyone had shark repellent and spear guns.

# 27

Coach Barkley watched as the last of the players, from the pick-up game left the court. Eddie Dreyer was the lone player remaining. Eddie could not have known the Coach was watching the scrimmage. Only half of the court was lighted; it was dark on Barkley's end of the gymnasium. The coach watched as the ball hit the rim and bounced away. Eddie was shooting free throws; Barkley counted five hits, five misses. He had seen enough.

"Hey stud," he yelled. "It's time to shut the place down."

The coach walked out of the darkness and toward Eddie.

"Hey Coach. You know if I had a key, I could lock this place up and you wouldn't have to worry about being here," Eddie said.

"How soon you forget. We tried that when you were a freshman. Remember?" the coach responded.

"Yeah, I remember; it worked out great," Eddie answered.

"That's not what the administration thought. They were not happy with you running up the electrical bill by shooting basketballs at three in the morning. They chewed on my ass for an hour," Coach Barkley said.

"It's a university. I major in basketball. I was prepping for a test. They let the eggheads stay in the library all night. They should let the athletes study late."

"No they don't. The library closes before midnight," the coach said.

"It's the first rule I will change when I run this place," Eddie said and flashed a big grin.

He turned and fired up another free throw, another miss.

"I'd vote for you but for now, let's play by the rules," the coach advised with a slight smile.

"Fine. The shots aren't falling tonight anyway," Eddie said as he retrieved the ball.

Eddie tossed it in his bag and grabbed a towel. He mopped sweat away as he and the coach walked toward the locker room.

"Eddie, are you pushing too hard?" The coach asked.

"No."

"The trainer says you are."

"That's why he's a trainer and I'm a player."

"Eddie, he's trying to be the best at what he does just like you're trying to be the best at what you do. Don't come down on him. He wants you to make it back."

Eddie stopped and slung the towel around his neck and held both ends tightly.

"Make it back? I am back. I just need to fine tune," Eddie said.

"You can fine tune at a slower pace. You're doing more harm than good, son," the coach stated.

"You are not me and you are not a doctor," Eddie snapped.

"No, I'm your coach."

"Yeah, well this is the off season. I can do whatever I want. So, back off Coach."

"I'm tired of you barking at me, son. We are not equals."

"No, we aren't and I'm not your son," Eddie said defiantly.

"There is no reason for you to be angry with me. You shouldn't be looking around for someone to blame unless it's yourself," the coach barked.

"You have your opinion; I have mine," Eddie said.

"Just remember my opinion carries a lot more weight," the coach stated.

Eddie turned and leaned in closer to the coach's face.

"There's a bunch of people who would be interested in what Eddie Dreyer has to say about how this program is run," Eddie threatened.

Coach Barkley could not be intimidated by Eddie's physical presence. His first thought was to move even closer to demonstrate his fearlessness. The coach thwarted the negative emotions and chose to give reason another chance to prevail.

"You have a shoulder that limits your movement, Eddie. And your left hand is not as capable as it used to be," he said with a controlled and compassionate tone.

"Eddie, the doctors expected the injuries to affect the way you play but the recovery is stymied because you are pushing too hard. Your way isn't working out. I'm suggesting a different approach."

"Your opinion doesn't mesh with my plans," Eddie said.

"Your plans? As the coach I make the plans."

"Not for me you don't."

"Really?" Coach Barkley said in disbelief.

"Nope. If I had listened to you last year, we would not have won as often as we did. And the Cougars would not have lost to the Raiders, if I had been playing. Your plans did not work," Eddie said.

Coach Barkley stared at this person thinking who is this? Eddie's ego was off the charts. The coach lost interest in reeling him back to reality. Coach Barkley wanted to paddle him like a disobedient child.

"If you hadn't been an idiot, I would not have had to change plans. Was it your plan to be an idiot? Is it part of your master plan to break all your bones so you will know what it is like to be average? Tell me more; what other plans do you have, genius?" The coach yelled into Eddie's face.

"You don't understand competition or excellence," Eddie yelled. "You have no idea what it takes to be the best."

Coach Barkley looked down. He had reached his limit. When he looked back up, he took a step closer to Eddie and leaned to within two inches of Eddie's chin.

"The best? Hell Eddie, you aren't the best. You used to be the best in this little pond. But you know what, right now you aren't even the best on this team," Coach yelled without moving back at inch.

"Who are you fuckin' kidding? " Eddie said as he laughed.

"I'm not kidding. I watched the little four-on-four game you guys played. Verdell ate your lunch and DJ must have scored a hundred on you."

"That was not a real game and I'm not completely healed," Eddie responded.

"Yeah, that's what they all told you, didn't they Eddie?"

"Why are you messing with me?"

"I'm not messing with you," Coach Barkley answered. "You want to treat me with disrespect. You want to make it clear to me that you run the Eddie Dreyer show."

Coach Barkley began to walk around Eddie. He walked in a tight circle and barked as he walked.

"You want me to know that I am just a figurehead. You're telling me I can't coach. Well, I appreciate your candor, son. Oh sorry, I meant Mr. Dreyer. It takes a lot of pressure off me. I don't have to motivate you, coddle you, or massage your precious ego. Damn, I can just relax and tell you the truth. Man, what a relief. Now I can tell you, you won't even make this team."

"Coach, have you lost your mind?" Eddie asked.

"Please call me Phil. It's obvious; I don't know how to coach special talents like you."

Eddie picked up his bag and walked the remaining steps to the locker room.

"Thanks again, Eddie. It's a real relief knowing you have everything worked out."

Coach Barkley walked to the control panel and turned the lights off. He took several deep breaths on his walk back to his office. He knew he had gone over the line; the coach knew the difference between manipulation and maltreatment. But of greater concern to Coach Barkley was a feeling that he had stumbled upon the truth. Eddie Dreyer may not make the team.

# 28

Harmon Evans was taking the day off. He and Helen saw the new Tom Hanks movie at an early matinee. She suggested they have wine to go with the cheese she bought. Harmon listened as she described a romantic twilight at the beach. Helen bounced several innuendos off of Harmon's useless armor. Harmon parked the car at Captain Bluebeard's to grab a bottle of wine.

As owner of a bar, everyone wants to say hello. Harmon could not understand the thrill of saying, "Oh, look, it's Harm; he owns the joint." Maybe they thought it would get them better drinks or free drinks. However, Harmon Evans prided himself on being selectively generous. He waved to a few people and tossed out a couple of "How ya' doin's," but he kept moving. Helen was in the car and nothing in the bar could match what she was offering.

He went behind the bar, pulled a bottle of Wine from the wall, and sat it on the lacquered mahogany bar. He reached into the rack and grabbed three wine glasses.

"Hi ya', Boss; thought you were taking the day off," Dexter queried.

Harmon grabbed the bottle, glasses, and started out from behind the bar.

"I am, Dex. So long," Harmon responded.

"Hey, since you're here__," Dexter said as he chased after Harmon. "Eddie Dreyer's in the corner and he's shitfaced. I tried to cut him off but he started threatening me."

Dexter leaned in and whispered to Harmon, "I didn't want to call the police on the star of our basketball team."

Harmon turned to look in the corner. He handed the glasses and bottle to Dexter and walked toward Eddie Dreyer. Harmon sat opposite Eddie.

"Hey, Eddie. How's it going?" Harmon asked.

Eddie's head was hanging; his hands were toying with the glass. He tilted the fluid toward the edge and back. A mindless game was being played. He righted the glass and looked up.

"Hiya' Harm."

"How many of those have you had?" Harmon asked.

"I'm not spilling so I'd say, not enough," Eddie remarked.

Harmon reached across the table to take the glass. Eddie tightened his grip on the glass. Harmon released his grasp.

"I don't allow students to get shitfaced. You're done. Let's go," Harmon said.

Harmon stood up and towered over Eddie. He hoped Eddie would listen to reason. Harmon wanted to avoid confrontation. He watched as Eddie continued to sip his drink.

"I paid for this; I'm finishing it," Eddie said belligerently.

"Hey, take your time. I'm gonna' go make a phone call. Who would you like me to call, Coach Barkley, your dad, or the police?" Harmon said.

"I turned twenty one two months ago and I'm not breaking any laws. I walked over here and I'll walk home. You can call whoever you want. And tell them how responsible I'm being."

Harmon wished he had not tried to bluff Eddie. Eddie Dreyer did not know how to back down and intoxication only strengthened his resolve.

"It will be your last. I will instruct the entire staff not to serve you. So, finish up and get out of here," Harmon told him.

Harmon walked away. He went to the bar and instructed everyone that Eddie was not to be served additional alcohol. He picked up his wine and the glasses and left the bar. He opened the door and sat behind the wheel.

"That took a while. Is everything alright?" Helen asked as Harmon started the car.

"No. Eddie Dreyer is drunk," Harmon answered.

"There's always a drunk in your bar, Harmon."

"Not always," he said defensively.

"You know what I mean," she said and added," You cannot play daddy to every kid on this campus."

"Yes I can but it would mean I never get a day off," Harmon replied.

"No days off equal no romantic dates at the beach," Helen said.

"Yeah, that's not right. Harmon deserves to be with the pretty girl at the beach." Harmon said as he handed her the glasses and wine.

"Well, let's get going. I've got just the girl for you. With wine and soft crashing ocean waves, there's no telling how lucky you could get this evening." Helen pierced his armor again.

"Sounds a lot better than babysitting," Harmon said.

"Are you expecting company?" Helen asked as she held up three glasses.

"Suppose a mermaid comes ashore?" Harmon said.

"Suppose I break this glass against your head?" Helen responded.

"That's why I have a back-up glass, just in case I say or do something stupid," he said with a sly smile.

Helen returned his smile and slid across the bench seat. She weaved her arm under his. Harmon felt like a teenager when Helen touched him. He did not need much from life but Helen was the one thing he did not want to live without.

# 29

It was Labor Day weekend. Powers took his newspaper and coffee to his patio. Without a job at the university, his annual worry fest about class preparation, Tsar Harrington, and Freud aspirants was unnecessary. He poured a cup of coffee and sipped at it as he soaked up the morning sun. Powers breathed deep and scanned his backyard landscape. There was a little something extra in the air. He inhaled again; it was the smell of bacon frying from the McPherson clan.

"That which we call a rose by any other name would smell as sweet," Powers quoted taking a massive breath of air into his lungs.

Powers covered his toast with orange marmalade and took a bite. He raised his coffee cup and washed it down.

*I wish I had bacon.*

Powers continued taking small bites of his toast. He refilled his cup and opened the newspaper. The latest National Budget battle dominated the front page but a photo of Eddie Dreyer in his white Cougar uniform stole Powers' attention.

He spread the paper open and read, "Eddie Dreyer Suspended From Cougar Basketball Team."

He sat the toast on the plate and the coffee sat untouched as he read every word carefully.

"Eddie Dreyer, Conference MVP, while participating in a pick-up game of basketball in a park, assaulted a resident.

"He was "totally drunk when he got here," said Martin Hudson; a participant in the game. It was reported that Mr. Dreyer provoked several players.

"He reeked of alcohol and he bullied his way about the court. He was being a real jerk," said another participant.

"The game broke up and the recreational players left without incident. Eddie Dreyer stood at the edge of the park screaming obscenities at everyone. A resident walked across the street to request that Mr. Dreyer leave."

"I wanted him to realize the poor behavioral example he was demonstrating to the youth in the neighborhood," said the father of three.

The reporter wrote, "The former Cougar basketball player threw his basketball in the man's face; it bloodied his nose. The police arrived and after a struggle, he was arrested for public drunkenness, resisting arrest, and assault.

Coach Barkley suspended him from the team for Conduct Unbecoming a student athlete. The coach said he would meet with the university officials on Tuesday. They would decide the fate of Eddie Dreyer. He recommended Eddie get involved in an alcohol abuse program."

"We are certainly more concerned with Eddie's health than with his contribution as a basketball player," Coach. Barkley stated.

*Holy crap.*

Powers did not foresee this rain cloud on this sunny day. He picked up his cell phone and called Jim.

"Hello," Powers heard through labored breathing.

"Hi Jim. Are you enjoying the morning?"

"Absolutely. What better way to spend a beautiful Saturday morning than raking leaves."

"That's why I pay kids to do that," Powers said.

"You're cheating yourself of the true joy of home ownership, my man," Jim quipped.

"I know. Someday I will look back at these times and realize I missed the blisters on my hands, aches and pains in my back, and the hours I could have wasted," Power said.

"Still, there is a symbolism to it, a feeling of control. I change the season."

"Who am I to tell nature what to do or when to do it? She can change whenever she wants."

"Whatever. Speaking of wants, what do you want this morning?" Jim asked.

"I suppose you read the story about Eddie Dreyer."

"Oh yeah."

"Do you know any more about it, than what I am reading?" Powers asked.

"No, not really. They will kick him off the team, permanently. And I would not be surprised if they booted him out of school," Jim said.

"I thought the rules would magically bend for a star athlete."

127

"Nope, not once it is out in the open like this. They will circle the wagons. The university loves the opportunity to put on the war paint and battle for education. Athletes have no more importance on the campus than sociology majors, blah, blah, blah. It's not often they get to trumpet their cause. There will be plenty of righteousness to go around," Jim responded.

"What a bunch of hypocrites," Powers claimed.

"Not really. The truth is they believe the sociology major is more important, but with the money sports hauls in, can they really admit that?"

"So, they will use occasions like this to ride their moral war ponies," Powers stated.

"You got it. It is a damn shame. I don't know what has come over that boy. It will be a long time before we see talent like that again," Jim said.

"His injuries diminished his advantage on the court," Powers said with a tone of sadness.

"How do you know that? I haven't read about his recovery anywhere. I just assumed he was coming along fine," Jim responded.

"I'm not suggesting I know anything. I am theorizing," Powers said

"If Eddie's injuries have reduced him to mortal status, that would be a huge adjustment for a kid who lives for basketball," Jim added to the postulation.

"It is compounded by the fact that he is personally responsible for the injuries," Powers continued his analysis.

"So, doctor, you believe he has lost his superiority and is in deep denial," Jim asked.

"Among other issues," Powers said with a smugness his friends overlooked, often.

"Well, I know you won't tell me about those. And besides, these leaves won't rake themselves," Jim hinted.

"I am so glad you had a trite cliché handy to end this conversation. I apologize for interrupting your intimate affair with nature. Bye" Powers closed the phone.

He reached for the cup, tossed the cold coffee into the yard, and poured another cup from the carafe.

Eddie was in trouble. Powers was prepared for a break in the income flow. He was not prepared for Eddie to go nuts. Powers began to imagine embarrassing scenarios. He worried that a judge would

128

order Eddie to into therapy. Would they therapist discover the hypnotic suggestions?

Powers was certain the source of the suggestions would not be difficult to unravel. His mind was deluged. Every time Powers Meade believed road ahead would be easier, he rolled into another sink hole.

It was a new Fall season and as usual his Fall worry fest was at the top of his to do list, thanks to Eddie Dreyer.

*Was Harrington truly a worse worry?*

# 30

Eddie pulled three envelopes from his mailbox. He shuffled through them and tossed two envelopes into the recycle container by the door. He began ripping at the third letter as he walked into his apartment. He closed the door and pulled the letter from the envelope. The university had answered his appeal; the letter denied his request. The university would allow him to continue his education but the original ruling would stand: No basketball, no scholarship. Eddie was disappointed but not surprised. He did not intend to use his own money to attend a school that would not let him play basketball.

Eddie crumbled the letter and threw it away. In the eight weeks since the incident in the park, Eddie concentrated on exemplary behavior. He was attending class, doing his work, and attending the court mandated Alcohol Rehab Program. At first, he told them alcohol was not a problem. He quickly realized the sooner he admitted to being an alcoholic, the sooner he would be free from the program. Eddie decided their ignorance of his psyche was preferable to prolonged analysis.

He knew he was not an alcoholic and did not care what they believed. His addiction was competition. Alcohol was a quick fuck at closing time; it was not the girl of his dreams. He had hoped the release from the program and his cleaned up behavior would get him reinstated to the team. Those hopes were history. Anticipating the school's decision, Eddie had called a dozen schools seeking an opportunity to play basketball. Eleven responded with a firm "No" and one agreed to review his case after a year.

Cougar basketball practice had begun. The first game was Saturday. Eddie went to the gym to watch from the stands but Coach Barkley asked him to leave.

"Practice is open to players only, you know that," the coach had said.

The dismissive tone boomed like a gavel sentencing him to some black void where ordinary people gathered to cheer on the warriors.

Eddie leaned against the wall looking across the parking lot. He watched cars come and go; he watched the people in the cars. He was frustrated by the notion that all these people knew where they were going and what they were doing.

He re-opened the email from the Steelheads. It was time to turn the page. Thursday morning, Eddie drove to Gary, Indiana for a work out with the Steelheads. The scrimmage was over in twenty minutes and Eddie had been dismissed as not ready for the semi pro league.

*Not ready.*

Before the injuries, the Steelheads and any other team in this league would have bent over backwards to have Eddie Dreyer interested in playing for them. Now, he was not good enough.

The drive back gave him too much time to analyze his situation. He spent the first hundred miles criticizing the Steelhead coaches. He used the next hundred miles to compare himself to the Steelhead players. Hundreds of miles merely passed with fingers drumming to the music, flashes of Gary Peterson, and memories of he and Griff running through the sprinkler on hot summer days; days before the carcinogen of competition separated them.

Like quicksand, the lonely miles pulled Eddie down. With each attempt to share the blame for this quagmire the deeper he sank. The last hundred miles left him one lifeline to grab before he went under. Eddie began to face his own guilt.

Eddie blinked and hummed but could not block the thought. The extra had vanished; he was ordinary. He knew he could still shoot the basketball but the injuries robbed him of deftness, subtlety, and execution. He was now an average player. He could not say it out loud but he knew it was true. He proved it with every scrimmage, all summer long and the Steelheads confirmed it.

*I'm Average.*

Eddie pulled into the parking lot of his apartment. He grabbed his bag, went inside and lay down. His eyes were exhausted from the drive, his empty stomach growled for food, and the roller coaster of expectations flew up and down the rails. He went to the kitchen and filled a large glass with milk; he drank it all, without stopping.

Eddie stripped off his clothes as he walked. He pause at the full length mirror and looked at his physique. Leave it to a mirror to reflect only half the truth. He appeared flawless; he knew better, now.

He went to bed and lie there thinking about the unknown road ahead. He closed his eyes and the burning eased. The milk coated and

131

settled his stomach but peace of mind was beyond his reach, even when he stood on his tiptoes. Eddie had always known what he was expected to do, until now. Exhaustion overwhelmed him.

It was noon before he sat up in his bed. Eddie went directly to the shower and stood under the hot water for twenty minutes. Steam fogged the mirror and hung in the air. He dried his red skin and dressed. He walked to Captain Bluebeard's Bar. Football was on every television. A neon sign promoting Miller High Life Beer hung over a small table against the back wall; Eddie took it. A young brunette took his order. She returned with a tall glass of brown fluid with a thick creamy head on it. Eddie sipped at the beer and watched the blue team bang helmets into the white team. His sandwich came and Eddie ate.

He finished his beer and ordered another. He spied a newspaper sitting at the entrance to the kitchen. He asked the server if he could read it. She brought it to him. Eddie turned to the article about the Cougars opening basketball game. The article featured a question and answer session with the Cougars new starting point guard, Verdell Avery. Verdell's picture shouted, "Call me Mr. Congenial." It bellowed amiable. It was clear that Verdell Avery had won over the press. Eddie liked Verdell also but Verdell had his job.

No one wanted to talk to Eddie Dreyer. Eddie read every question posed to Verdell and every answer. Real tough journalism, he thought. Why didn't he ask what the people want to know? Can the new point guard fill Eddie Dreyer's shoes? Will the loss of Eddie's scoring make it harder to win? Will the team miss the Dreyer willingness to lead in tough times?

The reporter closed his article by concluding that Verdell Avery would keep Carlos Robinson below his average and the Cougars would beat the Wildcats. Eddie closed the paper in disgust, swallowed the last of his beer, left money on the table and walked out.

He walked back to his apartment. The alcohol buzz numbed the weariness that had him under siege when he entered the bar. The passing trees and buildings escaped Eddie's attention. Eddie was thinking about the article. A year ago, that newsprint would be about Eddie Dreyer's battle with Carlos Robinson. Eddie turned the corner, near his apartment. Abruptly he stopped.

"I held Carlos to twelve points," he muttered out loud. "Verdell's not that good. I bet Carlos hangs twenty five on him, easy" Eddie said so softly, he wasn't sure it was said out loud.

A smile covered his face and his head began to nod yes.

"I'd bet on it," he said.

A girl rounded the corner where he was standing and thought the smile was for her.

"Hi," she said, as she returned the smile.

"Hi," Eddie responded as she walked past him. Eddie wondered if she recognized him. With every passing day, fewer would.

Eddie rushed up stairs and logged onto the Internet. He typed in surefirewinners.com. Why not give them the business, he thought. They've worked for it. He set up an account for himself. Eddie deposited five thousand dollars from his savings account. He located the Cougar-Wildcat game and bet one thousand dollars on the Wildcats minus four.

Eddie drove to the store to buy some food and stopped at the liquor store for a bottle of Dewar's and a six of beer. When Eddie returned to his apartment and tuned the radio to the game. It was not on television; television broadcasts would have to wait until December when king football reduced its stranglehold on the viewing public. Three Dewar's later, Eddie paced the room. His voice filled the room alternately criticizing the Wildcats and the Cougars. No one was performing in the best interest of his money.

Verdell Avery calmly sank two free throws to preserve a victory for the Cougars. Eddie's one thousand dollars was gone but his resentment remained. Eddie pounded the back of the recliner until his sore shoulder sent enough pain notices to the brain to make him stop.

"Goddamn it!" He roared.

Eddie walked around the room rubbing his shoulder. He never wanted to lose at anything. Eddie did not hate Verdell or any of the Cougars. He merely believed his knowledge of Verdell's ability led him to a logical decision. Eddie truly believed Carlos and the Wildcats should have beaten the Cougars and covered the four points.

*Did I allowed emotion affect my analysis?*

Suddenly he said aloud, "Analysis? What analysis? I wasn't prepared to make this bet. I did it out of revenge. Bush league, Eddie; lame and bush league."

Eddie sat down behind his computer and logged on to the Internet. He pulled up the schedule for the conference. The Mustang game caught his attention. He reached over for some paper and a pencil to make some notes. The chatter continued to air from the radio. Verdell was describing his feelings; Eddie walked over and turned the radio off as Verdell thanked God for his ability.

"Right. Will you blame him for the ones you miss?" Eddie muttered as he walked back to his laptop.

133

Eddie analyzed every facet of the Mustangs-Warriors game. He wagered five hundred dollars on the Mustangs plus seven on Sunday afternoon; they needed twelve. Sunday night he bet one thousand dollars on the Yellow Jackets minus two. It was another loss.

The last minutes of Sunday night clicked off the clock with the same ease as his money disappeared from the betting account. He lost half of his money in two days but of far more importance to Eddie Dreyer was the fact that he could not predict a winner in a basketball game. They were teams he understood and players he knew yet he could not predict the outcome.

Hours ago, Eddie had dreamed of becoming a professional gambler. Now, the notion seemed preposterous. Eddie sat in his recliner with the last of the Dewar's straining to cover the bottom of his glass. He gulped it down.

With no time left on the Sunday clock and no scotch left to drink, Eddie wagered one thousand dollars on the Hoosiers and Eddie passed out.

# 31

Powers was lying in bed with a book in his hands. He had read the same paragraph three times. Had he been dozing for three minutes or thirty? He glanced at the clock; it was almost midnight. He closed the book and reached for the light when he heard the familiar ding of his computer. He got up to check the mail. It was from Eddie. Eddie was wagering one thousand dollars on the Hoosiers to win by twenty-four points.

Powers went to a betting site. He had six minutes to place Eddie's wager. He ran through some statistical records. The Hoosiers were the more talented team but the Condors had only one loss and it was by only four points.

"What's wrong with you Eddie?" Powers muttered to the monitor. "Why bet this game?"

Nothing had gone right since Eddie opened his own account and begun betting openly. Eddie made a large bet on the Wildcats. Powers jumped on board the gravy train. Eddie was wrong and Powers lost. Eddie bet twice the next day; Powers matched his bets. Eddie lost, as did Powers. Previously, Eddie had never lost two and the loss of three filled Powers with doubt. Two minutes left.

Powers could only imagine what provoked Eddie to begin openly betting. Had Eddie discovered the truth? Was he trying to trick Powers into losing money? Was he experimenting? Why was he suddenly incapable of picking a winner? Did consciousness cloud his judgment?

As the questions piled high, Powers cleared his head long enough to place the bet. Powers placed Eddie's bet but committed none of his own money. Powers needed answers about Eddie's state of mind. His farfetched plan was unraveling and his future was spiraling down the drain.

Powers awoke the next morning. Eddie's wager was his first thought. Three clicks later, he had an answer. Hoosiers seventy-seven and the Condors sixty-five. Eddie lost again.

Powers spent the remainder of his morning studying basketball game matchups and trying to believe in his own ability to select winners. He gave up and went for a walk.

Forty minutes later, he was near the campus. If asked, Powers would have denied he had walked toward the campus intentionally yet there he stood. He looked toward the center of the campus and decided to walk to the right instead. He did not want to go near the Psychology Building. As he neared the south border of the campus, he saw a familiar friend, Captain Bluebeard's.

Powers walked inside. Once his eyes adjusted, he saw opportunity sitting at a table near the windows. Powers walked over to the table.

"I see you are studying the sports page." Powers stated.

"I'm just reading."

"Powers Meade. Do you remember me?"

"Yes. You're the Psychology Professor."

"Not any more. My contract was not renewed."

"Neither was mine," Eddie said as he buried his head back into the paper.

"I guess it is hard to let go. You know these teams and players so well. I suppose there is very little drama for you. You know who should win and who should lose," Powers said as he sat down. "Do you expect the Cougars to repeat as champions of the conference?"

"Look, I'm just reading. I'm not looking for conversation."

The tone of Eddie's voice was unmistakable but Powers pressed on.

"Why all the circles and asterisk marks?" Powers asked as he pointed to the red lines.

"That's none of your business and I want to be alone." Eddie's said looking up with a glare meant to be intimidating.

"By all means," Powers said. "You probably aren't aware that I have been working on a book. Some of it is about game preparation." Powers stood. "If I ever reference you in the book, I'll send you a copy."

"If you ever reference me in a book I'll sue your ass off," Eddie responded. "I need the money."

Powers grinned, gave up, and walked away. Eddie went back to his study. Powers sat down at a table near the front and ordered a beer. He could monitor Eddie in a mirror. Powers watched Eddie typing notes into his laptop. Powers was convinced Eddie's bets at surefirewinners.com were not being made while he was under the influence of the hypnotic suggestions. He is trying to replace the competition of basketball with competition of beating the odds.

Powers left most of his beer sitting on the table and left. As he walked home, he continued his analysis of the broken basketball star. Powers was dumbstruck by Eddie's inability to predict games. During visualizations his accuracy was uncanny. Powers believed Eddie's loss of control had to be the answer. Powers had not pieced together how control explained the issue. He would continue to think about it.

Eddie would soon be out of money. Eddie's original five thousand dollar account had dwindled to nine hundred.

*What happens when he is out of money?*

Powers had grown accustomed to his unemployed unscheduled lifestyle. If Eddie Dreyer did not re-discover his winning ways, Powers would be forced to adapt his way of life. The rest of his walk was burdened with the unknown. Powers was beginning to think not working is far more taxing than being gainfully employed. A job. A book. A sense of dread crawled through his body.

"I do not have the will to start trying to write that damn book, again," he said as he rounded the corner to the final block of his walk.

# 32

Eddie left the bar and went home. He checked his phone as he walked. He pushed the voice mail button to hear the message from his father.

"Now, what are you going to do? What are you going to do with your life? How in the hell__," Eddie stopped the message and deleted it.

His father was not offering advice; he was venting from embarrassment. Eddie had no interest in his father's thoughts, feelings, or criticisms. He was not considering other options. He wanted to win this game, the gambling game. After spending the entire morning and part of the afternoon, researching games, Eddie was more bewildered than ever.

*What is wrong with me? Last night was just a fuck up. Angry and drunk is a bad combination. I know better.*

Eddie had lost a forty nine dollars. He knew he had to improve immediately.

Eddie opened the door to his apartment and tossed the keys on the table and sat down. He opened the laptop.

"I know this game better than anyone, I've ever met. I should be able to pick winners," Eddie said to the computer screen.

He began to review stats at the NCAA web site. He had nine hundred dollars left in his betting account and less than a thousand in his personal savings. He needed a win.

As a player, Eddie won; and then he would devote his time to improving his ability to win the next game. As a gambler, he was devoting his time to analyzing why his wager was a loser. This was very unfamiliar court for Eddie Dreyer. Once Eddie had determined an outcome, it was beyond his understanding when it turned out differently. Eddie wanted to change his focus through more research and more diligence.

He had reviewed every game on the Board. Still, only one game intrigued him, the game between the Seahawks and the Jaguars. The Seahawks were playing good ball despite starting three freshmen. The

Jaguars were starting four seniors including conference MVP candidate, Marcus Mobley. Eddie logged onto the Internet and searched for more information about the Jaguars and Mr. Mobley.

Eddie concluded that the youthful Seahawks would win if Mobley could be neutralized by fouls or injury. Holcombe, the left handed Seahawks freshman would difficult to handle for a handcuffed Mobley.

Eddie knew he was reaching for an upset that was not justifiable. It was not a good bet; there were too many ifs. His selection had to be made on the most likely scenario. The wager could not be made based on expecting misfortune. Yet, Eddie could not shake the images from his mind.

*I need to visualize this.*

He settled into his chair, closed his eyes and played the basketball game in his mind. He inserted miscues, mental mistakes, and bad luck. In his conjured version of the game, Marcus was limping. It was not a debilitating limp; he was disguising his discomfort. The leg was tender and affected his ability to go left. Marcus Mobley was assigned to defend the young freshman Holcombe. Marcus would have difficulty covering the talented left hander. Eddie envisioned Holcombe taking advantage of the injury and controlling the end of the game. Eddie saw the Seahawks upsetting the more talented Jaguars.

He opened his eyes.

"That's it!" Eddie blurted out.

Eddie had been conducting a basketball orchestra for the last seven years. He missed the control. Eddie wanted to orchestrate this one. The forecast of a limp seemed very real to Eddie. His mind toyed with the thought that Marcus Mobley was destined to suffer an injury and somehow Eddie had a premonition to be in on the news before anyone else. Despite the absurd nature of the thought it grew in his mind blocking reason.

It was six o'clock. These two teams would play in twenty-six hours. Eddie needed more information. He quickly packed a bag, got in his car, and drove five hours.

Eddie was sleepy. He pulled into a Wal Mart parking lot and fell asleep. The morning light awakened him. He followed the signs to the campus. The gymnasium was not hard to find. Home of the Jaguars was painted on the front of the building. He sat in the parking lot until someone unlocked the door. It was nine in the morning. Eddie opened his trunk and grabbed his ball and gym bag. He went inside. Eddie found the student in charge and asked if he could play for a while.

"The gym closes at four so we can set up for tonight's game," he said.

"I don't need that much time." Eddie said flashing a big smile to the student worker.

"Okay but stay on this end. On game day some players come in here early for a tension release session."

"No problem, Eddie shouted back.

Eddie knew Mobley was dedicated. As leader of this team, he would be in early to set an example. Eddie would see if that leg was injured.

"Hey, you need to leave your ID," the attendant said.

"I'll look for it. It's in my bag." He sat on a bench and pretended to look for the card. "Somewhere," he continued."

The attendant went about the business of unlocking doors and turning on lights. Eddie went into the locker room to change clothes. He was back on the court within minutes. He fired a shot toward the rim. The swish of the cords as the ball passed through whispered "You're the man, Eddie." Eddie retrieved the ball and continued dribbling and shooting, until a member of the Jaguars team walked on the court. Eddie watched him go through his ritual.

Eddie bounced a ball off his right shoe, intentionally allowing the ball to roll to the other end of the court. The player made no effort to stop Eddie's rolling ball. Eddie walked by and nodded.

"You're Marcus, aren't you?" Eddie asked.

"Yeah. Have we met? You look familiar."

"No. I doubt it. I'm new in town." Eddie walked closer and held out his hand. "I'm Larry Larson. I'm thinking of enrolling this fall."

"You gonna' try out for the team?" Marcus said as he sized Eddie up.

"Nah. I played in high school and a little in the Navy but I'm too slow for this level."

Eddie fired up a shot; it swished. Marcus matched it. They retrieved their balls.

"Hey, want some help warming up?" Eddie fired a bounce pass to Marcus without waiting for him to answer.

Marcus took it in stride and dropped the twelve-foot shot. He continued moving and Eddie hit him with another pass; he made it as well. Marcus moved toward the hoop and Eddie laid it up for Marcus to slam. Eddie fed him another bounce pass and gave a halfhearted block. Marcus drove by him for a shorter jump shot.

"See, I told you I was slow," Eddie said.

Marcus did not respond but threw Eddie a pass. Eddie pivoted and nailed the twenty-footer.

"You may be slow but you're shot's sweet" Marcus said.

"Yeah as long as someone doesn't cover me, I can hit that one all day."

"All day?" Marcus challenged the answer.

"Well, nine out of ten. Try me?"

"Fire it up, slick," Marcus passed the ball to Eddie.

Eddie hit five in a row but missed the sixth.

"Whatcha' got now, shooter?" Marcus was testing Eddie's mettle.

Eddie drained another shot. He took three passes and hit three shots.

"That's nine out of ten. Match that?" Eddie said.

"Nah, man. It ain't real," Marcus said. "That's not the way the game is played."

"You mean the game isn't about consistency."

"I didn't say I wasn't consistent," Marcus defended.

"Alright, I'll cover you. I don't think you can hit nine of ten," Eddie said.

Eddie passed the ball to him and moved out into his space. Marcus waited for Eddie to get within three feet, and then fired up shot that nailed the center of the net. Eddie retrieved the ball and brought it out to where Marcus stood.

"That's one but I wasn't ready," Eddie replied.

"You're never gonna' be ready for me, slick."

Marcus pump faked, Eddie went up, and Marcus drove around him.

"That's two. Not only will I hit nine of ten on you, I will hit ten of ten," Marcus said.

Small beads of sweat were popping off Marcus's shoulders but his smile and fluid movements were convincing evidence of his confidence.

"We'll see," Eddie said.

Marcus fired off two more. Then he smoothly drove by scoring with a soft layup. He drove past Eddie again; this time, he pulled up for a jumper. They were evenly matched physically but Eddie knew he could not compete with Marcus Mobley. Those days were gone. Eddie walked the ball out slowly. He was buying time; he was out of shape and struggling for air.

It was apparent; Marcus Mobley was not having a leg problem. Yet, the vision seemed so real to Eddie. Eddie could see the confidence oozing from Mobley. Marcus dribbled methodically looking for the opening.

Eddie knew what Marcus was looking for; Eddie had been there hundreds of times. Marcus wanted the slam. He needed to slam; it would be the exclamation point of superiority. Eddie reached for the ball; Marcus pulled it back and started his drive in the opposite direction. Knowing he was going to dunk, Eddie pivoted and leaped as high as he could for the block. Eddie could not reach the ball nor did he intend to. Marcus rammed it through.

Eddie did not see the shot. His attention was focused on the landing. As Marcus released from the rim Eddie did not try to prevent the crash of bodies. As they went down, Eddie deliberately forced his weight on Marcus's right leg. They fell hard to the wooden floor. Marcus was on the bottom grabbing his lower leg. Eddie felt pains shoot through his shoulder and neck as though the bones were re-broken. Eddie stood up quickly and offered to help Marcus.

"Are you okay, man?" Eddie asked.

Marcus refused to take Eddie's hand and stood up. He limped around in a circle.

"Shit, man. You had no chance of blocking that shot," Marcus yelled.

"Hey, I'm sorry. I guess I got caught up in the game. Are you gonna' be alright?" Eddie asked.

"Yeah, yeah, but we are through," Marcus said as he sat down to massage his knee and lower leg.

"That was only seven," Eddie said with a smile.

Marcus was not amused. Two other players came out of the locker room.

"Yo, Mo, whatcha' doin' man?" One of the players said.

"Loosening up, that's all," Mobley answered, not mentioning the pain in his leg.

Eddie grabbed his bag and ball; he did not bother to change clothes. He left the building. Eddie sat in his car; toweling off sweat and watching other team players enter the gymnasium. After twenty minutes, he went back in the gymnasium. He climbed to the top of the bleachers and sat in the far corner undetected. Marcus had a slight limp but it did not seem to be affecting his play.

Eddie went back to his car and drove back to his apartment. He sat in his recliner and closed his eyes. He pictured the game between the Seahawks and the Jaguars. He saw Marcus Mobley favoring the sore leg. Late in the game, when the leg was tired and tender, he saw the left-handed freshman taking advantage of the weakness. Eddie was relaxed amidst the chaotic competition. It was just like his playing days. He was orchestrating the outcome. He opened his eyes and bet his last nine hundred dollars on the young Seahawk team straight up.

# 33

In one hand, Powers held the latest bet from Eddie Dreyer; in the other hand, he held a statement of Eddie's wagering history since he was expelled from the team. Eddie did not know these players and yet he was risking his entire balance that the Seahawks would beat the Jaguars. Powers researched them on the Internet. The Jaguars were a decidedly better team. He could understand the boldness of the wager; Eddie's competitiveness never lacked confidence. Powers wondered why Eddie would pick a younger Seahawk team straight up.

Powers decided to gamble along with him. He spread twenty thousand dollars around five betting sites. Powers scanned his satellite listings for a broadcast of the game. He checked the internet for a scheduled streaming of the game. He could not find a broadcast of the game between the Jaguars and Seahawks.

He picked a novel, a red wine, and sat in his favorite chair to pass the next three hours.

At eleven, that evening, he tuned to ESPN to discover the score. He was hoping for a brief highlight or some helpful commentary. The reporters were covering all the Professional leagues and major college games. So Powers had his eyes glued to the scrolling sport scores at the bottom of the screen. A commercial interrupted the scroll before it reached the Seahawks-Jaguar game.

Powers sipped at the Pinot Noir and waited for the program to return. Moments later he saw the score. The Seahawks had upset the Jaguars. Powers did not leap from his chair nor did he scream exuberantly.

"Here's to you Eddie. Let's hope it's not the last," Powers said as he toasted Eddie's victory. The talking heads continued to preach and Powers finished his wine.

# 34

*Submit or Clear?*

The cursor hovered between the two buttons. Dexter Dalton stared at the screen on his monitor as though it contained a hidden message, as though there was a right answer. He stared so long his eyes were stuck; he could feel them crossed. Dexter shook his head.

"This is ridiculous. If I'm this torn, I shouldn't bet," he said out loud.

Dexter picked up the printout and looked at the column of statistics. It's early in the season but the Cardinals lead the conference with four wins and zero losses but had yet to cover the point spread on the road. The Tigers started the season one and four but were playing well at home. The six points could be money in the bank or it could wipe out his account. Dexter had lost six bets in a row. He knew a guaranteed winner did not exist. He knew a million things could offset the logical outcome. And it was obvious, the winning selection was not going to mysteriously appear on the screen, but he still believed in good bets and bad bets. Luck is only a factor, a factor missing from Dexter's formula lately.

Reaching a decision was difficult but mostly it was time consuming. Dexter clicked the button. His last one hundred and sixteen dollars were wagered on the Tigers plus six points. His confirmation was on screen; he printed it and put it in his file. Dexter checked the time and hurried out of the apartment. He was due at work at two.

# 35

There are moments, when a throat does not need to be cleared, when an error does not need to be erased, when nerves do not drive fingers to tap, and calculator keypads sit unused. In those moments of silence, the second hand of the large clock at the front of the room can be heard sweeping away time. April watched the hand move and unconsciously tapped her pencil to the beat. The girl to her left was irritated by the noise. She cleared her throat, and shot April an annoyed look. April was deep in thought; she did not hear the social signal nor notice the glance. Thirty-five minutes remained to finish the exam. She looked back at the paper on the desk, stopped tapping, and changed the eight to minus eight. April was through.

She had little to gather. She pushed the pencil behind her ear, clicked the calculator closed and walked to the front of the classroom. Everyone looked up, as though it were rude to leave. She gave a half-hearted smile to the TA, dropped the test into the basket and left the room.

April Pyle stepped into the sun and took a deep breath. The air was refreshing. She lowered the sunglasses from her pony-tailed head and strolled across the campus. It was nearly noon. She walked the central promenade, passed the Student Union and crossed the street to Captain Bluebeard's. April decided a midday buzz matched her mood better than Mass Marketing 301.

She walked inside the most popular bar near campus. April shoved the sunglasses back into her hair and gave her eyes a moment to adjust to the darkness. She ordered a pitcher of beer from the bartender and told him she would be sitting upstairs on the balcony. He nodded and began filling the pitcher as she walked away.

The balcony at Captain Bluebeard's provided the perfect escape. She chose a table close to the railing. The tall trees at curbside were pruned to accommodate the walking street traffic but a leafy canopy offered picturesque shade for the balcony patrons.

The beer arrived. April poured the glass full and drank several swallows. She smiled as she looked across the campus. Students walked in and out of doors like ants going and coming from the mound. She

146

put her feet up in a spare chair and rested her head back against the railing, soaking up the filtered rays of sun. She opened her eyes to grasp the glass of beer, took a drink and then returned to her restful position. The occasional sunray strained her eyelids but never long enough to be uncomfortable. The southern breeze constantly shuffled the branches to orchestrate a strobe light of sun and shade.

She refilled her glass and returned to her carefree position. A few minutes and few sips later, April noticed the sun was no longer filtering onto her face. She opened her eyes expecting to see a cloud blocking the sun. She saw Luke Clay; his tall lanky frame was eclipsing the sun. His NY Yankees cap was backwards, his ear was sporting a gold loop, his face was sporadically bearded, his sleeveless shirt proudly displayed a barbed wire tattoo on the right arm, and his jeans rode low, giving everyone a glimpse of his Joe Boxers. He smiled at April.

"Hey A. Whatsup, girl?" He asked.

"Hey Cliché. What are you doing out?" April responded.

"Why you wanna' do me like that?" He quickly responded.

"Like what?"

"My name is Luke Clay and everyone calls me LC," he said and sat down at the table.

"And my name is April, not A."

"So, that's it. I stop calling you 'A' and you stop calling me Cliché?"

"No. You're like the poster child for cliché," April said as she pulled her sunglasses back over her eyes.

"Yeah, okay. What's so great about your look?" Luke said pointing at her.

"I don't have a look. My hair should have been shampooed this morning but I ran out of time. Ponytail. Jeans, old Polo, and Sandals, I'm good to go. I honestly don't care if I've violated the fashion code," April said.

"Well you're the only one complaining about my look."

"That's because most southern folks are polite, Luke," she explained.

"You were raised down here. Why can't you be polite?" Luke wanted to know.

"I am polite," April said. "Be glad you can't hear the things I want to say."

"You're the most stone cold cruel chick on this campus."

"No sense running from the truth," she said as she finished the last swallow in the glass of beer.

147

She poured another. April motioned Luke to move to the left. He stood there puzzled.

"You're blocking the sun. Move over a little or sit back down," April said. Luke seemed offended. April recognized the need for additional southern politeness and added, "Please."

Luke sat and began talking about the Cougars. April heard "basketball" and tuned him out. She drank a few swallows, closed her eyes and let the sun warm her face. With her sunglasses covering her eyes, he would never know.

April reached for the beer.

"I'd offer you a beer but I know you athletes have rules to follow," April said to create a new subject.

"No. It's cool. I could have one if I wanted. Coach Barkley doesn't want us to drink but says that if we do, we better be responsible about it. But me, I believe my body is a__," Luke never finished.

"Temple? Seriously, you were going to say temple? Dude?" She shook her head and took another swallow.

It appeared Luke had taken all the abuse he could stand. He stood up.

"I gotta' go. I have a one-thirty Communications class. Coach won't allow us to miss classes. I'll see ya' around, alright?"

The disappointment in his voice and on his face was clear as he walked away.

"Now you're mad. You know I'm just bullshitting with you," April said to his back.

April raised her voice, "We've known each other since the third grade. I'm not trying to be mean. I'm just relaxing and having fun. Come on back and have one beer,"

Luke stopped and looked back over his shoulder.

"Nah, but thanks for asking, A__, April. Cya'," he said.

April watched him walk away.

*Was I cruel? Did I really hurt his feelings?*

Too late now.

# 36

Harmon wiped down the bar with his towel. He watched two students walk in the door and take stools at the far end. He went to the opposite end to serve them.

"A couple of beers. Bud will be fine," said the boy with the Metallica T-shirt.

"ID's, please?" Harmon requested without really hearing anything they say until he has proof of legal age.

"This is bullshit, you checked our ID's yesterday," said Metallica shirt.

"And the day before," said the second boy.

"I don't make a dime talking to you. What will it be? ID's our Cokes?" Harmon said as he placed both hands on the bar and leaned forward.

"There are other bars, where the bartenders are cool." Metallica boy said.

"I gave up cool for lent last year, decided I could live without it," Harmon said. "ID's?"

Both boys reached into their back pockets, pulled out wallets, and showed the identification. Harmon examined each under his magnifying glass mounted on the back bar. He was satisfied that each was legitimate. Harmon returned the wallets.

"Now, what can I get you boys?" Harmon asked.

"How about some courtesy? Is it possible for you to remember us tomorrow?" The black t-shirted boy demanded.

Harm did not react to the boys comment. He turned to the second boy.

"Apparently, your friend is not thirsty, are you?"

The second boy was speechless. Metallica spoke for him.

"Dude, what is your problem? Is it Alzheimer's? I said I want a Bud. This should be easy to understand. I'm a customer; you're a bartender; get my friend and I a couple of Buds," the boy said.

He twirled on the barstool to face his friend.

149

"You see Bobby; this is why our parents sent us to school. They don't want us to end up behind some bar, incapable of doing something worthwhile."

Harmon was a tolerant man although it was not necessary. Harmon was six-foot-two and carried a very lean and muscular two hundred and twenty pounds. His physical presence permitted him to choose his demeanor without reprisal on most occasions; he chose wisely. Harmon could have asked the boys to leave. He was not obligated to serve them but he let the remarks disappear among the clinking glass, bar banter, and background music. In the twenty-five years since Harmon Evans bought Captain Bluebeard's, he had seen a million kids come through the door. Every attitude imaginable had had already been demonstrated in Bluebeards.

Harmon grabbed two mugs and filled them with beer. He looked up when he saw Dexter walk behind the bar. Dexter gave Harmon a nod and started prepping lemons and limes for the evening.

"That'll be $3.50," Harmon said and placed the two mugs in front of the students.

Metallica tossed a five on the bar and clinked his mug against Bobby's. It was obvious the youth wanted to celebrate his conquest of the bartender. Harm returned and placed the change on the bar. He reached for a cord hanging from a large bell and began to ring it. After five clangs, he reached under the counter and pushed a button.

"Atta' boy Harm," someone in the bar yelled.

"Getting closer every day, Harm," sounded a second patron.

Heads turned as the electrical mechanism began to open the large treasure chest located on the wall behind the center of the bar. It was the showpiece of Captain Bluebeard's. It was six foot wide and was mounted from the wall at a forty-five degree angle. When the top of the chest was opened, customers could peer inside and view the treasure. When Harmon bought the bar, the chest was twelve inches deep and filled with fake coins. It was showy when the top was propped open.

Harmon had the chest re-constructed with thick glass. He had the door mounted on pneumatic rods. He could open and close the top with the push of a button. A bright light on each side of the chest lighted up. The chest was full of money, mostly one-dollar bills. It was apparent; there was a lot of money in the chest.

Clapping and laughing continued from the sparse afternoon crowd. The door reached its apex. Harmon Evans walked over to the chest and ceremoniously dropped the two ones inside. He held up both arms victoriously as the cheers waned.

Harmon combed his coarse red hair with his hand and nodded to Dexter. Dexter reached over to push the button; the Chest top started its descent. He laughed quietly.

Dexter took this job ten months ago. He had seen the money go in often enough for the novelty to wear off; it had not. The Jerk Chest still amused him. Dexter went back to cutting lime wedges.

He heard the Metallica shirted boy quizzed him.

"Hey dude; what the hell was that about?"

"I just got here, so I'm not sure," Dexter answered.

"You work here. You're telling me you've never seen that happen before?" Metallica asked.

"No, I see it happen almost every day, sometimes, several times a day. It's called the Jerk Chest. Every time someone acts like a jackass, Harmon puts the profits in the chest. There is about a dollar profit on a beer. He just put two ones in there, so I guess he just served beers to a couple of jerks. Did you see anyone acting like a jackass, in the last few minutes?" Dexter answered.

The two students looked at each other and then around the bar. They could see some patrons laughing. There was little doubt the laughter was at their expense. They mumbled to each other and moved to a table across the room.

Harmon walked up to Dexter and took a long deliberate look at the clock.

"If I put a dollar in there ever time you were late, I could retire much earlier."

"First, I'm not late. I walked in at exactly two o'clock. Second, you can't retire. Your only function in life is being ornery. You'd miss the joy of filling that chest and ringing that bell. How are you going to do that, if you are retired?"

"Quit wasting my limes. You're cutting them too big. Finish those, then check on the people upstairs," Harmon said.

Dexter nodded his acknowledgement and tried to cut the razor thin limes thinner.

# 37

The perfume trickled through his nose. He inhaled so long he thought his lungs would burst. He pulled it away from his nose and read the note a second time.

"Meet me at the Valley View Inn at four o'clock. We've waited long enough, baby. I already have the room. I can't wait to see you. Love Sondra."

Ray checked the time. It was three. He called Sondra but there was no answer. The Valley View was thirty minutes away. He grabbed his bag, threw everything he would need into it, and called Jerry.

"Hello," said the slow lazy voice of Jerry Thompson.

"J.T. Man, I need to borrow your ride," Ray said.

"What for?"

"Dawg, listen to me. Sondra is meeting me at a motel. You know what I'm saying?" Ray explained while trying to contain his excitement.

"Dude, right now?" Jerry asked. "We have to be on the bus at six."

"J.T., I'll be back by six, man. I got my stuff with me," Ray said. "I'll have ninety minutes of pleasure and I'll tell her to stay there so I can come back for seconds and thirds. It'll be a post game victory party for two." Ray laughed and nodded his head as he thought about the encounter.

"I don't think you should go, Ray. Tell her you'll meet her after the game," Jerry said.

"If this was Candace calling you, would you wait?"

"This ain't about me, Ray," Jerry responded. "Besides, you know I'd be telling her that I'm worth the wait."

"I've been waiting for this for a long, long time. I thought this day would never come. I gotta' go, Bro. Now, you gonna' let me use the car or not?" Ray asked.

"Yeah; sure but if you ain't back in time, Coach is gonna' be pissed."

"Hey, chill. I'll be back in time," Ray said. "I'll be over for the keys in just a minute."

Ray ran out the door, skipped the elevator, raced down the stairs and met Jerry at the door. He grabbed the keys from his friend's hand and ignored the disapproving glare. Two minutes later, he adjusted the music on the radio and began his drive to the Valley View.

He resisted the urge to drive over the speed limit. A traffic citation would make him late; he did not want to take any chances with this rendezvous. He drove into the parking lot of the Valley View at three fifty-five. He looked for Sondra's car; it was not in the parking lot. He pulled into a space at the end of the lot and waited. He watched for the yellow Camry. Ray could not believe his good fortune. Who knew; fantasy would become ecstasy today.

# 38

Dexter walked out on the balcony. He saw a girl holding her pilsner glass in a classic Hamlet pose. Her gaze was locked on the last couple of swallows. It could not be the look of a connoisseur appreciating the beauty of the drink; she was drinking Coors. It was more like transcendental meditation. The only thing missing was a chant.

He grabbed a tray from the corner station and cleared two tables of glasses and debris. He returned from the kitchen to find her attention still locked on the beer glass. He asked three other tables if they needed another round. All declined. Dexter walked toward the rail table hosting the deep-thinking patron. As he neared, he was hesitant to disturb her. He stopped a couple of feet away and just as he was about to speak, she spoke first.

"I need to pee. Why is it, all this yellow beer is going to come out clear and yet when I drink the same amount of water, it comes out yellow? She said without breaking her focus.

"I've never thought about it but then I'm not a science major," Dexter replied.

"Why does everyone have to identify themselves by some discipline?" She said drinking the last of her beer.

"I don't know but then I'm not a psychology major, either?" Dexter replied.

"You really want to tell me your major, don't you? " She said as she sat her glass on the table. She turned, raised her sunglasses, and stood up. "Obviously, it's important that you be identified as something other than a waiter. So, what is it, Pre-med? Pre-Law?"

"I'm not just a waiter; I'm a busboy, a go-fer, and a bartender," Dexter answered.

"Well, since we are being honest with each other. I want you to know that I am not merely a heavy afternoon drinker. I also enjoy beer in the evening."

"Speaking of drinking, can I assume you are done for the afternoon?" Dexter asked.

"Yup," she answered.

Dexter placed her empty pitcher and glass on his tray and wiped the table.

"You walked here, right?" Dexter asked.

"Yes I did," she replied. "Are you implying I might be too intoxicated to drive?"

"Just doing my job, ma'am," he said with a grin.

She gave Dexter a near sincere closed mouth smile.

"Excuse me," she said as she walked away.

Dexter turned to watch her walk toward the stairs; she was a little wobbly. Dexter cleaned another table and took an order. He went down the stairs. He watched for the girl to come out of the restroom. Dexter had not seen her on campus but he was sure she was a student. He wanted to meet her under normal circumstances; he suspected she would be an interesting person. He watched every chance he had, he never saw her leave.

Dexter began a normal shift of pouring beer, examining ID's, checking out ball games, and staying just busy enough to avoid Harmon's evil eye. Dexter loved his job and was never bored. He felt certain that Harmon liked him and trusted him, although Harmon had never said the words. But when Harmon took time off, Dexter was always scheduled to work.

The evening was flying by; any evening where one of Dexter's bets was a televised game kept him busier than usual. Dexter glanced up; with four minutes to go, the Cardinals were up by ten points; he only had six.

"A little D, that's all I ask," Dexter pled with the television.

Captain Bluebeard's had five televisions spread around. None of them were easy for Dexter to see. His best vantage point was at the far end of the bar. He wiped spills, made small talk, and over-serviced the drinkers at that end and Jenny impatiently waited at the server station, on the other end of the bar. She finally lost patience and yelled.

"Dex! Damn it."

Yelling in Captain Bluebeard's did not alarm anyone. Thursday crowds were no different than weekend crowds. College kids drank; days were irrelevant. Dexter hustled back to the other end of the bar to fill Jenny's order.

"Pitcher of Coors, three mugs and a Captain and rum," she ordered.

Lauren leaned in next to Jenny.

"The Sigma Chi's are luvin' the Guinness this evening," Lauren said. "I need six more."

155

Dexter gave the Coors to Jenny. She loaded her tray and left. Dexter began drawing the six Guinness for Lauren.

"A girl can't make money waiting on Guinness to quit foaming," she said. "I'll be back for 'em, Dex."

She smiled at Dexter and walked into the crowd creating a vacuum that turned heads to watch her walk. Dexter was one of them. He liked everything about Lauren except her smoking habit. The second hand smoke might kill him but it might not. Her smile was broad, dimpled, and bewitching. She winked a lot; her hazel eyes had an elfish twinkle that paralyzed him. Her hair was maroon, today. Last week it was platinum blonde. He wondered about her natural color but had decided it was simply unimportant. He did not care because it did not matter. Lauren was light years from his league. She was polite and friendly to him but Dexter was not on her radar screen. Lauren did not date, she interviewed. Dexter knew he lacked the minimum requirements.

All six glasses of Guinness were full and foaming. He rushed to the far end of the bar to check the score. One-fifteen remaining and the Cardinals were ahead by nine.

"Damn it!" he yelled.

They went to a commercial. Dexter rushed back to the six Guinness and topped each off, set them on a tray, and left them on the server station. As he was turning to get back to the game, he noticed Lauren bending down to tie her shoe. He stared; many stared.

*Miniskirts should never be out of style.*

Lauren finished and Dexter hurried back to the game. The Tigers were playing tight man-on-man defense. The ball was loose. Two guards collided; the Cardinal's guard was injured and the ball rolled out of bounds, last touched by a player in Cardinal red. The guard hobbled to the sideline. The whistle blew, a Tiger guard quickly fired a shot, nothing but net. The Cardinals lead dwindled to seven with thirty-nine seconds remaining. Dexter heard Jenny calling his name.

"Seven & Seven and two Bud Lights," she yelled.

Dexter did not look around; he held up his hand, without turning around, signaling her to wait a moment. Jenny called again but Dexter continued to watch the last few seconds of the game.

With their best guard out of the game, the Cardinals were having a difficult time bringing the ball up court. The Tigers stole the ball and drove for a lay-up.

"Yes!" Dexter yelled as the Cardinals lead was cut to five.

The Cardinals brought the ball in bounds and avoided the desperate foul attempts by the Tigers. Time expired with the score the Cardinals seventy-eight and the Tigers seventy-three. Dexter threw both arms into the air; skipped to the middle of the bar, poured two Bud Lights, and garnished the Seven & Seven with a split stem cherry. He brought the drinks to Jenny with a smile. Jenny did not smile back.

"I don't mind waiting Dexter Dalton, but that little stop sign action pisses me off. We can't all be Lauren. You owe me, asshole," she said and disappeared into the crowd.

*Let her rip me; I just started a new win streak.*

Jenny could not dampen his mood. He had correctly wagered on the spread and had increased his betting fund from one-sixteen to two hundred and thirty-two dollars. Dexter was feeling like a genius. He was smiling, filling drink orders and doing math in his head. Two thirty would become four sixty. He would keep doubling his money all the way to financial independence.

"It happens all the time," he said out loud to no one.

"Hey Dex, coupla' more beers here, okay, honey?" Lauren beckoned.

Dexter's fantasy switched gears as he winked at Lauren and headed to the server's station. "You know as a wealthy man, I just might have a shot," he mumbled as he strutted toward her.

# 39

With a Marketing textbook securely positioned against her bent knees April slept in a cushioned windowsill. She had not read a line in two hours. Studying was no match for the beer buzz; score it a TKO. She enjoyed drinking to a point where she was slightly out of control and had learned to stop drinking at the point where the stomach revolts and demands to throw-up. The ringing phone startled her. She grabbed the cell phone from the windowsill and pushed the talk button.

"Hello," she muttered.

"Hey, where are you? Didn't you say we would meet in the park at six?" The voice asked.

"Darren?" She said as she sat up. "Crap. I fell asleep. I'll be right there. Wait for me. Ok?"

"Hurry," he said and hung up.

April tied her shoes, put her hair in a tight ponytail, and left the apartment. She walked to the end of the block, and then broke into a slow jog. Five minutes later, she was at the park. She saw Darren at the entrance. He was off the path pushing against a tree. He bent over to stretch his calf muscles. Darren was an exercise enthusiast and incorporated stretching religiously but April knew his real motivation was to display his taut ass and lean legs. She slowed to a walk as she approached him.

"Let's go," he said unpleasantly and walked to the path.

"Yeah, hello to you also," April snapped.

"Unless we get started, the sun will set before we finish."

"Oh my God. No one can admire you in the dark. What was I thinking?" April said as she joined him on the path.

"I'm not late; you are. So, why is this about me," Darren said and began to jog.

"Darren, you want everyone to swoon as your tight ass parades by. You honestly believe every female out here is waiting for your appearance."

"Not all of them and not just the ladies. Well, who am I kidding; some of the guys notice also," he said casually.

"Egomaniac." April said.

"A healthy ego drives discipline. If you were more disciplined, you would not have been late."

His parental tone irritated her.

"I tell you what, Pretty Boy, don't talk today, just run."

April watched as Darren moved ahead of her. He was picking up the pace. He was not insulted by the Pretty Boy comment; she was stating the obvious. He would, however feel compelled to punish her for being late and upsetting his routine. She picked up her pace to match his.

They approached the first incline on the trail. Again, he picked up the pace. April was not athletic; she began running because it was a challenge and because her affection for beer was making it harder to stand naked in front of a mirror. She stepped up her pace to match his as they climbed a small hill. April struggled. She could not keep up with Darren if he chose to really turn it up. Darren was a cross-country star in high school and though not quite good enough for collegiate competition, he was more than capable of torching April. Still, she had a lot of pride. She wanted to stay astride him. If only the beer, bouncing between her belly and her bladder would cut her a little slack.

At the two-mile mark, April broke the silence in hopes that conversation would distract him enough to slow down.

"Ok, I blew off a class this afternoon," April said between gasps for air. "I went to Bluebeard's and drank a pitcher of beer."

Darren did not reply to her comment. The pace continued. They were starting another incline. Darren loved to lengthen his stride to 'overcome the gravity of the climb' he claimed; April did not endorse his strategy. She engaged again.

"The buzz of the beer felt really good," she spoke in a syncopated style befitting her lack of breath, "but I guess it made me sleepy."

They reached the top of the hill. The flat terrain provided soothing relief for April's panting lungs and burning thighs. It was a striking contrast to Darren's easy stride and effortless breathing. April had tried twice to carry on a civil conversation with Darren. She thought it was apparent; she was trying to apologize. She was ten minutes late; was that reason enough to ignore her?

"You're being a big baby. Why won't you talk to me?" April asked.

"Have I permission to speak? You said no talking today, run. I'm just doing as I was told," he said and turned to look at her. "You

159

expect everyone to obey your commands, right?"

"You're such an ass, an egotistical ass," April said. "I apologized."

"No. You didn't," he responded.

"Yes, I did. Weren't you listening?" She replied.

"You chose to get drunk this afternoon. That's your apology for being late?'" He asked.

"I didn't get drunk," April said defiantly.

"Denial; the first stage of alcoholism," he preached.

"I am not an alcoholic," she said through labored inhales.

"Fine, then let's talk about that apology," he said flatly.

"Let's go back to not talking at all," she yelled in frustration.

"As you wish, I think I'm going to sprint the last couple of miles. See you later, ok?" Darren said with a tone of indifference that froze what little oxygen was in the air around her.

"Yeah, whatever," she mumbled.

Darren picked up the pace. She increased her speed but realized it was pointless. The distance between them was increasing. She slowed down and watched him disappear around the curved path. When she reached the front entrance to the park, Darren was gone. It was dark; and without an admiring audience, there would be no reason for him to stick around. He lived a mile away. April suspected that he sprinted all the way back to his apartment without the pain she was feeling.

"Bastard," she said as she slowed to a walk and headed for home, wearily.

# 40

The back door of Bluebeard's opened into the kitchen. Harmon turned the gas on the flat top griddle as he walked through. Two light-switch flips later, he was measuring coffee. With the coffee perking away, he stepped into the bar.

Part of his morning ritual was to air out his establishment. He opened windows in the front and the back and hoped for cross ventilation. A bar is a gathering place where beer will be spilt. Every new fragrance of cologne and perfume will exit with perspiration. Perspiration is inevitable when opposite sexes gather to attract each other. Everyone is seducing regardless of the outward appearances. And that seduction has a scent. It all gets lost or tolerated in the laughter and chase. People leave and shower and clothes are laundered but bars have fewer options. Harmon tried to start each day as fresh as Mother Nature and six ceiling fans could get it.

On his way back to the kitchen, he reached up and tapped a framed napkin, mounted on the doorway. Harmon originally began touching it every morning as a reminder that Ernie O'Brien promised to sell him the building next door. Harmon wanted to convert the building into a loft home. It would have a fabulous bed, a plasma television, six recliners, and lots of shelving for his favorite things. He would not need a kitchen or a bar because Bluebeards would be next door. Harmon believed it to be the ideal plan.

It had been twenty years since Harmon first asked Ernie to sell the building to him. The first five years he said no. Then one evening seven years ago, Ernie scrawled a promise on a napkin and signed it. From time to time, Harmon tried to get Ernie to create an official document but Ernie would wink at him and say, "We'll talk about it over a couple of Whiskys, some evening."

Bottle after bottle ran dry yet the napkin remained the only evidence of Harmon's first option on the property. Harmon had the napkin framed and bolted to the wall; it was right under the autographed photo of Jesus Christ.

The photo had caused considerable criticism over the years. A group of Baptists picketed his business nine years ago but gave it up when they realized they were attracting larger crowds to the bar. Harmon had never met Jesus Christ in person but a man who looked remarkably like Peter O'Toole came in the bar one evening. He ordered a martini and asked Harmon to substitute the vermouth with additional gin. After several comments exchanged, the man asked Harmon to join him.

"If, I'm recognized, which is unlikely given the youth of this crowd, I do not want to be seen drinking alone. Alcoholics drink alone; or so I'm told," the man said.

They sat and sipped gin and talked about the sixties and changing times. Harmon never asked if he was truly Peter O'Toole but they did discuss films, including "The Ruling Class." Harmon went to his office and came back with a publicity photo from the movie. It was Peter O'Toole portraying Jesus Christ.

"This is one of my favorite movies. A kid who worked at the movie house down the street traded this photo for a pitcher of beer," Harmon explained.

"It's a very good likeness," the man responded.

"In this movie, Peter O'Toole had a great line__," Harmon was interrupted.

"You've decided, that I am not Peter O'Toole, have you?" he asked.

"You sure look like him," Harmon replied and continued. Harmon was beaming from ear to ear as he prepared to quote the line from the movie.

"A reporter asked him a question__"

The O'Toole look-a-like interrupted again, "I suppose you think I don't remember this line?"

"It was a long time ago," Harmon said giving the man an easy excuse. "Nominated for the Oscar, you know?" The look-alike said over the top of his martini glass.

Harmon studied the man's face, nodded yes, and continued.

"They asked him, how do you know you are Jesus? And he said, because when I pray, I find I'm talking to myself," Harmon said imitating a British accent. "I don't know why but that line cracks me up and it is profound."

"Without question!" He replied; and with surprising quickness, grabbed the photo and signed it J. Christ.

Harmon thought it was funny and they both laughed as they considered how the Almighty would take it. They concluded that a just Lord made allowances for multiple martini humor. The man left the bar without ever confirming or denying his true identity. Harmon was left with a fun evening and a story.

Harmon gave the Ernie napkin another pat as he walked into the kitchen. Ernie was old and he would never retire. Harmon was convinced the promissory napkin would disintegrate before Ernie died. He did not want to lose the opportunity to buy the building but he did not want to lose a good friend either.

He threw several slices of bacon on the hot griddle. He poured a cup of coffee as they sizzled. He flipped them over, cracked three eggs onto the hot surface and tossed two flour tortillas on the griddle as well. He flipped the eggs and chopped at the bacon. The medium fried eggs and bacon were slapped onto the warm tortillas. He placed his plate of food on a tray and walked back into the bar. He tucked the morning newspaper under his arm, sat the pot of coffee on a tray, stuffed a bottle of Tabasco into his pants pocket, and walked upstairs to the balcony.

Harmon unloaded his meal onto a table near the rail and watched the kids, across the street hurrying to their morning classes. He envied their youth. It was impossible to watch them without wanting to re-live the past. They had everything in front of them.

Every morning, weather permitting, he sat on the balcony; every morning he wondered if he should have taken a different path. Should he have gone to college instead of enlisting in the Marine Corps?

Harmon spotted a longhaired boy who had been in the bar the night before. He recognized him because he was wearing the same bright yellow shirt with a Legalize Marijuana slogan on the front. The boy was moving slowly; Harmon suspected he was fighting a doozie of a headache from too many beers supplemented by less legal highs. But no one blames the weed. Harmon smiled; no one wants to re-live past hangovers, just the party.

He pulled the Tabasco from his pocket, spiced-up the eggs and opened the morning paper. Every morning he decided the present was better than the past, plenty of parties, fewer hangovers.

# 41

April's Saturday morning ritual had not changed for months. She walked to the Starbucks on the corner, filled a large cup with a dark blend, and took the replica trolley to the Farmers Market. She strolled the aisles and examined the fruits and vegetables. April stopped at every flower vendor to smell and admire. She longed for the day when she would own land; she would plant and grow lots of flowers.

When she finished her coffee, she would wander back to a vendor and buy some fruit for breakfast. Today, April chose a peach, a plum, and cantaloupe on a stick. The cantaloupe vendor had come up with a great idea. He cut his melon into large bites and would skewer five chunks. For a fifty cents, it was a bargain and she could eat it without making a mess.

April walked and ate. Over the last six months, she had walked every street in a one-mile radius of the market. April was studying architecture on campus but out here was where she was learning. Every starry-eyed architect wannabe dreamed of designing the next Fallingwater, Sydney Opera, or Petronas Towers. April wanted to influence the environment but she had a passion for the daily rituals of living. She wanted to re-construct neighborhoods. Where once the Italians, the Polish, or the Germans would have dominated a neighborhood, April wanted to combine those influences and create American walking communities.

April sat on a bench and pulled her sketchpad from the backpack. Truttman Hardware had stood on this corner since eighteen eighty-two according to the embossed numbers on the cornerstone. She had no interest in the square box that housed tools, implements, screws, and nails. April was sketching the unique qualities of the artisanship. She sketched a corbel and cornice.

A small Mexican restaurant occupied the building next to Truttman's. April could smell the breakfast aromas every time someone opened the door. She was hungry; she paused to eat her plum and returned to drawing. She gave herself a mental pat on the back for eating healthy, when diet hell was right across the narrow street. She worked on the details of the cornice but her mind drifted.

She, muttered, "Screw it; that smells so good."

April closed her sketchpad walked into Carmelita's.

The eatery was not Americanized. She counted ten tables on the right side of the room and grocery shelves lined the left side. April was uncertain of procedure. She looked around the room hoping to find a sign.

*Should I seat myself?*

She became uncomfortable; she was the only person in the restaurant not of Central American heritage. From behind, she heard a male voice.

"Seat yourself."

As she turned to thank the man for the help, he spoke again.

"The window table is open. You enjoy views of the street, right?"

"Yeah," she said looking at him. "I've met you somewhere, haven't I?" April stared at him; she thought he might be someone she had seen on campus or someone introduced to her in a group.

"Yup. Yesterday you were enjoying the street traffic and a few beers at Captain Bluebeard and __," he could not finish.

"You're the busboy," she interrupted.

"Bartender, but who's kidding who? I bus tables, wait on people and mix drinks. It pays the rent and when the tips are right buys a great greasy breakfast. I'm gonna' take the window table. Would you like to join me?"

"Sure. Hey, I wasn't trying to insult you," April said. "Our meeting is a little foggy to me."

"A pitcher in the afternoon will do that to you, plus I'm not a memorable guy."

They walked to the table. He reached behind the bottle of Picante sauce and grabbed the two menus. He handed one to her. April studied his face as she would a building for its unique architecture. He was accurate; there was nothing unique about him. His hair was brown. He kept it short enough that it did not require attention. His eyes were brown and his average physical frame seemed unspoiled by the rigors of weight training and exercise. His smile was pleasant. He seemed harmless she surmised.

"What?" He said as he noticed her staring at him over the menu.

"Nothing. I was looking past you into the kitchen," April lied.

He turned to look behind him just as a young girl of thirteen or fourteen came to the table and asked if they wanted coffee or juice.

165

They both shook their heads no, and he added "No, gracias."

"I'm Dexter Dalton," he said as he extended his hand across the table.

"April Pyle, "she thought the handshake was bit hokey but she shook his hand.

"April, it's a pleasure to put a name to the face," he said and smiled.

"So, Dexter Dalton, is "gracias" all the Spanish you know?"

"Why no, Ms. Pyle; I can also pronounce "enchilada" and "tamale" and a wide variety of Mexican foods and beverages, like "margarita.""

"Okay. Well, you seem to be a regular here; what's good?"

"It's all good; if you like Tex-Mex style food," Dexter answered closing his menu. "I'm going to have chorizo and eggs."

"Chorizo is sausage, right?" April asked.

"Oh yeah. Greasy spicy orange looking sausage. It's chopped into the scrambled eggs. It is downright ugly but definitely bueno."

"Okay I'll assume that means it's good; I'll try it," April said. "But how about a moratorium on the Spanish?"

"Deal. Haven't you ever had Mexican food for breakfast?" Dexter asked.

"I had those breakfast tacos from McDonalds. Does that count?"

The young girl returned and they ordered. April noticed the newspaper Dexter brought. It was still wrapped in the plastic delivery bag.

"I can see you intended to read the newspaper while you ate breakfast. I won't be offended if you want to read it," April said.

"It can wait. I know what's in there. Car accidents, troubled dictators, tax arguments, diet trends, comics, and half the sports teams won and other half lost."

"Really? What about soccer? They tie, all the time. Nil to nil, and one to one," she said.

"Then they're both losers. If a game can end in a tie, it isn't worth watching, reporting, or worth the time to read about," Dexter replied.

April raised her eyebrows at the finality of the statement.

"Oops. Are you a soccer fan?" Dexter asked.

April started to say yes. She wanted to see if he would back off of his criticism, let it die, or dig a deeper pig-headed position. She decided against the strategy.

"No. I'm not a fan of any sport. They bore me after a few minutes. I don't see the point."

"Teamwork, common goal, strategy, these things bore you?"

"Those things do not bore me. Those things within the framework of a game bore me. I would rather see those things accomplish something useful."

"Are you telling me the basketball game between Greensboro and Chattanooga did not accomplish something useful?"

April watched him smile at her and she appreciated the fact that he was willing to make jokes about sports.

The breakfasts were delivered. Dexter looked at the girl's name tag and said,

"Thank you Anna. Could I have a Dos Equis, please?" Dexter looked at April. "You want one?"

April shook her head and said, "It's a little early for me."

She expected him to make some wisecrack about drinking, considering her behavior the day before. He let it pass and she was grateful.

Anna nodded and left. April moved her fork through the re-fried beans. He was right, the eggs looked brown and unappealing but the potatoes looked great.

She was not sure how to attack the meal. She looked up to see Dexter grab a tortilla and fill it with potatoes and covered it with a green salsa. He ate the eggs and beans with a fork and used the stuffed tortilla as a tool and a sandwich.

He swallowed and said, "There isn't an official etiquette to eating this stuff. However you tackle it will be acceptable. Do you like spicy salsas?" He asked.

April shrugged in a manner free of bias.

"Try the salsa verde, the green one. It's great."

An older man delivered the beer to Dexter.

April picked up a tortilla, covered it with the green salsa, and rolled it up. She began to eat the eggs. They were good. The chorizo was full of flavor; she chased it with a bite of the filled tortilla. Unconsciously, she nodded her head to signify her pleasure.

"Not too shabby, Huh? And only three ninety-five, this is a great deal for us poor starving college kids," he said then grabbed his stomach to feign hunger.

He poured his beer into a glass, raised it, and smiled.

"Long live Mexican food!" He toasted.

167

April mumbled agreement and returned his smile without showing the mouthful of food. She watched him drink the beer. It looked refreshing. The only reason she was not having a beer was to appear in control. April did not like to make decisions based on appearances. She signaled to Anna.

"I'll have a Corona, no lime," she ordered. "You want another?"

"I believe I will. Do Equis, please," he said."

Anna again nodded and left.

"Is this the really hot sauce?" April pointed to a small red bowl.

"Nope." Dexter reached around behind the napkin holder and showed her a bottle that looked like Tabasco but was labeled in Spanish. "This here is the hot stuff."

The elderly man returned with the beers and took Dexter's empty. He watched April shake the bottle onto her tortilla.

"Go easy, senorita. Muy caliente," he said softly.

He walked away. April mixed beans and potatoes on a fork, tasted them and tasted the hot sauce slathered tortilla. Muy caliente, indeed, she thought. She grabbed her beer to ease the heat and saw Dexter staring over the top of his beer bottle.

"What?" She asked.

"Hot enough for you?"

She could see that Dexter was choking back a laugh.

"Holy shit. What's in here?" he asked using her hand to fan her mouth.

"Special Habanero peppers. Too hot, huh?"

"I can take it." April said.

"No doubt in my mind. I just met you but I can tell you are not the backing down type," Dexter said and then stuffed more food in his mouth.

"How come you aren't eating this stuff?" April asked.

"It's too hot for me," he said.

"You big Wuss." April challenged.

"Yes ma'am. That's me, just a big ol' wuss. I can live with that."

April could feel the burn all the way down. It was good in moderation but it was really too hot for her. She pushed her plate away.

April agreed, "It's too hot for me also but you have to try different things or life is pretty boring."

Dexter held out his beer, inviting her to toast. "To trying." She brandished her Corona to the center of the table, "To trying." She added and clinked his Dos Equis. April returned his smile.

The next thirty minutes were spent getting to know each other. April asked about bartending. Dexter talked about Captain Bluebeard's. He asked where she was from. She talked about her life in a small southern town. Dexter countered with coming to Carolina because it was green. He grew up in New Mexico.

They had one more beer and nibbled on chips. They had a pleasant time and did not discuss sports or architecture. April was surprised. She enjoyed the chance encounter but doubted they were heading in the same direction.

They paid their tabs and went their separate ways. She looked over her shoulder to see Dexter reading his newspaper as he walked. She suspected he went directly to the Sports section. She headed home having had a very pleasant morning.

# 42

April stood in front of the mailbox. It had become a stressful routine. She was expecting a check from her scholarship fund. It had never been late before. School had been in session for almost two months. April arranged for her payments to be divided into thirds for the semester. She paid the first third, certain that the money would arrive in time to pay the remainder and replenish her personal account.

Relief trickled through her veins like caffeine as she pulled the familiar envelope from the box. She opened it as she walked back to her apartment. The relief was momentary. The letter stated the money would not be coming. April re-read it. No misunderstanding, the treasurer had embezzled the fund dry. The letter went on to explain he was being prosecuted. Justice would prevail, however April would not be receiving the five thousand dollars. She failed to see the justice.

She slammed the door shut.

"Fuck!" She yelled into the empty apartment.

April's intelligence came in handy at test time; but it was no match for her poor discipline. She was not frugal. The three scholarship checks covered her expenses and permitted her to enjoy the college experience. She would have to make the next payment from her personal account; it would be drained. April had no idea where the third would come from. If she found a job, she would not earn enough in time frame available.

She fell on the futon and stared at the letter. As she processed the repercussions of the loss of income, her thoughts were interrupted by the drone of the news on the radio. The news headlines of the day seemed the same as the news of yesterday or last month. She turned it off. The only news that April cared about was not being reported.

*Where is the outrage for me?*

The radios should be reporting real injustice, "April Pyle Stranded in Third year of College? "Creative Phenom Desperate for Funds to continue Studying Architecture."

She knew her personal problems paled in comparison to real tragedy but right now, she just did not care. She wanted her check. She wanted to shed the stress. She wanted a beer. She wanted a friend. One of the side effects of individualism, sarcasm, and skepticism is a shortage of friends.

Out of beer, she opted for exercise. She changed clothes and jogged toward the park. April hoped to clear her mind and review her options. She was running too fast but could not slow down. Her breathing was labored and out of control, and the chorizo coated eggs were unhappy being jostled. With her thighs burning and lungs begging for air, she began to cry.

The pity party was unavoidable. She stopped running, sat with her back to a large tree, and sobbed. She lost track of time but her weeping was fading to a muffled whimper when she heard footsteps. She looked up to see Darren's spandex body peering down at her.

*Ah, shit. If I close my eyes, will this rich boy from a blessed gene pool just disappear?*

There would be no magic in April's day. Darren squatted next to her.

*He can see I've been crying. Great.*

"Hey, did you hurt yourself?" he asked.

"No," she said as she wiped her eyes and stood.

"Ok. Well, are you alright?" Darren asked.

Darren put his hand on her shoulder.

"I'm fine. I'm heading back home," she said and started walking back toward the path.

"Do you need some company?" Darren asked.

"No, but thanks for asking. I'll talk to you later, ok?"

April jogged off.

She heard him say, "Alright, I'll see ya' later."

She waved without turning around.

Everyone had a role in April's life. Darren was a running partner and elusive date. Ursula was a neighbor and study partner. Luke was the boy next door, a touchstone. Kenneth was the creative rival that kept her in check. But the role of friend was unfilled. She wondered if she had blown an opportunity to develop a genuine friendship. It would not have been the first time. April slowed to a walk and ambled home feeling very alone.

# 43

The professor finished early and everyone began to walk out. Dexter checked his watch. He walked to Bluebeard's and arrived forty-five minutes early for his shift. He walked in, filled a glass with Coke, grabbed the newspaper, waved to Harmon, and trotted upstairs. He settled into a chair at the smallest table.

He looked at the front page and scanned the headlines. War and economic gloom stood like weathered street signs leading to the sordid parts of town. Dexter turned to page two and discovered invitations to learn more about deep conspiracies, corporate greed, and death in the name of some God. He re-folded the section and set it aside.

*That's enough of that depressing crap.*

He picked up the sports section.

"If life isn't like sports, it ought to be," he said out loud.

Dexter believed that somewhere in the pages, hope would rear its defiant head and beat the odds. Somewhere in these parables, a bully will be humiliated and chronicled as a loser. The sports page is the scoreboard. Winners wear a ring; losers are naked. Winners feel the pressure and sparkle like a diamond; losers feel the heat and wilt. The sports section is where the final score anoints a king and decrees status. Arguments are settled. Just once, Dexter wanted to see the main section of the paper report, "Taiwan 68 China 65 –Freedom Reigns in Asia." Squabble settled on the court.

On page three, Dexter began reading an article about Titus Lockwood, a former Cougar assistant coach, having remarkable success as a head coach in Arkansas. A shadow interrupted his concentration. Dexter looked up to see Harmon staring at him.

"What?" Dexter said as he used one finger to hold his place on the article.

"Even when you are here on time, you can't start to work on time," Harmon said to him as an answer.

Dexter tapped his cell phone to check the time.

"Shit," Dexter said as he gathered his paper and ran downstairs.

172

"You're starting late so you can leave early?" Harmon yelled as he followed Dexter down.

"Sorry Harm," he yelled taking steps two at a time without turning around.

Dexter tied on his apron as Harmon leaned against the bar and stared at him.

"Dex, what was so important in the sports page?"

"Nothing in particular. I just lost track of time," he said as he unloaded the mugs from the dishwasher.

"How much do you gamble?" Harm asked without making eye contact.

The question caught him off guard but he answered it without pausing from his work.

"Four or five days a week, maybe."

"How much have you lost?" Harmon asked now looking into Dexter's eyes.

Dexter looked at him searching for an inkling of why Harmon was asking these questions.

A man sat down on a stool; he signaled to Dexter as he yanked his tie loose from his neck. Dexter glanced back at Harmon, held up one finger and walked down to pour a beer for the salesman with the frustrated look on his face. Harmon had not moved; he was still leaning against the bar waiting on an answer. Dexter retuned.

"Harm, do you want to lecture me on the evils of gambling?"

"Nope. It's not evil. I've made a bet or two over the years."

Dexter asked, "So, you're just curious? You're not trying to get all parental on me?"

Dexter slid menus in front of two students, three stools away.

"If I had been one of your parents, you would have been bigger and better looking," Harmon said. "I'm just curious; why do you bet?"

"To bump my income a little. You know I could stop if you would give me a big raise," Dexter said.

"A raise wouldn't keep you from betting," Harm stated.

"Probably not. I like it too much. I do research and I have some decent instincts. I make selections that should win and half of them don't," Dexter explained.

"It all boils down to luck, doesn't it Dex?" Harmon asked. "I mean, if every player performs as expected, if no one gets injured, if no one gets too tired, or suddenly develops diarrhea you would win most of the time."

"And I would too, if it weren't for those damn point spreads," Dexter replied.

"So, really it's just luck, right?" Harmon asked again.

"Luck has a lot to do with it," he responded.

Dexter walked a few steps away and took an order for food. He hustled it over to the kitchen window. On the way back, he filled two mugs with tap beer and pushed them in front of the two customers, collected the currency from the counter and put it in the till.

Dexter looked up and Harmon was still leaning against the bar. Dexter grabbed a towel from the counter, walked back toward Harmon and said, "Okay Harm. Lay on it on me. What is it you really want to tell me?"

"I was hoping you would come to the conclusion that betting on basketball games is a pointless pastime."

"There, now, don't you feel better? You've done the right thing. You've given a young man advice. And I appreciate it," Dexter said as he clapped Harmon on the shoulder.

"You're right I do feel better. Now, when you lose your ass, I'll be able to say I told you so," Harmon said as he straightened up. "That, I will enjoy."

Dexter watched Harmon walk toward his office.

"Thanks Dad," Dexter yelled. "I'm really going to think about what you said."

Harmon turned and looked over his shoulder and yelled back, "Be careful Dex; thinking can lead to early maturity."

Harmon went into his office. Dexter shook his head.

"Why do old people want to stop young people from having fun?" He mumbled.

"Hey Dex, we need two more beers," came a shout from his left. Dex nodded and pulled the lever. He sat the two mugs in front of them and collected the cash and the empty mugs.

"I bet he drank and smoked and chased women and gambled when he was young. He survived but now he doesn't want me to have any of that fun," Dexter grumbled as he put the empties into the washer.

"Pointless. I tell you what's pointless, Harm. It's pointless to believe I will stop having fun just because you say it's too risky." Dexter said toward the Office Door just loud enough to not be heard by Harmon.

Dexter straightened up and looked around. He saw Lauren at the server's station. His face erupted into a glowing smile.

"I could stop gambling for her," he said as he walked toward the server's station.

# 44

The white clad painter was standing on a ladder applying a bright gold coat to the stripe that went the length of the hall. The blue and gold stripes had been on these walls for over forty years. The campus was covered with reminders of Spartan pride. This was one of them. He applied the paint in a very deliberate manner. His thick glasses would not inspire confidence but the glistening gold line was perfectly straight.

The painter heard the sound of a door open and close. Three students were walking toward him. They were laughing and joking with one another as they walked. The ladder covered most of the hallway. The first student crouched to walk under the ladder. The second grabbed him by the arm.

"Say man, that's bad luck," he said.

The painter watched the boys below him; he grabbed the ladder with one hand and stabilized the paint can with the other.

"Oh, thank you. My momma would have slapped me upside the head if she knew I was about to walk under a ladder," he responded as he rolled his eyes and squeezed past the painter.

The second boy followed him acting as though he were walking on a high wire. All three laughed. The third boy ducked his head and started under the ladder.

"Please don't walk__," the painter was saying as he pushed his foot further inside on the step. The foot caught the shoulder of the boy. The boy straightened a little. The painter seemed to lose his balance and grabbed at the paint can. The painter hugged the ladder but dropped the paint can.

The heavy can, like a bomb, exploded on the sandal-clad foot of the boy. He screamed. The top came off the can and the gold paint shot up his leg and the white wall. The boy crawled out from under the ladder and grabbed at his foot. His path out toppled the ladder; the painter leapt off and stumbled to the hallway floor. The painter got up, picked up the can, and pushed a lid on it, concealing the lead weight wedged in the bottom.

"Are you okay?" The painter asked.

176

"It hurts like a son-of-a-bitch," the boy howled.

"Ya'll better get him over to the infirmary. I'll clean up this mess," the painter told them.

The trio left with the hurt boy in the middle supported by the other two. The painter opened a can of paint thinner and within a few minutes, the gold spot was erased. He did not finish the stripe. He packed up his paints, tarp, and ladder and left. He put everything into a truck and drove away.

The three students arrived at the infirmary. A nurse assisted Jason to the examination room. The doctor entered a few minutes later. Jason sat on the table, staring at his blue swelling foot as the doctor examined it.

"Nothing's broken, right?" Jason asked the doctor.

"Jason, I told you we are waiting on the x-rays to come back. I can tell you that you won't be walking on it for at least a week."

"A week? I have a game in three hours."

There was a knock at the door. Expecting the x-rays the doctor said, "Come in."

It was Coach Rogers.

"J, what the hell happened?" He said as he looked at the foot. "Shit, that does not look good. Doc is that thing broken? He can't play like that, can he?"

"Coach, please calm down," the doctor said.

A second knock at the door was the nurse with the x-rays. Doctor Talbot slammed them into the light box.

"That must have been a really heavy paint can. You can almost make out where the rim line impacted the foot. The good news: None of the bones are broken but that paint can ruptured some vessels and really bruised the tendons. It's going to be tender until that swelling and bruise dissipates. Tell your trainer to put him on a rest, ice, compression, exercise program, and maybe he will be ready to go in a week."

"Goddamn it!" The coach said.

Coach Rogers was concerned for Jason's health but his mind was already working on a back up strategy for the game. He was depending on his defensive specialist.

"Coach, I think if we wrap it good, I'll be able to play tonight," Jason said.

The coach looked at him without speaking.

The Doctor looked at the Coach and said, "Don't even consider it Charlie. This thing could bother him for the rest of the season if you don't let it heal."

The doctor glared at them both waiting for a signal of agreement. They both nodded their heads.

The painter stopped at the dumpster. He tossed the overalls tarp, and brushes inside. He hurled the lead-laden paint can through the door; the metallic crash echoed through the alley. He stepped up into the rented truck and drove away.

# 45

The bar curved and ended at the wall. April sat on the last stool. It was a crowded night and her left elbow brushed the wall with every sip of beer. A student in the chair behind her bumped his head into the small of her back every time he roared back to laugh. He apologized the first time.

She smiled and mouthed, "No problem."

He continued to bump her. She tried to ignore it, writing it off to crowded conditions but she suspected he was getting some kind of erotic kick from it. She did not understand it but she let him have his thrills.

April felt a little guilty about being at Captain Bluebeard's spending money on beer when she had just discovered she was going to be five thousand dollars short of income this semester.

*Part of the college experience is drowning one's sorrows.*

It was two dollar beer night; so, she was building character and doing so economically.

She saw her new acquaintance, Dexter Dalton walk in. He walked behind the bar, poured a tap beer, and ambled among the crowd until he saw his friends at a table. The table of friends included the cheap thrill artist behind April. They high-fived and traded insults as though it were the ante for a poker game. Dexter did not see April and she did not turn around. April could hear most of their conversation; they were loud.

"Hello, earth to Dex. What are you doing?"

"Ah, nothing," he said as he turned back to the group.

"Ohhh. You're checking out the tattoo?" The questioner said. "I saw it earlier. You can't miss it, the way that short blouse creeps up the back and those jeans ride so low. Kinda' hot, huh?"

'Oh crap, why did I have to wear these jeans?' April thought.

"It's cool. There's a red circle with four question marks. The question marks have a common dot and a vine crawling between them," Dexter explained.

April continued to look toward the front door and sip her beer. She was hoping they would change the subject and leave her alone.

"Yeah. I wonder what it means," Dexter said.

"It doesn't mean anything," Dale blurted out, "Chicks get tattoos for three reasons. Number one: they want to say, 'Fuck you,' to their parents. Number two: they think it makes them look cool. And number three: they think it makes guys horny. Their reasons are no different from ours."

"The philosopher has spoken. Nothing more need be said. Next topic please?" Said the friend with the Buddy Holly glasses.

The group laughed.

"Well, let's just ask her," Dale said as he tapped her shoulder. "Excuse me."

April wanted to ignore him as she had for the last hour as he bumped his head into her repeatedly but it would be impossible. She twirled around.

"I took a trip to Malaysia after my freshman year to view the work of Cesar Pelli. Are you familiar with the Petronas Towers?" She raised her eyebrows and continued, "It's not important. While I was there, I had this tattoo etched into my skin to remind me to question the norm and strive for perfection. That answers the question about why it is there and what it means. Now, about your theory, let's see my choices were rebel against my parents, make me look cool, or make you horny. Both of my parents have tattoos; they don't care. That eliminates number one. Cool is an attitude and does not require your approval. And if a man is breathing, he is horny. It requires no work from us, whatsoever. Three strikes, you're out."

April said and turned back to the bar and again hoping they would leave her alone. She heard applause and then a series of shots were taken at Dale. She did not hear Dale defend himself. She assumed he was accustomed to being put down. April felt someone pushing his way to the bar. It was Dexter. He wedged himself between April and the guy next to her, reached across, clinked his glass against hers.

"Well done. Sounded a little testy but for the most part well done."

"Friend of yours?" April offered a very small olive branch.

"Define friend," Dexter said. "I hang out with lots of people. Dale is one of them."

"Friend enough that you feel a need to defend him," April asked.

"Defend him? He's just having fun. Come on, I'll introduce you," Dexter said.

Before she could object, Dexter had his hand around her shoulder and was turning her on the barstool. He yelled to the group.

"Hey, this is April."

They turned to look and Dexter looked at April.

"April, this is Rod, Robert, Paul, and Dale." Dexter named the table.

"Glad to meet you, April. I guess my tattoo theory belongs in the shitter, like the rest of my theories," Dale said.

"It's a pleasure to meet you, Dale," she returned the courtesy.

The other three offered hellos as well. Paul found an empty chair and insisted that she sit with them. April felt railroaded but sat anyway. They spent a few minutes talking about majors. The guys posed a united front in asking about architecture and trying to get April to open up. She was uncomfortable in the role and swung the conversation back to them.

"Really, let's not talk about school. What were you talking about before Dexter turned the conversation to tattoos," she looked at Dexter as if to say, "It's all your fault."

"Robert was trying to convince us ballgames are determined by oddities more often than by skill and talent," Rod said looking around for agreement.

April scanned the room for the server. She was going to need more beer if she was going to listen to college boys talk about sports.

"Oddities. Like what?" She asked.

"Take tonight's game. The Cougars win but would they have won if Jason Poe had played?"

"That's just the way the ball bounces," Paul said automatically.

"Jason is not the star of the Cats team," Dexter reported. "He's strictly defense."

"Exactly. If he plays, does Verdell drop thirty points on the Cats?" Robert asks.

The comment silences the group. They all lift their glasses to drink.

"It's still not an oddity," April said. "If he's injured and we know about it, then it's a factor, not an oddity. We can calculate it. No star defender, whoever he guards scores more points. It's a shift in the balance."

"What if you didn't know beforehand? Boom. It's game time and Jason Poe is sitting on the bench with his foot wrapped. It may not be an oddity but I guarantee you the oddsmakers are going to be unhappy with the shift in the balance, as you put it," Robert said.

"What was the line on the game, Dex?" Paul asked.

"Cats minus four," he answered.

"They lost by three. Jason Poe could easily have held Verdell to his average or less. I just think it's odd. Another example could be the Bulldogs-Knights game," Robert said.

"Why? What happened?" April asked.

"Ray Jefferson sat on the bench the whole game. Without him, the Knights lose. They were favored by eight," he said.

"Why didn't he play?" Dale asked.

"The official reason is disciplinary action taken by the coach," Dexter said. "But a friend of mine is their trainer and he told me Jefferson was waiting for his girl at some motel and she never showed. He missed the team bus. He drove to the game by car but the coach was mad and decided to make an example of him. So, he sat the whole game. And dude didn't get any on top of that."

"Ah, poor thing," April said.

"Eight points? That's like a toss-up. Four baskets? The game was too close to call," Dale offered his opinion.

"No, Dale. Eight points is a lot," Dexter said.

"Really? So, you took the Bulldogs and eight?"

"No." Dexter answered.

"If it was a lot of points, you should have jumped on it," Dale said.

"It wasn't the best bet on the board," Dexter replied.

"Whatever," Dale said.

"You two are side tracking the issue," Robert said. "Jefferson sat. It was unexpected and the game was decided because of it. Oddity decided the game not talent."

"Some games are decided by the unexpected but not most," Paul said.

"Most games are not decided by talent," Robert said.

"What difference does it make? It's just a game," April chimed in.

April knew the boys at the table would circle the wagons and begin firing on her rather than one another.

"It is just a game. But to answer your question, it makes a huge difference, because those of us who wager on these games, win and lose money based on details like this," Dexter said.

"Yeah, like Jason Poe? That was freaky. A paint can drops on his foot on game day. That was a big turn of events. Anyone who knew about the injury, even a few minutes before the game could have made a bundle," Rod said.

"Yeah, what are the odds?" Paul responded.

April waited for the apology for the pun; it never came.

Rod added, "That's why they play the game. On any given night the best team can lose."

Clichés among the sports minded flow from their mouths like the word fuck from a Marine. It has no meaning. It merely fills dead air.

*It's a fucking shame.*

"You said a bundle. What's a bundle?" April asked.

"You can nearly double your money," Rod answered.

"Or you can make more by betting parlays," Robert added.

April looked to Dexter for clarification.

"Two or more bets connected. Both have to win for you to win. It compounds your money but obviously it is twice as hard to win."

"I made almost seven hundred dollars on a three team parlay last week," Paul said.

"That was sweet; especially since you lost seven bets in a row. You're almost back to even now," Dale said.

"I know but you will always be the worst gambler at the table, Dale. Our parents don't keep propping up our accounts," Paul replied.

April listened as the boys sniped at Dale and then one another. She hoisted the beer to her lips and thought about what she had just heard. Bundle. Seven hundred. Parlays.

*Double your money.*

She finished her beer and stood. April exchanged pleasantries with the group. As she walked home that evening, she wondered if she could make money by wagering. She picked up her pace. The sooner she could get home the sooner she could do some research on Internet gambling.

"Double my money," she mumbled to herself over and over.

183

# 46

April watched the slide change, she could hear the lecturer's drone, but her mind was not interested. Nothing was going right. She stayed out too late, drank too much beer, had a headache, felt queasy, and a Thunderstorm had knocked cable out. She fell asleep waiting for it to come back up.

The lights came up and applause disrupted April's daze. She put her hands together half-heartedly. She closed her note-less spiral and filed out with the other future architects. The sun was bright. April reached up to her head to pull sunglasses over her eyes; they were not there. Perfect, she thought, as it should be today.

Her body was on cruise control, headed straight toward Starbucks. She stopped, as if she were lost. She stamped her foot down in mock determination.

*I'm going home to brew coffee.*

She had to start cutting costs. She jaywalked the street and saw Dexter walking toward her. Dark sunglasses shielded his eyes and he was drinking from a tall Starbucks cup.

"Sunglasses and coffee, I hate him," she mumbled.

"Hiya' April. How do you feel this morning?"

"I'm dragging ass. No coffee this morning. I'm heading home to brew some, right now," she said holding her hand over her eyes to block the morning sun.

"That's crazy. Let me help you out. Lucky for you I'm double cupped."

Dexter separated the two cups and poured half of his into the second cup. He gave one to her.

"You don't have to do this. I'll be home in ten minutes," April replied.

"Take it. I never finish the big ones anyway. When's your next class?" Dexter asked as he slurped coffee through his lips.

"Ten thirty." April sipped. "Thanks for the coffee. I owe you one."

"No worries. You want to sit down?" Dexter asked.

"Sure, but unless you can halve your sunglasses, let's sit in the shade."

They walked back across the street and chose a bench under a tree. They sat without speaking for a few minutes. It seemed like an eternity to April. Her headache seemed to amplify every noise, including her own coffee slurping.

"Ok, I get the whole 'question the norm' ideology but why four question marks?"

She blinked a few times trying to fast forward to his segue. It dawned on her; he was talking about the tattoo.

"Why knot?" She answered annunciating the letter K.

"Oh, I get it; question the question, question the questioner, question the answer. That sort of thing?" Dexter replied.

"I meant Knot, with a K. I thought one dot with four marks made a cool knot-like design. As far as I am concerned, it can mean whatever you want it to mean," April explained.

"Fine with me. It's too early for philosophy, anyway," Dexter said.

April was grateful.

"So, will you forgive me for introducing you to those bozos last night?" Dexter said.

"They weren't bozos. They were alright. As a matter of fact they started me thinking about sports, she replied.

"You mean like, sports is a ridiculous waste of time?"

"No," she said with limited sincerity. "I mean, 'Yes' in the bigger picture sports is a big ol' waste of time; however, if I can make money from their foolishness, then I have developed a sudden interest."

"You want to bet on sports?" Dexter asked and faced her.

"Maybe. If I were interested in this Internet gambling, where would be a good place to start?" She asked.

"Start? As in learn how to bet or to place a bet? What do you mean by start?" Dexter said still reeling from the thought.

"What's to learn about betting? I assume one team is favored over another and the penalty for picking the favorite is balanced by points. How hard is it to understand? I want to know where to find statistics. Where can I compare the teams?" April replied.

"Take it easy; I didn't mean to insult you. I shared my coffee, remember?"

"Yes, I remember, thank you again," she said.

"ESPN is a good place for statistics on individuals, teams, and conferences. There's tons of shit there. Or you can pay a professional service to break it down for you and even advise you on who to bet on," Dexter said.

"You pay a fee? Do you get a guarantee?" April asked.

"Nope. But they will give you another pick for free."

"What good is a free pick if you lose your money on the first one?" April asked.

"I don't know. I never used one. I know that really good handicappers hit about sixty percent of the time," Dexter said.

"Sixty percent?" she repeated over a sip of coffee.

Her disappointment was easily apparent.

"Sixty is sensational. If you're expecting more, you should consider another money making business," Dexter said.

"All right, thank you," April responded.

"Are you really gonna' start gambling?" Dexter inquired.

"I think I can make money betting on basketball. All I have to do is predict winners more than fifty percent of the time. I don't get emotional. I'm not attached to any of these teams. I don't have any favorite players. I'm not likely to get (all) poetic over someone's potential. I will predict the outcomes based on the facts," April stated.

"Well, as long as you have it all figured out," he said.

Dexter struggled to hold his laughter and April noticed.

"Sarcasm noted," April said. "I have to go to class. Thanks again for the coffee."

Dexter waved it off and said, "You buy me a steak dinner with your first winnings and we will call it even," he said.

"I wouldn't bet against me, if I were you," April said.

"Don't worry, I don't do sucker bets," he said as he watched her walk away.

April sat through her ten-thirty class with inadequate attention as well. She hurried home, opened her door, dropped everything, and logged onto the Internet. She went to ESPN and dug into the college basketball conferences. She printed out seven weekly schedules with the matching standings. She found a website that listed the point spreads and printed the lines for the games to be played that evening. She took the print outs and propped up into her favorite spot, the pillow cushioned window seat.

She tucked the page of point-spreads under a pillow. She decided that she would reach a decision without being influenced by the odds. She settled in with her pencil and began to study the information. A few minutes later, she narrowed her focus to the Puma-Bears game. The Pumas were in first place; the Bears were tied for last place. The Pumas were averaging thirteen more points per game than the Bears. She reached a conclusion. The Pumas were playing at home and would win this game by the average margin.

April pulled the page of point-spreads from under the pillow to check the betting lines. The line read Pumas minus nine points. April's immediate reaction was joy. She was sure the Pumas would win by at least nine. Then reason squeezed a question from her throat.

"Why so few?" April said out loud. "It should be higher."

She reached for the laptop to dig a little deeper. The Pumas average thirteen more points every game than the Bears. Everyone should bet on the Pumas.

*I must be missing something.*

She searched for the hometown newspaper for the Pumas. After nosing around for thirty minutes, she found the news that could be affecting the line. Starting guard, Damian Ethridge was out for the season with a broken fibula. His replacement, Stephen Lincoln, was a diminutive five foot six. However, Lincoln was noted for giving taller players fits because of his quickness and tenacity. He averaged ten points a game as Ethridge's backup. Lincoln was not Ethridge, April noted but he should not be a liability for the Pumas against the Bears.

"We will miss Damian but Stevie will do a great job," Coach Gerrard was quoted as saying.

To be thorough, April checked the local newspaper for the Bears. She found no information that would lead her to believe the Bears could stay within ten points of the Pumas. She had no choice but to go with the logic. The Pumas were the better team and she was going to place her first bet on them.

Her Yahoo search brought back two million websites on betting. After surfing for two minutes, she settled on a betting service. April deposited five hundred dollars, read every instruction on the website. With the inexplicable confidence of youth and the apprehension of an old soul, she placed a fifty-dollar bet on the Pumas minus nine.

She briefly considered wagering a larger sum. The analysis seemed strong. This could be an opportunity to bet more and win more. She remembered the discussion about parlays and how they can compound the payout. Given her need for tuition money and her lack of discipline, April shut the computer to avoid the temptation.

187

She stared at the laptop for a few moments. It was chocolate candy begging to be eaten. She had no difficulty picturing the laptop as the temptation, not the wagering. April could open that laptop and with four mouse clicks wagering again. She could continue to wager until all her money was gone from the account. A slight shiver ran through her body. She stood abruptly. She walked toward the kitchen staring at the laptop the entire time.

*Damn, forget meth, this is scary.*

# 47

Most Sundays, Little Stevie remembered spending with his Grandma and Grandpa. He and his father would go for a big lunch. Stevie loved Grandpa Lincoln's farm. It was a dairy farm. It wasn't much of an operation but they managed to raise and feed five kids. None of those kids stayed home to become the next generation of Lincoln dairy farmers. Four of them were doing well but Stevie's daddy struggled. To Stevie's dad, Sunday's meant two things: a good meal for Stevie and a sermon from the senior Lincoln.

But to Little Stevie, it meant something entirely different. It meant playing in the hay barn, throwing rocks at the pigeons, tossing pointed sticks at targets, testing the beehives, and riding the big swinging gates. It may have been uncomfortable for his dad but it was Disneyland to Stevie.

In the late afternoon, Stevie would hear his dad yelling for him to come in. It was a dreary drive back to the dumpy little apartment in the city. Stevie was five the first time he remembered stopping at the Knotty Pine. He remembers it because a nice woman with really big earrings bought him an orange soda. His dad would stop off there for a beer on the way back to the city. Little Stevie liked this part of Sunday also. His dad would sit at the bar and talk to a bunch of men; Stevie explored. Someone always offered to buy him an orange soda.

The most fascinating part of the Knotty Pine was the pinball machines. He watched the men play. He asked questions; he was relentless but cute.

"You want to try?" They would ask.

He would nod yes unable to hide his enthusiasm. They would stack wooden boxes so he could reach the flippers.

Many of Stevie's childhood passions passed by but the pinball intrigue remained. Eventually, he had to pay for his own games. Stevie dropped a lot of quarters into Pinball machines. He never felt stress when he was working the machine. He could block out the rest of the world.

Stephen Lincoln was never able to shed the Little Stevie label. Now, twenty-one years old, he stood five foot six and weighed a slight one hundred and sixty pounds. He stood in front of the pinball machine. His fingers hit the flippers with perfect timing. His arms moved the machine gently without tilting. The sounds, though loud, frequent, and varied, had no effect on Stevie. The score counter rolled perpetually. His mind was in tune with his objective, his fingers were reacting with precise timing, and lady luck nursed his needs. The Strange Science Pin Ball Machine did not stand a chance and Stephen Lincoln's size was not a factor. He would set another High Score this afternoon.

Stevie was unaware that the player to his right was not faring as well. His ball continued to be swallowed by the black hole, as his flippers swung like Mario Mendosa. He was pounding on the machine. The tilting alarm was on continuous ring. Stevie glanced to his right and then back to his game. He refocused on his own objective as the arcade manager came over and urged the abusive patron to calm down.

"You, piece of shit!" The player yelled at the machine.

The player stepped back to kick the machine. The manager grabbed him by the shoulder. The kick missed the machine but his big black motorcycle boot crashed into Stevie's hand.

Stevie let loose the flipper buttons, grabbed his right hand with his left and began to hop up and down. His hand was throbbing with pain. A slight cut on the backside trickled blood. He spun around looking for the raging man who had kicked him. He was gone.

He turned back and stared at the machine. It had tilted from the kick. "Game Over," it read. Stephen Lincoln had entered the Arcade walking tall, prepared to demonstrate size did not matter. Now with his hand swelling and throbbing, the kick of a boot had tilted the machine fifty points shy of the high score. Stephen Lincoln walked out the door and into the cool night air as Little Stevie once again.

# 48

He untied the boots and stripped all the black leather clothing from his body. He shoved it in a duffle bag and took a shower. He re-dressed, poured a Dewars, and sat on the bed with his laptop computer. He accessed the Internet and placed a bet on the Bears plus nine points. Road victories are not easy for mediocre teams but the nine points and a third string guard should push the odds just far enough.

He poured another Dewars and powered up the television. It did not matter in which hotel he was staying ESPN was always a feature. He studied schedules on the Internet as he listened to the reporting of hockey, football, and tennis. His attention was reserved for basketball. The reporting ended and a basketball game between South Florida and Alabama-Birmingham began. He divided his attention between the television and the Internet. Preparedness is the lifeblood of the successful.

He did not watch basketball for enjoyment. He noted tendencies and prepared counter measures. He continued reading articles, forums, and watching campus chat rooms. He came upon a thread of conversation suggesting that the seven-foot center of the Tigers might prefer male company to female company. Eddie began to imagine Riley Remmington's reaction to pressure.

*How would the twenty-year-old Riley handle himself if the public knew of his sexual preference?*

He turned off the television and closed his laptop. He had decided where his next competition would be. One must be willing to exploit to win. Many are afraid to win; Eddie was not among them. Soon Riley Remmington would be face to face with his own desire to win.

# 49

Powers sat at the bar. He emptied the bottle into his glass and watched the head bubble over the rim and dribble down to the bar surface. He picked it up to take a swallow and saw the towel appear out of nowhere.

"You're wasting good beer and making a mess of my bar," Harmon said.

Powers took the towel, wiped the bar and the bottom of his glass, and tossed the towel back to him. Harmon watched the towel land at his feet.

"Nice toss. Who taught you to throw, you're girlfriend?" Harmon asked.

"No one taught me. I had to choose between sex and athletics. The choice seemed obvious, to me anyway."

"Big ladies man, are you?" Harm said as he tossed the dirty towel in hamper in the corner.

"I would not say big. I would certainly say adequate."

"Well, professor, are you in here looking for ladies this evening?"

"No, just having a beer," Powers replied.

"I think this is the first time I've ever seen you in here alone. Where are your buddies?" Harm asked.

"Finishing class work, I suppose. The unemployed enjoy greater freedom," Powers said with his best upper crust brogue.

Harmon bent down, reached under the counter for a clean towel and slung it over his shoulder.

He walked closer to Powers and asked, "Unemployed? How does that happen? I thought you guys got life time contracts."

"Ah, yes. Tenure. Tenure is a marvelous lifestyle. The department head did not like me very much. He offered me freedom as a consolation," Powers explained.

"So, what are you doing; looking for another teaching job?"

"No, I have lost interest in training youth to become social workers and shrinks," Powers answered.

"Are you practicing Psychology or Counseling?" Harmon probed.

"No. Working with Eddie Dreyer revealed my weaknesses. I am not a healer."

"No one can fix Eddie. He's completely broken," Harmon stated flatly.

"I am curious; why do you believe he is broken beyond repair?"

"Eddie doesn't believe in right or wrong. He only believes in winning," Harmon said.

"Would you not agree this win at all costs attitude is related to the way he was taught and the environment he experienced?" Powers asked.

"Sure, but it's not an attitude; it's his vision of the way the world works," Harmon said.

"Psychologists, given time, would unearth the origin of his philosophy. They would help him see the irrationality of the objective. They would compare it to winning with honor and guide him to a healthier choice," Powers explained.

Harmon half grinned and said, "I'm sure that's what they would try to do. But Eddie would exploit them. Eddie Dreyer versus the psychiatrist. In Eddie world, there is no right or wrong. It's just another game to him. The psychiatrist doesn't stand a chance. You should know; look what he did to you."

He looked directly into Powers eyes.

"No offense," Harmon said.

"None taken," Posers admitted. "He was a challenge. I was not up to it."

"Did you have any success with the hypnosis? I mean any at all?" Harmon asked and turned to wave at an older gentleman.

"Hypnosis?" Powers asked.

Fear unleashed a rush of adrenalin. Powers could feel juice tingling throughout his body. Jim and Natalie were controllable but Harmon Evans was certainly not.

"Yeah, Eddie told me he was going to push you to use hypnosis."

"I am still bound by confidentiality," Powers stated.

"Sure, sure professor. It's obvious you weren't successful or Eddie would still be playing basketball, not gambling," Harmon said.

Powers reached for his beer. He shook his head slightly and took a drink. He wanted to remain calm and appear ignorant of any information Harmon revealed.

"He gambles now?" Powers asked.

Harmon leaned in and answered, "Constantly. He reads everything he can get his hands. He has that iPad thing with him everywhere he goes. He is so sure the information is inadequate, he travels to games gathering first hand information. Not many people know as much about basketball as Eddie Dreyer. You want to talk psychology; I bet Eddie could fill a book about the psychology of a basketball player."

"You said he has to win. I suppose he is doing well." Powers responded.

"He must be. He's carting around a gazillion dollars of technology. He's connected to the Internet constantly. He's driving a couple of different vehicles. He runs big bar tabs and pays with cash. He moved out of his apartment; He just goes from hotel to hotel," Harmon said.

"Do you think he is happy with this new lifestyle?" Powers asked.

"I never think of Eddie as happy or unhappy. I only think of him as winning or losing. But it is kind of sad. He lost all the camaraderie, the kinship of team, and the adoration of fans. Most of us would be devastated. I would be." Harmon said. "But then Eddie never did it for anyone else. He does not need an audience or applause. He does not need anything but an opponent."

"You may be right Mr. Evans. Maybe you should be an analyst?" Powers suggested and took the last drink of his beer.

"I get more sad stories here than I can handle. No thanks. Get you another beer?"

"No, I better head home," Powers said.

"Well, good luck on the job search," Harmon told him.

"Maybe I will become a gambler. Now that I know the money is good." Powers quipped.

"I've seen you throw, professor. I'd bet you're a little short on sports knowledge."

"You would win," Powers answered with a smile.

Powers waved to Harmon and walked out. On the drive home, he thought about how lucky he had been. He had hypnotized a college student without being disgraced professionally. He had taken advantage of the hypnosis for profit without being exposed. Then the student gets drummed out of basketball. The meal ticket, the golden child of basketball could not pick a winner. Powers loses a ton of money. It seems Powers Meade's plan for wealth would be destroyed by bad luck.

As proof that good luck is a forgiving mistress, Eddie decides to become a professional gambler. He starts picking winners again and continues to bet at surefirewinners.com. Eddie places bets three or four times a week. Powers selects the same wager. Eddie's hit rate is extraordinary. Powers rakes in tons of cash.

Most men would worry themselves to death. Every day they would wonder when is this luck going to run out? They might, they should wrestle with sound sleep nightly. Powers did not. They would be afraid good luck would turn and abandon them. Powers did not. Powers Meade walked in the door of his house happy and worry free. He was at peace with the belief in good luck. Some are just born lucky.

*Lucky me.*

Powers sat. He checked his laptop. His Notes popped out for easy viewing. The one note that caught his eye was a reminder to hire a CPA. Powers was willing to gamble on good luck but not willing to tempt the Federal government or the IRS.

# 50

April dressed, poured the travel mug full of coffee left early for class. She hoped to cross paths with Dexter. Losing her first wager put April in a foul mood. She took a seat on the bench across the street from Starbucks. April was hoping to cross paths with Dexter. Mr. Predictable strolled in and out of the coffee shop. April called to him from the bench.

"Hiya' April," he said while dodging a bicyclist and a jogger. You look a lot better than yesterday."

"You know that's not exactly a compliment," April said.

"It wasn't meant to be. I was merely stating a fact. Were you looking for a compliment?"

"No. I think everyone who knows me, knows I don't care what people think about me," April explained.

"Oh, you care. This is just part of your hard-ass façade," he said to her.

"Whatever," April said with a near roll of the eyes. "What do you know about the Bears-Pumas game?"

"Nothing. Why?"

"Come on Dexter; you know basketball. Who was supposed to win?"

"The Pumas, I guess. They are in first place in their conference," he reasoned.

April responded, "Yeah and the line was nine even though the Pumas have a twelve point scoring advantage. Even with Ethridge out, the Pumas at home cover nine, right?"

"Holy shit. Who are you and what have you done with April?" Dexter said and added, "I don't know you well but I know this out of your norm."

"Come on. I'm serious. I lost fifty dollars and it doesn't make sense," she said.

"You want the truth?" Dexter asked and watched her nod yes. "Shit happens. That's it."

"Shit happens?" April repeated.

196

"Yeah," Dexter repeated without considering a deeper explanation.

"If I can't depend on the best team to win, most of the time, then I cannot make money betting on basketball," April told him.

"The best team does win most of the time. Most of the time only has to mean fifty-one percent of the time. You only picked one game," Dexter said.

"I get the math. I can't afford to lose money," April said.

"Then don't gamble. I'm pretty sure the only people who make money gambling are the gaming houses, and of course, liars. Liars seem to do very well," Dexter replied.

"How does lying help?" April asked as though she was missing an important variable in her equation.

"I mean they are lying about winning," Dexter answered.

"Would you quit fucking with me? I'm not in the mood."

Dexter stood up, picked up his backpack, and took a couple of steps away.

"I like you. Maybe I'm a masochist but I like you but not right now," Dexter said. "I'm going to class."

He took a few steps, turned around, and added, "Oh, and without a sense of humor about gambling, you're going to need a twelve step program eventually. See ya' later."

April did not say a word. She sat there until Dexter was out of sight, then she began her walk to class.

"He likes me. What the hell does that mean?" She said as she walked.

# 51

Dexter kicked his computer, took a deep breath, and pressed the Power button. Despite the clicking and clanging and the electrical hum, the mysterious box came to life. The monitor blinked and showed the log-on window.

"Only three tries this time. Not bad, you pile of junk," he said to the machine.

The old desk top computer was all Dexter could afford at this time. With a gun to his head, he would admit he could pick up a good used laptop but he would have to back off the partying and gambling. He was not willing to make that sacrifice.

Dexter typed in his password and opened the file containing his term paper for Kinesiology. He read over the last few paragraphs, changed a few words, and began typing new thoughts. He would finish this evening and polish it up in the morning. Dexter was pleased with his research and his diligence. He would submit this paper by the due date without pulling an all-nighter.

One hour later, the paper was complete. Dexter reviewed the betting lines for the evening. Then he checked his email. He was surprised to see email from April.

*Where did she get my address?*

He clicked the email and with eager anticipation he read it slowly. She explained that she sent emails to ten different name combinations and figured one of them would be correct.

*That answers one question.*

She asked if he would drop by her apartment to discuss a game between BYU and Utah. She gave her address. As letters go, it was anticlimactic. Dexter stared at the letter burning bright on his monitor. He scrolled up and down looking for a hidden message, looking for some subtle innuendo. It was not there. April did not indicate that she had an interest in him. He told her he liked her; he could only conclude she was not interested.

*Where's the apology for the way she acted earlier today.*

"This chick is a one way street," he said to the email. "Figure out your own bet."

Dexter closed the email and continued his own research. He focused on the Southern Conference. The most intriguing game on the board, to Dexter, was the Georgia Southern-Citadel contest. He placed a bet on Citadel plus seven. He knew the Eagles would win but hoped the Bulldogs would keep it close in their home gym.

With his bet placed, he could not resist the temptation to check out April's game. He was unfamiliar with the two teams. There are more than one hundred Division One colleges. Dexter believed it was better to keep track of one or two conferences.

"Only a fool would try to track them all," he mumbled.

Statistics loaded on the screen. BYU had a fourteen game winning streak at home but had lost all six road games. Dexter learned, Utah could grab first place with a win and they were getting an all-conference player back from scholastic probation. Dexter decided the nine points were not enough. If he were to wager on this game, Dexter would wager on Utah minus the nine points.

He resisted the urge to bet but resisting April's invitation was more difficult.

"I'm betting I'll regret this," he said out loud.

Dexter could almost hear voices from the walls agree with him. He made a few notes, grabbed his coat, and left for April's apartment.

# 52

He found the note taped to his door. He shouldered his gym bag and opened the note. He read the first part of the letter and closed it quickly. He looked up and down the hallway, stepped back in the room, closed the door, and leaned against it. He re-opened the letter and read:

"Do your teammates know? Is it hard for you to see all those cocks in the locker room? Have you picked out a favorite?

Right about now, you're saying, 'I haven't done anything.' But you don't have girlfriend; you've never had a girlfriend, and you don't want a girlfriend. No one has said anything because your seven feet tall, gangly, and unattractive. But you know there's a man for you out there, don't you Riley?

I bet you've been experimenting with a dildo or two? Where do you hide them? Do you worry about them being found? That's one big closet you're afraid to come out of, isn't it, Riley?

Wouldn't it feel good to let the world know? How about it, the first openly gay college basketball player? Once you've come out, maybe some boy will come forward dying to take the place of your dildo.

But you aren't the only person with problems. I'm struggling also, Riley. I can't decide to tell the newspaper about you or to tell your teammates. What do you think I should do? I guess it can wait until tomorrow.

Hey, I'm going to be watching you play this evening. I have a great seat – don't take that the wrong way Riley – I don't mean I have a great butt. Unlike you, I want girls playing with my cock. Have a good game! Remember, I'll be watching."

Riley Remington did not need to read the letter twice. He was not outraged; he was panic-stricken. He did not want anyone to know his sexual preferences. He had never had sex with anyone, male or female. Riley had been dealing with his sexuality for almost ten years. Neither sex excited him very much. He was uncomfortable around intimacy, period. The only truth in the letter surrounded his interest in pleasuring himself. But the least of the assertions were damning. He could not play basketball if his teammates thought he was odd and odd meant anything outside normal male-female fornication.

*As if any of that were normal.*

He went to the kitchen sink and burned the letter. He washed the ashes into the disposal and flipped the switch. Riley went to his closet and grabbed the box from his locked footlocker. He tossed the box into a trash bag. He triple tied it closed, grabbed his gym bag, and left the room. As he walked by the big dumpster near the cafeteria, he tossed the trash bag inside. He jogged to the gymnasium.

Riley Remington hurriedly dressed for the game. He concentrated on not looking at any of the players around him. He went through warm ups just like everyone else. His attention drifted to the bleachers. He searched the stands looking for the anonymous letter writer.

*Who could it be?*

He knew the truth was it could have been any one of the faces in the crowd. The letter said he had a good seat. Riley continued to sneak peeks into the crowd.

*Where is a good seat?*

Riley controlled the tip off but drew a foul foolishly. He tripped and fell to the court on top of his opponent.

"Get off me, you freak," the fouled player yelled.

Riley heard the word "freak" and his mind brewed with paranoia. Riley fouled him again on the other end of the court. It was intentional. With two fouls in the first two minutes, the coach pulled him out and scolded him. He sat on the bench and watched the Cobras take a twelve-point lead.

The Coach put Riley back in the game but poor play continued. Passes bounced off his legs, his shots were not falling, and he continued to pick up fouls. He was done before the first half was over. He walked off the court. He stood and stared around the arena, making a complete three sixty.

"I hope you're happy," he screamed into the stands.

Riley slapped a towel around his neck and mumbled, "I hope you are fucking happy."

The coach jumped up and met Riley on his path off the court.

"Who are you talking to?" Coach demanded.

"I have no idea," Riley responded. "Myself, I guess or some other demon."

"Demon? I wish to hell you were a Demon. At least a Demon would have done something worthwhile on the court. Sit, the hell down. You've done enough damage for one night," the Coach said as he pointed to a chair like a parent sending a child to his room.

Riley did not follow the order. He continued to stand on the court staring into the crowd. He did not know what he was looking to find. He was hoping the person who threatened him would reveal himself. Riley found nothing but disappointed fans.

As his fury slowly calmed back into reality he could see the Referee approaching and he could hear the Coach speaking. The coach leaned into Riley's face.

"If you draw a technical foul, I'll bounce your ass off the team," Coach said into his ear.

Riley Remington walked to the end of the bench and mopped his face with a towel. He continued to look up into the crowd picking out faces to scrutinize without basis. It was a half-hearted effort; the other half was searching his own soul for a practical way to live his life. He sat alone at the end of the bench and watched the Cobras beat his Tigers by eighteen.

# 53

Dexter stood at the door. He had changed his mind. As he was getting ready to leave, he lost control of his hand; it knocked on the door. The door opened and April smiled at him.

"I guess my email reached you," she said.

"Yeah. Am I the first one here?" Dexter asked hoping for a laugh.

"So far," April answered and smiled. "Come on in."

Dexter stepped inside and surveyed the one room efficiency. The space was better defined by what was missing. Dexter did not see plants, television, posters, pictures, candles, or furniture. The futon on the far wall had dual purpose. Her laptop sat on the table that would have served as the dining table. Her textbooks were lined up neatly on the floor in the corner by the window seat. Her sketchbooks were piled next to the futon with a lamp perched on top. Her only music source was the laptop with two speakers on the same table. Her kitchen was smaller than what many motels offered as kitchenettes. A two-burner stove, tiny microwave, three-foot refrigerator, and a sink barely eighteen inches wide.

April opened the mini-fridge and pulled two beers off the rack. She popped the top from both cans and handed one to Dexter as she walked by. She dragged the chair from the dining table closer to the window seat. She sat cross-legged in the window and motioned Dexter to take the chair. He turned the chair-back toward her, straddled the seat and sat down.

He wanted to ask why a student of architecture cared so little about her own environment. He wanted to say something clever and glib about interior decorators.

Instead Dexter said, "You know I only like two kinds of beer.

"Free and cheap?" She guessed.

"Exactly, Dexter answered. "So, you've heard that one before?"

"My dad's favorite line," April answered. "He used it more often than he should."

"Evidently, me too," Dexter said. "Do your parents visit very often?"

"No," April said. "And the whole "let's get to know each other's background" thing is really lame. At least mine is, I promise."

*I knew this was a bad idea.*

Dexter took a drink of his beer and wished his feet had left and his hand had not knocked on the door.

"How long have you been betting on basketball?"

"Since I was sixteen, so a little over five years," Dexter replied.

"Sixteen? How can you bet when you are sixteen? Internet gambling hasn't been around for five years, has it?"

"No, it hasn't but betting has been around for centuries."

Dexter plastered a big grin on his face and waited. He anticipated her wrath. April merely raised her eyebrows. He decided to finish the explanation before she unleashed something sarcastic.

"My dad owned a bar in northwestern New Mexico. I worked as a bartender after school and weekends. There was a bookie that frequented the bar and I placed bets with him," Dexter explained.

"A bookie? If it were New York City I could believe it but in Podunk USA?"

"We have all the conveniences of big cities, electricity, running water, drugs, and sin. Gambling is still a sin, isn't it?"

"Beats me," she said with an exaggerated shrug of her shoulders, followed by a swig of the beer.

"The Bookie would come into the bar every Friday. He would pay off the winners for the prior week and collect new bets," Dexter said. "It got ugly every once in a while. Sore losers caused most the problems."

"Your dad let you do this?" April asked.

"Son," my dad would say, "This is as good a time as any to learn how to throw your money away. So, don't let common sense interfere with a life lesson."

"And evidently you didn't."

"Nope," Dexter said as he took another drink.

"Well, that's good to know. If you are telling the truth, five years experience would be hard to beat on this campus," April said.

"Why would you assume I'm lying?" Dexter quickly defended.

"I didn't mean to suggest that you were lying. It's just a phrase," April replied.

Dexter's discomfort was clouding his ability to be civil. He did not like her abrupt style. He decided to get to the point. She only asked for an opinion on a bet; so he decided to stick the point.

"Ok. So who do you like in this BYU game?" Dexter asked.

"I think BYU plus nine is the way to go," April shot back.

"Really? Why?" Dexter asked.

"BYU scores seventy-three points per game and Utah averages sixty-one. And as I understand it, the BYU center has a five inch height advantage over the Utah center," April said confirming she had done her research.

"So, you're bigger in the paint and you score more on average per game?" Dexter quizzed.

"Yeah and don't forget BYU has won three more games than Utah."

"Sounds like you've got it all figured out. Place your bet."

"So, you agree with me?" She asked.

"Oh, no," Dexter replied.

"You would bet on Utah?" April exclaimed as she turned to face Dexter straight on from the window seat.

"No. I don't like the game. If I had wanted to bet on this game, I would have done it while I was doing my research. But I would bet you that you are wrong," Dexter said.

"Why, why am I wrong?" April questioned.

Dexter could sense her anger rising. She no longer sat casually crossed legged in the window seat. She was standing. Her eyes were blinking and her smile was gone.

*Bad idea, Dex; bad idea.*

"Look, I don't think you factored enough data. I think some of the variables give the advantage to the Utes." Dexter said as calmly as he could muster.

"What variables?"

"BYU doesn't average seventy-three points a game when they are on the road," Dexter stated.

"I thought of that. They only score sixty-four on the road but that's still better than the sixty-three Utah score at home, plus I have the nine points," April said with confidence.

"Yeah it sounds good. But Utah scores fewer points because they play tough man-to-man defense and that eats up a lot of the clock. Plus, how much difference do you think Rondell Demby will make?" Dexter asked.

"The guard who has been on scholastic probation?" April quizzed.

"Yeah, him," Dexter answer but was impressed she knew.

"None. The coach really likes Carson, his backup; he's started the last eight games. They are winning with him. The coach called him

205

a true point guard, a playmaker. Evidently, Dumbo shoots too much," April said.

"I'm sure you meant to say Demby," Dexter said. "Utah will have sole possession of first place with a win and the coach will play whoever gives him the best chance to win. Coaches like to talk big about TEAM but when it gets down to nut cracking time, they want somebody who can fill the basket. Demby averaged twenty-two per game last year. That's huge. He will not leave a weapon like that on the bench, especially against a high scoring team like BYU," Dexter said.

"That's all speculation. The numbers are in BYU's favor," April slapped her hand against the table. "My research says BYU; I'm right."

Dexter laughed and said, "It's all speculation. The numbers were in Auburn's favor, also. You weren't right then," Dexter debated.

"Screw you," April snarled.

Dexter stood up and sat his beer can on the table.

"Ok, that's it strike three. I'm out. You love to dish out crap but you can't take it. Thanks for the beer. Good luck with BYU," he said.

Dexter walked out the door. April was talking but he could not hear a word because his own voice in his head was too loud.

"This chick ain't worth it," he decided to mumble out loud.

# 54

April went to her laptop and placed a fifty-dollar bet on BYU. She closed the lid on the machine but continued to stare at the computer. She grabbed a fleece sweater and pulled it over her head, and walked out the door giving one last glance to the scary box..

Ten minutes later, she walked into Captain Bluebeards. She examined the televisions, found a game covered by ESPN, and took a seat close by. She casually watched the red team play the white team but her main interest was the scrolling scores at the bottom of the screen. Early in the first half, she noted BYU with a three-point lead.

"That's a twelve point lead for me, Dexter," her mumble was lost in bar room chatter.

She opened a sketchpad as the server placed the beer on the table. April began to draw the details of the wooden bar. The light was bad but it did not discourage her concentration. She finished her beer, at halftime, the white team was beating the red team comfortably, and BYU was still up by one.

A second beer arrived. April had not ordered it. The server said it was compliments of the guy in the blue sweatshirt. She turned to look. He sat three tables over and was watching the same red and white teams play. April did not recognize him and he did not look at her. He watched the game while making notes on his iPad.

He did not look like a student. But he did not look like an old letch trying to score with a co-ed. Unsure of the message, April sent the beer back. The server returned within a few minutes with four different brands of bottled beer.

"He said, pick the one you like," the server said and then added, "He's already paid for them."

"Do you know him?" April asked.

"He comes in regularly but I don't know him."

"Is he a student?"

"I really don't know. He watches games and buries himself in that iPad."

"I'll take them all," April said.

"Really?" The server asked in disbelief.

"Hell yeah. You said they were paid for?" The server nodded yes. "Why waste them?" April said.

April poured the darkest one in the glass. She did not turn around to look at him. She ignored him and watched the screen for the scrolling scores. The second half was underway and Utah had taken a two-point lead. She tried to busy herself with the sketches but her concentration was weakened by the sudden change in the game. She began work on the second bottle of beer from blue sweatshirt guy.

The buzz from the alcohol was beginning to set in; she was ready for the blue-sweatshirt-guy to make his move.

*He'll soon find out that free beer gets him nowhere.*

She put him out of her mind and doodled on her sketchpad. The intrigue of the woodwork waned; the Utes had taken a seven-point lead with five minutes to play; and blue-sweatshirt-guy was still anonymous. She stood up to take a trip to the restroom. The path she chose went directly past him. He never looked up from his iPad.

"What the hell does he think he's doing?" She said as she entered the rest room.

"Were you talking to me?" Remarked a girl at the mirror.

"No, just talking to myself," she said as she slid into a stall.

April finished and washed her hands and walked back to her table. She drank the last few swallows in the glass while waiting for the score to scroll by. Utah was up by twelve with under a minute to go.

"Fuck!" She said louder than intended.

She noticed a few people turn to look at her. They quickly went back to their conversations, seductions, and brain cell drowning. She poured the third beer from blue sweatshirt guy and took a long swallow.

On the TV, the white team finished with a fifteen-point victory and the scrolling scores revealed BYU had lost by twelve.

As she sipped on her last beer, Sports Center reported the highlights of the late games. Demby had come off the bench in the second half to score thirty points.

"Rondell Demby had a monster game. He missed eight games with some scholastic problems but his fresh legs and laser guided shooting were too much for the Cougars to overcome on the hostile Utah court," the television reported.

"Thanks a lot Dumbo," April said to the photo of Rondell Demby on the television.

April finished her free beer and stood to leave. She was prepared for blue sweatshirt-guy to swoop in and offer to buy another round; he did not. She walked toward the door. April was prepared for the wobbly walk home; but she was not prepared to see Dexter in the doorway. They both paused and stared at each other.

"Let's get this over with," she heard herself say.

She continued walking toward him but Dexter turned and walked back out the door.

"Great. One more momma's boy with hurt feelings," she said to no one.

Not only had she lost another fifty dollars but also Dexter's advice was accurate. The alcohol was unsheathing her caustic tongue. April was unhappy and she was itching to take it out on somebody.

*And what is the deal with blue sweatshirt-guy?*

She turned and walked back to his table. He was scrolling through screens on the iPad.

"Ok, what's the deal?" She asked with hands on her hips.

"The deal is, I like the way you look, your glass was empty, and so I ordered you more beers. I couldn't predict if you were leaving after one beer. I was hoping the additional beers would keep you here longer," he said.

"So you could look at me?" April asked.

"Yes," he answered.

"That's it. You have some sort of fetish, or what?"

"No, you stayed. That's enough for me. I won a bet with myself."

"A bet with yourself? You bet yourself that I would stay for beer?" April said as though insulted.

"Well, you look like a beer drinker," he said.

"What's that supposed to mean?" April said with a little more volume.

"It means you aren't a cocktail drinking sorority chick."

"Whatever. I hope you enjoyed yourself," April replied.

"Oh, I did. I won and don't forget I got to ogle you for an additional hour."

"Well, for the record; I didn't stay for the beer," April said trying to regain an edge in the conversation.

"Yeah I know. You were watching the game. What I don't get is why. VMI and Chattanooga? That's a battle for last place. I'm surprised either won," he said.

"I wasn't watching that game. I was watching for the score in the BYU game."

"Oh, you're a Mormon?"

"No. I'm a moron," April said. "I recently took up gambling and I lost money betting on BYU this evening."

"Damn. You didn't know Demby was coming back?" he asked.

"Yes, I knew. I didn't think he would make that much difference, she explained.

"You can know everything and still lose," he said to her.

"Evidently," April said. "You seem to know a lot. Not many people here know who Rondell Demby is. Why do you know so much?"

"Are you going to stand there until closing time or would you like to sit?" He asked ignoring her question.

April stood staring at blue-sweatshirt-guy. Her eyes darted back and forth trying to make sense of this meeting. He did not seem frightened by her aggressiveness; his confidence seemed unwavering. She got the impression, it did not matter to him, if she sat or not or if she left or not. She sat down.

"Had enough beer for the evening?" He asked and waved his glass for a refill.

"Yes. No more for me. What are you reading so intently? Your eyes rarely leave that iPad," April asked.

"I'm a professional gambler. I'm tracking games," he answered.

"You aren't a student?" She continued the quiz.

"I was but I quit," he answered.

"You weren't smart enough to make it in college but you are smart enough to gamble?" April said.

"Well, it depends on your definition of smart. I had a three point eight GPA. It was good enough for college but not quite good enough for gambling."

"Are you any good?" April asked in a softer tone.

"I hope you're asking about my gambling acumen, otherwise I consider that a very improper question, considering I just met you," he said. "By the way what is your name?"

"Why is it all guys think it's clever to turn every sentence into a sexual innuendo?"

"You know I think that's a great question. I think it's because we're horny, damn near all the time. Do you have a theory?" He asked.

"No. I don't have a theory. I just find it annoying," April responded. "Can we have a conversation about gambling without the sexual overtones?"

"No guarantees Dorothy," he replied.

"My name is not Dorothy."

"Until something better comes along, I'm going to call you Dorothy. Let's keep this professional, ok? How long have you been following basketball?" He asked.

"Counting today, three days."

"Ok, let me give you some advice. Stop gambling, Dorothy; you have no business betting on basketball," he said.

Blue-sweatshirt guy took another swallow of his drink and continued.

"You have no chance of winning. Is there anything else you want to talk about this evening?"

"You know, just because I'm not an athlete and I lack knowledge, does not mean I can't be successful. Every jock I have ever met is stone cold stupid. If they can learn it, I know I can," April replied; her tone was no longer soft.

"First, of course you can learn it but you are going to need a lot of money because you are going to lose a lot until that day comes along. Secondly, were the jocks stupid or just uninterested in your subject matter?" He asked.

"I'm going to stick with stupid, Percy," April answered.

"Clever, Dorothy. If all athletes are unintelligent, how do you account for those who become Rhodes Scholars?" He asked.

"Those are few and far between. Pretty damn rare, I think."

"Not as rare as 'sports-hating-women' who become successful gamblers."

"Don't label me. You don't know me," April warned.

"Don't tell me what to do," he said. "I've already labeled you; I've tagged you as a beer drinker, hothead, unsuccessful gambler, and athlete hater but I still like looking at you."

April was standing before he finished his sentence. She felt a little unstable from the beers but she was able to control her balance. She could feel her nostrils flaring in and out.

"Well, enjoy watching me leave pervert," she said.

"I preferred Percy but your call," he replied.

April said nothing and began walking.

"Hey Dorothy," she heard him yell. "Let me know who you like in the Seahawks-Dragon game, okay?"

April kept walking without turning or responding. She walked outside and took several deep breaths. The flow of adrenalin helped offset the beers. She walked home but blue sweatshirt-guy was dominating her thoughts.

"Who the hell does he think he is?" She said without realizing the volume of her angry voice.

A horn honked; she stepped back on the curb and waited for the car to pass and the driver to express his displeasure. She crossed the street and started across the campus.

"Why did he mention the Seahawks game?" She whispered into the night.

April went in her apartment hoping sleep would expunge the mysterious pervert from her mind. She hung her cap and her jeans on the chair. She pulled her bra out from under the t-shirt. She lay down and closed her eyes. Blue sweatshirt-guy was the first image she saw. His face was smiling and the pale blue eyes summoned her.

"Damn. I hope he doesn't look that good when I'm sober," she mumbled into the pillow.

# 55

Eddie Dreyer sat in his hotel staring at his laptop. He had logged into a Forum. Every ding sound was someone entering or leaving the Forum. He checked the latest ding. Not him. He was waiting for someone to log on; eighty minutes had past. He busied himself with research of an upcoming game in Virginia. The computer dinged.

"There he is," Eddie said. "ddawg44."

ddawg44 was the screen name of Reggie Fontenot. Reggie fancied himself as the best defensive player in the Colonial Conference. Eddie easily interpreted the screen name to be Defensive Dawg plus his jersey number forty-four.

Eddie knew Reggie's type. Reggie was a winner and would do whatever it took to keep his man from scoring. He stuck to his man; it did not matter how much he ran, Reggie kept up. He was allotted five fouls and he used them. Reggie had fouled out of all but two games this season. The last few minutes, he usually spent on the bench harassing players with his mouth. Every player he defended complained about his rough tactics. Some of it was warranted; much of it was soft-players who could not shake him. Reggie's big mouth and sweaty body rubbed opposing guards the wrong way. Eddie admired the commitment Reggie brought to the court but he knew how to play against him. Eddie began typing an message to Reggie.

"Hey Puppydawg, how's your game?"

Eddie watched and waited for Reggie to type a reply. Reggie could ignore the typed message from Eddie, he could totally block Eddie's messages, but Eddie expected him to respond. Reggie would not show fear.

"My game don't concern you, Spectator," Reggie typed.

"How do you know I'm a spectator? That shows limited vision. That's just another reason why Tyrone's gonna' hang a thirty spot on you, puppydawg," Eddie typed back.

"I told you last week, that ain't ever gonna' happen. You've obviously never seen me play or maybe you can't read the papers," Reggie wrote.

"I've seen you play and I read where you were going to hold Underwood to eight points. Dude lit you up like a Christmas Tree, puppydawg...Fifteen ain't eight," Eddie shot back.

"The dude scored six in the last two minutes, when I was out of the game," Reggie wrote back.

"Yeah, you fouled out and he spots up for six. You lose; your team loses," Eddie continued to attack.

"I do what I do; the team lost that game, not me. And what the hell do you know anyway, punk."

"What if I'm a scout? What if my job is to test your mental game?" Eddie probed.

"Scouts don't do that shit," Reggie responded quickly.

"Really. So, you know a lot of scouts, puppydawg?"

"I'm gonna' block you, bitch. I'm tired of your petty shit."

Eddie paused. He could feel Reggie's anger.

He typed another shot, "Go ahead but even with his sore wrist, Tyrone's gonna' school you."

The wait for the next reply was lengthy. The cursor blinked like a perturbed mom waiting on the truth to be spilled from a mischievous child. Eddie wondered if Reggie was now blocking his remarks.

Then Reggie chimed in, "You know what I think, I think you're Tyrone Traylor and you're trying to get inside my head because you're scared I'm gonna' shut you down."

"There's no room for anyone else inside your pea sized brain," Eddie typed.

"My pea sized brain knows you can't go left at all, brother and I'm sealing off the right. Every time you go right, there I'll be. All your points are coming from free throws because you won't get a shot off. I'm gonna' be in your face every minute," Reggie wrote.

"Perfect." Eddie said to the empty hotel room.

He typed back, "Listen puppydawg, I ain't Tyrone. Tyrone wouldn't waste his time on you."

"Whatever. Tyrone. What's the matter, man, can't sleep? You can't stop thinking about me shutting your ass down. The ddawg's coming for you; get ready for a Pit Bull," Reggie threatened.

"Somebody's gonna' claim top dawg status Thursday and my money's on Tyrone to put on a clinic," Eddie answered.

"We'll see, ass wipe, and if that wrist ain't sore, it's gonna' be," Reggie typed.

Eddie logged out without responding to Reggie's last message. Eddie knew from experience that teams talk about injured players; he knew that strategies were devised to take advantage of injured players. Reggie would go after Tyrone's wrist and he would foul out because of Tyrone's quickness. Tyrone was the best free throw shooter in the conference; he would score when Reggie fouled him and he would take over the end of the game when Reggie was gone. The betting line had Reggie and his Dragon teammates favored by four. Eddie would wager the Dragons would not cover the four points. He bet his five thousand on the Seahawks straight up.

Eddie checked out of the hotel and drove up the coast. He stopped by a Kinkos and printed five hundred copies of a legal sized sheet of paper reading: Poor Puppy Dawg. He walked around campus posting a few of the signs and left the remaining pile on a table in the gymnasium.

# 56

A dull headache had been her constant companion but she was determined to sweat it out. Running through an early morning hangover was an act of bravery in April's analysis. She slowed down to a walk. As she neared the apartment, April saw a note taped to her door. She unlocked the door, removed the note and went inside. She clicked her iPod off and pulled the earphones from her head and tossed the equipment onto the table. She toweled the sweat from her hands and opened the envelope. There was one sentence typed in the middle of the page.

"Did you pick the Seahawks or the Dragons?"

She knew where the note came from. Blue sweatshirt-guy must have followed her home. Questions mounted in her mind. Had the guy followed her? April reasoned that he might have been concerned about her safety. April remembered being a little wobbly when she left.

Would the guy really want to discuss a basketball bet?

Could those beautiful eyes really be interested in April?

Is this guy a pervert? A stalker?

"He knows where I live," she said still holding the note.

She felt uneasy and walked to the window to survey the area.

*Is he out there now, watching me?*

She decided she was being over dramatic. April walked over to the kitchen and filled a glass with water and began to re-hydrate her body. She stripped the wet clothes from her body and showered away the sweat and park dust. She toweled off and pulled a large baggy sweatshirt over her body.

A thought popped into her mind.

*He's testing me.*

He's probably made another bet with himself," she said as she pulled on a pair of jeans.

"Freak," she mumbled as she struggled to close the jeans.

She sat at her laptop and looked for information about the Seahawks game. April sipped at the water and chewed through the statistics. She concluded that the Dragons would win and cover the four points.

April picked up his note and looked at it. She examined it closer and discovered that blue sweatshirt-guy had drawn a frowning face inside the letter O of the word Dragons.

*The Dragons are the wrong choice?*

"This is Rondell Demby all over again," she said to the monitor. "Percy is trying to tell me I overlooked something."

April read the latest news from the local newspapers; she did not discover a reason to change her opinion.

"Goddammit. Screw this." April closed the laptop. She put a hat over her wet hair and a pair of sandals on her feet and hurried out the door. Ten minutes later, she was peering into the neon lit din of Bluebeards. April scanned the room; she knew he would be there. Her brain was working like a pinball machine bouncing her thoughts around in her head.

*He wants to be found. He wants to discuss this with me. He wants to tell me what I missed. He wants to show his superior knowledge.*

Ding. April spotted him against the back wall. She marched over to the table determined to shut down blue sweatshirt-guy's fun factory.

"Look pervert, there are laws against stalking and I will report you," she said as she stood over him.

"Come on Dorothy, call me Percy," he said with a faint smile. "Have a seat."

"No. I have no interest in talking to you," April said flatly.

"Then why did you come here?" He asked.

"I'm here to show you that I am not afraid and to tell you to leave me alone," she told him.

"That's it. Why can't we talk about this game? Does it have to be anything more than that? I'm neither a stalker nor a pervert. I like you, that's all. And right now the only thing we have in common is that we are both highly competitive," he said as he stood up. "Maybe we could talk about that."

He pulled the extra chair back slightly and gestured for her to sit down.

April had not seen him standing. He was tall and muscular and she could not look directly into his pale blue eyes. She stiffened her spine.

"You wanna' talk, call a friend," April said and turned to leave.

"You're the best friend I have," he quickly responded.

She turned back to see him shrug his shoulders.

"That's pretty messed up, Percy; not to mention pathetic."

217

"Percy? We're back on a first name basis? Come on, have a seat."

April thought she was glaring into his eyes to demonstrate her fortitude. But his eyes seem to being pulling her in for a comforting hug. His dimpled smile dismantled her anger.

*I have to quit looking.*

April turned her head and looked at the wall. She scrunched, and pulled her thick hair back tighter. She turned back around straddled the chair opposite him. She looked around the bar and signaled a server. April did not look across the table; her eyes tracked the server.

"Could you bring me a Carolina Blond?" April asked the server.

"Sure. Twelve or twenty ounce?"

"Twenty," April replied.

"You go it.," the server said as she turned and looked across the table. "Can I get you anything?"

April could see that the girl was not limiting his choices to the menu. Blue sweatshirt guy continued to look at April. He did not react to the way she accentuated "Anything."

"Another one of these would be great," he answered with a quick glance at her and a smile.

April turned and stared across the table.

*Why me?*

She considered asking pointed questions about his identity and sharp criticisms about following her home; instead, she allowed her intrigue to orchestrate the conversation.

"The Dragons should cover the four points," she said.

"I agree they should but it's really too close to call, isn't it?"

"Somebody wins every game," April countered.

"Yeah but the goal is to win a bet," he said. "Gamblers look for an edge, an oversight, a mismatch; gamblers are in search of the sure thing. Would you say this is a sure thing?"

It felt like a classroom to April. She wanted to learn but it was important that he knew she was informed and intelligent. The drinks arrived. She took a few swallow of the beer.

"There's no such thing as a sure thing," April said confidently.

"I agree," he said flatly and waited for her response.

"Then what's to discuss? You threw this game out for discussion. I did the research. The Dragons will win the game. You've got the laptop; place the bet," April said.

"I've already placed my bet. Would you like to place yours?"

"No. I'm done," April said to this mystery man.

"Never to bet again?" The devil asked as though he knew her resolve was no match for the lure.

"That was your advice," April reminded him.

"Yeah but I don't think you can resist," he said.

"What is this? Is it another bet with yourself?" April asked.

"No. Although I'm no longer a student, I will always be a student of human psychology. I don't think your competitiveness will let you quit," he explained.

"Well, you're wrong. You underestimate my determination."

April grabbed the chair with both arms and pushed back a little, to demonstrate her disinterest in wagering.

"So Mr. Professional gambler, how much will you win on the Dragons?" April asked.

"I didn't bet on the Dragons," he responded.

"Your money is on the Seahawks?" April asked.

She recalled a fourth grade teacher saying, "No, April that's the wrong answer."

It stung then; it stung April now. April had researched this game. She was convinced his choice was wrong.

"Why?" She asked without trying to disguise her disbelief.

"I think Reggie Fontenot will foul out early and when he does Tyrone Traylor will score at will. He will light the Dragons up. I think they will win the game outright. And I bet five thousand dollars. Without taking the points, I will make about seventy-five hundred."

"Are you shittin' me? Five thousand dollars, because you think someone will foul out of a game?" April nearly shrieked.

"That's why they call it gambling," he said as he finished the Dewar's and waved for another.

*He's lying. This is his line; it's how he impresses the girls.*

April stared at him and decided she was being played.

"I don't believe you," she blurted out.

"What don't you believe? The amount of money I bet?" He asked.

"Let's start there, April said to him.

"Let's assume, that I care," he responded. "Let's assume it is important that you believe me."

Eddie leaned his long torso halfway across the table.

"When I prove to you, that I am not a liar, what then? Will you lower the shields Captain Kirk?"

"Lower the shields?" April repeated. "Is this some elaborate scheme, a clever angle to hit on me; or are you really a closet Star Trek geek?"

"Do you think every guy on the planet wants to hit on you?" He asked but did not give her time to reply. "Let's deal with one issue at a time."

Eddie turned his laptop. The screen faced April.

"This is my betting service; take a look," he said.

April glanced at the screen but did not touch it.

"Go ahead. I'm already logged on," Eddie said. "Please, my privacy is irrelevant. I don't want you to think I'm a liar."

April's mind was once again rioting from indecision.

She pulled the laptop closer. April clicked on the My Account tab; it opened and revealed his current bet on the Seahawks and an available one hundred and eleven thousand dollars balance. It was impossible for April to remain calm. Her cool had evaporated like the last water drop on a hot skillet. Pop.

"Who are you? And don't say Percy the pervert," April demanded.

"My name is Eddie." He reached across the table and pulled his laptop computer back to his side of the table. He pressed a couple of buttons and looked back up to meet April's eyes.

"Just Eddie?"

"Just April Pyle?" He asked.

"You already know my name," she said feeling exposed.

April added rather sheepishly, "That doesn't surprise me." You found my name on the mailbox when you taped up your mystery note."

"No. I saw it on your sketchpad the other night. It's printed, very neatly," Eddie replied. "Your mailbox only says A. Pyle. I couldn't help but giggle when I saw it."

April restrained her smile. She had heard plenty of Pyle jokes through the years, but she did not want to lower her shields. She knew she would; it was just a question of when. She picked up her beer and slowly wet her lips as she processed the information. The sudden appearance of this guy in her life was intriguing but aggravating. He was the most unusual male she had ever met. Every alarm was ringing yet she did not feel alarmed. He broke the silence at the table.

"Dreyer, Eddie Dreyer is my name," he said.

He offered one answer; she wanted many more. April stepped out of the chair and turned it around. She did not need the chair back as a fence between them any longer.

"Eddie Dreyer, you have a hundred fucking thousand dollars in a betting account. Holy shit. Why would you leave that much money in cyberspace?" April said. "No, no, wait a minute, first, is it real? Do you really have that much money in this surefirewinners.com account?"

"Yes, I do. And no, I don't worry about the location of the money. I request a check every week and it comes like clockwork. I move around some and it still gets to me. I don't know much about the IRS but I assume I can declare what I take out. The rest of it just sits there." He responded in a very low key manner.

April stared as he finished the drink. She watched as he signaled the pony-tailed blonde. Another drink would be on its way.

"Did you win all that money?"

"Yes."

April was surprised at Eddie's simple responses. He suddenly seemed less conversational as if he had not anticipated the need to reveal his assets. He had seemed much livelier in the cat and mouse game of Dorothy and Percy. She continued to probe.

"That's unbelievable. Everyone loses. Even if you are on the greatest lucky streak of all time, you have to lose. Statistics dictate that."

"I lose but not regularly."

"I've done a lot of research. Sixty percent is supposed to be damn good." April stated.

She left the comment hanging in the air and waited for him to offer his success rate. He did not. She watched him scan the bar. The server came; he was not a sipper. Half of the fluid disappeared instantly. April could sense his discomfort with the barrage of questions but her intrigue was more important than his comfort level.

"You invited me to sit down and talk about the Seahawks and about competitive personalities," April said. "Have you changed your mind? Suddenly, you're not very chatty."

"I have not changed my mind about wanting to talk to you," Eddie said.

"But you don't want to talk about your account?"

"My account is irrelevant. It is what it is. Do you want to place a bet on the game? You could do it from here. You still have twenty minutes before game time." Eddie asked.

"I might but I still think the numbers are with the Dragons."

April was not confident enough to wager money on it. And Eddie's disagreement with her pick was unnerving. Eddie appeared to be raking in money with his picks.

Eddie said, "The Dragons are a good bet. It could work out."

Eddie leaned across the table again and into her space.

"I have a question for you. Do you believe anyone other than Reggie Fontenot can stop Tyrone Traylor?"

"I don't know. I didn't consider Reggie out of the game."

"Well, my bet is based on Reggie leaving early. Your bet would be with him in; that's the only difference."

Eddie paused to take a small sip.

"I played basketball most of my life. Skill, talent, and speed are useless unless it's on the court. I think Reggie is the best defensive player in the South. I also think he's so high strung that he can be pushed into carelessness. I'm going with Tyrone's cool over Reggie's hot head. However, the smart money is with you."

"Smart money. That's a stupid phrase. Let me borrow your laptop; I'm going to take a shot on your theory," April said.

Eddie pushed the computer across the table. April caught a glimpse of him ordering more drinks for the two of them. She pressed buttons on the keyboard, surfed to her betting service, and placed a bet on the Seahawks. And though the button was not on the laptop, she pressed something that lowered the shields.

# 57

Dexter watched as Eddie and April continued to talk, point, and drink. But their laughter bothered him most. They had sat together for over an hour.

Lauren interrupted his spying.

"Dex, you have to make these Dewars stronger," she said.

"He's getting a full measure." Dexter said.

"No he's not. I've been watching; you're pouring him short."

"He's already had four this evening. I'm responsible__"

"Save that shit Dex. Eddie is a great tipper. Don't screw this up. Besides, we've seen him put away a dozen of these, get up, and walk out. Come on," Lauren scolded.

Dexter poured a full measure and sat it down. Lauren smiled.

"Thanks, Dex," she said with her sultry voice.

Normally, a smile from Lauren froze Dexter but this time he barely noticed. He watched her deliver the drink to the table. Eddie did not run a tab. He handed her a five for a three-fifty drink and waved off the tip, the same routine every time. In a bar where college kids tip a quarter, if at all, Eddie was a lottery table.

Eddie did not turn his head to watch Lauren lean over; Lauren's breasts demanded attention but Eddie ignored them. Nor did he turn his head to watch her tight low riding jeans walk away. Dexter deemed him inhuman.

Harmon walked out of his office and stood next to Dexter. He looked across the bar and spotted Eddie.

"Dex, how many have you served to Eddie?"

"He's on number five. Are you going to cut him off?" Dexter asked; hoped.

"No," Harmon said. "Who's he talking to? I've never seen anyone at his table."

"April Pyle."

"You know her?" Harmon asked.

"Yeah. Kinda'."

"Does she gamble?" Harmon asked.

223

"She's toying with it. She's made a couple of bets and lost. I think she thought it would be easy to predict winners by using logic," Dexter said.

"Yeah, that'll work," Harmon said.

"Yeah, I know and I don't think chatting with Eddie Dreyer will help," Dexter added.

"That depends. If he tells her who to bet on, she'll win money," Harmon replied.

"Everybody loses," Dexter grumbled. "He's all talk."

"Eddie doesn't talk. Look at the money he spends, Dex. Look at the equipment he hauls around," Harmon said as he turned to the bar.

"So. He's a rich kid who fucked up at school and his parents fund his exploits while he gets his life back together," Dexter said with no chance of hiding the envy.

"Nope. His dad is a high school coach and his mother works at the YMCA. And besides, his dad has practically disowned him after he was arrested."

Harmon nodded toward the full dishwasher. Dexter began stacking glassware on the back bar.

Nikki called him; he filled her order.

He looked up at the television. At halftime, the Dragons were ahead by six. He wasn't betting this game so the score had no impact on him. He continued stacking Harm's glasses and envying Eddie's headway with April.

# 58

Powers offered David another cup of coffee; he declined.

"I need to go, Powers," David said and stood up.

"Alright. Are you sure you won't reconsider?" Powers asked.

"No. I think another accountant would be in your best interest. You need someone experienced with gamblers. It's kind of tricky deciphering wins and losses and earnings."

"Well, all right," Powers said.

"But Powers please think about my offer to attend church services this Sunday. I think the fellowship of our congregation could shine new light into your life."

"What you are really offering me is a support group to rid me of this demon. You hope that they could lead me away from a life of gambling," Powers said. "But I'm enjoying myself and making some money, so don't expect me to come."

"Well, at least you're honest. Most of the people I invite just say maybe."

"You are not misleading me about taxes, why should I mislead you about my intentions?" Powers said with a slight smile.

Powers opened the door and ushered David out. They exchanged pleasantries and David drove away. Powers went upstairs to catch the end of the Seahawks game and take the edge off the coffee. He poured a generous portion of Scotch whisky into his favorite crystal glass and sat comfortably in his viewing chair. With five minutes to go in the game, the camera was focused on a group of students chanting and holding signs. Poor puppydawg. Poor puppydawg. Poor puppydawg.

"These fans have rattled Reggie Fontenot this evening. We still have five minutes to play here at Terrell Coliseum, the D-dawg has fouled out and the Dragons cling to a two point lead."

The announcer continued his play by play but Powers turned the sound down. He picked up the laptop to research CPAs. He was not having much luck finding an accountant willing to advertise an emphasis in gambling income. He found contacts in Las Vegas but he was not sure how to check them out. He picked five names and sent email to each asking about their experience. He returned his attention to the game.

"The Seahawks are going to pull out an important victory tonight. This win will move them into third in the standings. Traylor got untracked in the last two minutes and buried three important buckets to give the Hawks a three-point lead, which they held. Your final again this evening, is the Seahawks seventy-three and the visiting Dragons seventy."

Powers shut the television off.

*Eddie is right again.*

Powers had made up his mind the only way to make a decision on the best CPA for his protection was to fly to Las Vegas and interview them personally. He clicked on Google and began his research with hotel rooms. He was immediately intrigued by the choices. He refreshed his drink and began his review of the Las Vegas accommodations.

# 59

Dexter saw the exuberant high five. It was clear to him that April had won her first bet and Eddie had helped. They must have had their money on the Seahawks.

*How did he figure that one out?*

"Gotta' be luck," Dexter mumbled. "Just wait, the worm will turn."

"The worm will turn?" He said louder accidently.

A nearby beer drinker asked, "Are you talking to me?"

"No, just talking to myself," he said and stuffed a portion of the towel in his mouth.

"God, I sound like my grandmother," Dexter mumbled.

Dexter busied himself at the bar trying to push April out of his mind. He had decided she was impossible to tolerate. He had been unable to enjoy extended conversation without her making it confrontational. Her self-defense mechanisms seem to hover like charged particles in the atmosphere, unnoticed, until her lightning strikes.

*So, why should I care, if she and Eddie Damn Dreyer are having a good time?*

Lauren called from the server station. Eddie had ordered another round. Dexter filled the order and watched Lauren serve them. He noticed April had moved into the chair next to Eddie. They were huddled over the laptop.

April sat in Eddie Dreyer's classroom. She was listening, nodding, and occasionally laughing. He had seen her smile, when they were together, but he could not recall seeing her laugh out loud. Dexter waited for April's lightning to strike but the storm clouds never formed.

*Dude's too lucky.*

Through fractured concentration, Dexter heard Harmon yell his name. He strolled into his office and found Ernie O'Brien sitting across the desk.

"Dex, have Nikki bring us a couple of coffees," Harmon said.

"Coffee? You want me to make coffee?" Dexter asked.

227

Ernie said, "You're right lad; sounds like too much trouble. Just bring us two whiskys."

Dexter left the room as the two men giggled like six year olds. He climbed the steps and pulled the bottle from the top shelf.

A student sitting at the bar said, "Hey, I'll have a shot of that; whatever it is."

"You can't afford it," Dexter answered and continued to walk toward the office.

He glanced at the clock on his way; it was twenty-five minutes until closing. He turned to look for April and Eddie. They were gone. He walked in and handed the bottle to Harmon.

"We only wanted a couple of glasses, Dex," Harmon said.

"Yeah, right. You fooled me once, boys, not again."

They laughed again.

Dexter smiled a little, shook his head, and left the office. He scanned the bar again looking for April. She and Eddie were not in Bluebeards.

"Bar's closing in 10 minutes; finish up," he yelled.

He began his routine to close and wondered just how lucky was Eddie Dreyer.

# 60

Dexter sat on the bench drinking the last of his coffee from the padded Styrofoam cup. He had ten minutes to get to class. He stood, swallowed the last gulp, tossed the cup in the trash container, and began his walk across campus. He would need to hurry; too much coffee meant he would have to pee before class. Dexter did not need the second cup but he ordered it to have an excuse for sitting there. He was hoping to see April.

His thoughts were not organized. He just knew he wanted to talk to her. He had questions. All of them could be bundled into a categories labeled the Handsome Funny Lucky Eddie Dreyer. Dexter knew he could not compete with Eddie. Somewhere buried in his head was a distinct memory that April had already told Dexter she did not like him 'that way.'

*Do I really want to know if she thinks of Eddie 'that way?'*

He walked into the building, hurried through the restroom, and took a seat at the back of the class. Dexter opened a notebook and listened as the lecture began. He penciled the occasional note; he highlighted reminders in the text and doodled around April's name.

He looked at his random artwork and imagined laughter erupting from April if she ever saw his childish effort. She had found plenty of ways to ridicule Dexter. There was no reason to provide her with more opportunities. He turned to a clean page.

"Name the four muscles involved in transverse abduction of the posterior deltoid. Let's see__," the professor said while looking at a list. "Dalton, Dexter."

"Shit," nearly slipped out of Dexter's mouth.

Dexter looked up. All he heard was his name. He looked at the board hoping to find a clue about the question.

"I'm sorry, could you repeat the question," Dexter asked?

"Yes, I could. Did you not hear the question?"

"No sir, I did not." Dexter told the truth.

"Very well," the professor said as he re-examined his list. "Warren, Randy, did you hear the question?"

"Yes." Came a response from the back.

"Will you name the muscles, please?"

"The deltoids, posterior and lateral, the infraspinatus, and the teres minor."

*Damn it. I knew that. Jerk. He could have repeated the question.*

Dexter sat in his chair uncomfortable and embarrassed. But he straightened up in the chair and intensified his eye contact on the professor. He was ready.

*Come on try me again, damn it.*

His telepathy failed. Class ended without an opportunity to redeem himself.

# 61

April woke up at nine. It was too late to make her nine thirty Building Pathology class; it would be her first miss. On any other day she would abandon vanity, certainly not a constant companion, cover her head with a cap and rush into the class a few minutes late. Today the cap might cover the hair and shield the eyes but it would not cover the headache. Recently beer was bothering her more than in the past. Of course, she was drinking more beer; it was easier to do when someone else was buying.

She rolled off the futon; she was wearing last night's clothes. April rubbed at her tender eyes as she walked to the kitchen. The first order of business was to start a pot of coffee. As the water began to gurgle, she stripped off her clothing and stepped into the tiny shower. She stepped in and allowed the water to cascade from her head to the rest of her body. It was warm; the steam soothed her strained eyes. She straightened and took three deep breaths, and exhaled slowly. Her lungs labored to expel the barroom air.

She lathered excessively and scrubbed hard. April stepped out of the shower, dried her face, and saw her image in the mirror. She was red from the water heat and the vigorous scrubbing; she felt decontaminated. The bar was an orgy for the senses but it was hell on the body.

She wanted to sit and begin healing. April filled a large mug with hot black coffee; this was not the time for a dainty cup. She adjusted the pillows in her window seat and leaned back. She held the mug lip-high with two hands. She peered through the window. It was quiet outside. The parking lot hosted five cars; by evening, there would be fifty. Responsibility had driven most people to work or class. It was extremely rare for her to miss an architecture class. Three sips later the guilt passed.

Eddie Dreyer was on her mind. With the slightest of effort, he could have been the first man to share her bed. They talked about basketball and he made it interesting. There had been electricity and laughter, yet he never hinted that they should leave together. She pictured her head nestled into his thick muscular shoulders. She saw her fingers ambling over his firm body.

A door slammed, somewhere in the building; April blinked the image away. She found it difficult to imagine Eddie would have an interest in her. The Eddie Dreyers of the world saddled up with the hot chicks. April's self-appraisal did not stretch far enough to include hot chick. Yet, more than once, he said, "I like the way you look." April filed the comment away as just another line.

*It had to be a line.*

She tucked strands of errant wet hair behind her ear while remembering Eddie had spent six hours charming her last night. Eddie should have reached to hold her hand, pulled her close for a little hug, or leaned down, cradled her head into his large hand and kissed her.

Instead, he smiled and said, "I had fun; see ya' later, okay?"

*What am I supposed to do with that?*

She tilted the large mug toward her lips and drank. April thought of herself as independent, intelligent, logical, truthful, and not hard on the eyes. Her goals and dreams had always been more important than relationships. She did not plan to live a mundane life. She wanted to see the world, all of it. It never occurred to her that seeing the world alone would diminish the experience. Adventure need not require a companion. But if the perfect man suddenly dropped into her life, she would voice little objection.

April did not believe opposites attract. The perfect man would share her dedication to architecture, construction, and art. He would be strong, confident, and passionate about his goals. She turned to look out the window. She drank the last swallow; it was cold. The cold shot exposed a ripple in her perfect plan. How would a man so focused on his own goals find room for April's plans? How could this perfect man compromise without sacrificing achievement?

Perfect man would have to be resolved at another time. April could not predict a basketball game correctly, much less the future. She tried to reel her thoughts back a little closer to the reality she knew. April was more comfortable believing a long-term relationship would never exist outside her dreams.

April refilled her coffee mug and grabbed a textbook. She read a few paragraphs but she was still distracted. Eddie was back in her thoughts. April's vivid imagination saw images that left her tingling; then she shut them down fearing no man would measure-up to her imagery. Eddie Dreyer was not even close to what she had always pictured. Yet when she closed her eyes, he was the picture.

She blinked; she was tired of pictures. Until one has walked the streets of Athens, The Parthenon is just a picture. Nothing clears up the details like experience.

"How many details could Eddie clear up?" she said to the windowpane.

April tossed the textbook on the floor and opened her laptop. She click the tab to her betting site and logged in. She had wagered two hundred dollars last night, at Eddie's insistence to "be bold" and she had won. She wanted to see the new balance. She saw the numbers; it was magical. She had not cleaned a table, served a burger, washed a dish, or sold a blouse yet she made nearly two hundred dollars in one night. Without the conversation with Eddie Dreyer, it would not have happened.

*He probably thinks I owe him something.*

Another picture, she blinked it away but not easily.

April concentrated on the information in front of her. She wanted to find another two hundred dollar winner.

# 62

Eddie Dreyer was driving the last hour of his five-hour trip. Interstate Forty put him in the heart of southern basketball. Little more than an hour separated the universities at Wake Forest, North Carolina, Duke, and North Carolina State. College basketball dominated conversations in diners, garages, offices, bars and dinner tables in North Carolina. Eddie had grown up in this area; he was expected to play in this area but he left for a smaller school that promised he could start as a freshman. He had many reasons for leaving. Fear of competition was not one of them. Eddie and the Cougars played the Tar Heels two years ago; Eddie posted twenty-three points and pulled down eight rebounds. The Cougars lost but Eddie had proved he could play with the big boys.

Eddie left the interstate and drove to a smaller campus in the area. The Marauders were not among the elite powers of this basketball haven; they were not even among the elite in their own conference. With a four and twelve record, the Marauders were seventh among nine teams. The league leading Eagles would be in town tomorrow. The oddsmakers favored the Eagles by twenty-four. Eddie thought the spread was too high but not high enough for him to put his money on The Marauders.

Marshall Kirkland played the center position for the Marauders. He was the only center on the roster. He stood six feet nine inches tall but weighed only two hundred and five pounds. Marshall inherited the job when a knee injury sidelined senior Tom Pulley and the backup suddenly quit the team. The Marauders had lost four straight since Kirkland became a starter. Marshall's weight was the problem. He was being pushed all over the court. Opponents were driving the lane without fear. The Marauders coach tried a forward at the position but it was robbing Peter to pay Paul.

Eddie parked at the Denny's; it was ten in the morning. He put on eyeglasses, grabbed his briefcase and went in the restaurant. He looked around and spotted Marshall easily. At six foot nine, his head was visible above the partitions. Eddie walked over and thrust his hand across the table as he sat down.

"Avery Walker," Eddie lied as he thrust out his hand. "I assume you are Marshall Kirkland."

"Yeah, call me Mars," he said and sheepishly shook Eddie's hand.

"Mars it is. So, the boys gave you a nickname. Is it a space thing?" Eddie asked.

"No. I gave it to myself. I'm a junior so it was easier at home to let my Dad answer to Marshall. I'm not crazy about Marshall anyway," he explained.

"All-righty, check this out," Eddie said and handed him a brochure.

It was another masterpiece created a Kinkos.

"How much do you really know about weight gain?" Eddie asked.

"Some. I've read through a few muscle magazines."

"I bet you've tried a few supplements with no results, right?" Eddie quickly added.

"Yeah, some powders I picked up from GNC. I saw the ads in the magazines."

"Ok, Mars, listen up. We call people like you hardgainers. I'm sure you've heard that before. If you were in school up the road at Duke or NC, they'd have a trainer assigned to bulk you up. But, your athletic department isn't rich. They aren't going to do that for you. Furthermore, the institutional academics aren't interested in allocating those kinds of resources," Eddie said.

"We have diet and weight training guidelines__," Marshall's words were cut off.

"How's that working out for you?" Eddie asked. "I saw the game against Liberty. They pushed you smooth out of the paint every time they wanted to go inside," Eddie lied.

He had not seen the game but the Marauders lost by eighteen; it was a reasonable bluff.

Marshall showed some fight and snapped back, "Look, when you called me you said you guaranteed you could help me gain weight fast. That's what I want to hear about. I don't want to hear from a stranger what I can hear all over town."

"Fair enough. Here's the bottom line. Hardgainers have to shock their system into gaining weight. You do that by eating excessively and training harder. Most of the time, you leave food on

235

your plate; you've done it all your life. I'm going to give you a weight training plan that works. It's hard but it will bulk you up. Second, I'm going to give you a meal plan. I only ask you to eat three times a day but you will also use this supplement three times a day. It's called a Meal Replacement Powder. This means you will be eating six times a day, three meals and three MRPs. You need a gram of protein for each pound of body weight. Strenuous muscle training, plus extra protein, and you will get bigger and stronger."

Eddie pushed the container across the table for Marshall to examine. He picked it up and seemed to be reading the label. He opened the plastic container and smelled it. He looked back across the table. Eddie was spooning the ice from a water glass. Eddie pushed the glass across the table.

"Put three heaping scoops in and drink it. I'll level with you, it does not taste great but it isn't horrible. I brought strawberry because I think it is the best tasting of the group," Eddie said.

"Right now?" Marshall asked.

"Right now. You might as well know if you can tolerate the taste."

"I just had breakfast," Marshall said.

"When? Two hours ago? Three hours ago?" He asked. "This is what it's about. Every three hours you need protein. If you're serious about gaining weight, you'll try it."

"I'll try it but first tell me why you are giving this to me free. Nothing's free. What's the gimmick?" Marshall said and leaned forward a little.

"Mars, you're right. Nothing is free."

Eddie pulled out three sets of photos and laid them on the table for Marshall to examine.

Eddie said, "Look, one track guy, one footballer, and a first baseman. You can see the before and the after. We've got maybe two-dozen success stories. Many others are using but they aren't disciplined and their success is minimal. I want you to buy our MRP and I am willing to give you three month's supply free. In exchange you let me take the photos for the before and after."

"I don't want people to know what I'm doing or__,"

Eddie interrupted, "We won't use your name. People are not going to call you and if you should become famous, we will stop using your photos. We have a very simple form; you will be able to see that we have stipulated your confidentiality. Plus, Mars I will exchange your photos with someone in Arizona or Washington. The photos you are looking at are from Nebraska, Texas, and Oregon," Eddie said authoritatively.

"You didn't say how much this stuff costs. I'm not rich," Marshall said.

"That jar supplements you for a week. It costs fifteen ninety-five," Eddie said.

"Sixty bucks a month." Marshall said, thinking, as he looked at the bottle. "How long before I see results?"

"You are going to feel stronger by tomorrow because of the extra protein for the muscles to utilize but the muscle mass won't show up for a month or so," Eddie replied.

"The season will be over in eight weeks."

"You've got to think long term, Mars," Eddie said. "You're a freshman. Start now; it will help. By next season you will have the body you want. Who knows how big the next freshman will be or if they will bring in a junior college transfer. Take control. I can't help you with your basketball skills but I can help you stand your ground. Go ahead try it. It's free," Eddie said.

Eddie immediately picked up his appointment book and ignored Marshall.

Marshall dumped the three scoops into the water and stirred until it was smooth. He stared at it. Eddie could see his mistrust. Eddie reached across the table and stuck a straw into the pink fluid. He pulled it toward him and took a long sip.

"Quality control," he said and took another smaller sip. "Yup, that's strawberry," Eddie said while removing his straw.

Having seen Eddie drink the concoction, Marshall pulled it back and began to drink. He licked his lips and started drinking again. Half of the pink drink was gone.

"I like strawberry and it tastes fine. So, what's next?" He asked.

"You take that jar and the weight training schedule with you and I will send you the additional jars. A man named Terry will call you within the next few days and he will schedule to take your picture. And that's it. An order form will be in the package I send you. Unless you have additional questions, I need to get going. I gotta' be in Chattanooga by tonight," Eddie explained.

"Who are you trying to recruit over there?" Marshall asked.

"I can't tell you that, Mars," Eddie said and broke into a smile. "Were you testing me?"

"No. Reflex question I guess."

"Don't disappoint me. Eat your lunch, drink another one of those this afternoon, and again tonight, ok?" Eddie said as he held out his hand.

"I will drink it and I will train. Thank you," he said with his first slight smile.

"Good luck against the Eagles," Eddie said and walked out the door.

Eddie drove away and headed to Chattanooga. Marshall Kirkland paid for his breakfast and headed back to become the big man on campus.

# 63

Powers walked up the jet-bridge and into the terminal at McCarran International Airport. He stopped and looked around. He was surprised to see slot machines lined up like the Sirens of Greek Mythology. The clinking coins falling into metal trays pierced logic as effectively as the seductive serenades of the Sirens seduced the Sailors of mythology. They were practically irresistible. With the strength of Odysseus, Powers walked on.

Powers had never been to Las Vegas; it was impossible to take it in stride. He gawked uncontrollably as he strolled.

He had settled into acceptance until the taxi driver turned onto the strip. He saw thousands of people walking the street. In a few short blocks he saw a helicopter take off, he saw Plymouth Prowlers and Hummers for rent. He saw the most unique architecture in the world. New York New York, the Bellagio, and the Eiffel Tower of Paris. His attention was imprisoned.

Twenty-five minutes ago, he watched as the airplane cruised past hundreds of miles of lifeless brown desert and now he was amid an oasis of color, neon, and life.

The driver pulled into the Paris Hotel & Casino; Powers craned his neck to view up the replica Eiffel Tower. As he walked to the desk, he bumped into a man. Powers did not see the man because he was watching a blonde cocktail waitress walk past. He apologized but immediately caught the scent of a brunette waitress and watched her walk. As if it were a stage show illusion, she disappeared and another blonde took her place. A lesson learned; he realized there would be a continuous flow of beauty and breasts in a variety of flavors. He need only stand still.

The legs of the Eiffel Tower were visible on the casino floor.
*Genius.*

His eyes followed it up to the ceiling. It was painted shades of sky blue with soothing dollops of clouds. As he stood there looking up, he thought they were moving. An elderly woman clad in stretch jeans,

239

rhinestone decorated sweatshirt, and fanny pack, brushed against Powers arm. The contact brought him back to earth; yet a much different earth than he left.

He found his way to the desk and checked in. He rode the elevator up, threw his bag on the bed and went back downstairs. Powers did not notice the window view of the strip, nor did he know, he could sit in the window and watch the Bellagio water fountains perform across the street. His only thought was to get back to the casino floor. The entire town was a museum of human imagination and human nature. Powers wanted to see it all. He abandoned his composure and let the baptism enrapt him. He walked and gawked.

He wandered into the sports book. Powers stared at the room. Seven large televisions covered the wall; the one in the middle was much larger. Each screen featured a different horse race from all over the country; each was in a different stage of readiness. Horses were racing on the middle screen and the overhead speakers increased in volume as the announcer called the race, "And GoneNDoneIt brings up the rear."

"Come on, grab the rail," screamed a man in front of Powers.

"Run six, run, dammit!" encouraged another.

The wall to his right supported a black marquee with illuminated red, yellow, and green lights. Every game in the country was listed by sport. Football, basketball, and hockey and all were categorized by college and professional. The odds were posted and while Powers examined them, some of them changed. His eyes caught Georgetown changing from a five point favorite to five and a half point favorites.

Powers scanned the remainder of the room; it was equipped with rows of tiered seating. Each seat sat behind a long bench table. Every person who sat had access to a personal television monitor. The gambler could select any event to track. It was Thursday; it was eleven thirty in the morning and the room was half full.

"It's WandaWillRun by two lengths, Marshall Willin, second, and DooWopUDo running third."

"Sonofabitch," yelled a bald man from the side of his mouth that was not chewing an unlit cigar.

Powers was in awe of the enormity of the business. A steady stream of people walked to the counter and exchanged money for tickets. What motivated them? Why would the seated man with the sore fist believe the six-horse would upset the favorite? How could anyone calculate Georgetown to be five and a half points better than Rutgers?

He found himself looking into the faces of these gamblers. They lose most of the time. Statistics do not lie. The regal Paris Hotel is not losing money. This city is being re-built and sustained by dreamy eyed bettors and gamblers. He left the room knowing that the only difference between them and himself was Eddie Dreyer.

Powers walked up to the bar and asked the bartender to make him a Bloody Mary with an extra shot of Absolut and Tabasco. He paid for the drink, an unnecessary expense in Las Vegas. He would learn one could drink for free. He could have sat down at a slot machine and within moments, a pair of breasts barely covered in blue would have brought him a drink for the price of a tip. It would be low-end booze and diluted but it would be free. His Bloody Mary was seven dollars; not gambling is expensive. He took a sip and gave the bartender an ok sign. The bartender nodded and picked up the dollar tip.

He took the elevator up to his room. He plugged in his laptop and turned it on. As he waited for Eddie's selection to register. He pulled the curtains all the way back and sat down. Powers placed his feet up on the windowsill and took in the magnificence of human engineering. The enormous hot air balloon, the fountains, the façade of New York New York, and the Luxor pyramid filled his view. Mountains stood in the distance: it was easier to believe he was seated in a theater and that the mountains were the backdrop scenery than to recognize them as the rugged walls of a desert.

Powers thought of his eco-friendly colleagues. They would see the sun painting those mountains in shades of orange and red and argue that nothing is more beautiful than the work of Mother Nature. Powers stood and pressed his face closer to the window to see farther down the strip.

"This is breathtaking. Mankind deserves a bit of praise as well," he said out loud.

Powers spotted a man on the street wearing a sandwich board that read, "Leave Lost Wages and Go Home to God."

"Good luck, Brother. You are going to have long day preaching here," Powers said.

Just as Powers was taking another drink of the tangy Bloody Mary, the computer dinged. He wiggled the mouse and there it was, Eddie's selection. The Eagles minus twenty-four. Powers stared at the computer with his face snarled. Eddie had never given up that many

241

points. Eighteen was the most Powers could recall. This was an unusual pick. Powers was not compelled to wager any of his money; his only obligation was to bet Eddie's money. Just like the people downstairs in the Sports Book, Eddie loses. Not very often but he does lose.

He placed the bet for Eddie. If Eddie were wrong, Powers would feel victorious. If Eddie is right, there's always next time. Powers needed some intrigue in this relationship. Challenging Eddie would give him something to anticipate this evening. Powers passed on the opportunity. It was an easy decision; Powers was anxious to see more of the city. He left his empty glass on the table and went downstairs to explore more of the man-made marvel.

# 64

April had narrowed her choice of games to three. She thought each was a good bet. She checked the time; four hours had passed. She had missed a second class and decided to miss the third. Her justification; two hundred dollars will help pay the tuition. She could always make up the class.

She went into the kitchen. She spread peanut butter on bread and folded it in half. She took a bite and poured a large glass of water. She heard ding from her phone; it was a Text. It was from Eddie.

"I'm 8-2 in the last 10 bets. Who's your bet tonight?"

"Why do you assume I am?" April text back.

Ding. "You believe you can be great at everything."

"I can," she sent.

Ding. "So?"

"Looking at 3 but I think I like Tennessee at home -7."

Ding. "Somebody's gotta' win it."

"You like MSU +7 better?" April asked.

Ding. "No."

"What are you saying?" April sent.

Ding. "I don't see an advantage in that game."

In frustration, April slapped the phone down, stood up and walked around for a minute. She heard it ding again.

Ding. "Not willing to risk money without an advantage."

April read the text and frustration monopolized her thinking.

"Every time I find a game that makes sense to me, some boy shoots it down, she said out loud.

April took a deep breath, picked up phone, and texted.

"Fine. What about South Carolina over Georgia Tech?"

Ding. "You don't need my blessings to place a bet."

April was not sure what she thought he was saying or what he intended but she was sure it angered her.

"Blessings? What are you the Pope?" She pressed Send.

Ding. "I am practically a God of gambling; but if you prefer Pope, I accept."

April tried to chill down. She knew he was being humorous.

Ding. "Eddie D, the Pope of the Holy Church of Gambling!"

Ding. "But I'm not sportin' that pointy hat. Maybe a baseball cap with Pope stitched across it. What do you think?"

"I think you are nuts," April sent.

"The entire Congregation of the Holy Church of Gambling is nuts," Eddie responded.

"I guess that makes me nuts, also."

Ding. "Oh yeah. No doubt. If you're going to continue to gamble, then you're nuts too."

"So, Pope, since all my picks suck, who do you like tonight?"

April typed the message and paused before she pushed Send.

*Do I really want his help?*

She sent it.

*Who am I kidding?*

At the very least she needed to hear his reasoning for a pick.

Ding. "Your picks don't suck. I can argue either side."

"Yet you bet daily," she typed.

Ding. "Money is always wagered on both sides. These lines are amazingly accurate."

Ding. They are designed to drive money to both sides."

"Not helping." Send.

Ding. "If there was only one right answer, I'd pick you to find it."

Eddie's last text caused her to perk up. She knew it was a blatant attempt to flatter her. Okay; she accepted it but what she really wanted from him right now was knowledge.

She focused and typed, "Yada, yada, yada. Maybe you are a Pope; you preach like one. What's you bet tonight?"

Ding. "The Eagles," read the text she received.

April checked the line.

"Holy Shit, your Excellency. You're giving up 24 points?"

Ding. "Yes,"

"Is this how you lose 2 of ten?" She asked.

Ding. "Possibly."

April scrolled around the web site and found some analysis.

She read, "The Eagles offense is designed to set picks and drive the lane. Marshall Kirkland blocks a lot of shots except when you put a big body on him. The Eagles don't have any big bodies."

244

She relayed some of the information to Eddie.

Ding. "I don't think he's going to play."

"Why not?" April typed.

Ding. "Rumor is he's taking steroids. I can't blame him; but it's illegal."

"If it's true and he's not in the game how come the line hasn't gone berserk?"

Ding. "24 is berserk."

Ding. "It was outrageous to begin with."

Ding. "The Eagles have to cover by 24…on the road!"

"Why a game at 24 but not my game at 7? My game makes more sense than this," April posted.

Ding. "If Kirkland doesn't play, two college kids have to play out of position against the best team in their conference."

Before April could respond, in came another text.

Ding. "The Marauders suddenly become dramatically smaller. The Eagles will see open paint. They are a team with four seniors; they will use the Marauders to send a message to the whole conference."

Ding. "Eagles will run away with this game." Eddie's sent.

"Sounds crazy to me," she responded.

Ding. "Not crazy, exciting. Imagine Kirkland sitting at one end of the bench, thinking I took a little powder to gain weight. BFD."

Ding. "Coach sits on the other end thinking I'm stuck at this nowhere college with inferior players and this kid is trying to destroy me."

Ding. "Can't you just see it? Hell, I can feel it."

April was reading the messages. She did not know how to respond to Eddie's pre-meditated script of the game.

Ding. "I'll bet they beat them by more than 30."

Ding. "That's how I see this game. How do you see your 7 point game?"

April hesitated. Doubt was creeping into her confidence. Then she said out loud, "There is nothing wrong with my analysis."

She explained her pick, "Tennessee is at home, where they have lost only once. The margins of victory and loss for the two teams favor Tennessee."

Ding. "If that's your rationale, bet it," Eddie sent.

April wanted Eddie to offer athletic perspective. Maybe he had and she did not recognize it. She leaned back against the wall and looked away from the phone. She also needed endorsement. That had always been the way it worked. She listened, she studied, and she made an A. The grade was validation. She had conquered. Nothing about the world of wagering was giving her endorsement. April had flunked two tests in a row. The frustration gnawed at her relentlessly.

Yet she followed Eddie once and she had won two hundred dollars. To April it felt like cheating off some other student's paper.

*Taking Eddie's advice is cheating.*

Gambling may be illegal but cheating is shameful.

"I won't do it," she said resolutely.

She typed, "I'm betting Tennessee -7."

Ding. "May the Gods of Gambling smile upon you."

Once again, April was unsure how to interpret his response. When they were face-to-face, she could read a smile, catch a raised eyebrow, or examine his body language but the text on the phone offered only words. Eddie could be shaking his head and calling April a "dumb shit."

She decided to change the subject.

She typed, "Where are you?"

"Chattanooga."

"What the hell for?"

"Research, scouting, you know, studying the scripture, all the mundane responsibilities of the Popedom."

"Popedom? Not sure that's a word," April sent.

"A lot of weight and power comes with the Pope Baseball Hat. Sometimes, words must be invented to describe reality."

"Well, good luck with that. Gotta' go. See you, when I see you," April sent.

Ding. "Go Vols!"

April placed her bet on Tennessee minus seven and closed the laptop. She put the iPod earphones on and laced her running shoes. A sweaty run would not erase the slothful day but it would force her mind to concentrate on breathing and coordination rather than college basketball and fantasies of Eddie Dreyer.

# 65

"These are fifteen rows back and nearly centered."

"How did you get them? The show is sold out?" Powers asked.

"This is Las Vegas. People come here to win. If you keep offering a profit, someone will take it."

"But I only need one ticket," Powers said.

"I know. You can buy both of these tickets for three hundred dollars or I let you have one for three hundred dollars, the man said.

"Or, I could just walk away and you would be stuck with two tickets," Powers responded.

"I wouldn't be stuck. I have the hundred dollars you gave me to search for tickets and I still have time to sell these tickets. Don't try to hardball me; I do this every day."

The man with the tickets offered a soft smile. He was neither threatening nor rude; he was conducting business.

"I will take the tickets. I've wanted to see "O" since the day I arrived," Powers said and handed the man three one hundred dollar bills.

"Oh and here's a little something extra for you." Powers flashed a big smile and gave the man a one-dollar bill.

Powers delighted in the tiny tip.

"Hey man, money's money. I'll bend over in a crowd to pick up a penny."

The man stuffed the bills in his pant pocket as he walked across the lobby. Two women, with lost looks in their eyes, began talking with him. Powers watched; within moments, they were opening Gucci handbags, exchanging money for tickets, and smiling. Powers handed his ticket to the usher and followed the man to his seat. It was an exquisite theatre. The details rivaled famous halls on the east coast or maybe anywhere in the world. The lights went down, a woman descended from the ceiling, and live vocal performers serenaded from the wings. It was a non-stop assault on his senses. They trapezed over the pool of water, dove into the water, and surfaced like dolphins. At times, it seemed they walked on water. Powers was impressed. When it ended, he stood and applauded. He was among the last to lower his hands to his side. He exited the auditorium.

It was nearing midnight as Powers approached the casino at the Bellagio. It was packed. Powers strolled the floor. He studied people at the craps table, marveled at the number of people willing to toss hundred dollar tokens at a game of blackjack, and watched as people crowded around a roulette wheel to predict where a ball would land. He rounded a corner and saw the art of Monet covering a hall. He walked past the security guard and examined the paintings. Powers was looking directly at the brush strokes of genius but his attention was divided.

"I want to live here," he said out loud.

Powers was profiling the reasons in him mind. First class shows, concerts, comedy, world-renowned restaurants, fine art exhibits, and enough psychology to satisfy any student of human nature.

Powers suspended his tour and rushed back to his room. He wanted to spend some time with his yellow legal pad. His brain was trying to deal with a melee of emotions. The confrontation of ideas and idealism was more than he could balance silently. He grabbed a drink from the bar and went upstairs. He sat his drink on the desk and slid into the chair. This would not be a list of pros and cons; this would be a list of things to do, Powers had reached his decision; he was re-locating to Las Vegas. The next big change in his life was under way. He paused to drink.

"This too is a stroke of genius," Powers said as he glanced out at the night's glamorous skyline.

"Well, for a mere mortal," he whispered.

Powers smiled and continued to write his to do list.

# 66

Billy Pettijohn entered the housing complex with his two roommates. Rodger left the trio to talk with a friend in apartment 4A. Billy and Dan continued up the stairs. Dan pulled an envelope from the crack between the door and jamb. It had Billy's name scrawled across it.

"Here you go, Billy. Maybe it's from coach; he wants to apologize for being so tough on you this week," Dan said.

"Oh yeah. The day he apologizes for anything will the first," Billy replied.

The coach had scheduled an extra session early last Monday morning. Billy complained. The coach confronted him. The squabble ended when Billy screamed, "Why ride us so hard? This isn't a championship game. It's just a game between two crappy teams in a second rate conference."

"Laps, now! Everyone," the coach had yelled.

After twenty laps and everyone cussing at Billy, the coach yelled, "Stop."

The team gathered around the coach. He gave a speech about pride, commitment, and losers. Most coaches would have sat Billy on the bench; some would have suspended him. Instead Coach Pullman decided to work his ass off.

He told the team, "Each of you are receiving a free education. That's why you are here, for an education. A diploma. That makes basketball your job. You are being paid to play basketball.

None of you are going to play professional basketball; that is not a career option for any of you. But, we pay you to play basketball. A scholarship is money, so the college pays you. I assume from Billy's comments that he wants to co-exist with me in an open and honest environment. Let's do that.

Here's some more honesty. This is a class just like all the others. Every class has an objective. That objective is to learn. Here in my class, the objective is to learn strategy, teamwork, and discipline.

Billy thinks that our record indicates that nearly every team in the conference can beat us. Billy wonders, why try? Why bust my ass? What difference does it make? I suspect many of you feel the same way.

Well, I don't care what you wonder about or how you feel. Open any book on the history of this game and you will find record after record of the less talented team winning the ball game. I will give you a strategy that will win. You will learn how to implement the strategy; that's what we do in this classroom. We don't pay you to win but we do pay you to follow orders and play. My strategy for the remaining games is your syllabus."

"Pettijohn, get in the paint. Low post drill, let's go," the Coach barked loudly.

The Coach had shamed Billy; made him feel like a loser for speaking impetuously. And physically, his legs and shoulders were paying the price for immaturity.

Dan opened the door and Billy followed him into the apartment. Dan threw his bag in his room and went directly to the bathroom. Billy walked into the kitchen, filled a glass with water, drank most of it, and then opened the envelope. He unfolded the paper and saw a one thousand dollar bill resting against the letter. He looked at the money expecting to see the face of Pauly Shore, Carrot Top, Bill Clinton, or even his own picture; he did not expect to see Grover Cleveland. It seemed real.

He read the letter, "Miss every free throw on Friday night and it's yours to keep. Please don't make us come back for our money. Miss them all. How hard can it be? You're the worst free throw shooter in the conference."

Billy reread the letter and stared at the money. He heard the door to the bathroom opening; he stuffed the money into his sweatshirt pouch. He picked up the water glass, envelope, letter, and walked toward his room.

"Who's the letter from?" Dan asked.

"Brenda," Billy lied without breaking stride.

The explanation must have been satisfactory; Dan did not ask additional questions. Billy closed the door to his room and sat on the bed. He held the money up to the light.

"What am I doing? I don't know what the hell I should be looking for," he whispered.

If a joke was being played on Billy, he wanted to unravel the mystery before the laughter started. Strangled by disbelief, Billy turned to the Internet; he verified Grover Cleveland as the official face of a one thousand dollar bill. It might be counterfeit but it looked real.

Billy stuffed both the letter and the money into the sweatshirt pouch and walked into the living room. He told Dan he had to go to the bank and left. As Billy walked across campus, he knew the money was about gambling but he wondered why anyone would have an interest in the game on Friday night. Billy's team was in last place and their opponent, the Phantoms, had only one conference victory.

*Who cares about this game in Chattanooga, Tennessee, except Coach Pullman?*

Billy walked into the bank and looked around. This was not his personal bank. He walked up to a teller. He smiled and tried to speak calmly.

"Hi. I received this as a gift from my uncle but he's a bit of a practical joker. Can you tell me if it is real?" Billy asked.

"Sure," she said with a pleasant smile.

Billy drummed his fingers on the counter as he looked around. He spotted the surveillance camera; his fingers froze. He turned his head to look away from the evil eye. He straightened and relaxed feeling less comfortable than before.

*I'm not guilty of anything, but I feel like I am.*

He decided to focus his attention on the space directly in front of him. The teller returned and laid the bill on the counter.

"Your uncle sent you a very nice gift," she said with another huge smile.

"Really! It's real?"

The teller nodded her head. "It sure is."

"Could I get it broken down into twenties?" Billy asked.

"Certainly."

Billy took the money and left the bank. The money was in his wallet. He could feel it because it was much thicker than usual. He had been bribed. Billy was unsure how bad it felt. He could certainly find a use for the money but the Coach's strategy for this game was going to feature Billy heavily; he would be fouled frequently. The Phantoms knew he was not a good free throw shooter. The letter demanded that he miss them all.

Billy felt frightened. He would give the money back, if he knew where to give it. Perhaps, he would just keep it and wait for them to come get it. What would they do? Who are they?

*Maybe I should tell the Coach.*

251

Billy reached his apartment and went to his room. He crashed onto his bed and tried to deflect the darts of guilt while imagining a use for the money. His phone rang; it was Brenda.

After a few minutes of conversation, he arranged to meet her for dinner. Billy Pettijohn started the day being told he was being paid to play basketball. His day would end being paid to play basketball poorly.

# 67

Dexter rubbed his towel in tight circles; the spilled beer disappeared. He topped off the glass and placed it back on the coaster.

"Sorry, just clumsy, I guess," she said.

"Don't worry about it, he said with a warm smile.

He turned and saw Harmon walking toward him. Dexter winked.

"Stop giving away my money," Harmon instructed.

"Come on, Harm. I haven't had an early shift in weeks. I get off in ten minutes and I think she likes me. I top that off, give her a smile and, well you never know about the generosity of women," Dexter said as he glanced back at the lady in the dark blue business suit.

"You dream all you want, just quit giving away my beer," Harmon said.

"Grouch."

"Loser," Harmon said and nodded toward the woman.

A dark blue suited man sat down next to her and loosened his tie. He held up his arm to signal for Dexter's attention; his watch and ring glistened in the overhead lights.

"Dex, that man with your woman, would like a drink," Harmon said.

"Yeah, yeah, yeah, I see him," Dexter grumbled.

Dexter served him a beer and left the two of them to laugh and flirt.

Dexter saw Juanita getting ready to take his place behind the bar. He walked in the back and collected his backpack. He waved to Juanita as he slid under the bar door. As he stood up, he saw April taking a seat at the far end of the bar. He stopped walking and stared at her. April did not see him; her attention was on a notebook. Dexter started walking again but he continued to watch April. He had decided to leave unnoticed, when April looked up.

*Smile and walk away.*

Dexter could feel the corners of his mouth rising but he knew it was mechanical and insincere. Dexter could not walk away. He changed course and walked closer to her.

"Hey, how's it going?" Dexter asked her.

"That depends. Which April do you want to talk to?"

"What do you mean?"

"Here's the deal Dexter. Every time I talk to you, your feelings get hurt and you run away mad. I am what I am. If you want me to be nice all the time then you're wasting your time. I can't do that. So, you see that April doesn't exist."

"So, you plan to wander through life being mean to everyone and you expect the whole world to adapt to you?"

"I don't expect anyone to do anything. I don't force myself on people," April told him.

"You think I'm forcing myself on you?" Dexter asked.

"Aren't you? Haven't you told me you like me? Isn't your motivation to have us be a couple, or to hang out, to date, or to become romantically involved?" April said.

Dexter sat down on the stool next to her and stared straight ahead. He was afraid to answer the question. If he said yes, she would crush him; he knew she did not want that kind of relationship. If he said no, he would be positioned as a friend.

"No April I gave up on that," Dexter said. He voiced his words with a frigid calm. He changed the subject to demonstrate he was over her.

"Still checking the basketball lines. So, you didn't quit betting?"

Dexter watched April's eyes. She was squinting as she peered back at him. He was sure she did not believe him. But April broke the gaze and took a drink.

"I'm certainly contributing money to the gambling services," she said.

"Not winning?" He asked.

*Good, as long as we discuss anything but relationships.*

"Nope. Four bets, four losses. Tennessee lost two nights ago and last night Duke lost at home. I think I'm a jinx. These teams should pay me to not bet on them," April said.

"When you were in here with Eddie Dreyer the other night, you two were celebrating. Did you have a winner?" Dexter asked.

"Yeah. That was nice. I took his advice; I bet two hundred dollars and won."

"What made you take his advice?"

"He seemed so sure Reggie Fontenot would foul out and that the other team would take control in his absence," April explained. "He talks a good game. Plus I was on my fourth beer."

"Eddie knows basketball. Maybe, you should get his input more often," Dexter suggested.

"I tried to get him to agree that the Tennessee pick was a good pick but he said he couldn't find an advantage for either team. He put his money on the Eagles minus twenty-four," April said.

"Damn, that's a lot of points," he said to her.

"I know, right?" She said with a raised voice.

"So, have you had a chance to talk with him since?" Dexter tried to deliver the question without sounding like he was snooping on the extent of Eddie's relationship.

"No. We were trading Texts about games. I still can't believe Eddie took the Eagles minus twenty-four on the road and won," she said. "How scary is that?"

She finished her beer.

"Yeah, they won by a bunch, right?" Dexter asked.

"Thirty-seven. It seems that toothpick Kirkland started taking steroids. The coach suspended him. The team played without a true center and started three freshmen. And Eddie knew Kirkland was on steroids." April waved at Juanita for another beer.

"How did he know? It wasn't in the papers," Dexter asked.

"I don't know but I do know he researches. He travels to campuses and watches players and talks to people. That's all he does. He seems to be able to get inside their heads. I think he visualizes games and individual match-ups."

"When he played, he used to visualize his own games. I suppose he still uses the technique," Dexter replied.

"What do you mean?" She asked.

"Eddie used to go through a pre-game ritual where he would almost put himself in a trance. He would play a whole game in his head," Dexter explained.

April asked, "How do you know that?"

"He didn't try to keep it a secret. Nearly everyone knew." Dexter said as a thought occurred to him.

"You do know Eddie played for the Cougars, right?" Dexter asked.

"Here?" April questioned.

"Yeah. He was a stud. Conference MVP until the injury. How could you live here and not hear any of this. He was in the papers almost daily for three years," Dexter said surprised.

"I proudly plead guilty to being ignorant of everything related to sports prior to become a lousy gambler," she said.

"Eddie's life was basketball he didn't like to lose. He would do whatever it took to win," Dexter said.

"You mean he cheated?" April asked.

"Cheated, took advantage of weaknesses, pushed the limits of the rules, engaged in mind games, antagonized coaches, used team mates, was a ball-hawk, anything that could be done he did it."

"You don't seem disappointed in his behavior?" April asked.

"I loved watching him play. He was unflappable, supremely confident. He knew what had to be done and he would do it. Not all his team mates loved him but they loved riding the victory train." Dexter told her as though he were reminiscing the past glory.

"Hmmmph. How come you don't get mad at him for being mean?" She asked.

"It's a simple explanation. I have a double standard," Dexter answered.

"Meaning, it is okay for a guy to do mean things but not okay for a girl to say or do mean things? Is that what you are saying?" April said as she gripped the beer.

"No absolutely not. I mean I have one set of standards for humans and a different set of standards for the mentally disturbed," Dexter explained.

"You think Eddie is mentally disturbed because he is committed to winning?" April asked as she turned to stare into his face. She continued, "Eddie's natural course of action is to take control and because of that, you call him disturbed?"

"What would you call a guy who saw his future go down the drain, lives in hotels, associates with no one, is pickling his liver with whiskey and uses people to get what he wants?" Dexter stated.

"I call him a winner," April said. "Maybe he's a loner; I know something about loners. They find it difficult to make small talk. Many times loners just aren't interested in other people. Maybe they are not normal, but acting abnormal does not make them mentally disturbed."

"April. You think you and Eddie share a similar mental makeup?"

"I don't know. I only talked to the guy once and I was nearly drunk. I just think he has moved on from playing basketball. Now he gambles and he wants to be the best. That's consistent behavior. But it sounds like, you think he's less than human because of his devotion,"

April said with obvious sympathy.

"I'm not implying he is less than human. I am separating him from those of us who like human interaction. Part of me would love to experience the kind of success Eddie has experienced but I know I would never make the sacrifices he makes," Dexter said.

Dexter reached out and touched her forearm.

"Hey, I'm sorry. It's obvious you like the guy. I'm not trying to trash him, I'm just discussing what makes him different, and that's all." Dexter said and removed his hand.

April turned back toward the bar and drank more beer. She looked down at her notebook.

Dexter was waiting; he would like to hear her comment on whether she liked Eddie. But Dexter could sense the uneasiness and decided to change the subject one more time.

"So, who do you like tonight?" He asked nodding at her notes.

"I've narrowed it down to two options. I'm taking Maryland minus five or I'm resigning from the Holy Church of Gamblers," April said.

"The Holy Church of Gamblers?" Dexter asked with a smile.

"Yeah something Eddie came up with. He said he knew so much that he must be the Pope of the Holy Church of Gamblers. I'm beginning to think I know so little I shouldn't even be a believer." April reasoned.

"Hey, I don't claim to be a preacher or a psychologist, although I play one behind the bar most nights," Dexter said. "But, if you aren't having fun, quit. It should be fun."

Dexter watched as April stared into the mirror behind the bar without responding to the advice. He waited and considered what he would say next. April continued to stare into the mirror. Dexter looked into the mirror to make eye contact thinking it might snap her gaze. Instead, he saw the reason for April's hesitation. Eddie Dreyer was settling into a table along the back wall.

# 68

Powers tore the pages from the yellow legal pad and spread them across the bedspread. They rested there like a large unsolved puzzle. He placed them in a line, as though they led to some logical conclusion. He scanned through the six pages of words, numbers and question marks. He turned to look at the clock. It was after three in the morning. Powers could not remember the last time he was awake at three in the morning. Sleep had not entered his mind. He decided to take a break from his yellow brick road and go down stairs. Will the casino be bustling with people, even in the wee hours of a Wednesday morning?

The elevator doors opened and his ears intercepted the siren symphony of casino sounds. Powers followed his ears to the roar of a Craps table. Thirteen people crowded around the oval erupting in periodic cheers and sighs. He paused to take it in.

*Splendid; just splendid.*

He looked around; it was not crowded. Fewer grandmothers wandered the floor with plastic cups full of nickels and many of the dealers had gone home to family a normal life. But normal casino life continued.

Powers walked to a table full of Asian men playing Kai Pow. He watched; he did not know the rules of the game but he was intrigued. Over the dealer's shoulder, Powers saw the Sportsbook and remembered Eddie's bet. He walked into the empty room and examined the large marquee of scores. He located the game. The Eagles ninety-one and The Marauders fifty-four. Eddie picks a team to cover twenty-four, on the road, and wins. Powers smiled as he re-entered the casino. He thought how uncanny that anyone could pick winners so consistently; he also thought about the lost profit opportunity. He should have followed Eddie's selection. Eddie's quote rang in his head, "Betting against me is gambling."

Powers stood near a Blackjack table and watched four players pushing chips and waving hits. He decided he would play.

He stepped over to the cashier cage and traded a one-hundred dollar bill for twenty chips. He went back and stood near the table palming the chips from one hand to the other like a child playing with a Slinky. A cocktail waitress interrupted his study and penciled gin and tonic on her pad. Powers tipped her when she returned and took an empty chair at a black jack table.

Powers pushed a chip toward the dealer and the Eight of Hearts fell in front of him. A moment later, the Six of Spades fell next to it. Powers looked at the other four hands and watched hit, hold, bust, and hold. He could hear the other players offering senseless chatter.

"It's just not my night," came a voice from his right.

"Whoa, the cards hate me," said the lady at the left end.

The dealer looked at Powers with an implied impatience. Powers tapped his cards and watched as the Eight of Diamonds spoiled his rookie outing. The dealer totaled nineteen. She paid the man with twenty and collected all the other chips and cards. Powers went with the double up to catch up theory. He drew nineteen; the dealer drew twenty.

"Damn, You got the mojo working for the man tonight, Darlin'," said the man with the hairy arms to the Dealer.

Powers wanted to leave the table. Ignorance was rattling him but he could not allow the other four players to classify him as a quitter or a cheap amateur. Pride threw common sense out on the streets like a bouncer roughing up the town drunk.

He pushed four chips to the Promised Land. He was rewarded with an Ace and a Nine; they lay there confidently on the green table. The dealer drew twenty-four. Powers could not contain his smile. He reached for the eight chips, and then hesitated. If I am to live the life of a gambler, let it begin now. He left the eight chips on the table and waited for his cards.

# 69

April could see that Dexter was watching her as she stared at the mirror. She could not break her gaze. She wanted Eddie to notice her. She wanted him to initiate a wave, a smile, or anything that would indicate he had an interest. She needed to gauge his interest.

Eddie continued his walk to the far wall without looking around. He sat alone. April should have recognized that Eddie could not have known she would be at Bluebeards. But the emotions she had been juggling lately clouded her reasoning. All she felt at this time was that she was being ignored.

Dexter broke through the confusion and said, "April, did you see Eddie Dreyer come in or are you just enamored with your reflection in the mirror?"

"I saw him," she said with an apparent tone of disappointment.

Dexter said, "I'm going over there and talk to him. Maybe he will lay a pearl of wisdom on me and I can make some money tonight," Dexter said. "Come with me."

"I don't think so. I think maybe you're right. I should quit gambling," she said.

"Great I give good advice and now it's going to cost me money," Dexter responded.

"You don't need me. Go over there by yourself," April said and signaled for another beer. "You know him, right?"

"Yeah we've met but it's not like we're buds. You know him. He'll invite you to sit down. That may not happen for me," Dexter said.

"Dexter, this is insulting. You just want to use me for your own selfish reasons," April blurted out.

"Yeah. But I would gladly let you use me," he said with a big smile.

"Big deal. What do you have that I want?" She asked. But before Dexter could respond, she continued. "Just trying to be cute, Dexter. Don't take it wrong."

"Really, so there's something about me you like?" He asked.

April swung around on her stool to face him. She stared at him, mostly astonished at his resilience.

Her beer arrived; she picked it up as she stood and said, "Come on let's go. Talking about gambling is less taxing than watching you try to get into my pants."

April began the walk across the room.

"Hey, I'm interested in your mind, as well," he said as he followed her.

They reached the table where Eddie was already deep into his laptop.

"Hi Eddie. How was Chattanooga?" April asked.

"It's just like every other place. I can't tell them apart," Eddie responded.

"Just another day at the office?" April said.

Eddie Dreyer looked up from his computer. He flashed a smile at April and then turned his attention toward Dexter.

"Dexter. Dexter Dalton, right?" Eddie said with his hand extended.

Dexter shook his hand and wondered why some guys got all the winning cards from the deck of genes. Tall, broad shouldered, pale mysterious eyes, square jaw, and gleaming teeth; a Royal Flush. And as if he needed an ace up his sleeve, he was dealt athleticism.

"Yeah. I'm surprised you remember me," Dexter said.

"You taped my ankle once when Tagge was out of town."

April did not want to listen to two guys talk about taping and locker rooms.

"Do you mind if we sit down?" She asked as she pulled a chair back from the table.

"No. Have a seat." Eddie said as his eyes cut back and forth between the two of them.

April sat opposite Eddie leaving the chair next to him for Dexter. April could sense Eddie taking a defensive posture. She watched Eddie's eyes; he looked like a gunslinger preparing to outdraw two opponents at the same time.

Eddie's drink arrived. He took a few quick sips. It was obvious his second drink would arrive soon. Dexter asked for a beer as April sat hers on the table.

"So, what are you guys up to?" Eddie asked.

"Dexter wants betting advice," April said.

She knew the bluntness of her comment would make Dexter squirm. And right on cue, Dexter snapped his head around to give April a disapproving look. April responded immediately.

"Don't look at me like that; it's true. I don't like to play games and I don't think Eddie does either. Do you Eddie?"

"No." Eddie responded. "Dexter, what makes you think I can give you profitable advice?"

"Harm told me you win a lot."

"Eddie wins eight out of every ten; don't you Eddie?" April remarked flippantly.

It was like playing with dolls. She remembered holding a doll in each hand. Each doll did just as April would command. The doll would say exactly what she wanted to hear.

*Both of these boys are irritating in different ways. Let's see how they like it.*

April said, "That's what you told me. You weren't just bullshitting me, were you?"

She knew this would make Eddie uncomfortable.

Dexter blurted out, "Eight out of ten? That's unheard of."

"I do win eight out of ten," Eddie said softly, confidently.

"Damn. Then you are the Pope of the Holy Church of Gamblers," Dexter said.

April watched as Eddie turned to look directly and solely at her. April felt a small pang of regret. The Pope conversation was an exchange between two people getting to know each other. Eddie probably considered that conversation private. April rarely felt unjustified for her crassness; this time she wished, she had been a little more sensitive.

Eddie said, "Suddenly, we've all become very intimate."

April knew trying to read Eddie was a losing exercise. He seemed to be responding very calmly. She was beginning to believe that no matter what she said to him, she could not hurt him. The realization offered her a little clarity.

*If he's not in to me, then nothing's private.*

"Works for me. So, Pope, you know I lost my Tennessee bet," April said.

"Yeah by only three points; the Gods can be so unkind," Eddie said and took another sip of his drink.

"But not to you," she said.

"Perhaps, I'm a bit more religious. The devout travel a lonely path but a path to the one true reward," Eddie said with a smile. "Victory."

Dexter broke in and said, "Okay, where I come from this conversation would be considered blasphemous. Am I the only one worried about sudden lightning strikes?" Dexter asked.

April and Eddie ignored his comment.

"Or maybe, you're just the luckiest gambler on the planet?" April said.

"April, jealously is not your color; confidence is your color."

"So the info on the Marauder kid wasn't lucky timing; it was a product of your devotion to scripture, to be faithful to time honored gambling doctrine?" April asked.

"Absolutely. Demonstrate devotion to the objective and the Gods provide," Eddie replied and waved for his second Dewar's.

Dexter interrupted again, "Seriously, a lightning bolt aimed for the two of you might singe me, as well."

"Dex, do you really think our conversation has the highest priority on God's to-do list?" Eddie asked.

April watched as Eddie smiled at Dexter to soften the words he had hurled at Dexter. He was not belittling Dexter; he was being gracious, trying to include Dexter in the threesome. He was hoping for levity and perhaps a subject change.

It angered April to think that Eddie could wrestle the control of the conversation from her. April tightened her grip on the Dexter doll. She turned to face Dexter. She pulled hair back behind her ear and touched his forearm. She knew it would get his full attention.

"Dex, who is Marshall Kirkland?" She asked.

"I never heard of him."

April told him, "He's the center for the Marauders. Eddie knew Kirkland was on steroids and would be suspended. And without his tall skinny ass in the paint, the Eagles drove the lane all-night and won by thirty-five. The line was twenty-four. Eddie took the minus twenty-four," April reported.

April slowly removed her hand and turned to look at Eddie. Eddie reached across the table to put his hand on April's forearm.

"Let's keep the facts straight. The Eagles won by thirty-seven," Eddie said.

"My apologies," April faked sincerity, looked at Eddie, and pulled her arm from Eddie's touch. She returned her attention to Dexter.

"You're a member of the Holy Church of Gamblers; would you have taken minus twenty-four on the road?" April asked him.

"No, but truthfully giving anything over seven points scares me," Dexter said.

Eddie pressed the glass of Dewar's to his lips, sipped, and asked, "Dex, do you gamble a lot?"

"I don't know about this church-thing but I do bet a few games a week," Dexter said.

"How are you doing? Are you ahead?" Eddie asked.

"I'm ahead of zero," Dexter answered.

"Why do you bet money? Do you have money to lose?" Eddie asked like a polished attorney moving in for the confession.

"No. I'm broke but I like trying to figure out who's going to win. It's a challenge to choose whether the oddsmakers are right or wrong."

"Yeah, that's cool; I get that; but why risk money? Why not just keep score?" Eddie asked and then he tapped a few keys on his laptop.

April could not figure out why Eddie was taking the role of an analyst. His motivation worried her.

April interrupted the two-way conversation. "Because it's a waste of time."

"It is; isn't it?" Eddie said, turning his attentive smile to April.

"I don't need additional time wasting activities. I am busy doing things I want to do," April said. "Why would anyone invest time matching wits with an odds maker? For a job like that I want to be paid."

She looked at Dexter. Dexter raised his eyebrows but did not respond. She turned to look at Eddie.

"You wouldn't just keep score; why would you expect anyone else to?" She asked.

"Not everyone is like me. I'm just interested in human nature," Eddie said and paused to sip his drink. "What Dex thinks and what motivates you are both interesting to me."

"Well, what motivates you?" April said hoping to unsettle his calmness.

"I just want to win. I'm not a "would've" guy. I have no patience for the guy who stands in the background and tells everyone what he "would've" done. Step up and put your money where your mouth is or shut the fuck up. So, for me, I'm either all the way in or all the way out," Eddie said.

Dexter responded, "That's understandable, man, because that's the way you played ball. You were definitely all the way in."

April could see that Dexter's admiration was genuine.

"Let's not talk about my playing days, okay?" Eddie's suggestion had a tone of finality to it.

"Sure. I didn't mean to stir anything up," Dexter said.

"I know; it's cool. People who prattle about the glory days are pathetic. Let's keep it current," Eddie said.

She wanted to rattle Eddie. She sensed a probe into his past might be a cage rattler.

"It's only pathetic, if someone relives the past over and over again. I don't know much about your past. I didn't know you played for the school until Dex told me, a few minutes ago. So, what's wrong with talking about the past? Does the Pope have something to hide?" April asked.

Eddie showed no emotion to the comment; he ignored April's question and directed a question to Dexter. "Are you betting this evening, Dex?"

"I was leaning toward the Greensboro-Appalachian game but I haven't__,"

April did not give him time to finish.

"Wait a minute."

April slapped both hands on the table.

"You didn't answer my question. Why do you decide what will be discussed and what will not?"

"Because this is my table, my life, and I can make choices. I decided to let you sit down. I decided to answer some of your questions and I decided to not answer this one." Eddie answered calmly." And now, I choose to order another drink."

He waved to the server, and then continued. "It is not a one-way freedom, April. You can choose to talk about gambling with us, if you would like."

*Talk with us or leave. Is that what he just said to me?*

It seemed clear to her that Eddie would be satisfied no matter which option she chose. April continued to be puzzled.

*What makes me think this guy likes me?*

She watched Eddie turn his attention to Dexter.

"You're leaning toward ASU, aren't you?" Eddie asked him.

"Probably. What do you think?" Dexter asked.

"I think it's a good bet. It's better than Greensboro plus...what, six?" Eddie said.

April watched as Eddie clicked a few keys on his laptop. She knew her frosty gaze was having no effect on Eddie.

Eddie looked up and said, "Yeah, it's still six."

265

*He doesn't think I'll leave. Well, I'm out of here.*

She stood.

Eddie said, "April, don't be mad. It's such a waste of time. I played ball; I was pretty good. I got injured. I made a bad decision. I've found something else to do. I've moved on. What do you say? Let's have some fun."

He put his hand on her arm and smiled.

"Come on. Who are you betting on this evening?" Eddie asked.

Eddie's beguiling charm left April feeling connected. He was not offering an apology but he was answering her question. He told her about his past and now he was politely asking her to join his conversation. Maybe Eddie sincerely wanted her to stay.

*He must care a little.*

He removed his hand from her arm. Dexter bridged the brief silence with a show of support for April.

"She's quitting," Dexter said. "She has decided gambling isn't fun for her."

"Really?" Eddie asked.

April could feel her pulse racing and her eyelids blinking quickly. She knew that her face still showed anger or at least, confusion. She wanted to demonstrate control. She had been in this position hundreds of times in the past. This type of interaction was exactly why she did not have friends. April felt most concessions were just name changing for losing. Lashing out with inarguable logic is what she likes. She believed her strong will should be blind and furious. She preferred to whirl like a tornado through situations like this one. Her insensitivity startled people. Most would walk away rather than listen. In the aftermath, she was alone but victorious.

But at this moment, April knew that Eddie was right. She could choose to be mad or decide that it was unworthy of anger. She wanted to stay and she wanted to be reasonable. They were bending over backwards to include her in the conversation. She was not mad at Eddie. She was aggravated because she liked Eddie but was unsure where he stood. She was jealous because Eddie was able to select winners and she was not. April did not want to stop betting but logic told her, she could not win. She decided to explain her reasoning and listen to Eddie's reaction.

"I'm not quitting, Dex; I'm eliminating gambling as a means of making money," she said. "I started because I wanted to make money. That was my objective. I now realize that there are too many variables. Consistently predicting these games is impossible. Therefore, I cannot

266

make money. So, there's no reason to continue."

Eddie was holding his glass to his lips but sat it down without drinking to respond to April.

"Yeah, I understand that. It's a control thing. Hell, you're an architectural engineering major; you juggle a zillion tasks at once. I look at some building being constructed and I see a pile of bricks and boards. You know where everything is going to go. You have the future in your hands. In my world, the future is in the hands of a twenty-year-old boy and when I'm depending on him; his hands are sweaty and shaky," Eddie said.

"Exactly." April agreed. "I see ten boys running around a small area; it's chaos. I know there is a designed play and yet half the time, no one scores. As an architect, I can plan a beam to be put in place and securely stationed and it happens, every time."

"That's because there isn't another team of de-constructors blocking the nail guns," Dexter chimed in.

"That strengthens my point. That makes it even harder to predict who will win. It's no way to make money," April said.

"But that's the fun of it," Dexter said.

"No winning, no money; no money, no fun. That's the bottom line to me. So, it seems to be a waste of time," April responded.

"Then how do you explain Eddie's success?" Dexter asked.

"I have no idea." April turned and locked her gaze into Eddie's pale eyes. "How is it possible that you defy the odds, Eddie?"

"Yeah, what's the secret, Pope?" Dexter asked with a smile.

Eddie said, "What I do is simple. I pick the right game by finding the player that is definitely a factor in the team's success. Then I visualize a scenario where he fails. I put my faith in human failure. That's why I like to study human nature."

April thought he stated it clearly and succinctly. This was not an off the cuff response of a bragging bar drunk; this was a philosophy he practiced. It caused her to wonder if his life work was celebrating human failure because of his past. She wanted to know but she knew to question him would be futile.

Dexter said, "Really. Then, would you mind telling me who you've selected next and why?"

"My money is on the Cats. I'm betting against the Wolves because I think they've given up on the season. Furthermore, I think Billy Pettijohn will set a record for the most missed free throw opportunities in a single season. I think he may actually be trying to get the record. These are the worst two teams in the conference but I think the Cats plus four is the bet," Eddie stated without hesitation.

"You are betting real money that a kid in a small college in Tennessee wants to be the worst free throw shooter in conference history? Athletes don't want those kinds of records. He would be embarrassed for the rest of his life," April exclaimed.

"Maybe. Maybe he hasn't even thought about the future. Maybe he just wants to get even with a coach who's riding his back. Maybe he's busy thinking about his girlfriend. Maybe he doesn't care and just wants to end the season. I can imagine a butt-load of reasons why he will miss shots other than the fact that he's not very good but you know I can only think of one reason why he would play well. Pride. Only pride would lift his game. I don't think he has enough of that to do well," Eddie stated.

The comment left April cold. She was disappointed that Eddie would analyze a person and conclude that he lacked pride. To question the heart of a twenty year old was icy cold.

"Whoa. You don't know him, Eddie. How can you question his heart?" Dexter asked.

"Easily. He's a big stiff, who was big enough to land a scholarship at a small school. He has been unable to hold his own against the other nine centers in the conference. He has no history of winning. He's a guy who will leave school with an accounting degree in a few months and probably be a fine CPA. He has figured out his place in life. Many people don't. His heart is not in basketball and it won't take much for him to throw in the towel," Eddie said.

"Dude, that is stone cold analysis," Dexter said.

"Not really. You've been around practices, Dex. Have you ever heard a coach say? 'Your opponent cannot go to his left so cut him off every time. Get in his head. Make him understand that he is inferior to you. Demoralize him. He'll screw up at the end of the game. He'll buckle under the pressure," Eddie asked.

"Maybe not those exact words but I've heard coaches preach meaner tactics than that," Dexter said.

"I'm just following through on what I know is strategy. The Cats coaches know that Pettijohn is the worst free throw shooter in the conference. They want him on the line. It all boils down to individual players. Pettijohn will lose this game. I'm betting on it," Eddie said.

"No wonder I can't make money doing this. I thought it was about statistics and trends and maybe home court advantage," April said.

"Nope. The oddsmakers have already figured that part out. My job is figure out which side of the line will prevail. That means players. It's a team sport but individual players execute or fail," Eddie said.

He turned to Dexter. "So, if you still want to bet on Appalachian, you can use my laptop," Eddie slid the computer toward Dexter.

"What if I want to jump on your bet?" Dexter asked.

"It's your money but remember, I lose a few," Eddie said.

April watched Dexter take the computer as she had done a few nights before. He punched keys and a minute later, he pushed the laptop back to Eddie. No one asked on whom he had wagered and he did not offer to reveal his selection.

The trio sat for a few minutes sipping their drinks. No one was talking. Dexter's bet had left a void. Dexter finished his beer, shook hands with Eddie and said goodbye to April.

April watched him walk out of the bar; her buffer was gone. Eddie ordered another Dewar's and offered to buy April another beer.

She considered saying "No" but responded, "Sure, why not?"

# 70

The dealer was waiting; the four seasoned bettors were waiting. Powers stared at the two cards. His hand showed seventeen; he knew he should hold but he wanted one more card. His last four chips were stacked out on the betting table like the Leaning Tower of Pisa, only he feared his small tower was about to tumble. What was the chance a four or smaller would come slicing through the early morning Casino air? What was the dealer holding? Powers wanted to win this hand, even though he realized it was out of his hands.

"Suckers take a hit, Slick," said the man next to him. Without looking in Powers direction.

"Stay. It's the smart thing to do," Powers heard him say.

Powers waved his hand over his cards. The dealer showed fifteen and drew a Nine. The Leaning Tower doubled in size and straightened up. Powers reached across to collect his chips and noticed his watch gleaming under the lights. He turned his wrist to check the time. It was nearly six in the morning. He picked up his eight chips and stood to leave.

"Thanks," Powers said to the player to his right.

"Just trying to speed up the game," he replied.

Powers paused to look at the man.

He said to him, "Well, thanks anyway and good luck."

Powers walked away shuffling the chips in his hands. He stopped by a cashier's cage and converted them to forty dollars. He had been up all night. It had been nearly three decades since he was up all night. Powers was tired and knew sleep would come easily after he lay down. The elevator opened on his floor and he strolled to his room. His bed was still covered with the yellow brick road to a new life. He picked up the yellow pages of notes and stacked them on the desk.

Powers undressed. He pulled the covers up around his neck and stared at the ceiling and thought about his first blackjack experience. The ceiling made a nice blackboard to do the math. The chalk scribbled numbers for him to review. Powers started with a hundred dollars but lost that and pulled out another hundred. He lost that and traded another hundred for another twenty chips. He stared at the imaginary blackboard. He looked at the number, two four zero. He had lost two hundred and forty dollars. The total bothered him.

Powers had lost bets of five thousand dollars on basketball; those losses did not affect him like this. Two-forty. The blackboard disappeared into the acoustical plaster of the ceiling.

The psychology of the situation was intriguing. These were not Eddie Dreyer's decisions. Only Powers could decide to bet and only he could decide to hold or take a hit. Powers could not blame Eddie or anyone for the loss. Powers knew he could learn. Learning is what he had always done.

*I can learn to play this game, as well as anyone.*

Powers left the table on a winning note. Two-forty. He had paid a fee to learn valuable information and guidance. He had paid tuition to learn the field of psychology; why should he not pay tuition to learn to wager? He thought about the warning signals of an addiction.

*Am I already in denial? No, losing is merely tuition.*

He wondered if he was rationalizing. Was this what it would be like to walk up the steps to addictive gambling? He blinked his eyes a few times to clear the thoughts from his tired mind.

Falling asleep was not happening as quickly as he anticipated. He went to the cabinet, housing the television, and opened the doors. He returned to the bed and used the remote to surf channels. He found the Travel Channel. It was airing a program about beating the odds in Vegas.

The sun was sneaking up behind the mountains. The morning traffic, like ants leaving the mound to scavenge the desert floor, was packing the freeway dutifully. The bustle of a new day included Powers scribbling notes on his pad as the television detailed tricks of the trade. Powers was in class; sleep would have to wait.

# 71

The numbers on the alarm clock clearly read ten fifty-five. April squeezed her eyelids together forcefully, and then re-opened them. She had read the clock correctly but the numbers were small and red; her clock numbers were large and blue.

She sat up. Daylight outlined dark curtains. A loud motor whined from an air conditioner. Her eyes adjusted; she was in a hotel room.

Her pulse quickened; she must have come here with Eddie. She listened for noise in the bathroom. Nothing. She got out of bed and turned on a light; she was alone. April went to the bathroom. Her beer filled bladder needed relief. She sat down and saw a note attached to her purse. She reached over and picked it up.

"Ms. Pyle, I had to leave early. Research doesn't come to me; I have to go to it. You were out cold, so I didn't disturb you. I'll be back from Greenville Sunday. How about dinner and a movie...or something? And since it was my idea to bring you here instead of your apartment, please use this money for a taxi back to your place. Eddie."

April crumpled up the note and tossed it in the can, set the fifty-dollar bill on the counter and flushed the toilet. Her pulse was slowing. One mystery was solved; a second still loomed. Attraction, heavy drinking, hotel room, most people would have fumbled their way through sex. This would be the morning after, the morning of shame or regret or with good luck, elation. There was no sex and Eddie was gone and April was not sure what she felt.

She looked in the mirror; she was wearing yesterday's clothes.

*Is he gay or was I so drunk that I passed out?*

April decided to freshen up before leaving. Water is free at a hotel. She stripped her clothing off and stepped in the shower. The water stream was warm and soft. The pressure had a massaging effect on April's drained body. She could feel her energy level rising as the water cascaded down her body. She stood with her eyes closed without moving a muscle for several minutes. She breathed with the precision of a metronome, getting lost in her own thoughts. April could feel her lungs being regenerated with each humid and misty breath. A beer belch brought her back to reality.

She used excessive amounts of free soap and shampoo, rinsed, and stepped out. The mirror was opaque from the steam. She had instinctively closed the bathroom door when she entered, though there was no need. She opened the door to allow the steam to escape.

She sprawled naked and spread-eagle onto the sheets to cool down. April's mind was still dealing with last night. She wondered if there might be marks on her body, some evidence of lust to support the 'passed out' theory. April sat up and walked over to the full length mirror and examined her body.

*Nothing.*

She felt a moment of depression.

*There's something about me that doesn't turn him on.*

She rotated her torso to see if her breasts were perky enough. She thought they were average. She craned her neck to examine her butt. It seemed average as well. April wondered if average was good enough for the intoxicating blue eyes of Eddie Dreyer. April turned to face the mirror straight on.

This is who I am; take it or leave it.

It seemed like a very hollow threat since Eddie had left.

She walked back to the bed and sprawled again. April reached for the remote and powered up the television; she chose ESPN.

A momentary scare surge through her body as she realized she missing more classes. A month ago, her classroom attendance was exemplary, she rarely watched television, and considered sporting events as a ridiculous use of time. Yet yesterday she blew off three classes, today she was blowing off another three, lounging naked in a hotel room, and reviewing the basketball scores from last night.

The scare passed and April was left with the guilt. She had a clear vision of a sensible April, standing on a shore beckoning her to wade no deeper and come back. She blinked it away.

April stood to get a glass of water. As she walked by, she noticed the score for the Wolves-Cats game. She walked closer to the television and stared at the information. Cats sixty-eight and Wolves sixty-seven. Eddie wins again.

"Son-of-a-bitch," she said and tossed the remote on the bed.

"How does he do it?" She screamed at the television. "Why didn't I listen? Why didn't I take the bet? No, I have to do things my way. I could have used the money from that win. Shit. Shit. Shit."

273

April picked up her clothes. She pulled her jeans over her naked body. She put the bra on and covered it with the t-shirt. She shoved her panties into her back pocket. She brushed her wet hair straight back and down, grabbed her purse, threw the hotel shampoo, lotion and soap inside, and walked out the door.

April entered the elevator and slammed her fist on the first floor button. Rode down, stepped out into the sunlight and began the long walk back to her apartment. She would return the fifty dollars to Eddie, if she ever saw him again. April was mad but she was equally bewildered by the anger. She walked and talked. Occasionally, her thoughts were voiced out loud. Every ten strides or so, April was on a new topic.

"I'm going to get back on track."

She walked another block.

"Eddie is not right for me; I'm going to put an end to this."

She came to a stop.

"An end to what?"

April continued to walk, talk, and curse.

She reached her apartment and opened the door without having reached any resolutions she could keep.

"That long walk is the only healthy thing I've done in two days," April said as she stared out the window.

*Why am I trying to blame someone else? I'm such a moron.*

# 72

Dexter sat shotgun as Dale Klaussen sang off key. Dexter hit the scan button on the radio. The green LED numbers race for a new signal.

"Hey, man! That was a great tune," Dale yelled.

"It is when you aren't singing it," Dexter mumbled back.

The radio stopped on a country station.

"Way down yonder on the Chattaho__"

Dale hit the button and said, "I can sing as good as that guy."

"Oh yeah. You sound just like him," Dexter replied. "If he was being hit in the throat with a hammer."

"Screw you."

"No thanks. I'm holding out for someone less hairy and who can carry a tune," Dexter told him.

The radio stopped on a station in Greenville. Rob Thomas blared from the speakers. Dexter looked at Dale. There seemed to be a mutual agreement to lock the station.

Dexter read the remaining distance to the ECU campus on a roadside sign. And Dale continued to sing but it was low enough to be only a minor annoyance to Dexter. The miles passed without incident.

Dexter looked up and said, "Just eight more miles. Then the fun begins."

"Dex, it's a seminar on shoulder motion therapy. Nobody mentioned fun, in the marketing material," Dale reminded him.

"You're focus is too narrow. There will be students from dozens of schools here. Some of them will be chicks," Dexter said.

"What makes you think those chicks will be any different from the chicks that ignore us in Charleston?" Dale asked genuinely.

"They don't know us. They have no pre-existing notions about us," Dexter answered while nodding his yes as though he had reached a brilliant conclusion.

"I'm thinking they will just decide they don't like the way we look," Dale said.

"Speak for yourself, my friend. I can turn on the charm. I'll do fine."

"Absolutely. I've seen you at work. How is that assault on April Pyle going?"

"I'm not really into her," Dexter replied.

"Oh really, because I thought you were," Dale responded.

"What would give you that idea?" Dexter asked.

"You. You told me she was way different than any other girl. You told me, you found her irresistible. I interpreted that to mean you were highly interested in her," Dale said.

"She is different but she is also moody and mean; and she's hanging with Eddie Dreyer," Dexter said.

"Eddie D? How does a chick like her get into Eddie D's crowd?" Dale wanted to know.

"Eddie doesn't have a crowd," Dexter replied. "He hangs out alone. And get this; he's a professional gambler."

"Are you shittin' me?" Dale asked.

"Nope. I've seen him at work. He's raking in mega bucks. He's uncanny." Dexter turned from the side window to talk more directly to Dale.

"He gave me a tip yesterday that I would never have believed, but it won. I won a hundred bucks. I can't imagine how much he won."

"Damn. A quick phone call to me wouldn't have killed you, Dex. I like easy money, also."

"It was too late. I got my bet down seven minutes before game time. Maybe, next time," Dexter sounded sincere.

They pulled onto campus and parked near the Physical Education Department building. They both grabbed backpacks and walked toward the building. Dale nudged Dexter in the side.

"Hot chick at three o'clock," Dale whispered.

She walked nearer. Dexter raised his eyebrows.

"Well, hot for a PT major." Dale added.

"Dale, I don't need a wingman. You worry about you. Dex will take care of Dex."

"Whatever."

Dexter neatly printed Dex on his nametag and examined Dale's tag. It was barely decipherable. He chose not to comment. They both opened their program and studied it. Dexter closed his and walked toward the auditorium; Dale followed. He took a seat near the same female Dale had ogled outside. She did not look up from the thick novel she was reading.

Dexter pulled a notebook from his backpack and clicked his mechanical pencil to advance the lead. He wrote the date at the top of a page, looked up at the clock, and began to doodle as he waited for the symposium to start.

Three men dressed in sweaters sat down at the front of the auditorium stage. A young woman walked from behind a curtain walked to the podium. She tapped the microphone.

"Good Morning. I'm Thomasa Hidalgo. I am pursuing my doctorate here at ECU and have orchestrated this symposium."

"Now, she's definitely hot," Dale whispered to Dexter.

"Oh yeah, but why waste admiration on something you can't have?" Dexter said.

Dale did not respond his eyes were glued on Ms. Hidalgo.

Dexter glanced at novel-reader to his left; her attention was fully focused on the front of the room. Ms. Hidalgo sat down and the purple sweater guy came to microphone. He started discussing the construction of the human shoulder. The lights went down and slides were shown.

As purple sweater guy talked, some students, like Dexter, scribbled in their notebooks but most pecked away at tablets or laptop. It was like dozens of miniscule sized women walking their high heels down a marble hallway.

Dexter found the typing noise annoying. He refocused and took his own notes quietly. Purple sweater guy finished his portion of the presentation. There was a light applause. The lights came up; ninety minutes had passed. Ms. Hidalgo returned to the podium and told everyone to take a fifteen-minute break.

Dexter watched as Dale went to the front of the room to ask questions about graduate study at ECU. His strategy for talking to Ms Hidalgo was not unique. Dale had plenty of company. Dexter walked outside.

He saw the blonde haired novel-reader sitting under a tree reading her book. Dexter walked toward her.

*Must be an interesting book.*

He knew it was a line and she would know it was a line but how else does a conversation get started?

With just fifteen feet to reach novel reader, Dexter's attention was diverted by a tall male accompanied by a female walking into the gymnasium. He stopped to study the figure. It looked like Eddie

Dreyer with a girl. She was tall and her skirt was short.

As Dexter stood there, looking to his right, novel-reader stood and walked toward him. Dexter found it difficult to take his eyes off the leggy-woman at Eddie's side. Novel reader stopped next to Dexter; he broke his stare to look at her.

"My lighter crapped out; do you have a light?" She asked.

"No. I'm sorry; I don't smoke."

She managed to give him a slight grin and walked toward a boy smoking near the entrance to the auditorium. Dexter watched her walk away. He would cross her off his list. Smokers had to be super hot to keep his interest; she was not.

He looked back at the gymnasium. Could that have been Eddie? If it were Eddie, who was that goddess with him and maybe this would change April's opinion of Eddie. Dexter looked at his watch; he had seven minutes left on the break.

He jogged over to the gymnasium. The door was locked. Dexter jogged to the other side, locked. He went to the back and found an open door. He went inside; it was dark but he could see light at the far end of the gymnasium. He could hear a female voice; the faint sounds were indecipherable. Dexter walked toward the light.

The old gymnasium was small with the bleachers pulled out. It resembled thousands of high school and small college gymnasiums. As he neared the court, he could see the girl and a tall male. It was not Eddie Dreyer.

Dexter walked under the bleachers. He did not want to be seen. He could hear the couple talking. Dexter walked quietly to the middle of the bleachers and squatted to peer out between the rows. He could see them and now their words seemed to echo in the empty gymnasium.

"We don't have all day," she said and dropped her jacket to the floor.

The jacket was not hiding a blouse or t-shirt. It was hiding a pair of breast that stood straight out and her nipples had hardened from the cool air.

"Damn, girl. I don't believe this," the boy said as he squeezed the basketball.

"You'll believe it in a minute. I'm not called Dream Maker for nothing."

She stepped closer and slid her hand between his legs.

"Whoa," he yelped and took a step back.

"You're not queer, are ya'?" She asked.

278

She reached behind her to unzip the mini skirt. The unzipping sound halted his retreat, instantly. It was too tight to just fall to the ground. He stared as she shimmied out of the skirt and stood naked before him.

"Hell no," he said trying to sound as macho as possible.

She paused there for a moment with her legs apart. The boy with the basketball stared uncontrollably at the light shining through the dark hair between her legs.

She took two slow steps forward and took the basketball from his hands. She kneeled and rolled the ball down the court. She reached up and yanked his shorts down to the floor. He stood motionless as she pulled his jock strap down to the court as well.

"This is crazy; somebody will walk in here," he said.

"Not a chance. I locked the doors behind me," she said as she fondled him and caressed him with her lips.

Dexter was frozen. His heart was pounding and his jeans were straining to accommodate his growing penis. He cut his eyes left and right. He too was concerned that someone else would enter. Dexter knew the back door was unlocked.

When he looked to the right, he caught a glimpse of movement. The boy at center court was groaning but Dexter's attention was focused on the movement he saw to his right. He stared intently; he saw it again. Someone was standing under the bleachers on the other side. Dexter thought he heard a slight noise but it was impossible to be certain.

The naked leggy girl continued to coerce moans from the boy at center court. Until that moment, Dexter had assumed the uninhibited performance he was watching only occurred in porn videos.

But as tantalizing as the soundtrack at center court was Dexter could not forget about the second voyeur. Dexter trained his eyes on the last place he saw movement. His eyes adjusted to the darker conditions away from the court lights. Dexter could see feet; he knew someone was there and it had to be Eddie Dreyer. Dexter had seen him come in the door. Why is Eddie here? How could he have known this sexual encounter would go down? What kind of pervert is he?

*Hell, what kind of pervert am I?*

An uncontrolled guttural groan drew his attention to center court. The girl looked up at the boy and said, "That's like a fantasy come true, ain't it boy?"

She stood up and stepped into her mini skirt, picked up her jacket, and with two quick zips, the show and the service were over. Dexter froze as she walked within a few feet of his hiding place. His fear of being discovered elevated his heartbeat. His heart beat faster still as the leggy-girl passed.

*Only two garments from naked.*

Dexter heard the back door open and close behind her. His erection began to diminish. The boy at center court was pulling his shorts back up over his startled damp genitals.

Dexter had decided to leave when he saw a paper airplane land and scoot across the floor. A streamline paper airplane lay a few feet from the basketball player on court. The boy's head snapped in the direction of the darkness.

"Who threw that?" The boy's voice echoed in the empty gymnasium.

"Dream Maker, are you still here?" He asked with a slight hopeful smile. "Now that you've had a taste, you want it all, don't you?"

He stood there and the cockiness began to fade when no one replied to his question. He reached down to pick up the airplane. After looking at it, he opened it up. He appeared to be reading a message. The boy looked worried; he ran toward the dark end of the court. Dexter could hear him searching around. He saw the boy heading toward the control box. He began flipping light switches. Dexter knew that within a few minutes the lights would make him totally visible. As the boy searched the bleachers on the right, Dexter exited into the daylight and ran as fast as he could toward the auditorium.

None of the seminar students were outside. Dexter stepped inside the doorway and watched the gymnasium door. The boy came outside. Dexter could see his disturbed face as he intensely searched the area for whoever tossed that airplane onto the court. The boy went back inside; Dexter continued to scan the campus.

Dexter tried to convince himself that another student was playing a joke on the boy at center court. But he could not shake his original image of the tall boy and the girl entering the gymnasium. It had to be Eddie.

Dexter went back to his seat and tried to keep his mind from blurting out the thoughts inside. At the next break, he left and did not return. Dexter eventually found his way back to the car. He sat inside and waited for Dale. The daylong seminar passed and Dale returned.

"Where have you been?" Dale asked.

"Let's go home," was all Dexter said.

Dale prattled on about Ms. Hidalgo and a few other females who showed no interest in him. Dexter could hear him rambling but he could not have told anyone what Dale had said. His every thought was focused on the events in the gymnasium. Miles passed.

"Could you be any quieter?" Dale asked. "Are you sick or something?"

"What are you talking about?" Dexter responded.

"We've been driving for two hours and you haven't said a damn word," Dale said to him.

"Yes I have."

"No, Dude. No, you haven't. Yeah. Maybe. Could be. These are not conversation starters, my friend. They are dead ends. What the hell are you thinking about? And where were you for the second portion of the seminar. You missed nearly everything we came to learn," Dale said.

Dexter looked out the side window. He did not want to tell Dale what he saw but he thought it might help to hear the words out loud. And maybe a fresh perspective would be helpful.

"I thought I saw Eddie Dreyer today," Dexter said as he turned from the window.

"Eddie Dreyer? At ECU? Why would Eddie Dreyer be at ECU?" Dale questioned.

"I don't know. That's what I can't figure out," Dexter answered sounding totally confused.

"Did you talk to him?" Dale asked returning his eyes to the highway.

"No. He was going into the gymnasium. I went over to see what he was doing."

"What was he doing?"

"I don't know. I didn't find him," Dexter answered.

"Maybe you were mistaken. Maybe it was someone who looked like Eddie."

"Maybe, but it sure looked a lot like Eddie." Dexter said and continued. "Anyway, I went inside and I saw someone hiding under the bleachers spying on a basketball player."

"What?" Dale asked trying to understand.

"Ok. When I went in looking for Eddie; I didn't find him. But I did see this basketball player standing near mid-court, talking to a girl. I walked under the bleachers and stood in the dark. I wanted to see what was going on. Long story short. This chick strips down naked and gives the basketball player a blow job."

"You're lying." Dale practically screams.

"No. And this chick was hot. I got a boner just watching. But while this dude was getting off, I saw someone watching from the other side of the bleachers and I think he was taking pictures," Dexter said.

"What are you saying? The guy who you thought was Eddie D was like a voyeur or something?" Dale asked. "Well it could not have been Eddie Dreyer. Eddie D has no trouble pulling chicks. No reason for that stud to hide in the dark and take pictures."

"Fine, but someone was over there. After the chick dressed and left, the watcher tossed a paper airplane onto the court, like a calling card to let the player know he had been watching."

"Come on. Dex, you don't have to lie to me. You ditched the seminar because it was boring. You spent the afternoon with that novel reading chick. But this shit is not believable," Dale said.

"Yeah, I'm having trouble believing it myself," Dexter said and returned to the passing highway markers out the side window.

"So, what did you do with the rest of the afternoon?" Dale asked.

Dexter ignored Dale's disbelief and continued to tell his tale.

"I think there was a note written on the airplane because after he looked at it, he freaked. He ran to the other end of the gym and started flipping all the light switches on.

So, I ran out. He didn't see me. I went back to the auditorium but I knew I wouldn't be able to concentrate, so I wandered around the campus and walked the streets. I was hoping to see Eddie," Dexter explained.

"First, you want me to believe that one of the smoothest smartest basketball players, I've ever seen, is some kind of pervert. And now you want me to believe that he is stupid, so stupid that he would hang around the scene of the peek-fest?"

"Yeah, I knew it was a long-shot."

"Long shot?" Dale said through a rolling laugh. The Bengals win the Super Bowl or the Cubs win the World Series, those are long shots. Eddie Dreyer a stupid pervert is a damn fool's bet."

"Maybe you're right. But I could have sworn I saw him," Dexter said.

"If I was you, I'd stick to the story about the guy getting sucked off at mid-court. That's awesome. That'll leave guys dreaming. That's a story. If there were a peeping Tom, I'd leave it that way. I wouldn't make it a peeping EddieD," Dale said.

Ten minutes later, Dale drove into the parking lot of Dexter's apartment. Dexter grabbed his backpack and opened the car door.

"Dale, do me a favor. Don't spread this around. I'm not sure what to make of it, yet. And I don't want people coming up to me asking me to tell them about it."

"Alright, but it won't be easy. And if I get drunk, I can't promise you it won't come out. If someone mentions blow jobs, I might explode keeping this inside."

"Just make an honest effort, Dale. Okay?"

"Dude, you are going to owe me big time," Dale said.

Dale drove away. Dexter checked his watch. He hurried inside, dropped the backpack and rushed back out the door. He walked at a brisk pace toward Captain Bluebeards. Dexter pushed open the door and paused a moment to allow his eyes to adjust to the darkness; he cleared a table on his way over to the bar.

"Thanks, Dex. I gotta' split. If you really need me, call me on the cell phone," Harmon said.

Dexter knew he was seeing Helen this evening.

"Don't worry about it; have a good time."

Dexter moved behind the bar and was summoned immediately by Lauren. He walked down to the server station and smiled at her. She looked sensational. Like a perfect Martini, Lauren's genetics came out of the shaker blended for intoxication. She had chosen a tank top designed for maximum tips. Few would notice her genuine smile; discover she had a compassionate heart, or benefit from her innate common sense. The price of the oversight was over tipping.

*I bet she has a healthy bank account.*

"Geez, what does a girl have to do to get her drink order filled?" Lauren asked.

Dexter ran through several options for responding to that question. He chose conservatively.

"What do you need, Lauren? You know I'm here for you, honey."

He flashed a smile and gave her a wink.

She asked for a pitcher of Budweiser and four mugs. She smiled and threw him a "Thanks."

He watched her walk away and selfishly indulged in a little basketball court fantasy of his own.

*If luck were a lady, it would be Lauren.*

# 73

April stormed into her apartment and slammed her purse on the table as she kicked her shoes across the room. A small lamp toppled to the floor; a casualty of a shoe missile. She found one beer in the refrigerator; she took it and lounged in her cushioned window seat. Several long swallows and ten seconds later her beer was half gone. She ran her fingers through her hair to pull it back. April could not get comfortable in her window seat. She stood up and felt the back of her jeans. She pulled the panties from last night from her back pocket and tossed them into the chair.

*Much better.*

She sat back in the window seat and stared out the window, there was nothing to see but fading white stripes of the parking spaces unoccupied in the mid-afternoon. April looked back into the apartment. She stretched across the chair for her laptop to check her email.

She scrolled through dating service proposals, porn invitations, and a debt consolidation offers. Junk, junk, junk. Block, block, block. April looked at the remaining mail. A math question from Ursula, a reminder from her dentist about a cleaning, and a notice from her Internet betting site.

She opened the betting mail. She had won a bet. Her new balance was eight hundred dollars. April did not remember placing a bet. She recalled the discussion with Eddie about the bet; she remembered him pushing her pretty hard to "bet the wad." But April did not remember wagering her last four hundred dollars on the game. She went to the web site to confirm the balance. She logged in and clicked on the Available Funds tab. Yesterday, it read four hundred dollars; today it showed eight hundred.

"Eddie did this."

She sat the empty bottle on the table.

"At some point, when we were at my site, he must have placed this bet. Or maybe he did it after we got to the hotel room."

"Son-of-a bitch! Who in the hell does he think he is? It's my goddamn money and my fucking life."

April stood and went to the refrigerator for another beer. The light beamed on the empty shelves.

"Shit," she said and slammed the door close.

"I'm keeping that money and if he thinks I owe him something, he's in for a big disappointment."

Once again, April was confused and angry. She grabbed her sketchpad and left the apartment. Somehow, she had to get back on track. Her angry strides ended eight minutes later. She sat on the ground opposite Captain Bluebeard's Bar and began to sketch.

Architecture is reason, beauty and control. April craved the trinity today. She sought asylum from the compromises of human interaction. Bluebeard's Bar was not as it had always been. It is rare that an architect creates a design that goes unchanged. An ordinance, a tree, someone with too much money, someone with too little, or someone with a smaller dream can chip away at the original design.

She turned to a clean page and began to redesign Bluebeards. She concentrated on functionality first and then penciled in design preferences. How interesting it would be to discuss this re-design with the original architect.

Control is temporary. Architects live with compromise or their sketches remain dreams. April was sketching but she was also reviewing her beliefs. She paused to look at all the buildings on the block. Each had changed to some degree. Change is inevitable.

She continued to sketch and think about the difference between bullheadedness and idealistic stands and compromise. April was uncertain she could survive the reality of business with the control issues she carried.

*Hell, I don't know if I can survive in any reality.*

She finished the sketch, admired it for a moment, then, tore it out and crumpled it. She left Bluebeard's unchanged. She wished she could do the same with her personal life. April's sketchpad was full; to date none of her dreams had become reality. "Your hardheadedness," as her mother described it, "is going to lead to a lot more misery than is necessary, April. Right can not only stand alone, it can stand lonely in a crowd."

She knew her intolerance was a starved tiger but she was unsure how to tame it or if she wanted it tamed.

April's stomach growled; it was loud enough to startle her. She closed her book, tucked it under her arm and crossed the street for a

285

sandwich and beer. April would feed the growl in her stomach and work on the tiger later.

# 74

Powers tucked the crisp starched shirt into his pants and smartly aligned his buckle and button line. He was satisfied his appearance was uniform. He stepped out into the hallway; the garishly colored carpet was an instant reminder that he was in Las Vegas. He still found it hard to believe. The elevator opened and Powers rode to the casino floor. Today the ringing bells, metallic clink of coins, and cheers of "Wheel Of Fortune!" were in unison. Like a parent grows selective to the relentless babble of inquisitive children, Powers was becoming immune to the call of the casino floor. He strode past hundreds of machines without noticing them or the faithful gamblers.

Powers stepped into the restaurant; the hostess guided him to a table in the courtyard. He ordered coffee and Eggs Benedict. Breakfast at eleven was so far removed from his routine; he again found it hard to believe the changes in his lifestyle. A three-day weekend had become a life-changing trip.

Today marked his tenth day in Las Vegas. Today would be his last day in the Paris Hotel. Powers was moving into a condominium. The banker did not even blink as Powers counted out the two hundred thousand dollars in cash. He had come to Las Vegas in search of a tax expert to handle the finances of a gambler. He found Guy Beck and a new home.

Powers would be flying to Charleston in a few days. He would ship the things he truly wanted and leave the house mostly furnished. Powers had devised an elaborate plan to create a special scholarship that included his house as living quarters. It would not be difficult to find students who want to live dirt cheap in a restored home two miles from the campus. He would give the details to Guy when he returned. Guy was certain he could work it as a tax advantage for Powers.

The Mexican man who had greeted Powers with "Bon Jour" brought his eggs.

"Will there be anything else, sir?" He asked.

"Yes. I would like a Bloody Mary, please."

"Right away, sir."

He wondered why the waiter used 'Bonjour' for the greeting but did not follow through with "Monsieur" rather than "Sir."

He shrugged off the inconsistency and cut into his eggs and tasted his first bite. The food was delicious. He savored his meal as he watched the people stroll past. It was Sunday although it is difficult to distinguish one day from another in Las Vegas. No calendars, no clocks, and no daylight. It was Sunday in reality world but in Las Vegas it was Lucky Day; everyday is Lucky Day.

"Here you are, sir," the waiter sat the vegetable laden drink on the table.

"Thank you."

Powers sipped the spicy concoction and continued to analyze the parade of dreamers. He imagined little cartoon bubbles above their heads.

"Stand aside losers; this is my lucky day," was assigned to the man dressed by Hilfiger.

"My luck has to be better today," was slapped over the head of the sweatshirt reading "Virginia Is For Lovers."

To the woman with the perfect blue-haired perm he attached, "I've waited a lifetime for my lucky day."

Powers looked up from a bite of food and saw a man in shower-shoes, uncombed hair, unshaven, and barely awake. He looked perfect for, "Okay, you bastard, give me my money back."

Powers looked for his waiter; the attentive man came to the table immediately.

"I'll have another Bloody Mary, please."

The waiter nodded his head with a slight bow and hurried away. Powers continued to eat his breakfast and watch the ants scurrying to feed the queen. This was the mother lode for analysts who wanted to specialize in gambling. When is it addictive; when is it abusive? Powers could throw his celery stalk out onto the casino floor and no matter where it came to rest; it would be lying next to a Doctorial dissertation.

"Here you are, sir," the waiter said.

"Thank you."

Every person walking the floor knows the only thing separating winners and losers is good luck. Powers watched them wander the casino floor as if they possessed an internal divining rod that would lead them to the lucky machine that will spit out fortunes. Like the prospectors, who came a century before them, most will not strike it rich. Most will put the last quarter in a machine, watch it spin, and go home with the empty cup as a souvenir. Most will spin a tale about how close they were to a fortune. Most of these prospectors believe they win by skill and lose by luck. Rarely is reality unmarred by distortion in Vegas.

Powers finished his breakfast and savored the last few swallows of his Bloody Mary. He walked outside and saw the taxis unloading a new wave of prospectors. Powers paused to look at them one by one.

He realized how fortunate he was to have Eddie as a meal ticket but the casinos of Vegas had a pretty sweet deal as well. He ambled down the Strip thinking, I'm no more unethical than the casino executives. After all, Powers was only manipulating the mind of one individual not millions.

# 75

Harmon stuck his finger between his neck and shirt collar. He slid it back to front several times. It did not help; it was still tight. He tried two fingers. Relief would be denied until the tie was off and the collar unbuttoned. He wore it at Helen's request but he was uncomfortable and he wanted her to know it. Helen either ignored his theatrics or was too focused on the ceremony to notice Harmon's protest.

Harmon knew it was best that she did not see his antics. He knew exactly what her words would be.

"Stop acting like a little baby."

Harmon removed his finger with a slight sigh. He tried to forget about it. A discussion about tight collars at a wedding was sure to be trouble. Helen would start quoting Freud and Nietzsche. Harmon decided the discomfort was less painful than a preachy psycho-lashing from Helen.

He and Helen sat in the fourth row. They watched as the couple exchange vows. The bride was Helen's best friend from work. The happy couple kissed and everyone applauded. The soprano tried to sing over the shuffling feet and whispering voices. The bride and groom walked past with smiles as wide as the aisle.

"There goes a lucky man," Helen said to Harmon. "She's too good for him."

"None of us are good enough," Harmon mumbled back.

"You don't have to mumble, Harm. The truth shouldn't shame you," she said with a smile.

They walked out of the church and stood on the walkway. Helen spoke to a few people. Harmon stood among the strangers, smiling occasionally, and trying to remember the names of people he had met. For a bar owner, Harmon Evans had an unusual trait; he was not happy among crowds. Most of his time was spent catering to crowds of strangers; solitude was his favorite free-time activity.

Couple by couple and family-by-family people began to drive away. Everyone was heading for the reception. Harmon opened the car door for Helen; she buckled the old lap style seat belt as he walked around. He started the car and pulled in behind a red minivan. They followed the minivan along the tree-lined street for a few blocks.

"Harmon would you pull over for a moment," Helen asked.

"What's the matter? Did you forget something?" He asked.

"No. I just need a minute."

Harmon pulled the car over to the curb and pushed the column lever up to the park position. Helen unbuckled the seat belt and slid across the roll-and-pleated bench seat; she kissed him. She reached up to his neck and began to untie the tie, tossed it in the back seat, and unbuttoned the top two buttons. She ran her hand across his chest.

"Is that better, baby?" Helen asked.

"A little too good, actually. Are you sure we have to go to this reception?"

"Yes, but I find a man with patience to be very irresistible," she said.

She kissed him again and slid back across the seat. Harmon watched as she pulled her skirt back down toward her knees.

"Patience. Okay, I've got a little patience left in the tank. But remember you've asked me to wear a tie and have patience, in the same day," Harmon said as he pulled the car back into the traffic.

"My gratitude will not disappoint," she said.

Her normal gratitude amazed Harmon; special gratitude might be more than he could handle. He loved Helen deeply. He could not imagine facing the day-to-day ritual of life without her. Helen was a petite woman with short hair and large eyes that looked like pools of melted dark chocolate. She was independent and opinionated; yet thoughtful and passionate.

Helen Gerald did not believe in a free ride. She grew up among the have-nots but hard work gave her a modest lifestyle. She was Shift Manager on an assembly line. For twenty-two years, she has been the most dependable employee the owners could ever desire. Garrity Services had lost scores of employees because Helen refused to allow workers to cheat the system. Eight hours meant eight hours.

"Mr. Garrity pays you to work. If you are going to take his money, then do the work. He does not force you to work here. If you don't want to work, every minute for eight hours, do yourself a favor, go work somewhere else. I will not permit you to do less than the rest of this crew," she would preach.

Older workers could recite the sermon verbatim. She expected more from everyone.

Harmon looked across the seat at Helen.

"Watch where you're driving, Harmon," she instructed.

Harmon refocused his eyes on the road. Helen had never married. Harmon thought about asking her. He had thought about it every day for the last four years. He feared she might say no and a small part of him feared she would say yes.

He also found himself wondering why she did not ask him. Helen was a very straightforward woman. The first time they ever went on a date, she asked him. The first time they had sex was upon her request not his. If she really wanted to marry any man, she would not hesitate to ask. He did not think about marriage often because it always ended the same way. Harmon would worry that asking her to marry him might destroy their relationship. That he would not want to do.

He pulled into the parking lot and drove to the front door, where Helen's sister, Paula stood waiting. Helen exited and Harmon drove away to park the car.

"Such a gentleman you've got, Helen. Drops you at the front door," Paula said.

"He's just thinking about his car. He wants everyone to see it and then he wants to park it away from all the other vehicles. He doesn't want anyone to ding his doors. Where he's going to park, he knows I would be complaining about the walk. That's why he drops me off," Helen said.

"It's a beautiful car. Tom whines every time he sees it."

Paula deepened her voice to mock her co-worker.

"A 1964 Galaxy 500 with a 390. Damn, that's a fine car."

Helen smiled and said, "It's a guy thing. Back when they were teenagers, girls weren't putting out as easily as they do today, so they turned to cars."

"Helen, that's a pretty broad statement to make about girls today," Paula said.

"Hey, I was trying to be funny not philosophical. Lighten up."

Harmon walked up with Tom.

"Man, that's a sweet Galaxy 500, Harm. Wish I had one," Tom said.

"Yeah. I wouldn't trade her for anything," Harmon said.

"Really? Not for anything?" Helen asked as she laced her arm around his.

Harmon did not respond to the comment but his mind went on high alert.

*What did she mean? She would never make me choose between my car and her, would she? Damn it.*

# 76

Dexter saw April walk into the bar. She walked directly to a table on the far wall. Lauren took April's order; she dropped the food order in the kitchen and requested a beer. Dexter drew the mug and watched Lauren deliver it. Dexter watched as April's first sip drained the mug half empty. He broke his gaze and filled a few orders from patrons sitting at the bar. He watched as Lauren delivered the food to April's table. Two bites into the sandwich, April finished the beer and Lauren was back at the bar for a second mug. Dexter drew the tap, gave it to her, and stared in April's direction.

"Dude, I'll watch her walk; you get me the beer I asked for. Deal?" Said a guy holding an empty mug.

Dexter filled his mug and took his money without responding to his comment. Normally Dexter would be guilty of watching Lauren walk, however this time he was wishing he could go talk to April. He wanted to discuss Eddie and he still held out hope that April would discover a soft spot in her heart for him, if there were any soft spots.

He checked the clock. It was eight-thirty. With Harmon gone for the evening, Dexter was committed to work until closing. Even if she came to the bar, he would not feel comfortable discussing Eddie with so many listeners nearby.

Dexter continued to service the patrons at the bar and fill the orders for the servers but he kept a watchful eye on April. She finished her sandwich and started on her third beer. She did not appear to be in a hurry. She seemed content to sip on her beer and work in her sketchpad. Shortly after ten o'clock, James Breman settled in at the bar with his friend Carla. James was also a bartender at Bluebeards.

"Hey Dex, how about two Tanqueray martinis?" James asked.

"Hey James. Hi Carla. How's it going?" Dexter said.

Carla gave him a so-so hand wave and a smile. Dexter leaned over to speak to James.

"Can I talk to you for a moment?" Dexter nodded toward the end of the bar.

"Sure," James said.

They walked to the server's station.

"What's up?" James asked.

"James, you know Harm will dock my check if I serve you Call Drinks for free."

"So, don't tell him," James told him.

"He has a way of finding things out and I don't want him on me."

"Dex, don't be such a suck-up. When I'm on duty, he lets me drink whatever I want, so what's the difference?" James said.

"The difference is you aren't on duty and you want me to make and comp martinis all night," Dexter said. "Look, I don't mind if you want to be BMOC for Carla but I'm not gonna' serve you Top Shelf Gin for free. I didn't want to tell you in front of her."

"That's fucking great Dex. Are you trying to tell me, that you never try to impress chicks with free stuff here at the bar?" James said.

"I never said I didn't. I have comp'd a drink or two but I never came in on your shift and expected you to take the fall for it," Dexter said.

Dexter glanced across the room and saw that April was almost finished with her beer. He had no way of knowing if she would order a fourth or leave.

"I've got a proposition for you, James," Dexter offered.

"What?" James asked with no intent of hiding his anger.

"Cover the rest of my shift for me?"

"No," he said immediately.

"You could save face," Dexter said. "You could tell Carla you are doing me a huge favor, plus then you could serve anything you like."

"You've got over three hours to go, Dex," he complained.

"And if your charm can keep Carla here for three hours, the alcohol will make you look better," Dexter said with a smile.

"Screw you Dex."

"Come on James. This is a no-brainer; you save face and save money," Dexter said.

"Fine. Why do you want off so bad?" He asked.

"I'll be honest with you; I'm gonna' try to impress a chick."

Dexter grabbed two mugs, filled them with tap beer, and checked to see that April was still at the table. She was.

295

"Really, which one?" James said as he looked around the room.

"The one on the wall wearing the baseball cap," Dexter said as he started off with the beers.

"Those will be the last free drinks you get tonight," James said as he hoisted the bottle of Tanqueray from the top shelf and walked toward Carla.

Dexter stood beside the table. April was peering intently into her sketchbook.

"Do you have room for another beer?" Dexter asked.

"How much will it cost me?" She said without looking up.

"It's free," he said as he offered it to her, continuing to stand and waiting for an invitation to sit.

"It's free but I do have to invite you to sit and talk."

"Correct."

"I've already turned down two drinks at the same price," April responded.

"Yes, but I've already been briefed. You won't have to set me straight. I know you aren't interested in a relationship," Dexter said subduing his regret.

"That's an excellent point and I think I have room for one more beer," April said and took the beer from Dexter and motioned him to sit down.

"So, what did you do today?" Dexter said. It was a lame start but he had to start somewhere. He could not open with, 'Do you think Eddie could be a pervert?'

"I slept late and did a lot of sketching," April responded and added. "Have you been here all day?"

"No. I went to a symposium at ECU today," Dexter answered.

"Was it interesting?" She asked while continuing to draw in her sketchbook. She was on politeness autopilot.

"It could have been but I sort of skipped the second half of it," Dexter answered.

"You went all the way to ECU then ditched the seminar. I didn't know Greenville was that fascinating," she replied.

"I did see something unusual," Dexter said.

"Yeah? What?" She said looking up from her pad and downing some beer.

He was nervous and unsure he wanted to go down this path with April. There was no doubt his motives would not hold up to scrutiny. April was not attracted to Dexter so there was nothing to gain by destroying Eddie Dreyer. However, April might be able to shed some light on where Eddie was today. He decided to tell his tale.

"I saw a chick take off her clothes and give a basketball player a blowjob," Dexter said and lifted his beer to his lips and swallowed several times.

"What?" April was staring intently at Dexter with her eyebrows raised high.

"Yup. That's what I saw and I also saw someone watching the deed being done," Dexter added.

"You mean some voyeur other than you?"

"Yeah, but I discovered them accidentally. This guy knew it was going to happen and planned to watch," Dexter said.

"How do you know that?" April asked.

"Because, after the chick left, this guy threw a paper airplane onto the court. It had a message on it. The basketball player read it and started hollering in the dark. He turned on lights but the watcher was gone. I ran away also. He didn't find me watching either," Dexter explained.

"Dexter, is this the truth?" April searched his eyes.

"Yes ma'am," he said crossing his heart.

"Damn. Now there's a story for the grandkids. Do you know the player?" April quizzed.

"No, but I think I know the voyeur."

He drank more beer hoping it would slow his racing heartbeat.

"Really, who?" She asked. "Was it Dale?"

"No. It was not Dale," he said with a grin as he imagined Dale's reaction to April thinking he would be voyeur type.

"Well, who then?" She asked.

"I'm not sure I should tell you because I'm not certain I'm right," Dexter was doing his best to leave the disbelief door wide open.

"Why not? Do I know him?"

"I saw a tall guy go into the gymnasium with this really hot chick but I was a good fifty yards away. It would be unfair of me to make this kind of accusation without concrete proof," Dexter said.

"Whatever. Just tell me who you think it was," April said.

"I think I better wait," Dexter said again.

"Why did you bother to tell me this shit if you weren't going to tell me all of it? I'm not trustworthy enough for you?" She asked.

Dexter saw the mood swing. Clouds were gathering.

"Let me guess. You thought it might keep us talking. You thought this might get you another little rendezvous. So, really, you're just scheming like every other prowler in this bar," April said.

She was about to launch another salvo but Dexter did not want to hear anymore.

He blurted out, "It was Eddie Dreyer."

"What? Are you insane?" She said calmly and softly as she glanced around the room.

"I saw Eddie Dreyer walk into that gym," Dexter repeated.

"Eddie Dreyer is some kind of pervert voyeur? Dexter, you don't want Eddie and me to hook up. I understand that. Do you think creating this story will keep us apart?" April asked but she seemed to be less angry, maybe even concerned for Dexter's feelings.

"I'm not making this up, April. I know what I saw. If I knew where Eddie was, I would confront him. And I promise if he tells me he was not in Greenville today, I will believe him. I need to know, one way or the other," Dexter said.

Dexter watched, as April seemed lost in thought. Suddenly, she stood with her sketchpad in hand. She finished the last swallow of beer.

"Dexter, I have to go," she said.

"April, don't be mad at me. I needed to tell someone. I am not getting any joy from this. I did not tell you to gain an advantage. I__" Dexter did not finish because he did not know what to say.

"I am not mad at you but I have to go. Thanks for the beer. I'll talk to you later."

April walked away.

Dexter took his time and finished his beer.

*I shouldn't have told her.*

He stood and walked slowly toward the door.

As he passed the bar, he heard James yell, "Hey Dex, I'm glad to see the switch worked out so well."

He was laughing and toasting with Carla.

*Damn, I wish Harm would drop by and catch that bastard giving away the profits. It wouldn't make things right but I could use a good laugh right now.*

Dexter walked into the night air.

# 77

April walked quickly toward home. She cried most of the way. Each time she wiped tears away with the sleeve of her shirt, a new pool appeared. Dexter was telling his farfetched tale when Eddie's note flashed back in her memory. It said he would be in Greenville. Dexter could not have known that information when he sighted someone who looked like Eddie going into a gymnasium. It was too coincidental for a skeptic like April.

She was prepared to confront Eddie about making bets with her money. She was ready to discuss why he would take her to a hotel. She was eager to explain why leaving money for a taxi is insulting. And she might be ready to discuss how they could have been in a hotel, uninhibited by alcohol, and not have sex. But she was not ready to confront Eddie about voyeurism. Can it be possible that Eddie Dreyer is a peeking tom pervert?

April did not want to believe it. Eddie might have lied about his whereabouts because he did not want to be found. That was one of only two hopes she could hold. The other possibility was that he was in Greenville but was not Dexter's mysterious voyeur. But dread of Dexter's version was much stronger than the thin hopes fading to the back of her mind.

Eddie Dreyer led a mysterious life. Could it be that normal sexual relations do not excite Eddie? April's pace quickened; she was oblivious to the people and scenery she passed. She groped for explanations for his sexual indifference and the trip to Greenville. Maybe Eddie can only get off by watching other people? April concluded Eddie had something to hide; kinky sexual problems might be it.

She opened the door to her apartment, went in, and locked the door behind her. April went to her window seat and sobbed some more. Her thoughts turned to self blame. She felt foolish for thinking she was so selective and yet had selected so poorly. Reality began to pile on the pressure. She wanted to confide. She wanted to trust. She was tired of hearing her own propaganda. April wanted to hear a new reality. More than she could ever remember, April needed a friend.

# 78

Harmon pulled the car up to the front and hopped out. He hurried to the passenger side to open the door for Helen. As independent as she was, she waited for him to do it. They buckled up and drove away.

"Thank you Harmon. I know social affairs are not your favorite outings and I appreciate you going," she said as she reached over to touch his arm.

"Anything for you, honey but you did mention something about showing your gratitude?" Harmon said knowing his reminder sounded childlike.

"Would you prefer that I attack you here in the car or wait until we get back to my place, so that I can exhibit a little creativity?" Helen said in a breathy whisper.

"I'll take door number two," Harmon answered without hesitation.

The radio was broadcasting a basketball game. Helen turned the dial on the radio searching for music. News, talk shows, and ball games crackled through the dashboard speaker. Harmon hoped he was not in for another lecture.

"How can you truly enjoy the beauty of riding in this car without music? Have a new system put in."

He had heard the lecture a dozen times.

Tonight she searched in silence.

Harmon did not want to alter the original design of the car.

*I want it to stay original. The AM Radio is perfectly fine.*

She could nag but she would not win this one.

Helen finally stopped turning the dial; the speaker was broadcasting tunes from the fifties and sixties. It seemed to please her and it suited the automobile. Fifteen minutes later, Harmon pulled into the driveway of Helen's small house. He turned the key; the engine and Elvis went silent. "Return To Sender" continued to sing in Harmon's head. They went inside.

"Harmon, pour us a couple of whiskys, would you? I'll be right out," Helen said as she went into the bedroom.

Harmon poured two glasses and took a seat on the sofa. He set the glasses on the coffee table, picked up the newspaper, crossed his legs, and waited on Helen to return. He only turned two pages before she returned and sat beside him. He reached for the glasses and offered one to Helen. They clinked the glasses together.

"Here's to young love," she said.

"Here's to their wedding bliss," Harmon added.

"I meant our love," Helen said as she moved the whisky to her lips.

"That's even better; ditto," he said.

"Harmon, why haven't you asked me to marry you?" Helen asked as she pulled the glass from her lips.

Harmon was taking his second sip of the whisky. He was expecting a little conversation about the wedding, a little seductive banter, and then some very satisfying sex. He was not expecting this question. He had no idea how to respond. He watched as she drank. Harmon knew Helen. She would sit there silent as the Sphinx until he answered. Helen did not bail people out, once she had put them on the spot.

"Why haven't you asked me?" He countered.

"Once you have answered my question, I will answer yours."

"Because we have a great relationship and if you said "No", that relationship might be damaged, changed, or maybe even ruined."

Harmon chased the response with a large swallow.

"I haven't asked you because I knew you couldn't turn me down. I needed you to ask me, so that I could be sure you really wanted to share your life with me," Helen said.

"So, are you proposing?" Harmon asked.

"No! I just told you, I need you to ask."

"Are you telling me you would say yes, if I asked?"

He finished his drink and cradled the empty glass with both hands.

"No. I'm just curious about how you see the future," she responded.

"Well, your curiosity has created the awkward moment I feared. Do you want to get married?" Harmon asked.

"Are you proposing?"

Harmon stared into her eyes. He could not decide how to respond. He felt as if he were being tested. He did not want this to be

302

how she remembered his proposal.

"No ma'am," he said. "I'm just curious about whether you intend to be married. You have lived without it for forty years."

Harmon hoped she would reveal a missing piece of information.

"It's always been a day-to-day decision. I have not premeditatively chosen to be un-wed. It has just worked out that way. Are you looking for general beliefs?"

Again, Harmon was not sure how to respond. He shrugged a little; she continued.

"What's not to like about marriage? It's a partner who enjoys spending time with you but can leave enough space for individual freedom. And I think a spouse and a friend are two different things. Too often a friend will candy-coat the truth; a spouse can't do that. Spouses are too important to each other. A spouse has to be a crutch, a hard-ass, and a lover. Would I rather have a spouse than a friend? Any day," Helen said answering her own question.

She finished her whisky and sat the glass on the table.

"Okay, it is apparent to me that you have thought about true love more than I have," Harmon said trying to hide his embarrassment from her.

"Really? Or is it that you've never bothered to write down your thoughts?" Helen said as she opened a drawer under the coffee table.

She pulled out small journal. She handed it to him. Harmon opened the book. Page one was filled with sentences. Many were crossed out. Page two was the same. He kept turning page after page. Half way through the journal, Harmon realized, she had been trying to define marriage for a long time.

"Wow. I guess you are still looking for the right words," he said.

"The words are in there. I can pull the right ones together at the right time," Helen said. "I bet that if you were sitting home nights, rather than standing behind a bar, nursing drunks or listening to people who have given up on love, you might have written something very similar."

Helen moved much closer to Harmon.

Harmon said, "I wouldn't bet on it. I'm not that good with words."

"I'd bet on you Harmon but you don't have to start writing."

She turned his head and kissed him.

"Maybe you can come up with another way to express yourself."

"Oh, it's gratitude time?" Harmon said.

"Oh yeah. I never leave a debt unpaid," Helen said as she stood and reached for his hand. Harmon took her hand and followed her to the bedroom but he would have followed her anywhere.

# 79

Dexter straightened his shoulders and knocked. His palm felt sweaty; he wiped it on his pant leg. The door partially opened and neither Dexter nor April spoke. They stared at each other, as though they were communicating telepathically but in different languages. Uncertainty diminished and April opened the door completely and stepped aside. It seemed to be an invitation. Dexter was taking nothing for granted.

"I know it's late but I was hoping we could talk about some things," Dexter said.

"Yeah, me too. Come on in," April said.

April walked over to the window. She threw one pillow to the right side and kept the other. She sat with her arms wrapped around her knees.

"Have a seat," she said.

April hid behind her tucked knees and peered over the top like an archer looking down from a castle wall. Dexter had never studied body language but this looked defensive. He moved the pillow against the window and leaned back. He was not comfortable; he tried several positions.

"Pull up a chair, Dexter. You don't have to sit in the window."

"Thanks."

He carried the chair from the table near April, turned it around backwards, and straddled it. His barrier was in place and the chair-back would provide a place to occupy his nervous and sweaty hands. They sat like generals on opposite sides of the battlefield; the knee castle and chair-back shield both weighing their options. Dexter was first to test the middle ground.

"Okay. First, I think of you as a friend. I want you to think of me as a friend. I did not intend to upset you. Well, maybe part of me would like to knock Eddie down a notch or two but mainly I wanted to talk to someone about what I saw. You were my best option."

"Yeah, I realize that, Dexter.

"Then why did you bolt?" He asked.

April turned to look out the window. It was dark, it was late, and there was no movement. April's head turned back toward Dexter; she rested her chin on her knee.

"Dexter, I'm flattered you think of me as a friend and I could use a friend. I don't have anyone I trust. It's my fault. I'm a loner. I have never felt it necessary to explain why I do what I do or say what I say."

"I'm not sure what that means. Does it mean a friend has to agree with everything you say or do?" Dexter asked.

"No, of course not. I'm trying to say that I am perfectly capable of making decisions. I don't want people walking around thinking that I need help to have a happy life," she added.

"So, you think someone is keeping score? You think there is a Who's Who of people who made it own their own?" Dexter asked but remained calm despite his disapproval of her ego-centered responses.

"Maybe," she said.

Dexter wondered if she had thought this through.

"Well, that's messed up. You don't want a friend; you want a fan club," Dexter said.

"I don't need worship!" April's temper was apparent but she paused and added, "But I can live without condemnation. I'm not always wrong," she said in a soft voice.

"No one is always wrong and no one is always right. You'd agree with that, wouldn't you?" Dexter asked.

"Yes," she said and tucked her chin back between her knees.

"Here's what I think," Dexter had decided to take his shot. "You're scared and most of what you say is meant to keep people at a distance. It will not work on me. I think there is room for us. I think we can talk, laugh, yell, agree, and disagree. I call that a friendship. How about it; wanna' be friends?" Dexter smiled and hoped the chair-back would shield him from a violent rejection.

"Yes, we can be friends; but remember, I am what I am. I don't want to tiptoe around you. I want to be me." Her tone was purposeful and uncompromising.

"Okay, so you get a nice, sensitive, well mannered listener and I get a scary-smart, opinionated, intolerant talker. Yeah, sounds perfect; it's a deal," Dexter said as he offered his hand to consummate the arrangement.

She reached out and shook his hand, then withdrew to the protection of her kneed castle. Dexter wanted to know the truth about

Eddie; he decided to ask his toughest question first.

"What is the deal with you and Eddie?"

April turned toward the window.

"Couldn't we start with something a little easier?" April answered.

"No. You said you had some talking to do. So, talk. If homeboy's in your pants, I need to know," Dexter said.

"Nobody is in anybody's pants. Geez, Dex. There is nothing going on," April answered.

Dexter felt a smile coming from the answer but he restrained it and continued to probe the subject.

"But you like him. I can tell."

"I am intrigued by him. He's so aloof and he has killer confidence. I'm attracted to that," April said. "But, to tell you the truth, I can't tell if he wants to be with me or not."

"If he doesn't, why does he send you email, hook up with you at Bluebeards, and spend so much time talking to you about gambling and stuff?" Dexter asked.

"I have no idea. Maybe it's because he's really messed up, after all, you think he's a Peeping Tom," she said.

"I said it looked like him. I hope it wasn't," Dexter said.

"It was. I'm sure of it," April said with a slight whimper.

"How can you be sure? You weren't there," Dexter countered.

"Eddie told me he would be in Greenville on that day. That has to be more than coincidence, don't you think?" April answered.

"Holy shit. He told you he was in Greenville?" Dexter stood up and took a seat next to April on the window bench.

"When we left Bluebeard's, we were both pretty tanked. He took us to his hotel. When I woke up the next day, he was gone. He left a note saying he would be in Greenville to do some basketball research," April explained. "Some research."

Dexter said, "As long as I couldn't prove Eddie was in Greenville, I held out hope that I was mistaken but now, man, I don't know what to think."

"I know what to think and what to do. I'm going to find his ass and call him a pervert to his face. The presumptuous bastard is going to hear a few other opinions as well. That night, when we were getting plastered, he bet my money on a game, without telling me. I had four hundred dollars in my account; he bet it all." April was loud.

"But you won" Dexter said.

"Yes but that's not the point. I don't___,"

307

"I know; you don't need him making your decisions for you," Dexter interrupted.

"Exactly."

Dexter slapped her on the bent knee and stood up again.

"Friend, I have to get some sleep. If I hurry home, I can snore for four hours. I have to work tomorrow but I finish at four. Can you come by?" Dexter said.

"Friend. Some friend. You lightweight. I have a million more things to say. This is your idea of staying power?" April asked.

"Yup. Get used to it. This will teach you to wait until the last minute to pick a friend. You should have known all the good ones would have been picked by now. I'll listen again in twelve hours," Dexter said and slowly moved toward the door.

April got up and followed him over. Dexter opened the door and stepped outside.

"Thanks for caring, Dex, really," April said.

"No problem. If I hadn't taken this shot, I would have been stuck with Dale as my only friend," he said.

"Liar. You have lots of friends," she responded.

"Not like you," Dexter said.

He smiled at her and walked away. Dexter started the engine and drove toward his apartment. He felt happy with himself, sleepy but happy.

# 80

April awoke feeling rested. It was nearly eleven o'clock. Dexter's visit had a comforting effect on her mood. She visited Ursula to catch up on a couple of her classes that she blew off. The load wasn't too heavy. She knew she could get caught up. April settled into her window seat and began to read a textbook. She was enjoying the ease of the day.

The familiar ding of incoming email interrupted the silence. She pulled the laptop closer. The calm of the day evaporated. It was email from Eddie.

"Hey, since you never agreed to have dinner with me, I have decided to travel to Orangeburg to check out the Bulldogs. But I will come back to Charleston in a couple of days and I would still like to have dinner with you. Yes or No?"

"Also, here's a tip for you, use it if you want. The Bruins will not cover the six points. Pendleton will not play the whole game. He's sick. Take the Cowboys and the points. Gotta' fly, Eddie."

"Pendleton isn't the only sick one; you pervert," she said to the screen.

April phoned Bluebeard's.

"Good afternoon, Captain Bluebeards," said the voice.

"Could I speak with Dexter Dalton please?"

"This is Dex. Who is this?"

"It's April. You don't recognize a friend's voice?"

"It's kinda' loud in here."

"So, I hear. What's all that clanging?"

"Harmon is ringing the Jerk Chest bell," Dexter explained.

"The what?" She asked.

"I'll explain later. What do you need?" He asked.

"Are you still planning on come over after work?" April said a little too loudly trying to be heard over the Bar noise.

"Sure; if you want me to? I can be there by four fifteen," Dexter replied.

"Great; see you later," she said and hung up the phone.

She walked to the kitchen for a glass of water. As she passed the laptop, Eddie's gambling was flashing in her mind like a neon sign on a chocolate shop. "You want some you know you do" it tempted.

She returned to her textbook. She hoped to get the wager out of her mind; it did not work.

*There is no future with him but why should I pass up the opportunity to earn eight hundred dollars?*

April grabbed the laptop and logged onto her betting service. The line was still six points but game time was five o'clock. She had one hour to decide.

"This is exactly the kind of thing I should talk over with a friend," she said aloud.

She closed the textbook and tossed it onto the chair. April waited for Dexter. She left the web site on screen and stared out the window to the parking lot waiting for Dexter's arrival. She saw him pull into the parking lot. He looked up and waved; she waved back. She met him with an open door and a warm smile.

"Thanks for coming. Would you like some water? I'm out of beer," she said.

"No, I'm good."

April walked to the table, pulled the two chairs close together, and sat in one of them. Dexter took the other.

"Okay, let's test this friendship thing. I have a decision to make and it must be made in the next forty minutes," April explained.

"Cool. What's the dilemma?" He asked.

"To gamble or not to gamble."

"Well, the other night you swore off gambling. Because, as I recall, you decided that Gambling often results in a loss of money," Dexter said. "Money you cannot afford to lose."

"But what if I had a tip from Eddie?" She said.

"Damn, that's like money in the bank."

"That's what I thought. What do you think? Should I?" She asked.

"I think we have two dilemmas. Maybe I want in."

"Great. I thought you were going to be the voice of reason," April said with a sincerity that left her feeling vulnerable.

"I am the voice of reason. There's a reasonably good chance we can make money. Only an unreasonable person would pass that up." Dexter paused and added, "Unless, you have reached some decision about your feelings for Eddie and this has become a principle thing."

"Eddie and I aren't going to happen. We are both too independent and uncompromising, plus we do not have anything in common."

April continued, "And I believe he's on a road to destruction. No one can be so wrapped up in gambling and still lead a normal life. I'm not a psychologist but he's a mental case."

"I was only gone for twelve hours. How did you get to here? Maybe you don't need a friend, after all. It sounds like you have this decision under control. But let me ask you something. Are you going to tell Eddie you aren't interested or just avoid him?" Dexter asked.

"Run away? I don't think so. I'm not going to respond to his emails. If he calls or I bump into him I will tell him, I'm not interested," April said.

"Then, my advice, don't use his tip. He might accuse you of being two-faced. You don't want to hear him say that," Dexter said and gave her light pat on the back.

"Yeah, that's what I thought. I better log off before the urge gets too strong," April said as she lifted the laptop from the bench seat.

"You know I'm not attracted to Eddie; and I gamble all the time. I often wager based on a tip," Dexter mumbled meekly.

"You turd! You want me to tell you the tip, so you can use it?" April said.

"Well, you are acting on principle; so should I." Dexter defended his request.

"On principle?" April said through a devilish laugh. "Okay. Eddie says the Bruins will not cover the six points against the Cowboys."

"May I use your laptop for a moment?" Dexter held out his hand as he asked.

"Why not? You're using me; you might as well use my equipment," she told him. "Slide over here."

Dexter clicked the mouse a few times and waited for the Bruins page to load. He reviewed the record, statistics, and the home versus road records.

"The game starts in ten minutes Dexter. Are you telling me you would second guess Eddie Dreyer?" April asked astonished.

"Well, yeah. The Bruins should easily cover the six. They beat the Cowboys in Fort Worth by ten three weeks ago. It sure seems they would do the same on their own court," Dexter said and continued to look for individual match-ups.

"Eddie said Pendleton was sick and would not play," April added.

"He's the power forward; he gets a lot of rebounds. Let's look at his stats." Dexter said and clicked on Michael Pendleton. The stats popped on screen before the photo. Dexter intently studied the statistics until the picture loaded.

"Holy shit!" He yelled.

"What? What did you find?" April asked leaning closer to the laptop screen to see.

"That's the guy I saw getting the BJ at center court," Dexter bellowed.

"Are you sure Dexter? Are you positive?"

"Yeah. There's no doubt. I saw him clearly. That's the guy," Dexter said.

"So, on Saturday, he's getting his cock vacuumed and Sunday he's going to be too sick to play basketball. Did he look sick to you?" April asked.

"He looked healthy and fit," Dexter answered. "And uh, oh so happy."

"What guy wouldn't? Men are doomed by their dicks," April said, sat back, and crossed her arms across her chest.

"Why get mad at us? More importantly, why take it out on me? Shouldn't all that anger be directed at the chick that chose to go out there and do it?" Dexter asked.

"First it is not anger; it's pity. And second yes they are both pathetic," April said.

"Okay, I'm a brand new friend. This can't be the right time to discuss your sexual hang ups but let's get back to Eddie; he watched them do this?" Dexter reminded her.

"I don't have sexual hang ups," April fired back. "Great sex comes with trust and trust takes time. And fantasies are dreams. Not all dreams come true. And I don't know what to think about his involvement," April said.

"Whoever was watching, isn't a pervert; he's a blackmailer," Dexter said.

"What do you mean whoever? Eddie is blackmailing this kid," April snapped back.

"It's just too hard to believe. You didn't know Eddie the basketball player," Dexter defended Eddie.

"I don't have to. Was he talented? Was he assertive? Was he a risk taker? Would he do anything to win?" April asked in rapid fire succession.

She did not need his answer. "Of course he would. He's still doing all those things. But his goal is to win bets. He doesn't care about the money. He wants to do the impossible. He still wants to be the best. He's still controlling."

"I understand what you are saying but it's still hard to believe," Dexter replied.

"I bet this isn't the first time he manipulated a game," April said looking directly into Dexter's eyes and holding the glare.

"If you're right, and he has transferred his basketball drive to winning bets, there's no telling what he has done or will do. Eddie was a fearless player," Dexter said.

Dexter maneuvered the mouse, clicked a couple of times and arrived at his betting service. He typed in his user name and password.

"You are still going to bet on this game? Knowing it's rigged?" April's tone gave Dexter a chill.

"Yes, because I have nothing to do with what's going to happen," Dexter said without taking his eyes off the monitor. "And remember, it is still not a sure thing."

He typed in $650 and hit the submit button. He turned to face April.

"The Bruins could still cover the six and I will lose my entire balance. I'm still gambling," Dexter said.

"That's some interesting bullshit, excuse me, I mean rationalization. But if you can live with it, who am I to judge you," April said.

"That's the largest amount I have wagered in over a year and a half," Dexter said.

"Dexter, we have a more pressing matter to discuss than your courageous wager. What are we going to do about Eddie?"

"Do? What do you mean do?" Dexter said surprised.

"Eddie's blackmailing people. He's changing the outcomes of games," April said. "It's illegal."

"Well hell, gambling is illegal, I think," Dexter said.

April sat down and waited. She was not sure what she should do. She wanted to call the police. But she expected her friend to contribute some direction. Even if it was the misdirection of a college student guided by immaturity and male hormones.

Dexter said, "April, we have zero proof that Eddie has done anything wrong."

"You saw him. You can provide eyewitness testimony," said April.

"The eyewitness," Dexter made quotation marks with his hands, "was standing in the dark and the eyewitness never saw Eddie in the gym. The eyewitness does not know what was on the paper airplane. The eyewitness is not ready to get roasted by the authorities for what he thinks he saw. Or interrogated about my gambling habits. No ma'am; no thank you."

April could feel word upon word gathering in the back of her throat like a platoon preparing for attack. She choked them down. This should be a discussion, not a contest. But if she was willing to insult Dexter and make him feel like a coward, April was no better than Eddie Dreyer.

She took a moment to consider what Dexter said. His version of the gymnasium scene would be destroyed under cross-examination. Whether Dexter was driven to his conclusion by reason or fear did not matter; it was accurate.

"You may be right, Dexter but we can't ignore it, Can we?" April asked softly almost demanding agreement.

She reached over, grabbed his forearm, and gave it a slight squeeze.

Dexter replied, "We can't prove anything. Maybe we should tell him we know and warn him that we will inform the police, if he continues."

"I don't think that would stop him. He would just disappear from our lives and continue his blackmailing. We would never know," April said to him.

"Is it our responsibility to stop him?" Dexter asked.

April responded, "I don't know if we are obligated to do anything. But, to me, it feels wrong to do nothing."

"Then we have to confront him. If, after talking with him, we feel he is going to continue to break the law, we inform the police," Dexter said.

"Alright, I can live with that. We can talk to him on Tuesday. He's coming back from Orangeburg. I will email him. You want to meet him here?" April asked.

"No. Let's meet at Bluebeard's. He's still a large man capable of whipping my ass. He's less likely to do that in the bar crowded with people," Dexter said.

"Wuss," April quipped with a smile that she knew would disarm him.

"I can live with that. I'd rather be a walking wuss than a courageous and crippled hero," Dexter replied.

"Okay, well I'm a little behind on my studies. I'm going to try to catch up and crash early," April said.

Dexter said his goodbyes and left. April moved to the table and typed an email to Eddie. She asked him to meet her at Bluebeard's on Tuesday at seven. She sat in the window seat to study. Eddie was occupying space in her brain that should have been reserved for test material. She continued to pushed him aside as often as she could.

# 81

Powers placed the over-sized towel neatly on the back of the chair and sat down. He adjusted the chair to recline. He opened his book and began to read. The sun was hot but welcome. Every other day Powers came down to the pool at ten in the morning, sat in the sun for two hours and read books. The pool was for exclusive use of the condominium owners. He was getting quite tan and meeting people. Most were employed in the gaming industry and worked second and third shifts. Many lounged by the pool midday.

"You look ridiculous," Jim said.

"Look around Jim; you are the only one sitting under an umbrella. You're pasty white. Get out here and get some color," Powers said.

"Whisper that from your deathbed. Academicians have surrounded you all your life. Someone somewhere must have mentioned the harmful effects of the sun," Jim told him.

"Have you ever seen all the old rich people in South Florida? They are brown and healthy and did I mention old?" Powers replied.

"I came out here to visit not to roast. Let's go back inside," Jim requested.

"We will, in a little while," Powers said as he reclined.

"Well, at least put the book down and tell me how all this is possible."

Powers had asked Jim to come visit several times but he had declined every offer. Powers came up with a plan. He arranged for Jim's wife to visit her relatives in Albany. She was thrilled. Jim was left without an excuse to come visit Las Vegas.

"You are going to find this hard to believe but have I made a lot of money betting on basketball games," Powers said.

"You don't know squat about basketball. Tell me you rob banks; that would be easier to believe," Jim dismissed Powers claim.

"Anything can be learned. I do not have to dribble between my legs or nail a three-pointer to understand the game," Powers said defensively.

"Gamblers are not this successful. Statistics, logic, and reason dictate that you cannot accurately predict games. The best team does not always win__," Jim was cut off.

"Stop, stop, stop. I have a ton of money; I won it. Your disbelief is illogical and annoying. I had some help. Remember Eddie Dreyer? I learned a lot about basketball and betting from him," Powers said as he rose and walked under the umbrella to pour an orange concoction into his tall plastic glass.

Powers turned to Jim and asked, "Are you thirsty? Would you like a glass?"

"What is it, orange juice?" Jim asked.

"Bingo, buddy," Powers said and poured the second glass and handed it to him.

"Cheers," Powers said.

"Yeah cheers," Jim echoed and took a drink and added, "Yikes, what else is in this thing?"

"Tequila, grenadine. It's called a Tequila Sunrise," Powers answered.

"Holy crap Powers; it's ten in the morning."

"It's ten in the morning in Las Vegas, Jim. We are not breaking the Law. You are not driving; you are not scheduled to drive. You have no schedule to keep. You are on holiday, my friend. Live a little. Lighten up. On second thought, don't lighten up, get out here in the sun," Powers said nearly giggling at his own joke.

Powers resettled in his reclined chair. With hair slicked back, head reclined, and Ray-Ban sunglasses resting on his thin nose, he felt cool. He imagined the sparse pool crowd approving of his slim golden tan body. He took another drink of his spiked orange juice and sucked in his stomach as a brunette spread her towel nearby.

"You look silly, like a misplaced Jersey mobster, only without the gold jewelry and chest hair," Jim said.

"Look around Casper; as I said, you are the only ghost hiding in the shade." Powers said to Jim without looking at him.

"But none of them look as pretentious as you," Jim accused.

"I am pretentious. You think I should be ashamed of that?" Powers asked.

"I give up." Jim pulled his chair closer to Powers and asked, "How did Eddie Dreyer help you become a professional gambler?"

"Eddie had a fixation on the betting lines. I questioned him. He said he did not bet on games. He used the lines for motivation. By the end of a session, I was convinced Eddie did not wager on games. I kidded with him. I suggested that with my new knowledge of his psyche, I might be able to make some money wagering. I asked him if he had any tips for me," Powers lied as though it were actually the truth.

"That seems very unprofessional and certainly unethical," Jim exclaimed.

"I was joking, at the time. Trying to bond, I suppose. However, Eddie does not bond. But his answer was intriguing. He said, "Gambling is a foolish risk. People who bet on these games have no control over the outcome. I'm a guy who has to have control. Here's a tip, betting against me is gambling," Powers said.

"How did that help you?" Jim asked. He was confused by the answer. Jim grabbed the bottle of lotion on the table and began to lather his pasty white limbs.

"I knew Eddie's confidence was high. I had given him suggestions during hypnosis to deal with the expectations of his father. I knew Eddie would play well. I opened an Internet betting account and placed a bet. He won; I won. It was exhilarating. I began to consider the possibilities. I was losing my position in the department. I needed a new challenge. Gambling kept eating at my interest. I placed another bet on Eddie; I won again. That's how it started," Powers said as he re-filled his empty glass.

"When Eddie got injured and subsequently bombed out of basketball and school, how did you continue to win?" Jim asked.

"I continue to win because Eddie bets on basketball." Powers said in a matter of fact way that dumbfounded Jim.

He continued, "I created an Internet wagering business. It's called surefirewinners.com. Eddie uses it to place bets. When I see his bet, I mirror it. He wins nearly eighty percent of the time," Powers said.

"I can't believe this. Eddie now gambles?" Jim said in a whisper. "How? I mean, out of all the gambling sites on the Internet, how did he find you?"

"Because during hypnosis, I gave him the suggestion," Powers stated.

Powers had not intended to tell anyone but there it was floating in the air like a fragile soap bubble. It was released; it was shared. The burden was lightened. Until Pop.

"Are you insane? Do you know how wrong that is?" Jim was whispering, as though every sun worshiper were FBI agents monitoring their conversation.

"Yes, I know but I can live with it. I am not hurting Eddie. Eddie has chosen gambling as a post basketball career. He needs a place to wager. I provide it," Powers responded.

"Powers I cannot believe what you are telling me. I do not know what to say. What am I supposed to tell people who ask about you? Do you expect me to lie?" Jim was licking his lips and massaging his forehead. "You should not have told me."

"Jim, no one is going to ask about me. What would they ask anyway?

"So, what is old Meade up to these days?"

You will say. "You're not going to believe it but he moved to Las Vegas and became a professional gambler."

"You are kidding, they will say."

"He's always been a little different, you will say."

"That's true, they will respond."

"And the subject will change to Harrington, student apathy, right-wing-conservative insensitivities, or employee benefits," Powers said with a wave of his hand as though it were that simple.

"What happens if Eddie stops gambling?" Jim asked.

Powers took off the Ray-Bans and attempted to show interest in Jim's confusion. Jim was right; Powers should not have told him the truth. Powers hoped the strength and length of their friendship gave him permission to do so. It was an error in judgment. Powers would not tell him about the triggering mechanism. As long as Eddie was alive, he would go through his visualizations and every time he does, Powers will receive a wager. Powers would not argue right versus wrong on his actions. Powers worried that Jim could not live with knowing.

Powers knew he needed to offer Jim a lifeline.

"Yes, that will leave me without a source of income but I am investing this money. If I need more money, I will write a book and get back into teaching," Powers lied to his friend.

"I wish you would go back to teaching right now. This will be difficult for me. I am not one of those people who believe Butch Cassidy and the Sundance Kid were heroes. Because they managed to steal money without killing people does not absolve them. What they did was wrong; what you have done is wrong," Jim said.

319

"Jim, Eddie is making ten to fifteen thousand dollars a week. If he placed his bets at another site, he would be tracked. When his acumen became apparent, the directors of that site would bar him or they also would use him. Eddie is going to wager. With me he will not get ripped off," Powers said.

"And that makes it right, Powers?" Jim said to him. "As psychologist, we effort to help people control abusive behavior. You're not helping Eddie. You're enabling him. And I am pretty sure gambling online is illegal," Jim continued to lecture.

"Jim, what are you asking me to do? Your friendship is important to me. Hell, you are my only real friend," Powers said.

"Be a professional. If you were hearing this tale from a patient, what would you tell them?" Jim asked.

"Alright. I get the picture. Let's not role-play. I have nearly three quarters of a million dollars plus I own this condo and my house in Charleston. I will dismantle my website and hope the stock market does not destroy this nest egg," Powers said.

"Meaning you will stop gambling?" Jim asked.

"Probably not. It means I will disconnect my association with Eddie Dreyer. I have become a fan of the casino tables. Black Jack, Roulette, and even Craps are very exciting to me," Powers said.

"You mean it? Just like that you will stop?" Jim asked reaching to touch Powers on the shoulder.

"I told you; I do not want to lose my only friend," Powers responded.

"I'm flattered. Now, what are you going to do about Eddie's gambling addiction?" Jim said.

"Do? I will do nothing. He does not have an addiction. It is a job, a profession, and a career choice. You can smother me in guilt and friendship but you cannot affect Eddie Dreyer. I have worked with him. He manipulated me and he manipulates everyone. He treats everyone like an opponent. He studies you, finds your weaknesses, and uses them against you. It's not what he does; it's what he is. I cannot help Eddie Dreyer," Powers said.

"Okay. I know you do not like him. You have taken revenge by using him. Maybe you should just call it even. He is on his own again and you are on your own. That may be the only compromise possible."

"I'm giving you my word that I will dissolve surefirewinners.com and effectively end my chance at financial independence. Is that what you are asking me to do?" Powers asked.

"That's exactly what I am asking," Jim said.

"And when Eddie discovers the site is gone, where will he exercise his wager?" Powers asked.

"That is an interesting question. Driven by a hypnotic suggestion, how will he fulfill the command? The frustration might break the link; the association could disappear, couldn't it? Jim said.

"It might; I do not know. It will be frustrating. I could have the webmaster automatically re-direct the site to a list of other gambling entities," Powers offered.

"No; you are still enabling," Jim said louder than before.

"Easy, calm down, I was just thinking out loud," Powers said.

"Obviously the kind of thinking that got you into this mess," Jim said.

Ignoring Jim's remark, Powers said, "I know Eddie well enough to know that if the checks stop rolling in, he will find another arena to compete in. His ego and drive will not permit him to fail. Money is now tied to his success. The hypnotic suggestion will be obliterated by his will to succeed."

Jim said, "I suppose that is possible. At the very least it forces him to deal with his demon in a more open environment, rather than as your pawn."

"Okay, have you taken your last shot at me?" Powers said.

Powers picked up the thermos and shook it. It was empty. He stood up, gathered his towel, and the two glasses.

"Let's clean up, have some lunch and then I will show you around town," Powers said.

"Sounds great. I want to see why you would want to live in this place," Jim replied.

"Well, it is hot, dirty, foolish, and replete with sex and sin but there are some downsides as well," Powers quipped.

"You know. It's hard to tell if I'm visiting an old friend or hanging out with a stranger," Jim said as he followed Powers back to the condo.

Powers took another look at the brunette; he patted Jim on the back and said, "A little of both, Jim, a little of both."

321

# 82

Dexter stood at the servers' station at the end of the bar. He was sipping on a cola, talking to co-workers, and watching the front door. Harmon patrolled behind the bar. James Breman was bartending. Dexter exchanged flirtations with Lauren and checked the door; he was expecting April and Eddie. Dexter did not see Harmon lean in behind him.

"Dex, are you here on a day off just to interfere with the staff doing their job?" Harmon asked.

"I'm not slowing anyone down. Besides, with my charm and good looks, I'm a drawing card for this place. You should be paying me to stand here."

"Bring that mirror of yours to Bluebeards. I need to look in it. Maybe it will lie to me also. I always wanted to look like Robert Mitchum," Harmon said.

"Robert who?" Dexter asked.

"You don't deserve to know. Why are you staring at the door?" Harmon asked. "Are you expecting that chick?"

"What chick?" Dexter answered.

"The one you've got the hots for," Harmon said.

"Yeah, I'm waiting for her but it's not like that; we're just friends," Dexter said, convincing no one he wanted it that way.

"My condolences," Harmon said.

"It's cool. April will make a great friend. She's honest and straightforward. I respect that. It will be good for me," Dexter said.

"Yeah; it will be like having your mother around," Harmon said as he walked toward the on-duty bartender.

"Great. Thanks for the image, Harm." Dexter yelled to the back of Harmon.

Eddie Dreyer walked in the door carrying his normal backpack of technology. Dexter watched him walk to the far end of the room. Like every other time he had seen Eddie enter, Eddie walked with his eyes on his destination. He did not check-out the women. He did not

322

look to see if he recognized anyone. Socialization and fraternity were not important to Eddie. Eddie was important to Eddie. And Dexter could not take his eyes off him.

"Hey Dex, are you going to answer me?" Harmon asked.

"What? I'm sorry; I didn't hear you."

"I said, James is looking for someone to switch with him tomorrow. Can you do it?" Harmon asked.

"Yeah, I'll work it out with James."

"Good, Harmon responded. "Why are you staring at Eddie?"

"I'm not staring."

"That's good. I thought since the chick blew you off, you were going over to the other side," Harmon said to him.

Dexter flipped him the finger over his shoulder without looking at him. He could hear Harmon smiling as he walked away.

He saw April walk through the door. Her baseball cap was curled on the brim to perfection; it would be the envy of any ball player, were it not for the Minnie Mouse embroidered on it. She had it pulled down low on her forehead; her tight ponytail hung out the back. Her shoulders were back and her stride was lengthy and purposeful. She reached Eddie's table but did not sit down. Dexter could see Eddie greet her with a big smile. Dexter did not know what April said but it was obvious, Eddie was upset. April continued to talk; Eddie did not. His smile vanished. Eddie closed his laptop computer and shoved it the bag. Dexter watched as Eddie stood and brushed past April on his way out the door.

April did not turn to watch him walk away nor did she try to continue the conversation. She turned to look around the bar. Dexter began walking toward her. April sat at the table Eddie had vacated. Dexter took the chair next to her.

"I thought you were going to wait for me to come over," Dexter asked.

"I changed my mind. I'm just not good at beating around the bush," she replied.

"So, what did you say?"

"I asked him why he blackmailed Michael Pendleton."

"That was your opening line?" Dexter exclaimed, "What did he say?"

"Nothing. He shut down and started packing his stuff as I was asking him who else he was blackmailing," April responded.

"He didn't answer that either, did he?" Dexter asked.

"Nope. He didn't try to deny it. He didn't try to defend himself. He didn't look mad or hurt. He acted as if he realized he was in the wrong place. So, he and his poker face of confidence just walked off," April said.

"Now what? Dexter asked.

"I don't know. I have no idea where he's going," she answered.

"April, let's get out of here. I don't want someone to overhear this stuff about Eddie," Dexter whispered and glanced around the room to see if anyone was listening.

"Fine. By all means, let's not slander the name of a low-life-blackmailer," she said as she stood.

April walked toward the door and Dexter followed. They walked across the street, found a bench on campus and sat beneath a dim quarter moon. Dexter waited for April to initiate the conversation. He expected her to break into a rant about Eddie's silence. He grew tired of waiting.

"Option One: It's over. We go about our business and consider this an interesting piece of history. Option Two: Go back and reconsider Option One," Dexter said.

"Option Three: We expose him. We tell the police or we post a warning on the Internet or start a blog, or tell a newspaper," April said while craning her neck to study the moon.

"Or Option Four: reconsider Option One," Dexter repeated.

"Four sounds a lot like number two," April said as she ceased to study the sky and turned her attention to Dexter. "What are you afraid of? You saw Eddie go in the gym; you know he was there."

Dexter sensed her frustration was being held on a leash. He hoped a strong one.

"I'm not afraid. I just don't see the benefit of being involved. I don't want to have my name dragged all over the airways and newspapers as the narc trying to destroy Eddied Dreyer," Dexter told her.

"You would prefer to let Eddie go around abusing people? You want to sit back while he bullies his way around campus after campus?" April asked as she searched Dexter's face.

Dexter knew the right response was to say something about doing the right thing. He knew that someone should stand up to a bully but he was busy thinking about himself. He thought about the movies where the guy telling the truth on the witness stand is made to look like a fool. He imagined his own death as Eddie sought revenge. Just as he was about to mumble another compromise, a small paper airplane landed at their feet. They both looked down at it and saw the two shoes appear. They looked up.

"Bullying? Is that my crime?" Eddie asked.

Dexter tensed up; he was preparing to be hit. His heartbeat was beginning to race.

"Are you here to answer my question?" April asked.

"It was a stupid question. You asked "why?" It implied that I blackmailed someone and the answer to any blackmail question is getting something you want. I assumed with your GPA, you could have answered that question," Eddie said.

"Eddie, I was in Greenville. I saw you standing on the other side of the bleachers. I can't believe you are in the business of fixing basketball games," Dexter said.

Dexter stood up. He was scared. Standing did not improve his stature. Eddie was still six inches taller and fifty pounds heavier.

"I don't fix basketball games. I challenge players and coaches. I always have. The game is about pressure. Without pressure, it would be a shooting contest. I put pressure on Pendleton; he buckled. I bet he would; I made money." He turned to look at April. "And so did you," Eddie said.

"No. What you did was wrong. I did not want to make money off of someone else's misery," April said.

Dexter felt a lump in his throat. He had doubled his money on that bet but he did not say anything and neither did April. He was grateful.

"Really? Does it bother you when a coach targets a poor free throw shooter and puts him on the line time after time? The kid misses and misses. His psyche and confidence goes in the toilet. His team loses but someone wins a bet," Eddie said with a twinkling smile.

"What about when the crowd picks on some player and yells at him. Screaming "Air ball. Air ball Air ball." He loses; someone wins a bet.

"Your opponent falls and hurts his arm. You start banging on it because you know it hurts. His performance deteriorates. He loses; someone wins a bet."

"The game is half jubilation and half misery. Half the people lose every time they play," Eddie concluded.

"That's all part of the game; what you did is not part of the game," April said.

"Pressure is part of the game. It does not always come from inside the lines. Bill chooses Trudy as his girlfriend. Trudy starts demanding more time. Bill can't concentrate on the court. He plays poorly. His team loses; someone wins a bet. That's just normal human psychology. That's the way life is."

"These are ludicrous examples. I think you've lost it," April said too calmly for Dexter's comfort.

Now Dexter was certain Eddie would hit him. He braced for it. Yet, Eddie seemed unfazed by her attacks.

"They are choices April. Bill chose Trudy over basketball. Michael Pendleton chose to allow that prostitute to suck his cock in a public place. He chose self over basketball," Eddie said.

"Because you put him in that position. You are cheating reality. You're cheating Michael Pendleton and misusing your own talents." April's volume alarmed Eddie.

"I can disappear into the darkness just as easily as I appeared. And I will, if you feel it necessary to yell during this discussion. The two of you can go back to discussing your options," Eddie said.

April and Dexter looked at each other. They were unaware he had been listening.

"That's right I followed you over here," Eddie stated.

Dexter loved basketball. His number one wish, after blowing the candles out, had always been to possess talent like Eddie Dreyer. He envied great basketball players. He felt betrayed when those players strayed from their god-like image. Dexter mustered his courage.

Dexter asked, "Eddie you could do anything. Why this?"

Eddie continued to look at April as if he were waiting for her to respond to his last statement. She sat silent. Eddie turned to Dexter.

"Dex, let me be honest with you. I don't need hero worship. I don't need the roar of the crowd chanting my name. I stopped playing for the crowd when the game became work. And that was years ago. I play to win. Period. I do not give a shit about feelings or honor or moral victories. They keep score; somebody wins. I want that somebody to be me, every time. I cannot play like I used to but I still have the same desire eating at me hour after hour," Eddie said succinctly and without emotion.

Dexter opened his mouth to speak but Eddie resumed talking.

"I know you are about to tell me what a great Coach I might be. Right now, it's hard to imagine that coaching could feed this obsession. This is what I do. It's all I have ever done. I challenge basketball players. That's what I'm doing now, plain and simple." Eddie said.

"Dude, you may hit me but I gotta' tell you. That's messed up. Can't you see it's wrong to fuck around with people like this? You aren't even playing. You had no right to screw around with Michael Pendleton," Dexter said.

"Dex, I'm not going to hit you. I don't hit anyone," Eddie said. "Pendleton choked. I would not have released those photos. He's just a piss poor poker player. I bluffed; he folded. It's my new game. I'm a gambler gambling." Eddie spread his arms wide like a preacher calling to the lost flock.

Dexter struggled mightily to accept the image he was watching. The Eddie Dreyer he knew was a dedicated tactician, who walked onto a court, shredded the defense, and quietly left the scene. But watching Eddie stand with his arms spread wide, spewing distorted wisdom and guidance, Dexter saw an assassin.

"You have to stop," April chimed in. "I'll report you."

She stood to make her point. The three of them danced for control though no one's feet moved.

"No you won't. Neither of you have really thought this through," Eddie said as he shook his head from side to side while looking down.

"Dexter does not want to tell what he thinks he saw. And I promise you Michael Pendleton will not cooperate. Where would you begin looking for the hooker? Do you think I hired her in Greenville? You think if I paid her two thousand dollars, I wouldn't spend a few hundred to fly her in?"

He turned to face Dexter.

"You saw her, Dex. Did she look like the average tramp on a corner?" Eddie asked.

Dexter took his eyes off of Eddie to intercept April's look. He had no idea what his face was revealing but he knew he had no answer for Eddie Dreyer's assessment of the situation. Dexter could tell by the look on her face that she was not searching his face for instruction or reassurance; she was giving him one last chance before her short fuse detonated. Eddie played to win but April did not take losing quietly. Dexter was scared but decided to voice exactly how he felt.

"April, we hurt more people by reporting Eddie than we help. Michael Pendleton would be ruined. At a minimum, he would be dropped from the team and lose his scholarship. You know, it's not easy to come up with the money to stay in college," Dexter said.

"Yeah it would suck for Michael Pendleton but he could have walked away from the hooker," April said with an unusual calm.

"And what about tomorrow? Do you think Eddie is through playing Satan? He has some other schmuck in his sights right now. He just came from Orangeburg. I bet somebody at South Carolina State is about to make a choice. Dexter, other than the victims, we are the only people who know what he's doing. Can we just look the other way, while he continues to blackmail people?"

Her sincerity was not laced with anger or resentment. She was really asking him, friend to friend, would it be possible to be uninvolved. Dexter did not know the answer. He decided to address Eddie instead.

"Eddie you will get caught. Nobody is perfect. I found out; someone else will. One of these players will report you. Somebody with more courage than I have will take you down."

"It's hard to imagine. The odds are against it. Your discovery was just luck. Pure dumb luck.

"No. You messed up. You didn't think of everything. You left a door open for the hooker but did not think to close it. That was a mistake. If you made one mistake, you can make another. As a matter of fact, your new career is a product of past mistakes. You could not control yourself against Gary Peterson. You made a mistake and it cost you a professional basketball career," Dexter said.

Eddie moved to within inches of Dexter's face.

*He said he wouldn't hit anyone.*

He wanted to believe it and so he repeated it to himself.

*He said he wouldn't hit anyone.*

Eddie's presence made it hard to believe.

"I've never been intimidated by anyone, so don't imagine that you can get the job done. Here's the bottom line to think about. Your very smart girl friend said the most important thing. You and she are the only ones who know. Think about what that means," Eddie said.

He turned and walked through the shrubs on the opposite side of the path. In less than a minute, he was no longer visible.

"What did he mean by that?" Dexter asked April as his eyes remained locked on the darkness behind the shrubs.

"I'm not sure. Was he threatening us?" April asked.

"He wants to intimidate us. It's what he does to competition. He has to defeat us," Dexter said.

"Yeah. Okay, but what does that mean? What could he possibly do to us? He is not violent. He has never attacked anyone, right?"

"Not that I know of but I'm not sure this is the same Eddie Dreyer, I once knew. This guy is scary," Dexter said.

"You'll get no argument from me. Let's get out of here," April suggested.

"Sounds good to me. Would you like me to drive you home?" Dexter asked.

"Yes, I would. Thank you," April said with a slight smile.

"The pleasure is all mine ma'am," he answered.

He took her arm, laced it through his, and walked to the car. Dexter was happy to have April at his side. He walked tall but through his fragile courage, he covertly cut his eyes left and right, scanning the darkness for the demonic Mr. Hyde and paper airplanes.

# 83

Dexter unlocked the door and went inside. He walked up the stairs and out onto the balcony. Harmon sat on the balcony, eating his fried egg sandwich and washing it down with a Dr. Pepper. Dexter saw the morning sun leafing through the overhanging tree and the sounds of the city bustling around him. Harmon was reading the morning newspaper.

"Mornin', Harm. How about sharing your coffee with me?" Dexter asked. He stood there with a cup extended and a quizzical look on his face.

Harmon lowered his newspaper and peered over the top of his bifocals.

"Good morning, Dex. I am ready for a cup of coffee. You go downstairs and fill a carafe, bring it back upstairs, and I will share it with you," Harmon said.

"Who drinks that stuff in the morning?" Dexter said as he motioned with his head toward the Dr. Pepper.

"You worry about your health, I'll worry about mine. Now go get the damn coffee or you can scrub the floors," Harmon said, still peering over the eyeglasses.

Dexter did not respond; he went downstairs. He came back up with the carafe and two cups. He sat down and filled both cups.

"Do you mind if I read the sports page?" Dexter asked.

"No, go ahead. I'm finished with it," Harmon replied and reached across for the coffee.

Dexter laid the newspaper on the table and began to read the articles. He slurped the hot coffee and turned the page. He went through the scores of the games the night before. He read that the Grizzlies had defeated the Falcons by fourteen.

"I bet that surprised you, Mr. Perfect," Dexter mumbled.

"Don't mumble Dex. I don't want to work that hard to hear you," Harmon said lowering his paper. "What did you say?"

"Sorry. It's not important. I was commenting on how bad the Falcons must be this year," Dexter said.

"Did you read the recap?" Harmon asked.

"No, should I?"

"I'll save you some time. The mascot, you know the kid with the oversized Grizzly costume, ran out on the court to argue a call. He pestered the referee, so persistently, that a technical foul was called on the bench. One minute later, he ran out and pants a Falcon player and chest bumped the official. The referee called another technical foul and security had to remove him from the building. The Falcons may be having a bad year but at least their mascot isn't making a fool of himself," Harmon said.

"In a meaningless game, why would he do that?" Dexter commented. "The guy had to be high."

"College kids. I don't try to figure them out. I just laugh at them and take their money," Harmon responded. "But, that game must have pissed off a few gamblers. The line was fifteen. That mascot doesn't clown up the end of the game and the Grizzlies cover the point spread."

"How in the hell do you remember a line from that game? What do you do, memorize all the games? Do you have a photographic memory?" Dexter quizzed.

"No, Eddie Dreyer was at the bar last night. He mentioned it," Harmon said.

"I suppose Mr. Lucky had the Falcons and the points."

"Yup, his research seems to pay off but after a while you have to admit he is one lucky son of a bitch," Harmon said as he raised his paper back up to continue reading.

"Yeah, lucky," Dexter said.

Dexter sat looking at his Sports page but his brain had shifted gears. Dexter knew that Eddie was in Orangeburg. Did he influence a mascot? Could he have done that? Dexter knew the answer; Eddie was capable of anything.

Dexter's confusion was interrupted by a cell phone ringing. Harmon picked it up and clicked the talk button. He stood and walked away to talk.

Dexter poured coffee from the carafe and leaned back; he put his feet up on the rail, and gazed across the campus. He saw someone sitting on the bench across the street. He sat up to get a better look at the person sipping on a Starbucks cup. Harmon stepped into his view.

"Dex, get your feet off the rail. Day after day, I have to ride these damn kids to quit putting their dirty big-ass clodhoppers on my railing. I shouldn't have to tell the staff. Do you want a permanent job painting and repairing it, without pay?" Harmon bellowed.

"Sorry, Harm. I forgot. Oh, and by the way, clodhoppers? Dude the generation gap is eating you alive," Dexter said.

"The bigger the gap the better," Harmon said and wiped at the imaginary dirt on the rails.

He sat down and continued. "That was Helen. You won't believe this but that Grizzly mascot is her nephew. Helen just got off the phone with her sister. The sister is bawling her eyes out. I'm listening to Helen rant about this boy and trying to figure out why she called me. Then I hear it. Helen thinks a male influence would be helpful."

"Why doesn't his father do it," Dexter suggests.

"She's a single mother. The father never was in the picture. He split. I don't want to go to Orangeburg and I don't want to get involved," Harmon said and then added, "Beautiful day, and now it's off to a really ugly-ass start."

Dexter did not know whether to smile or not; he did not. He wanted to tell Harmon that this was probably the work of Eddie Dreyer. He wanted to tell him that he believed Eddie was blackmailing students to affect the outcome of games. He wanted to share this burden with someone but he could not.

"That's what Moms do; they overreact. They have a hard time believing their baby could have been drinking or high on something. Hell, someone probably dared him to do it," Dexter suggested. "Or it was a bet of some kind."

"That may be but it sounds like the kid may get kicked out of school. Helen wants me to go with her to talk to the boy. They are trying to set up an appointment with the Dean to discuss how he can keep his ass in school," Harmon said.

Dexter saw an opening. If Harmon went down and talked to the mascot, he might learn that the boy was blackmailed. If Harmon learned the truth, he would not sit on it. He would do something.

"Maybe you should go. Your woman needs you. You know relationships are a two way street, Harmon Evans." Dexter tried to sound parental or least funny.

"Yeah, I'm going to take advice from you. How's your love life Casanova?" Harmon asked.

Dexter stood up, trying to look resentful. He collected the carafe and his cup.

"That is none of your business. I'm not the kind of guy that brags and boasts," he said as he turned to clock-in for his shift.

"Hey Casanova, don't forget these dishes," Harmon said pointing to his breakfast plate.

Dexter grabbed a bus-tub and walked back to the table. He loaded everything inside. As he was turning to leave, he noticed the male figure across the street was now standing. Dexter could clearly see that it was Eddie Dreyer. Eddie held his Starbucks cup up in toasting fashion. Dexter did not acknowledge the toast. He turned and walked away.

Dexter wondered why Eddie was across the street.

*Eddie followed me this morning.*

Dexter walked down the stairs. As he walked, Dexter realized that Harmon should not talk to the Grizzlies mascot. If Harmon talks to the mascot and discovers the truth, Eddie will not believe Harmon accidentally stumbled upon the truth, he'll think I told him.

He dropped the bus-tub in the kitchen, and clocked-in. He stepped behind the bar, and began stocking the liquor to replace the near-empties. He found himself wondering if Eddie was capable of violence. He worried about the line. Everyone is always talking about the "the thin line between sanity and insanity." When and what makes people cross that line?

Dexter finished the stocking and began cutting lemons and limes. It does not take much concentration to cut a lime into wedges but it took more than Dexter was allotting. He cut his finger.

"Damn it," he said and reached into the drawer for a Band-Aid.

He covered it and continued to work. Dexter was crossing his own line. He was no longer curious about what Eddie might do, Dexter was afraid of what Eddie Dreyer would do.

# 84

She typed "April" on the bottom line, paused with the cursor hovering over the Send button, and wondered how Darren would react to the letter. Darren and April had drifted apart over the last few months. They passed each other on the campus but neither offered to stop and exchange pleasantries. The separation grew because she had tired of his arrogance and he of her insensitivities and lack of discipline, but mostly because she was exercising less and gambling more.

Her delay in sending the mail was evidence of her insight. She knew by opening this door she would have to reveal her gambling activity to Darren. Darren would criticize her. He would not spare synonyms to point out the frivolous, senseless and destructive aspects of gambling. By clicking the Send button, she would be consenting to a sermon, consenting to control her temper, and conceding to the need for help.

April re-read the email. It was concise but detailed. She clicked Send.

As the senior columnist of the campus newspaper, Darren had received several awards for his reporting, which led to his internship with The Seaboard Post. April was certain he would respond to her email despite the state of their relationship. He would see the value of the story instantly; he would want to expose the blackmailer. April did not name Eddie as the blackmailer. Curiosity would compel Darren to respond.

The more April thought about it, the more she realized that Darren would have to curtail his desire to criticize, if he wanted to learn more about the evidence.

"If Dudley Do-Right wants to ride in to save the day, he's going to have to get off that goofy looking high horse," April said as she snapped her fingers, rather proud of her reasoning.

April walked away from the computer. She had motivation to control her temper long enough to endure Darren's sermon but she also recognized Dexter was going to be a problem.

She did not expect him to outwardly show his disagreement but she expected a total freak out to be brewing inside. He had been adamant; he did not want to be involved in trying to stop Eddie Dreyer. April saw the look on his face as Eddie made a convincing argument that Dexter would suffer from the publicity and so would Michael Pendleton. April worried about their new friendship. April knew she should not have made this decision without discussing it with Dexter. But she rationalized that at the end of the discussion, he would still say "No" and she would still contact Darren.

*Why waste time?*

"Good job, April. Just another of the many examples of why you have no friends," she said out loud and frustrated.

April called Dexter. His voice mail answered. She left him a message asking him to meet her at Captain Bluebeards at eight.

She went to the bathroom and took a shower. She walked by the laptop and saw the email alert. She opened it; Darren was in disbelief and asked to know more. April emailed back and asked him to meet her at Captain Bluebeards at eight thirty. She hoped that the thirty minute cushion would be enough to cool Dexter and formulate a plan for Darren.

She pulled the oversized T-shirt over her head and tucked the shirt bottom into her jeans. She stared in the mirror. At first, she saw a wet ponytail pulled through the back of her baseball cap, a well-worn five-year old T-shirt, and comfy jeans. But the longer she peered into the mirror, the more obvious it became. She was staring at a warrior ready to do battle.

The usual April would not be able to manipulate these two boys. She was dressed to belittle and antagonize. Her history and reputation were tied to this image. The mirror screamed, "I don't care"; "take it or leave it" and "screw you." The typical April persona carried a chip too large for one shoulder. She considered her appearance for a few more seconds and decided a softer image was required tonight.

She took the shirt and hat off, and loosened the ponytail. April fumbled around under the sink cabinet, dragged out a blow dryer, and dried her thick chestnut brown hair. She went to the closet and chose a low cut tank top. It was green and yellow. Her mother had given it to her at Christmas.

"April these colors soften your face and accentuate your eyes," she had told her.

April was unsure what her mom was advocating with the low cut neckline and did not ask.

She draped the lightweight chiffon yellow shirt over her shoulders and buttoned only one button. She unzipped the baggy jeans; they fell to the floor. April took the brown stonewashed jeans from the hanger and pulled them on. The skintight fit was rare for April. She turned to look at her butt in the mirror. Considering the lack of exercise, she was surprised by the tight and thin look. She turned to face the mirror. April pulled the bottom of the tank top down, knowing full well it would not stay down. If it did not, more cleavage would be exposed. Her midriff would peek through the unbuttoned shirt. She stepped back; this was definitely an abnormal April.

"Alright Mom, I hope you are right. I hope this makes these boys look into my eyes without wanting to kill me."

She walked across the room picked up her purse and left the apartment.

# 85

Every car on the highway was zooming past the blue Monte Carlo. Eddie looked down at the speedometer; he was doing fifty. He was driving fifteen miles under the speed limit. He wondered how long he had been crawling along. He sped up. Eddie rubbed at his eyes. He was tired but fatigue was not affecting his driving. Eddie Dreyer was distracted and confused.

The trip to Boone had been a smooth one but an hour ago he pulled into a roadside park to take a short nap. Had he not been wearing his seatbelt, Eddie might have hit his head on the steering wheel, he awoke so abruptly. It was a dream that startled him. It was a dark and disturbing dream, with vague characters. He began to drive and though Charleston was only sixty miles away, Eddie pulled into another roadside park.

He leaned his seat back and thought about the dream. Eddie remembered strings attached to his arms and legs. The strings seemed delicate but were too strong to break. Eddie looked up to find the source of the strings and discovered he was a puppet. He tried to run away but the strings pulled him back. Eddie could see a giant puppeteer above him but the face was masked by the shadows.

Eddie opened his eyes and grabbed his bottled water from the cup holder. He squeezed several drops into his hands and tried to soothe his eyes with the cool water. He laid his head back and left his eyes closed. Within seconds, he saw dangling strings and heard a voice say, "surefirewinners."

He snapped his head up and repeated the words out loud, "surefirewinners? Have I forgotten to place my bet? Could I be that tired?" Eddie reached into the back seat and pulled his iPad to the front. He opened it and powered it up. He opened his email program and found the receipt for his bet.

He read, "Mountaineers plus five."

*The bet's down.*

337

He lowered the window to get some fresh air and vent some frustration.

"Eddie Dreyer is in control of Eddie Dreyer," he said to the windshield as though the imaginary puppet master could hear him.

The sense that he was out of control angered him and adrenalin surged through his body. He started the engine and re-entered the highway traffic. He set the cruise control to sixty nine miles per hour and took ten slow deep breaths to calm down. He raised the window, analyzed the dream, and talked out loud.

"This is obviously a guilt issue. I am not feeling guilty. Guilt is a condition. The condition exists for the players I have challenged, not for me. They made their own choices. I put them in situations where they must choose and they chose. I have never followed through on a threat and I wouldn't.

"I threatened Duane Brown. He popped an easy three-pointer as time expired to win the game. He stood at mid-court, pointing his finger around the gymnasium, as though he were calling me out. He chose to defy me; he chose to win. That's a man. He suffered no repercussions from me. I lost ten thousand dollars on that basket."

"That's the way the game works. It ain't about luck; it's about preparation, skill, and guts. Duane has guts. Phil Roker, Abdul Donia, Enrique Lawson, all of them had guts; all of them chose to preserve their honor. All of them chose to win at any cost. And none of them suffered consequence from me. I bluffed; they called."

All the other Michael Pendletons' of the world are losers. It's a game; games are to be won. Guilt is a pest to the weak. I am not weak. I refused to be influenced by something as trivial as guilt."

Eddie stared down the dark highway. He felt better after speaking his mind. Charleston was only minutes away. The adrenalin had chewed up the miles and he felt like he had just slam-dunked on an impenetrable defense. Guilt was history; it was done; yet, Eddie was still bothered by the puppet master and the voicing of surefirewinners.com.

He pulled into the parking lot of the hotel. With his backpack on one shoulder and a tote bag on the other, Eddie registered for a three day stay. He went upstairs to his room. He tossed everything on the desk and lay down on the bed. He turned on the television and clicked to ESPN. He watched the scores scroll by as the station covered a hockey game. Eddie saw it go by, The Cobras eighty and the Mountaineers seventy-seven, another winner for Eddie.

"You're a loser, Earl. You're no Duane Brown." Eddie said loudly.

He turned the television off. Eddie lay there looking into the dark. The curtains swayed to the flow of the air conditioner. The light from the hallway and the outside alternated choreographing his ability to see clearly. In a rather dark moment he saw a flash of the puppet master. This time he recognized the face.

In a flashback, Eddie thought it looked like professor Powers Meade. Eddie blinked several times but could not recreate the scene. He sat up and swung his legs over the side of the bed.

"Why would I dream that Meade is controlling me?" He asked of the dimly lit room.

Eddie sat there wondering why this professor was in his dreams. How could this betting service and this professor be related?

He stood up, lifted the cover to his laptop and went Google. He searched for betting services. Google came back with over four million results. Eddie clicked through twenty-five pages; surefirewinners.com was not listed. He quickly clicked through another twenty-five without finding his service. Eddie clicked on a few different services. The only advantage of surefirewinners.com was a slightly better payout than the other sites.

*How did I ever find this site?*

Eddie turned the computer off and lay down. Moments later, he turned the lights off and gave in to his exhaustion.

Before he fell asleep, he whispered, "I'm coming to see you Powers Meade. I don't know your role but I will find out. No one controls Eddie Dreyer except Eddie Dreyer."

# 86

April saw him standing in the doorway looking around the room. She waved; he waved back and started toward her. Dexter was thirty minutes late. Darren arrived fifteen minutes early and was already seated at the table. Her plan to break the news to Dexter first was now shot. Darren had wasted no time. He was asking questions about the blackmailer. He was anxious. April was not sure how to proceed; she started with an introduction.

"Dexter this is Darren."

"Hey Dexter," he said holding out his hand. "Darren Benefield."

"Dexter Dalton, but call me Dex," Dexter said shaking his hand.

"Deal; and you can call me Darren," he said with a half smile.

"Don't like people calling you Dare, huh?"

Darren shook his head in agreement but did not respond.

"I thought you would be here by eight," April said to Dexter.

"I couldn't. I was stuck in the training room helping with player rehab and__," Dexter answered but the end of his response tailed off to a whisper.

April waited a few seconds for him to finish. But he did not; instead he was staring at her. She could see in his eyes that Dexter seemed to be at a loss for words.

"Dexter, why are you staring at me?" April asked hoping to gain an upper hand by being aggressive.

"I'm sorry but damn, you look great!" Dexter said. "Where have you been? I've never seen you dressed up."

"Dexter. Don't be a pig. It's cleavage. Stop staring."

"Don't sell me short. I see the chest show but I also noticed how your eyes seem to jump and sparkle and that your hair is thick and shiny. April, you look hot! I'm not sure I can quit staring," he said.

"Stop." April ordered him and watched as Dexter slowly turned his attention toward Darren.

"So, Darren, how do you know April?" He asked.

"I met her last year in a Philosophy class. I ran into her one day at the park. We started running together," Darren explained.

April saw Dexter look at her with inquisitive eyes.

"I haven't run as often as I used to. I've been distracted lately," April said defending her exercise program.

Dexter leaned a little closer to April and said, "They're more green than brown. I never noticed before."

April tilted her head trying to understand what he had said.

*What the hell is he talking about?*

"Your eyes," Dexter said. "Tell your parents they did a nice job with that."

Darren asked Dexter, "So, how did you meet April?"

"I'm a bartender here. The first time I met her she was having an afternoon beer or three. The second time I bumped into her at a Mexican restaurant. But the main activity we have in common is our gambling habit," Dexter said.

Darren turned his head to look at April. She could sense Darren was trying to put pieces of a puzzle together. But her mind was asking another question.

*How come Darren isn't ogling me, like Dexter?*

April quickly said, "I am not addicted to gambling. I quit, remember?"

"That's true. With my own two eyes I have seen her pass up really good opportunities," Dexter said as he waved for Lauren to come to the table.

"Wow, that doesn't sound like the April I know. She would never risk money and hope to get lucky. Nope, that does not sound like the analytical April I know," Darren said.

Lauren arrived and Dexter ordered a pitcher of beer and asked for three mugs.

"None for me; thanks. Could you bring me a glass of tea?" Darren asked.

"Sure, Honey," answered Lauren. "Sweet Tea?"

"Unsweetened, please," he answered and turned to Dexter.

"So, you bet a lot, do you Dex?" He asked.

"Daily," Dexter answered.

"Are you rich?" Darren asked.

"Hell no. I work in this bar forty hours a week, minimum," Dexter said turning his full attention to Darren.

"Have you amassed a sizable bankroll from all this betting?" Darren continued his barrage of questions.

"Nah. I hit a good one every once in a while. It's kind of a fifty fifty thing," Dexter answered.

"What would you say is the primary reason you continue to do it?" Darren asked.

"Damn Darren, are you a psych major?"

"No. I'm a Journalism major."

"Benefield," Dexter slightly mumbled.

Then he remembered.

"You're the guy in the campus newspaper.

"Benefield: From The Field," Dexter said.

Darren nodded without any additional reaction.

"I've read some of your stuff. You always seem to find the less pleasant aspects of life to write about. Wasn't your last one about a drug addicted football player?" Dexter asked.

Again, Darren nodded.

"I certainly wouldn't want to be one of those articles," Dexter said.

Darren lifted his hand like a stop sign and said, "You aren't my next article, Dex. I'm not here to gather facts about you or your gambling."

Dexter said, "Great. That's a relief."

"However," Darren continued. "April piqued my curiosity about the world of gambling. I haven't heard from her in months; now she wants to talk to me about a potential blockbuster blackmailing scandal."

April saw Dexter's head snap in her direction. She could feel his stare and suddenly she felt desert dryness in the back of her throat. Dexter was no longer distracted by her cleavage and she felt the sparkle of her eyes had lost their luster.

April moved her purse as Lauren sat the pitcher of beer in front of her. April reached for the pitcher but Dexter beat her to the handle. He filled two mugs and pushed one toward her.

"Thanks," she said and took a drink.

She continued, "I called Darren because I thought he might be able to expose the guy that is going around blackmailing people to influence the outcome of basketball games."

"Really! Anybody I know?" Dexter asked still staring at April in disbelief.

April knew he felt betrayed. She thought about taking him by the arm and walking away from the table to explain but Darren interrupted her thoughts.

"I am ready for more details. But April, are you sure it is wise to involve Dex?"

"What? You don't think you can trust me with your story?" Dexter asked.

"No offense, Dex. It's just that I would not want a bunch of people wandering around babbling about this. If what she says is true, I might be able to catch him in the act. But if he learns he is being tracked, he might just quit or move," Darren said.

"I'm not likely to babble, Dare," Dexter said intentionally trying to provoke Darren.

April saw Darren's smile disappear, as Dexter glared at him.

"Okay, stop it. This is not how I intended to do this but I don't have a choice now."

She turned to face Darren.

"Darren. Dexter knows everything I know, but he does not want to get involved. He believes exposure will bring bad press his way and destroy the life of some basketball player."

April turned and put her hand on Dexter's arm. She softened her voice.

She whispered, "Dex, I had planned to discuss this with you before Darren arrived. But you were late getting here. Please don't be hurt or mad. I think we can bring Eddie down without involving you."

April kept her eyes glued to Dexter's face. She desperately wanted to console him and preserve their friendship. Darren broke the silence.

"How is Dexter involved?" Darren asked. "Dexter gambles. I know that much. What else should I know?"

April left her hand on Dexter's arm but snapped her head in Darren's direction and leaned toward him.

"Darren, you don't know shit at this point. Without more information from me; you have no idea what direction to take. You have zero chance of making this into a story. This gets done my way or it doesn't get done. Take it or leave it," she said.

"Well, that certainly sounds more like the April I know. And how do you see this going down?" Darren asked.

"If I give you information about the blackmailer, you will promise to follow him and generate new evidence. From that evidence, you will build your story and the story will not mention us. You will

343

write a story as though you discovered this person by accident. You will not mention that you received a tip or that you overheard it somewhere. It has to be your discovery," April demanded.

"That means I am starting my story from a lie. I do not have to do that. I have the right to protect my sources," Darren said.

"Nope. No deal. The blackmailer knows we know. He is very unstable. If he suspects we put you on his trail, we're doomed. I believe he is capable of anything."

April stood up.

"I did not come here to bargain with you," she said to Darren then turned to look directly into Dexter's eyes. "Or lose a friend."

She turned and fixed her sternest stare on Darren.

"My way or I walk," she said to him.

"Sit down." Darren requested. "Please."

April sat.

"I'll do it your way," Darren said.

"We have his word for it? That's it?" Dexter asked.

"Nope." April reached in her purse and pulled out a small tape recorder. "He's going to be taped saying he agrees to do it this way. I will make it my lifelong goal to ruin his journalistic integrity, if he involves either of us."

"This is absurd. Why is my credibility in question? I've never broken my word. I'm not sure this level of distrust works for me," Darren said.

"That's your decision to make," April responded.

As April waited on Darren to choose, she felt relaxed. She had planned everything except Dexter's tardiness. It did not matter if he said yes or no. She waited. A thought raced into her mind.

*Is this the way Eddie feels when he puts players into pressure situations?*

Darren took the recorder and taped a message that satisfied April. She turned and handed the tape to Dexter.

"I know you want to do something. Is this acceptable to you, Dex?" She asked.

"Yeah, under one condition," Dexter said.

"What else could you possibly want?" Darren asked.

"Easy Dare, this has nothing to do with you. April, you have to promise to dress up one more time," he said with a smile.

"Damn it. I knew this would come back to bite me in the butt," April said.

"Do you agree?" Dex asked her.

"Fine," she said sounding irritated but inside she was flattered.

344

"If the little love-fest is over, can we get on with the details of this story?" Darren asked.

Dexter refilled the two beer mugs and began to tell his tale about the gymnasium in Greenville. April added details about the subsequent meeting with Eddie. Darren only looked up when he was not scribbling notes, which was not often. April felt unburdened and ordered another pitcher of beer. She listened as Dexter talked about seeing Eddie across the street yesterday and he suggested Eddie might have something to do with a Mascot incident in Orangeburg.

Lauren brought the beer and reached across the table to set it down. April could not help but notice Lauren's largely exposed breasts.

*Damn! Those are real and real nice. Now that's cleavage.*

Darren's head was buried in the yellow legal pad; he did not notice Lauren's irresistible flesh. Dexter, however, threw his story-telling machine into neutral and paused to admire Lauren's display, like aficionados pause to admire great works of art.

Lauren walked away and April said to Dexter, "Come on; you see those every day."

"Yeah I know." Dexter said as he turned his attention back to April. "A lot of people don't. It reminds me of the importance of luck."

Darren looked up from his note writing. "What are you two mumbling about?"

"Luck." April said as she adjusted her tank top. "We were just talking about luck."

# 87

Eddie Dreyer closed the door behind him, shoved both hands deep into his pants pockets and began walking down the hall. He was looking down and deep on thought. The recently polished squares of tile passed by one by one. He saw a pair of running shoes approach but collided with the walker before he could look up. A pen fell to the tile and Eddie's eyes met a man who had been reading as he walked.

"I'm sorry; I should have been watching where I was walking," said the man as he bent down to pick up the pen that had fallen during the bump.

"It's alright. I wasn't paying attention to where I was going either," Eddie said.

The man straightened up and adjusted his eyeglasses and took a lengthy look at Eddie. Eddie could see it coming.

"You're Eddie Dreyer, aren't you?" He asked.

"Yeah," Eddie responded looking around.

Eddie was anxious to leave the building.

Before he could step around the man, the bumped man extended his hand and said, "I'm Jim Oberling, a professor here, and I'm a big fan of yours. You're one of the best college ballplayers I've ever seen."

"Thank you," Eddie said as he shook the waiting hand.

"I expected you to catch on with some pro team by now," the professor said as he let go Eddie's hand.

"That didn't work out. Turns out I'm not as good as you thought I was," Eddie remarked with a very thin grin.

"No, you were exceptional. If you had not injured that shoulder__,"

Eddie interrupted, "No offense sir, but I don't play the 'what if' game. It just did not work out."

"Sure; sure. It was impolite of me to probe. Well, how are you doing? Are you back in school?" He asked.

"No. I'm just here on campus looking for a professor. I just discovered he doesn't teach here anymore," Eddie replied.

"In this department?" The man asked.

Eddie did not answer at first. He was uncomfortable in the psych building, although he was unsure why. Eddie did not want to leave this man with the opinion that he required help. But it occurred to him that maybe this professor might have some information.

"Yeah. Professor Meade, but the aide said he was no longer here and she had no idea where I might find him. I'll just drop by his house," Eddie said.

"He's not there, Eddie. He moved," Jim said.

"Oh, do you know where I can find him?" Eddie asked.

"He moved out of state. Listen, Eddie, if you need someone to talk to, I could give you the names of some very good counselors," Jim said in a sympathetic whisper.

"No, that's not it, professor. I'm okay with my life; I've moved on. Professor Meade came to me, back when I was playing, to interview me about my visualization techniques. I started doing them in my early teens. They were very effective for me, kept me totally focused. Professor Meade said he wanted to study me and put together a book about visualization potential. At the time, I wasn't interested; but now I thought it might be a way to make some money. Maybe we could help each other out," Eddie explained.

"He's not teaching any more but he might still have some interest in writing that book. Why don't you give me your email and I will pass it on to him," Jim said.

"Well, I'm not really wired at the moment. Hey, just forget about it. It was just an idea. It was nice meeting you, Professor Oberling. I gotta' run," Eddie said and he walked away.

Eddie heard the professor say, "Good luck to you, Eddie."

He walked out into the bright sunlight. Eddie pulled the sunglasses on his head down over his eyes.

*Luck. Meade is the one who will need luck, when I find him.*

# 88

Darren recognized the girl at the front desk. He did not know her name but could remember having a class with her. He walked over, sat his notebook down on the counter, and smiled as he read her nametag.

"Good afternoon, what can I do for you today?" She asked.

"Hi Jeanette. My name is Darren Benefield. I'm an intern with The Seaboard Post and I'm working on a story about basketball player Eddie Dreyer. Have you heard of him?" He asked.

"I've heard of him," she said.

"Is he staying here or has he stayed here recently? Darren asked.

"Our policy is to protect the privacy of our guests. I can not reveal that kind of information," she parroted instinctively.

Darren wanted to remind Jeanette that they both took the same Spanish class two years ago but he preferred to wait on her to make the connection.

"Jeannette, if I step outside and call this Hotel on my cell phone, and I ask for Eddie Dreyer, wouldn't you connect me or tell me that you do not have a guest named Eddie Dreyer?" Darren asked her.

"I would, unless the guest specifically requested anonymity," she replied continuing to be polite.

Darren opened his notebook and pulled a photograph of Eddie from the pocket. He placed it on the counter and pushed it toward her.

"This is Eddie Dreyer," he said and watched her face, as she looked down at the photograph of a student in a basketball uniform. She studied the photo. Darren was hoping for a sign that she recognized him.

"Is he registered here?" Darren asked again.

Jeanette stepped behind a monitor and typed on a keyboard below the counter. She stared at the screen and said, "Mr. Dreyer is registered here but has asked to remain undisturbed."

"By undisturbed, you mean you will not ring his room or give me his room number?" Darren replied as he put the photograph back into the notebook.

"That's correct and Darren, the Hotel will not permit loitering. Last month, when Darius Rucker was in town for a concert, some fans suspected he was staying here. They tried to hang out here in the lobby. They hoped to catch him when he came downstairs. They were all removed from the property by the police," Jeanette said.

"Hey, I'm not a nut job. I'm a journalist. I just want to find him and write a story. I will not violate your policies," Darren said.

He was offended and it showed. He wondered if she had called him by name because she remembered or because he had introduced himself.

"I was not questioning your professionalism. I was doing my job," she said.

"Yes, I know." He softened his tone. "We had a class together. Two years ago, I think. Spanish, maybe?" Darren said.

"Maybe. Two years ago is a long time," Jeanette replied.

Another employee joined her at the counter; the nametag read, "Donna." Darren looked at her, smiled and said, "Hi." He returned his attention to Jeanette. "Well, thanks for the information, Jeanette. Maybe I will see you around campus," he said and smiled.

"Maybe and you are welcome," she replied.

Darren walked across the lobby and out the door.

Donna gave Jeanette a gentle nudge. "Damn girl, I thought we were agreed to buzz each other when the hot ones come through." Donna continued to watch him go through the glass doors.

"Sorry. It must have slipped my mind," Jeannette said through a grin.

"Oh yeah, I bet. Do they teach ya'll to be selfish over at that college?" Donna asked.

"No, but my momma didn't raise a fool." Jeanette responded.

# 89

"Do you know what time it is?"

"Of course I do; it's nine in the morning," Jim answered.

"In Charleston, Jim," Powers said. "In Las Vegas, it is six."

"You were always up at the crack of dawn," Jim said.

"That was before I started staying awake until the crack of dawn," Powers complained.

"Not my problem," Jim said.

"It will be your problem, when I hang up on you," Powers responded.

"Go ahead and I won't tell you about Eddie Dreyer."

Powers sat up in the bed and turned the light on. He swung his legs out over the edge and stood up.

"What about Eddie Dreyer?" He asked as he pressed the phone tighter to his ear.

"He was in the Psyche Building today, looking for you."

"Are you sure it was him?" Powers asked.

"I talked to him, Powers. He's trying to find you." Jim said.

Why?" Powers asked.

"Why? How do I know? Maybe he needs help? I offered to direct him to some counselors but he cut me short and denied needing any help. He says he wants to talk to you about a book idea you had, something about visualizations. But I think he has figured out that you are behind that website of yours. You closed that down, right," Jim asked.

"I am in the process," Powers answered.

"It's been nearly two weeks. You promised; you gave me your word," Jim said with a raised and stern voice.

"I am doing it. The Webmaster is making it difficult. He wants to buy the business from me," Powers lied.

"Tell him you have only one customer. He will lose interest," Jim countered.

"It is in the process of being closed down," Powers restated.

"Eddie must have discovered what you did, Powers."

"Jim, that may be possible but if it is, then it is over. He will no longer use the site and he will quickly lose interest in trying to find me," Powers replied.

"I'm not so sure. Eddie Dreyer does not strike me as the kind of person who gives up on anything."

"He is not perfect. He has serious mental issues. He cannot relate to his father or mother and has built his own little world to micro-manage. I am not part of that world," Powers told Jim.

"Maybe he really wants to talk to you about this book idea. You didn't tell me that you approached him about visualizations," Jim said.

"I highly doubt that his sudden appearance in the psych building had anything to do with a book," Powers said with authority.

"Maybe he really needs the money."

"Jim it is impossible for Eddie to spend all the money I send him. It has nothing to do with a book. He knows I dropped a suggestion into his brain and now he wants to punish me, somehow. He cannot do that if he cannot find me," Powers stated. "You didn't tell him where to find me, did you?"

"Of course not, Powers. I'm running late for a class. If I don't hurry they will walk but I wanted to get this information to you as soon as possible."

"Thank you, Jim. You are indeed the best friend I have. Don't worry; this means it is over. I am going back to sleep. You go teach and I will talk to you later, okay?"

"Alright. Bye," Jim said.

Powers listened to the dial tone for a moment, clicked the end button, and tossed the phone onto the bed. He filled a glass with water and drank to moisten his dry throat. He was not as calm as he led Jim to believe. Powers sat down on the edge of the bed and wondered if it was truly over. It was an important moment; the revelation merited rational thought but Powers lay down and turned off the light. He removed the cell phone from under his right hip and placed it back on the night table. He tried to think but sleep carried a solution he needed more. The consequence of an informed Eddie would have to wait.

# 90

Eddie knocked on the door and waited. He stepped back to make it easier for the person on the other side of the door to see him. Eddie was dressed like a magazine advertisement for Eddie Bauer. The khaki pants were crisp; the polo shirt was bright. Eddie heard rustling feet at the door. The peep hole would not reveal a threat. His hair was in place; he was the picture of clean cut. The door opened.

"May I help you?"

"Hi. My name is Rex Carlson. Is Professor Meade home?" Eddie asked.

"Professor Meade does not live in this house. The three of us rent it."

"He moved?" Eddie asked.

"He does not teach anymore," the boy said.

"He isn't with the college anymore?" Eddie asked.

"No."

"Wow, this is surprising," Eddie said and reached up to scratch the back of his head.

"Professor Meade created a special grant that allows us to live in the house while we attend school."

"For free?" Eddie asked.

"Almost. We pay fifty dollar a month, apiece."

"That's a sweet deal. I've been in here many times. He said as he patted the door frame. "It's a great old house. Who got his old office with the street view?"

"Not me. I got the downstairs bedroom."

"But that ain't bad either. Where did he move to?" Eddie asked.

"I don't know for sure but I think Las Vegas."

"Professor Meade? In Las Vegas?" Eddie said.

"Well, that's where we mail the rent checks."

"I'll be damned. Are all of you Psyche majors?" Eddie asked.

"None of us are. It's a requirement. Psychology and Athletics are like the only two majors ineligible to apply."

"That's an odd stipulation for a Psychology professor," Eddie said.

He opened his iPad. "Hey, would you happen to have that address in Las Vegas? I would like to mail him a thank you letter. He really helped me get a great internship up in Pittsburg."

"I can give you the address where the checks go. It's probably some accounting firm but maybe they can hook you up with his home address."

"That would be great," Eddie replied as the boy walked to a table in the foyer and retrieved a sheet of paper.

He peeled off a mailing label and handed it to Eddie.

Eddied closed the iPad and stuck the label to the outside cover.

"Thank you," Eddie said.

"Not a problem and good luck to you."

"Good luck to ya'll as well," Eddie said, shook the boy's hand and he walked toward his car.

Eddie opened the car door and slid in behind the steering wheel. He peeled the label from the cover. Eddie opened the iPad and typed the information into his contacts app and closed the cover. He continued to stare at the label.

He started the engine and said, "How many puppets is this guy stringing along, and how?"

Eddie drove away with his thoughts focused on a new opponent in Las Vegas.

353

# 91

The remaining sips of coffee were cold; Harmon toyed with the cup nervously. He listened as Helen and her sister repeated the same questions. He watched them; they were in constant motion. Walking around the room, hovering like buzzards. Routinely they would swoop in and fire a question at the boy. The order of the words did not matter; they wanted to know why and he was not answering. The two women were showing no signs of tiring. The boy sat in the chair silent and unafraid.

Harmon wanted to leave the room. He was not related to any of these people. He had never met Jimmy Gerald before today. Jimmy had done something stupid but many do. Trying to find a reason behind a stupid college stunt is like trying to understand the male sex drive.

Harmon loved Helen and sitting through this inquisition was absolute proof. His devotion to her was the only force strong enough to keep Harmon in the room.

He decided to set the cup on a nearby table. He stood. It caught Helen's attention. She walked over and whispered to him.

"Harmon, we need your help," she said in a whisper.

"Honey, this is a family thing; I am not family. I'm not even their friend," Harmon replied.

"We are not having any effect on Jimmy. If he is using drugs, we need to know. I was there the day he was born. I've watched him grow. I can't stand it. I do not want to see him destroy his life. It has to be drugs. He has to admit it so we can help him," she said.

"I can see you are distraught. I know you are in pain but I can't see how I can help," Harmon replied.

"Jimmy has never had a male influence in his life. Maybe, he will talk to you, man to man," Helen suggested.

"From what I can see, we'll be one man short," Harmon said.

"This is not funny, Harmon. The last thing I need is for you to make jokes," Helen unhappiness was crystal clear.

"Yeah, okay, I'm sorry."

Harmon began to squirm as he felt Helen's eyes sear into his.

"Honey, I don't know how to talk to a boy. I have no experience as a father figure." Harmon explained.

"Really? You seem to do well enough in Bluebeards. They keep coming back," she said.

"That's because I serve them alcohol. And furthermore, I don't take any shit off of them. And I embarrass them when they act like adolescents instead of adults licensed to drink."

Harmon found it difficult to keep his voice to a whisper.

"This is important to me," Helen said.

Harmon looked into her eyes. He knew what that meant. It meant love trumps reason. He wanted no one to doubt his love for Helen.

He put his hand on her shoulder and said, "I will get an answer from the boy. You and your sister take the car and go for a ride. Don't come back in the house until you see us sitting on the front porch."

"Harm, what are you going to do?" Helen asked.

Harmon reached into his pocket and pulled out the car keys. He held them out for her to take. He did not answer her question.

"If you want my help, go get your sister and leave," he instructed.

Helen took the keys and walked across the room. She took her sister by the arm and led her to the door. She protested but followed her out. Harmon could hear them arguing all the way to the car. He locked the door. The click of the deadbolt sounded like thunder in the suddenly quiet room.

Jimmy turned his head to confirm what he had heard. He stood up, looked at Harmon, and walked toward the back door.

"Don't go out that back door," Harmon commanded. "I can stop you and I will."

"This is none of your business," Jimmy said.

"I know that but Helen told me to get some answers and she is my business," Harmon answered.

"I have nothing to say," the boy said defiantly.

Harmon walked across the room in long slow strides. He stood directly in front of the boy. His imposing size had an effect. Jimmy took a step back. Harmon began to unbuckle his belt and pulled it loose from the loops. Jimmy was perplexed and it showed on his face.

"What? You're gonna' try to scare me into talking?" Jimmy said as he tried to stiffen his stance. "I'm not afraid of you."

355

"Yes you are," Harmon said as he took hold of both ends of the belt in his right hand. "I have no interest in being your friend. I'm after answers and I do not intend to waste my time reasoning with you."

"Meaning what?" Jimmy asked.

"I sat here and watched you treat your mother and aunt with total disrespect. You're acting like a five-year-old child. I'm going to treat you like a five-year-old child. I am going to give you an old fashion whipping if you don't answer the questions they were asking. I'm going to grab you by the arm, turn you, and start whipping your ass with this belt."

"You think I'm going to stand here and let you do that?" Jimmy said as he kept his eyes glued to the moving belt.

"No. You'll struggle; you may even get in a shot or two but you're soft, son. I'm going to keep striking your ass with this belt until you cry like a little girl. And when you've had enough, you'll tell me what I want to know."

"Dude that's assault. I'll have you put in jail," Jimmy yelled.

"No, Dude, it's an agenda; this is assault."

Harmon grabbed the boy and clutched tightly on his arm where it meets the shoulder. With fluid movement, he swung the belt through the air. It landed and wrapped around Jimmy's thin hips. Harmon pulled it back to swing again.

"Stop it!" Jimmy screamed.

Harmon landed the belt a second time and then a third. Jimmy struggled but Harmon's strength and size blocked any chance of freedom. Jimmy hit Harmon in the neck, back, and kidney. Harmon felt the dull pain and responded by lashing with additional power. Jimmy groaned and pulled but Harmon continued to swing the belt. It continued to land on his butt, hips and legs.

"Stop it! Goddamn it," Jimmy begged. "Quit!"

Jimmy was beginning to cry. He was no longer trying to hit Harmon. He was sobbing and pulling at his arm and shirt. He kept trying to reach down and cover his legs from the belts strikes but quickly pulled his hand back up when the belt struck his bare flesh. Harmon brought the belt back and paused.

"I told you how this was going to go. Do you know how to make it stop?" Harmon asked with the belt drawn back.

"Yes," he said through cries and tears. But I'm not talking."

"Let me give you another forecast. No one is coming to rescue you. I'm going to continue to whip you until you talk. It is just a matter

356

of time. My arm is much stronger than your will," Harmon said directly into Jimmy's face.

"Don't hit me, please," Jimmy begged again through whimpers.

"That's not the answer, I'm looking for," Harmon said as he unleashed three quick strokes on the boy's butt.

Jimmy cried with each strike. Harmon drew the belt back to continue.

"Stop it!" Jimmy yelled at the top of his lungs. "What do you want to know?"

"Your mother asked you if you are doing drugs, are you?" Harmon asked as he held the belt in mid swing.

"Let go of me." Jimmy replied as he squirmed.

Ignoring the tears and the crying, Harmon lashed him twice.

"No. No. No," Jimmy screamed through the crying. "I am not taking drugs."

"Then how do you explain your behavior?" Harmon asked.

"A guy bet me I wouldn't do it," Jimmy answered.

"You ruined your life at the college because of some bet?" Harmon said. "You chest bump a referee and pants an opposing player for a few dollars?"

"It was more than a few dollars," Jimmy responded.

"How much?" Harmon demanded.

"Two thousand dollars," Jimmy said through the tears.

"You're lying. I'm going to start swinging this belt again. Liars really piss me off, son," Harmon yelled.

"I'm not lying. I still have the money. It's in the envelope he gave me. I haven't spent a dime of the money."

"Show me," Harmon said.

"Can you let go of my arm? It really hurts," Jimmy asked.

Harmon loosened his grip and removed his hand. Jimmy used both hands to wipe the tears from his face and walked toward his room; Harmon followed. Harmon watched as Jimmy rummaged the top shelf of his closet and retrieved an envelope. He handed it to Harmon. Harmon looked inside and quickly counted twenty one hundred dollar bills.

"Who gave this to you?" Harmon asked.

"I don't know the guy," Jimmy said.

"You made a bet with a stranger and expected him to pay off?" Harmon's disbelief was hanging in the air like a threat.

"He paid me in advance," the still whimpering boy said.

"Paid you in advance?"

Harmon took his eyes off the money and stared into Jimmy's eyes.

"Son, that's not a bet. That's a payoff. You were paid to perform that little stunt. Don't you realize you were paid to affect the outcome of the game?" Harmon explained.

"No, I didn't. We won that game by fourteen points. I thought it would be funny," Jimmy said rubbing at his sore arm. "It was funny; everyone was laughing."

"Yeah, but they have stopped laughing now; and you're just an idiot suspended from school," Harmon reminded him.

"I didn't think they would kick me out of school. I thought they might reprimand me or suspend me. I was prepared to live with that. Two thousand dollars is a lot of money," Jimmy said.

"Yeah, it's a lot of money. But now you are an embarrassment to your mother and your aunt; you have been expelled from school and somewhere some gambler has used you to make money," Harmon said.

"Don't you think I know that? If I had it to do over, I wouldn't do it. But I can't undo it," Jimmy's voice trembled; he stopped short of crying.

"Why didn't you tell the school the truth? Why haven't you exposed the kid who paid you?" Harmon asked.

"I don't know him. He's not on our campus. He must go to school somewhere else. Eastern Shore, maybe; that's the game he wanted to affect," Jimmy suggested.

"Come on. You and I are going to sit on the porch," Harmon said.

"Why?" Jimmy demanded.

"Your mother and aunt will come back in when they see us sitting there," Harmon told him.

"I'm not going to sit on the porch like we're buddies or something," Jimmy said.

"Son, are you really that stupid?" Harmon asked slowly. "Nothing has changed in the last five minutes. I can make you do whatever I want you to. Stop talking like some bad-ass. I just watched you cry like a baby. Get your ass out on the damn porch."

Jimmy walked out the front door; Harmon followed him. Harmon leaned against the doorjamb and Jimmy leaned against the wall.

"When my mom finds out you beat me, she'll call the police," Jimmy said.

Harmon walked to the edge of the porch and sat down. He looked over his shoulder at Jimmy.

"You're probably right, Jimmy. I'm gonna' sit right here and worry about that," Harmon replied.

"You want to sit down, Jimmy or is that ass a little sore?" Harmon asked him.

Jimmy did not answer. Harmon tried not to chuckle; he failed.

# 92

The bed was not much softer than the floor. He laid on it thinking the same thoughts he had thought over and over since she had left.

She had said to him, "You've changed."

"How?" He had asked. "In high school, I lived for basketball. In college, I lived for basketball. For the last five years, I have lived for basketball."

He told her, "The only changes I've undergone were changes you demanded. You threatened to leave, if I didn't stop cussing. I stopped. You demanded I stop smoking. I stopped. You insisted I was an alcoholic. I stopped drinking."

Laura was the only woman he had ever loved. They had met when they were both fifteen.

*I love her; what else could I do?*

Titus was just one win away from a third consecutive twenty-win season. His accomplishments were turning heads in the world of college basketball but the woman he had loved for twelve years was less impressed.

Titus Lockwood rolled over and looked at the clock. It read four thirty; he sat up and turned on the light. He wrapped his hand around the Jim Beam bottle and pulled it into his lap. Today would have been his sixtieth sober day. Together, they had marked a big bold 'W' on the calendar. Heck of a winning streak until now. Titus was at a total loss.

*How could this have happened.*

He coached; she sought a Master's Degree. He obsessed over winning. She and her MBA friends obsessed over the best route on the corporate freeway. Two careers moving forward. She was having late night discussions on economics; and he filled his late nights traveling the state, recruiting players. Both of them were fulfilling requirements for success.

*So, what the fuck happened?*

She spent time in weekend conferences on employee motivation. He used his time to groom young men to function as a team.

*Did we need more in common; was that it?*

Titus tried to fit in with the new friends but the road map of a small college basketball coach lacked significance to the newly christened lieutenants of industry. Titus sat through dinners and parties practically ignored by everyone.

*I love her; what else could I do?*

But she left anyway. Like the corporate CEO she hoped to be, she imposed her way of life on Titus, and then moved on for a better deal. Titus was left surrounded by questions.

*Was it the money?*

Titus knew his next Head Coaching job would be bigger, better, and more money.

*Surely, an MBA could see that? Was she ashamed of me?*

Titus did not have the answers and he did not understand her reasons for leaving. He knew the answers would not erase the absence but the void was like holding a deflated basketball in a gymnasium without an air pump.

He put the bottle on the table, picked up the Winston's, and shook a cigarette from the pack; he lit it.

"No Laura, no rules," he said through the smoke drifting to the ceiling.

His lungs burned as they tried to adjust to the smoke just as his heart was trying to adjust to half of a life. Laura and basketball, he always thought of his life as fifty-fifty. Laura had joked that fifty percent of his time was all anyone could stand.

*Should I have given her less or more?*

Titus opened the bottle and poured the plastic cup nearly three quarters full; he topped it off with Coke. The air conditioner in the small motel room clicked off. The television in the next room mumbled through the wall as the carbonated bubbles begged for attention. He drank three big gulps.

"No Laura, no rules, goddamn it." Titus said and swallowed.

He took another long pull on the Winston and felt his head lower to his chest. He preached to his players to never hang their heads, never admit defeat. Yet here he sat, head hanging. He raised his head but only to take another drink of the Coke flavored Jim Beam.

*What would they think if they could see me now?*

# 93

Darren reached over and picked up the cell phone.

"Benefield," he said.

"Can't you just say hello, like everybody else?"

"Is this April?" He asked.

"I thought you were going to call me after you checked out the hotels?" April responded.

"I am busy. I would have called, when it was convenient to do so," Darren said.

"Where are you?" She asked.

"April, the less I tell you the better my investigation will go."

"It is not just your investigation and what do you mean by that?" She wanted to know.

"I mean you are personally involved. Eddie did not return your affection. It's practically a vendetta with you," Darren said.

"It is not a vendetta and I did not throw myself at him. He was interested in me," she said trying to remain calm.

"Your version is interesting, though a professional would say you are in denial," Darren answered back.

"Screw you Freud." April charged with a raised voice. "I want to know where you are."

"I don't think I can trust you to act rationally," he said coolly.

"If I'm not acting rationally, why did I involve you in the first place?" April said.

"Because you needed help," Darren replied.

"Listen, you asshole, I know the reason you won't tell me is because you know where Eddie's staying," April said getting louder. "It's a small town Darren, I can find you."

"Calm down. I have found the hotel. I am sitting in my car and watching for Eddie to come back. The next time he leaves, I'm going to follow him," he explained hoping it was not a mistake to tell her.

"Which Hotel?" April asked.

"April."

"Which Hotel?" She re-asked.

"Let me do this my way. I will keep you informed every step of the way," Darren finished his sentence to a dial tone.

April clicked the off button. She picked up her purse and left the apartment. The choice was a long walk or a short bus ride. She chose the bus. Ten minutes later, she was on a search mission for Darren's black Nissan Pathfinder. She walked around the Historic District. She walked around every hotel she came to. She walked for nearly an hour and then she spotted the Pathfinder. She walked toward the vehicle. April could see Darren. He was turned sideways, using opera binoculars to watch the front door of the hotel. He did not hear her walk up to the window.

"What, no disguises?" She said through the passenger side window.

Darren's left elbow flew into the steering wheel, the rest of his body jerked, as his head snapped around to confront the intruder. April leaned into the window and rested her angelic, innocent, and smiling face on the window frame.

"That was not funny. You're lucky I didn't turn around swinging; you could have been hurt," Darren said while wiping his eye. The opera glasses poked him during the surprise.

"Yeah, I'm lucky like that," she said. "I'm lucky you didn't die of a heart attack."

"I'm thrilled for you. Really; I hope you can continue to have laughs by being childish," Darren responded.

"Childish? Oh, you mean like you not telling me where you were," April said.

"I still think you should not be here. He will recognize you, then what?" Darren said as he turned his head to re-watch the front door.

"Darren, get a grip. You do not have this under control. Eddie could come in one of the side doors or enter through the parking garage. You would miss him," April told him.

"I will spot him eventually,' Darren said. "As you can see__," he held up a small notebook. "I am logging the vehicles."

April took the notebook and flung it into the back seat of the Pathfinder.

"You go watch from the lobby. You will be able to see anyone who enters the elevator. I will sit here and watch for a vehicle I might recognize. Then we can't miss him," April said.

"That will not work. If you do not recognize a vehicle, we will not know what car to follow, when he goes back out," Darren said.

"Fine, I will sit here and make your little log," April said.

"I don't need you here. I can do this by myself," Darren said reaching into the back seat to retrieve his notebook.

"That's irrelevant because I am here and I do not intend to leave," April said smugly and walked to the front of the Pathfinder and sat on the hood.

"If Eddie drives by, he will see you; and then everything will be ruined. April. Please come back over here," Darren said hoping the additional politeness would strengthen his request.

April heard him but she did not move. She wanted to be certain that Darren would relinquish some of his control before she talked to him. He continued to make requests for her to return to the driver side window.

She was smiling again and enjoying her stubbornness until Darren honked the horn. Caught unprepared, she jumped and slid off the front hood. April turned to look at the enterprising journalist. Her stance was wide and un-amused. She watched as Darren's determined face gave way to a smirk, followed by rolling laughter.

"Funny. Are we even now?" April asked when she reached the window.

"Pretty much," Darren conceded.

"Now can we work together?" April asked with a smile.

"Like you said, I have no choice. I'll take my cell phone and my laptop. I will pretend to be working. If I see him I will call you; if you see him you call me," Darren said while gathering his equipment.

April opened the door. Darren stepped out; April replaced him behind the wheel.

"Hey Sherlock, should we use code words or something?" April asked.

She watched as Darren walked away without acknowledging her comment.

"I swear you have no sense of humor," she yelled to his back.

# 94

Eddie began a journal in his laptop. The noise in the bar faded to a hum as he typed about the places he had been and the people he influenced. He backtracked to record his feelings for his father, mother, and Griff. He recorded the guilt and voices. He stared at the words. The guilt and voices are gone.

He noted, "When did they go away? Why? How?"

He began to make notes about Powers Meade.

"I don't remember meeting with him, yet I know Harmon paid Powers Meade to counsel me."

As he recalled thoughts and activities he typed the memories into the journal. He wrote what he recalled about the time Meade interviewed Eddie about his visualizations. He noted the website surefirewinner.com. He recorded the slim chance that he would have ever found surefirewinner.com on his own. Eddie typed everything, regardless of the order it occurred to him.

The professor moved to Las Vegas. Why? The images of a puppet master seemed to be Powers Meade. Could he possibly control Eddie? Could Eddie have been hypnotized without knowing it?

His eyes were glued to his laptop screen. The metronome blink of the cursor captivated Eddie as he thought. He slipped deeper and deeper into the computer screen. He felt as though he was slipping into a trance. Though Eddie was surrounded by noise and light, he was in darkness. He saw steps and a light at the top. He walked up the steps. He saw his family on a basketball court. He spoke with them and entered a control room. He came out of the room ready to play ball. He walked to a computer and typed surefirewinners.com.

Clang. Clang. Clang. A bell rang. Eddie's head snapped in the direction of the noise. He saw Harmon Evans with his hand on a rope. Clang. Clang. The chest door was opening. The bar was erupting with laughter. Eddie felt a little dizzy. He turned his attention to the laptop and found Surefirewinners.com filled the screen.

Eddie stared as if it were an alien language.

*I was talking to my family.*
*No, I was writing a journal.*

He glanced at the Task Bar on the computer. The journal was open; but he did not remember opening the betting site.

"It must be hypnosis. He must have hypnotized me," Eddie muttered out loud.

Eddie began typing notes about what he remembered of the dream.

"I talked with Griff. He said he forgave me. My parents said I should play my own game."

"Two thoughts that once troubled my game were eliminated from my conscience," Eddie typed.

He stopped recording his thoughts while he pieced it together in his head.

*He hypnotized me. I must be highly susceptible because of my own training. He must have planted a suggestion that every time I did a pep talk, I would go to this web site and place a bet. He must have mirrored my activity to make money.*

"Son of a bitch!" he said out loud.

Eddie did not notice the people who turned to look at him.

Eddie's brain was flying from point to point.

*For all I know, I may have been clucking like a chicken at the same time.*

Powers Meade had beaten Eddie. Only a handful of people could make that claim. Eddie loathed the thought of being manipulated by the professor. Like a tsunami, revenge decimated all other thoughts. Eddie would not allow this man to get away with this deception.

Eddie used both hands to massage the back of his neck. He returned to the laptop and recorded his suspicions. He packed up and left Bluebeards. He made one stop on the way back to the hotel. He was in and out of the bookstore and pulling into the parking garage before sunset. Eddie went to his room; it was time to develop a game plan for Professor Powers Meade.

# 95

April watched Darren walk into the hotel lobby. She picked up the logbook to familiarize herself with how Darren had been recording the information. She looked up to see a red truck enter the parking garage. She made a note in the book even though she knew it was not Eddie. She recorded the information on twelve vehicles. She was getting hungry and thirsty.

She opened the door and walked to the back of the Pathfinder. She opened the tailgate and saw a cooler. Inside she found sodas and sandwiches. She took one of each.

"That-a-boy! I knew you'd be prepared," she said. "You little Eagle Scout."

April re-seated herself behind the wheel. She unwrapped the sandwich and took a bite. She looked up to see a blue sedan. She squinted and reached for the opera glasses. It looked like Eddie to her. She needed a closer look. She reached to turn the key in the ignition but it was missing. Darren had taken them with him.

"Damn it, Darren," April muttered into the night air.

April opened the door and jogged across the street. She reached the parking garage and went inside. She paused to let her eyes adjust while listening for the vehicle's motor. She heard it and moved forward. April could see the taillights; it was the blue sedan. She stood behind a column and waited for the driver to exit. She heard the slam of a closing car door and the squeak of rubber on concrete. The steps were getting farther away. April peeked around the corner and could see a tall male. It was Eddie; she was certain.

April had forgotten to take the cell phone. She ran back to the truck and quickly dialed Darren.

"Benefield."

"He's here. He should be inside by now," she whispered loudly into the phone.

Her phone went silent. Darren had hung up. A few seconds later, April spotted Darren walking across the street to the Pathfinder.

Darren picked up the logbook. He scanned the list.

"You didn't write it down?" Darren asked.

"I was too busy running to the garage to confirm it was him."

"You went over there?" Darren said throwing his hands into the air.

"Don't start, Darren. He did not see me. It's a blue sedan. Let's drive through the garage and I will point it out," April said as she situated herself in the passenger's seat.

Darren started the vehicle and drove into the garage. He drove down the second row slowly.

"That's it," April said as she took another bite of the sandwich.

"That's a Chevy Monte Carlo. A new one." Darren said as he recorded the license plate in his notebook. "Oh, and feel free to help yourself to my food."

"Thank you. You make a good sandwich. Sherlock," April replied. "If this journalist thing doesn't work out, they could really use you down at the deli in the union building."

# 96

Dexter gnawed at a tiny piece of dead skin next to the cuticle of his index finger. He managed to free the hard scratchy irritation.

"Dex, first, this is a restaurant and the Health Code Nazi's would cite me. Second: it's disgusting. You have a piece of dead dirty skin in your mouth. What do you intend to do with it? And don't say spit it on the floor. Don't answer; you'll just say something idiotic. Keep your fingers out of your mouth," Harmon said handing him a sheet of paper towel.

Dexter pulled his hand down and removed the tiny particle of skin from his tongue. He tossed the crumpled towel in the trashcan. He continued to file at the spot with his thumbnail.

"Why are you so nervous? Are you even listening to me?" Harmon asked.

"I've heard every word you said," Dexter answered.

"Are you worried about something? Classes going okay?"

"Classes are fine," Dexter mumbled back.

Dexter was worried and he was nervous. Harmon had spent the last fifteen minutes relating the details of his trip to Orangeburg with Helen. Dexter wanted to suggest that the briber could have been Eddie Dreyer but if he did, he would have to tell Harmon the whole story. Dexter could not predict how Harmon would react to the information. He could not predict how April and Darren would react to Harmon knowing. Again, Dexter decided to protect Dexter. His objective was to stay off the Nightly News.

Just as he was about to ask Harmon a question, Helen walked up to the bar.

"Hiya' Honey. What brings you in?" Harmon said.

"Harmon, you said I could come in and use your computer, remember?" Helen reminded.

"Yes, I remember. I was just giving you the opportunity to pamper me with sweet talk. But I can see, it's business before pleasure," Harmon said with a smile.

Helen reached across the bar, put her hand on his cheek, and gently stroked it.

"Harmon, I wouldn't trade you for a handsome man." She said and removed the hand.

"Thank you, Honey. You know where the computer is; help yourself," he said.

She walked around the end of the bar and into the office.

"That's because I'm the handsomest man you know," he yelled as she went through the door.

Dexter watched as Harmon shook his head and smiled. A broad smile on Harmon Evans's face was rare but it was more likely to occur when Helen was around. Dexter could see how much Harmon loved her. It was obvious that a man needs more than a bar in his life.

"Harmon," Dexter said to regain his attention.

"What?" He asked turning to face Dexter.

"What's Helen doing on the computer?" Dexter asked.

"Probably, gathering information on colleges?"

"Is she thinking about going back to school?" Dexter asked.

"No. And since I am paying you to stand around, you could be drying those mugs and glasses," Harmon said. "She's looking for another school for that dip-shit nephew of hers. She's always thinking of other people."

Harmon threw a towel at Dexter. Dexter grabbed it from the air, began to dry the mugs and put them away.

"I thought you told me everyone she works with hates her because she's mean," Dexter said.

"No. I said they are afraid of her because she is rough. But if you pay your dues, she's the best friend you can get. She will not rest until she helps you," Harmon explained. No one could have missed the admiration in his tone.

"But the nephew hasn't paid his dues," Dexter said.

"Jimmy is her only sister's only boy. I guess family rates an exemption," Harmon said. "And besides, before that bad decision, he made a lot of decent ones."

Dexter shoved a few dry wine glasses into the overhanging rack and decided to help Harmon reach a conclusion.

"Harm, when was the last time you saw Eddie Dreyer?" He blurted out.

"He was here earlier, just before you came in. Why?" Harmon answered.

"I've been wondering about his luck," Dexter said. "Statistics say it is impossible to be as lucky as he seems to be."

"Are you jealous or mad or bitter?" Harmon asked.

"All three, actually," Dexter said truthfully.

"Listen, I have never met anyone as focused on basketball as Eddie Dreyer. You've seen him. He has no life. He sleeps and then he gets up and starts his basketball day. Sure, he's lucky but haven't you ever heard the old saying – the harder you work the luckier you get?" Harmon asked.

"No," Dexter answered.

"That's not surprising," Harmon remarked.

"Hey! I work hard. If I didn't you wouldn't keep me here," Dexter said to Harmon.

"Just kidding," Harmon said through a slight chuckle.

"Harm, what if Eddie was in Orangeburg recently," Dexter asked and was immediately worried about saying it.

"What if he was?" Harmon asked.

"What if Eddie had bet the Grizzlies game and won?" Dexter more specifically asked.

"So? What's unusual about that?" Harmon responded sounding irritated by the confusing direction of Dexter's questions.

"He did all his research but he actually won because some mascot drew two technical fouls. What is that? Luck? Or did he know something?" Dexter asked.

Dexter was way over the line of comfort. He threw the towel over his shoulder and without conscious awareness; he began to gnaw at the finger with the calloused skin.

"Dex, get your hand out of your mouth," Harmon commanded. "Wash your hands. Why are you being so weird?" Harmon's tone changed.

"I'm not weird. I'm just curious. You said, Helen's nephew was bribed and it caused me to speculate on stuff, that's all," Dexter said.

"Speculate on stuff? Speculate that Eddie Dreyer bribed Jimmy Gerald?" Harmon said in a whisper. He moved too close to Dexter's face for Dexter comfort. "Is that what you are saying?"

"Isn't it possible?" Dexter answered.

Dexter felt cornered and a little frightened. He took a step to his left to create some space between himself and Harmon.

"Dexter, are you insane? Eddie Dreyer may not play basketball anymore but he sure as hell has not lost his competitive spirit."

371

"That's right. His competitive nature has pushed him to challenge people close to the game. I think he just wants to win. I don't think he cares how," Dexter said.

His voice had a tremble to it and he spoke softly; it must have been barely audible to Harmon. He watched as Harmon walked to the end of the bar. Dexter was wishing he could erase the conversation about Eddie Dreyer. He had no idea what was going through Harmon's mind but Dexter felt like he had indeed crossed a line. He reached for another glass to dry when he heard Harmon call his name. Dexter put the glass in the rack and walked next to Harmon.

"Dex, are you really dreaming this shit up or do you know something about Eddie Dreyer's activities?" Harmon asked.

Dexter did not want to reveal what he knew nor did he want to lie to Harmon. He stood there offering nothing but dry lips and a racing heartbeat. Harmon reached toward Dexter. The sudden movement scared him. Dexter recoiled but Harmon's large hand clutched a shoulder. Harmon shook Dexter.

"Dexter, answer me," he said with a firmness that could not be ignored.

"I witnessed Eddie blackmail a player in Greenville. April and I talked to him about it. He admitted it was true," Dexter said. He searched Harmon's face and then added, "Harm. You're squeezing my shoulder pretty hard."

Harmon let go. His eyelids were blinking like a computer processing a command.

"Eddie is a blackmailer?" Harmon said as he turned his back to face the mirror. "Eddie could be the guy who blackmailed Helen's nephew? Dexter, is there any chance you are mistaken?"

Dexter did not answer; he just shook his head no.

"Harm, we didn't report him because I didn't want to be crucified in public. Eddie said it would be his word against mine and that the blackmailed player would never confess. I believed him. I just don't think there is any way for me to stop him."

"He's right. I would bet money Jimmy wouldn't testify either. Jimmy can get into another school. Years from now people will think of it as a funny prank. He can live with that but if the world knew he took a bribe, that's something he wouldn't want to live with," Harmon said.

"Other than you, me, and April, only one other person knows," Dexter said to him.

"Who's the other person?" Harmon asked.

"April thought it would be a good idea to tell Darren Benefield. He's a senior journalism major and an intern with The Seaboard Post. Darren is going to try and tail Eddie. He hopes he can create a story to expose him," Dexter explained.

"I don't think Eddie will stick around here now that you know. He can go anywhere. That son of a bitch, I wonder how many times he has done this," Harmon said.

"I don't know but I'm betting he stays busy," Dexter said.

"He is a hard worker," Harmon muttered. He removed his apron and without an explanation, walked to the office. He returned within a minute wearing a light jacket.

"Harm, are you leaving?" Dexter asked.

"Yeah."

"Where are you going?" Dexter said hoping the answer was anything but "To find Eddie Dreyer."

Harmon did not answer. Dexter called his name a second and third time but Harmon kept walking. Dexter heard a customer call his name; he walked back toward the middle of the bar but his eyes stayed fixed on Harmon. The student ordered beer but the only voice Dexter could hear was the one in his head.

*Idiot. Harmon will find Eddie. Eddie will know you told him and big bad Eddie D will come for you.*

"Yeah, if Harmon doesn't kill him," Dexter said out loud.

The student asked, "Dude, what'd you say?"

"Nothing, just talking to myself," Dexter answered.

"Well, when you finish, could I get a beer?"

Dexter pulled a mug from the overhang, filled it, and slid it in front of the student. He pulled his cell phone from his pocket and dialed April.

"Hello," she answered.

"It's Dex."

"It's hard to hear you," April said.

"Hold on." Dexter walked toward the office doorway and backed inside.

"Can you hear me now?" Dexter asked.

"Yeah, that's much better. What's up," she asked.

"I told Harm about Eddie," Dexter said.

Why?" April asked sharply.

"Does it matter?" Dexter replied.

Dexter turned around and saw Helen sitting at the computer and looking directly at him. He gave her a smile even though fear gripped his brain.

*Did she hear me?*

"April, I gotta' go. I'll call you back," Dexter said. He clicked the end button.

"I'm sorry Helen. I forgot you were back here. I hope I didn't disturb you."

"No. Do you need some privacy?" She asked.

"No, it can wait. Thanks, though," Dexter said as he walked back out to the bar.

"I am an idiot." Dexter's loud voice carried through the bar clamor.

"Hey," a student yelled. "Don't be so hard on yourself. You did a good job on this beer. Pour me another; it'll make you feel even better about yourself."

Dexter could not think of a sarcastic response. He did the only thing he could do; he poured another beer and waited for closing time.

# 97

Powers was accustom to mundane offices. He had sat in the offices of accountants, attorneys, and bankers. They imposed on secretaries or contracted decorators to paint and fill the space with trendy trinkets. He had sat in dozens of offices where Deans and Professors stacked dog-eared books, term papers, and memos into piles. They thought it was more colorful to hide behind labels like eccentric and eclectic than to be thought of as unorganized and lazy.

Every office, he had ever seen, was merely a place to perform work.

"Offices' are a nuisance," they might claim.

"Creativity, is better used for one's leisure environment," he had heard them say.

Powers always wondered if their homes were any better.

This office was different; it was an extension of the man. Powers sat down and soaked up the character of the room. Nothing was out of place. If one object were moved, the man behind the desk would know and he would re-position it, immediately. Powers could see artistry and craftsmanship had liberated plain walls, stain-free carpet floors, and primary human clothing. Here, it was understood that an office is another opportunity to showcase. Money holds no beauty. Here, money had been exchanged for art, quality, and creativity. This place, this office, and this professional made Powers feel comfortable.

Powers had been exchanging from the first day he earned a paycheck. 'Beyond his means' was never a deterrent to owning finer things. His colleagues considered him arrogant, pretentious, and wasteful. What people did not know about Powers was that he lived in that manner because he found no joy in the merely functional. Powers Meade wanted everything to reflect the epitome of artistry. He did not care how his peers perceived him. He admired finer things for what they were, not what they represent.

The man in the crisp white shirt pushed a folder across the desk. His golden cuff link glittered under the desk lamp; the pinstripe in his navy blue jacket was so faint, it hardly seemed worth the effort to loom. Powers lifted the folder from the burled cherry-wood surface. He opened it. The financial investment portfolio was not intimidating but neither was it interesting.

Powers thumbed through the pages with his displeasure in check. He had not received a wager from Eddie in five days. Powers could only assume, Eddie knew about the hypnotic suggestion and had the strength to overpower it. Powers knew, he would need professional help to protect his money and he understood the importance of taking control. Yet, now that the bridle was securely jammed into his mouth, he felt rebellious. He had tasted freedom; he wanted to run with the lead horses.

"I can see by the look on your face that the suggested budget is distasteful," the man said.

Powers watched the man across the desk shaped his hands into a loose praying position. His manicured fingertips tapped together. It seemed to imply impatience to Powers.

"It certainly represents a change in my lifestyle; the last few months have been nirvana. This is a step back into reality," Powers said as he closed the folder and replaced it on the desk.

"Have you changed your primary goal, Mr. Meade?"

His calm voice carried an unmistakable confidence. His plan was flawless; it was unreasonable for Powers to challenge it.

"That's difficult to answer, Mr. Kessler. This is the first time I have ever had a set of goals. It is rather like trying on a swimsuit. I am more comfortable clothed," Powers said with a small smile.

"I suspect it is for first timers," he responded.

Kessler did not smile but he did manage a head nod and then continued as though he was missing something important.

"Have any of the variables changed since you and I first spoke? Have you acquired another source of income?"

"No. I just want a larger wagering account," Powers stated.

"The probability of increasing your wealth through gambling is statistically impossible. The greater the sum allocated for the portfolio, the greater the probability of financial gain," Mr. Kessler said without saying yes or no to Powers request.

Powers picked up the folder again and looked at page after page of monotonous numbers. He imagined receiving his monthly stipend like a welfare check. He knew he would have three days of intrigue, followed by twenty-seven days of thrill-less waiting. The reality bridle was too large for the mouth of Powers Meade.

"Mr. Kessler, please send me a bill for your time. I have changed my primary goal. Though I never really thought about it this way, my goal is to be lucky. I never planned to be wealthy and yet I have acquired a healthy sum," Powers said as he stood.

"As you wish, Mr. Meade. Good day to you and I hope you are successful in the pursuit of your primary goal," he said as he rose, walked around the desk, and extended his hand.

They shook hands and Powers walked out into the Nevada sun. He was mildly surprised that Kessler was not more persistent. His passion to sell the investment plan was invisible, as though he could take or leave the business.

Powers would go home, sit by the pool for a few hours, and try his luck at the Mirage.

*Yes. The Mirage seems appropriate tonight.*

# 98

The twin tailpipes of the Galaxy 500 rumbled one last groan as the ignition was turned off. Harmon looked at his watch as he closed the car door. He had traveled the sixty-nine miles in a little over an hour. He walked hurriedly to the door of the house. He rang the door and stood impatiently. The porch light beamed on, the click of a deadbolt joined the chorus of crickets from the lawn, and the door opened. Jimmy stood there peering through a half opened door.

"What do you want?" Jimmy snarled.

Harmon raised a newspaper with a large photo of a basketball player. He pushed it very close to Jimmy's face.

"Is this the person who bribed you?" Harmon asked.

"I don't want to talk to you and I don't have to talk to you. So, go away," Jimmy said and started closing the door.

Harmon rammed his hand against the door. The loud slapping noise of Harmon's hand filled the room. The door reversed course and Jimmy was unprepared. The door hit him in the shoulder. He stumbled backwards. Harmon stepped in the doorway.

"You've got an awful short memory, boy. Is this the person who bribed you?" Harmon growled. "Don't make me ask again."

The noise alarmed Paula Gerald. She left the kitchen and rushed into the tiny living room.

"What in the hell is going on Jimmy?" She asked.

"He pushed his way in the house. No one invited him," Jimmy explained as he massaged his shoulder.

"Harmon, why are you here?" She looked at Jimmy and saw him rubbing the shoulder. "I will not let you whip my son again," she said as she stepped between Harmon and Jimmy.

Harmon did not look at Jimmy but he could feel a smug look on Jimmy's face.

"Paula, I simply want to know if this is the person who bribed Jimmy. I have asked him and twice he has refused to answer me," Harmon said holding the photo for her to see.

"That does not give you the right to hit my son," she said.

"I did not hit him. I stopped him from closing the door. The door clipped him; he isn't hurt," Harmon said trying to remain civil.

Harmon could see Jimmy grinning behind his mother.

"I just want him to answer the question."

Harmon focused his attention on Paula; he did not want to see Jimmy's sneering face. He tried to relax, to appear less hostile. Paula broke her stare and turned to face Jimmy.

"Jimmy, is this the person who gave you the money?" She asked.

"It's none of his business and it doesn't matter. The damage is done," Jimmy said.

Paula's eyes darted back and forth between her son and Harmon. She removed the towel that had been draped over her shoulder; and with lightning quickness, she began swatting Jimmy with the towel.

"Is he the one? Tell me. Is he the one?" She screamed as she flailed her towel at Jimmy's body. "Tell me; tell me."

"Stop it, stop, are you crazy?" Jimmy protested as his hands covered his face like a boxer pinned in the corner of the ring.

"Answer the damn question," she roared through the windmill of attacks.

"Yes. Yes. Now stop hitting me," Jimmy yelled.

Paula's kitchen towel fell to her side. Harmon spotted tears on her face. Jimmy started to leave but Harmon grabbed him by the arm and immediately Paula grabbed Harmon's arm. Harmon loosened his grip.

"Please, take another look at the photo. Are you certain this is the guy?" Harmon asked with the calmest voice he could muster.

"I'm positive. I'm sure I will never forget," Jimmy said as he sat in a chair and allowed his head to hang near his knees.

Paula watched her son walk out of the room. She turned and moved closer to Harmon.

"So, now you know who the blackmailer is. Tell me, Harmon, how is that going to help us?" She asked through the tears. "How, Harmon? How?" The tears fell faster until they formed a continuous stream. She used the towel to dry some away.

"I'm not sure yet, Paula. I know this boy. He used to be a great ball player. He was injured his junior year. His playing days were taken from him. He turned to gambling and was doing well. He was making lots of money and living in nice hotels in Charleston. But I didn't know

379

he was bribing people. When I was told it might be him, I had to know. Maybe Jimmy should press charges and put a stop to the guy." Harmon said.

Paula took the edge of the door in her hand. Harmon knew it was a command for him to leave. He walked back onto the porch and began down the path.

"Harmon, that's the last of it. We're burying the incident. We're done," she said to his back. "Make sure you understand me, Harmon."

He did not turn around. The porch light lit lawn went dark and Harmon heard the door close. He felt unhappy with what he had done. He could truthfully admit he did not care how the questioning affected Jimmy but he should have considered Paula's feelings.

He settled into his car, turned the key, and the tailpipes came alive. Harmon wished he had involved Helen before acting on his instincts. He hoped Paula would understand his need to know. Harmon would have plenty of time to think about Helen, Paula, Jimmy and Eddie Dreyer on the hour-long trip back. The angry drive up seemed much shorter than the atonement drive back.

# 99

"Who is Harmon?" Darren asked.

"Harmon owns Captain Bluebeards," April answered.

"Why did Dexter tell him?"

"He didn't say. He said he'd call back and hung up."

"What's Harmon's connection to Eddie?" Darren asked.

"I don't know," she said. "Eddie goes to the bar a lot."

"There must be a stronger connection; why else would Dexter tell him?" Darren wanted to know.

"Again, I do not know," April said as she leaned the passenger seat back.

"Does Eddie have a drinking problem?" Darren asked.

"Every college kid has a drinking problem. We have the freedom to abuse alcohol; so we do," April answered.

"I don't and I know many who do not," Darren stated.

"Yeah but you're a weirdo, a geek, and a nerd."

"Why do you associate Cool with following the herd?" He asked.

"Whoa, wait. You are accusing me of following the herd?" April said in near shock.

"No, of course not. You're precept is anti-herd. It's your thing," Darren said.

"I don't have a thing," April responded.

"Oh most definitely you do. You do not want people to understand you. You want to live with an atypical album of information and interests," Darren said.

He turned his attention back to the parking garage.

"I don't care if anyone understands me," April said.

"Yes you do. Most people won't put forward the effort to understand you so you don't get a lot of play. Instead of moving a little toward the middle so people have the opportunity to know you, you react by moving even further from the mainstream. It's your anti herd thing," Darren said. "A true Maverick."

"One of the things I hate most about college students is that everybody thinks they are Sigmund Fuckin' Freud. One or two semesters of psychology and everyone wants to break out their analytical skills. Believe whatever you want to believe Darren; I don't care," April said.

"Yes you do. But it's a different kind of caring. Architecture is the only thing you do for yourself. Every other piece of knowledge is stockpiled. You treat information the same way America and the Soviet Union once treated nuclear warheads. It's an arms race with you. You want to make sure your arsenal is bigger than anyone else's," Darren continued his analysis.

"I do not. Why are you blasting me, anyway?" April asked.

"Eddie Dreyer. No one truly knows him; so, you have to. Logic tells you can't get ahead by gambling but April is smarter than logic. The intelligent students don't get drunk because they are too busy being seduced by learning, but April can do both. You want to prove you can drink but refuse to hang out with the drinkers."

Darren had worked himself into frenzy.

"Doesn't that sound like a Maverick to you?"

April stared at him. She knew her nostrils were flaring; she could feel the rage pounding at her closed mouth demanding to be unleashed. She was stunned by his accusations but chose to change the direction of the conversation.

"Whatever." April said. "I'm not participating in your little mating dance."

"Mating dance?" Darren said while slapping himself on the forehead.

"Sure. I've seen this one before. One of two paths are available to me. I either go gaga over you because you are sooo deep or I become vulnerable to prove to you I am not cold, aloof, and anti-herd," April said. "Newsflash: I'm not doing either."

"It's not a newsflash to me, April. I have given up on trying to find common ground with you. Some things I can do; some things I cannot."

He slowly turned to continue looking at the garage. April did not know how to respond or if she wanted to. She sat quietly. It was near midnight and she was tired. Tired is often a place where people hurt each other's feelings. She did not want to hurt his feelings. Darren's assessment of her character was near accurate but hearing it out loud, left her feeling a little more lonely than usual. She was ready to go home and leave the investigation to Darren.

Her phone rang.

"Dexter?" She asked.

"Hey. Where are you?" Dexter asked.

"I'm with Darren. We have found Eddie's hotel and we are waiting for him to leave so we can follow him."

"I thought Darren was going to build a story and you and I were going to stay out of it,' Dexter asked a bit betrayed.

"Well, plans change," April snapped back.

"Meaning, you changed them," he replied.

"Yeah, but I'm going home. I'm leaving this spy crap to Darren."

Darren turned his head to look at April. She stuck out her tongue. He smiled. Her peace offering had been accepted.

*See, I can move to the middle, you shithead.*

"Well, Harmon just returned to the bar. If he's going to stick around, I'm going to try to leave early. Are you sleepy or could I come by?" Dexter said.

He did not get the immediate response he anticipated. He felt the need to clear up her possible confusion.

"I want to tell you about Harmon," he said.

"I'll be up. I want to know what's going on," April answered.

"Okay. Later."

Dexter disconnected.

"Okay Sherlock, your dreams are coming true. I'm going home," April said.

She opened the door and stepped out.

"Will you call me and let me in on this Harmon thing?" Darren asked.

"Yeah. I'll do that," April said through the open window.

"Bye, Darren. Don't fall asleep. Eddie is an unpredictable guy. He's probably in his room drinking scotch like it's water but he has an amazing ability to hold his liquor. Drinking will not prevent him from leaving the minute he needs to," she said.

April asked, "Are you sure you don't want my help?"

"I got this," Darren answered.

"Alright. Bye."

"Bye." Darren replied.

"April," he called to her.

April stopped and leaned back in the window. Darren leaned across and put his hand on hers.

"I wish I hadn't said all those things. I just had some stuff built up inside. If I had it to do over, I would say it much differently."

"Forget about it. So, you might have used different words and little less spittle but the meaning would be the same. I know what you are saying. Maybe you are right." April said. "See you later."

April walked two blocks down and waited for a bus. Fifteen minutes later, she settled into a seat near the back of the bus even though she was the only passenger.

# 100

Eddie looked away from the Google Map and glanced at the clock; he rubbed his eyes. No need to make travel notes, once he picked up Interstate Forty, nothing would change until Kingman, Arizona. His route was planned. Tomorrow morning he would begin a trip across country to Las Vegas. Eddie planned to confront Powers Meade. His initial reason for initiating contact was to demand the money in his account. He could not do that over the Internet; Powers would become suspicious. If Powers shut down the website and moved, it could become very difficult for Eddie to find him.

Eddie wanted his money but he wanted more. Eddie knew why Powers did it, to scam money off Eddie's expertise. Eddie did not know what he wanted from Powers; he just knew he wanted to face him. The drive would give him plenty of time to decide what he wanted to accomplish when he found the professor. But the absence of a clear-cut plan would not deter his determination to go.

With the trip details out of the way, Eddie's attention returned to the computer screen. He opened the basketball research tab. The notes he had written about the Rams basketball team in Arkansas were on screen. He briefly reviewed the data. He rubbed his eyes again and leaned back.

He opened a Word doc. His mind was awash with ideas. He closed his eyes briefly and allowed them to roll in like tidewaters until he saw one he really liked. The right plan came rolling in; he sat erect and began to type a letter. He took his time and edited frequently. He was satisfied; the letter would be effective. He finished and read it one last time.

Eddie printed and folded the letter carefully and slid it into the envelope. He sealed it and neatly wrote "*Malone Danbridge*" on the front. Eddie's plan was to hand deliver the envelope to the coach's office. Eddie sat the envelope on top of his iPad.

With the research completed and the letter written, Eddie was ready to relax. He needed sleep. Eddie wanted to leave before sunrise.

He looked at the clock and caught a glimpse of the Dewar's bottle, standing next to the lamp. It was a new bottle with an unbroken seal. Eddie had been working for hours but had not taken a drink. Earlier in the evening, Eddie grabbed the bottle and nearly twisted the top off but he stopped short. He heard the words of Dexter Dalton saying, "You made a mistake; you will make another."

Alcohol could have been a factor in the unlocked door in Greenville. Eddie remembered a nauseous feeling that morning. The feeling left him vulnerable to that mistake. He lifted the bottle by the neck and twirled it slowly in the palm of his hand. He scanned the label, as though he might find directions for use. Unlike regular medicine, it did not come with dosage instructions. If he had discovered instructions, it would not matter; moderation was not Eddie's style. Anything worth doing was worth doing to excess. This, he decided was not worth doing. He tossed it in the waste can. The clunking metal and glass sound bounced off the wall but the bottle remained unbroken.

Tonight neither the Puppet Master nor alcohol would control Eddie Dreyer. He was free to be Eddie Dreyer, a man in control. He shut the laptop down and packed everything away. Tomorrow morning he would shave, shower, dress and leave clean. It was time for a change of scenery.

# 101

Dexter stood in the doorframe, half in and half out. He watched as Harmon sat in the chair that had been occupied by Helen. Harmon had both feet up on the desk crossed at the ankles. His large boots displaced paper and sent a clipboard crashing to the floor. Neither the noise, nor the mess dislodged him from his position. He clasped his hands and lowered his chin to rest on the handmade perch. His eyes seemed locked on the wooden plank floor. He knew Dexter was standing in the doorway but he did not look up.

"Harm, where did you go?" Dexter asked.

"Orangeburg."

"You were gone less than three hours." Dexter said.

"Quit fishing for information Dex. I went to talk with Helen's nephew. The kid identified Eddie as the guy who bribed him," Harmon said and then added, "So, what?"

"I don't know, Harm. I've said all along, I don't know. Are you going to do something?" Dexter wanted to know.

"Like what? I can't report him. Jimmy won't testify and if he wanted to, his mother wouldn't let him. I guess I could go try to kick Eddie's ass but in case you haven't noticed, he's younger and bigger. We'd both get banged up and nothing would get accomplished," Harmon said.

Harmon broke eye contact. He was a realist but he felt a little ashamed that his age was a liability.

Harmon took his feet off the desk and stood up. Dexter cut his eyes toward the bar to be sure no one was requesting service. When he looked back, Harmon was directly in front of him and speaking loudly.

"And, you know what? This really has nothing to do with me. I used to admire Eddie as a ball player. That does not make me his keeper. Then Eddie started a new career; he was outsmarting the bookies. I got a kick out of that. Now, I find out Eddie is preying on weak people. He makes money by testing character. He hurts my girlfriend's only nephew. That's just bad luck. I can't punish him; so, I just won't admire him anymore. I'll blacklist him from my bar. I'm thinking that's enough. What do you think Dexter? Does that sound reasonable? Should I have to do more?"

Harmon paused while still staring into Dexter's confused face. He had not wanted to actually discuss this topic with Dexter. Harmon was merely practicing what he would tell Helen.

Dexter was not certain he should answer but he did.

Dexter answer, "Hey, that's fine with me," he said.

Harmon walked past Dexter and took a post along the bar.

"Dexter, go home. Last-call is in thirty minutes. I'll close up." Harmon told him.

"Are you sure?" Dexter asked.

"I've got nowhere to be. My mood is perfect for sending college students home before they do something stupid," he replied.

"Okay. Thanks," Dexter said.

"I'll see you tomorrow," Harmon said.

"Actually, I'm off tomorrow," Dexter said and turned to read his expression.

"Whenever," Harmon practically growled.

Harmon watched as Dexter grabbed his bag and headed for the door. Harmon turned his attention to the sparse crowd.

"Listen up; this is last call," he yelled over the noise.

"Hey it's too early," someone protested.

"It's my damn bar. You want to leave now?" Harmon barked at the young man.

No one chose to answer the question or challenge Harmon's order. Lucky for them.

# 102

The tap on the door was so soft; April mistook it for a clicking noise the refrigerator makes. The second knock was louder; she opened the door. Dexter stood motionless under the light.

"I could barely hear you knock. Were you afraid you'd wake the roommate?" April asked grabbing him by the arm and pulling him in the apartment.

"I didn't want to wake the neighbors. It's two in the morning you know?" Dexter said.

"Well, aren't you sweet?" April said closing the door.

"I prefer 'thoughtful' but whatever. So tell me about the stakeout," Dexter asked.

"Eddie came, we saw him, and Darren is still watching the hotel," April said.

"Wow, that's riveting. Tell me again." Dexter said.

"Dexter? It's not the movies. It's boring. The most exciting part of the day was discovering Darren's food stash in the cooler," she said. "Alright, tell me about Harmon."

"I told Harmon about Eddie," Dexter offered and waited.

He watched as April stared at him. She picked up a small pillow from the window seat and hit him with it.

"You smart ass. I gave you the Cliff Notes because there is nothing more to tell. You have more to tell, now tell," April said.

"I may have left out a couple of details," Dexter remarked.

"Last week the Grizzlies mascot interrupted the game by chest bumping a referee. A technical foul was called with only a few seconds to play. The shot was made and it affected the betting line by a point. The mascot was the nephew of Harmon's girlfriend. Harmon drove to Orangeburg tonight. The mascot identified Eddie as the guy who paid him to screw up the final score."

"That's the kind of proof we need to do something," April said as she crossed her legs and leaned back in the window seat.

389

"Nope," Dexter said as he shook his head no. He will not testify," "Darren is still the best chance."

"What about Harmon? What's he going to do?" April asked.

"I have no idea. I know he's mad. He went into a semi-rage thing while I was there. But I don't know if there is anything he can do. Harmon really likes Eddie. So, he's pretty disappointed. But it is hard to imagine that he will just sit and do nothing," Dexter shared.

"Well, shit. This doesn't help. What happens when Eddie shows up at Bluebeard's?" April asked.

"Eddie's a big guy but Harmon isn't afraid of him. He said he was going to refuse to serve him. I guess he intends to ban him from the bar," Dexter said with a small shrug of the shoulders.

"Eddie may not know how he figured it out but he will immediately assume it was you," April said.

"Yeah, that's the way I see it too." Dexter said as he took a seat next to her.

"What do you think he will do?" April asked.

"No telling. I think he's capable of anything."

"So you're scared?" April asked in a very soft tone.

"Don't look for the macho bravado from me. If I see him, I will turn tail and run. I have no interest in taking an ass whipping, if I can avoid it." Dexter said. "I don't think he will literally kill me. I hope."

"I don't think he will do anything except leave the area. He'll work somewhere else. It's not like this is the only place on the planet where basketball is played," April said.

"You may be right. If I were Eddie, I'd be more afraid of Helen Gerald." Dexter said. "Now there's someone with no fear."

"Helen is Harmon's girlfriend?" April asked.

"Yeah. A few months ago, she was in the bar to meet Harm. She was sitting at the bar while Harm was on the phone in the office. This barely legal punk sat down next to her even though there were empty chairs all over the place. I couldn't hear what was going on but I looked up just as she was about to twist his ear off leading him to the door," Dexter said with a big grin.

"She pushed him outside and screamed, "I'm going to convince someone in here to give me your momma's phone number and I will call her and tell her what you said," Dexter said mimicking Helen as best he could.

"I was laughing my ass off when Harmon walked out and saw her walking back in. He asked me what was going on. I told him what I saw. Harm just shook his head and says, 'Again?' And walked back in the office," Dexter was laughing as he finished the story.

"Good for her; she sounds cool." April said.

Dexter looked at April; she was laughing with him. Dexter photographed the moment. He wished he had a lifetime of tales that would make her laugh. She regained control and said, "Enough. I have to get some sleep."

"Alright, I'll take off," Dexter said.

He rose from the window seat and walked toward the door. April followed.

"April, do you really think Darren will call when Eddie leaves?" Dexter asked.

"No. That's why I'm going to get back down there tomorrow morning," April said.

"What time are you going?" Dexter asked.

"Three's a crowd, Dexter," she responded.

"Well, let's get rid of Darren," Dexter replied.

"Go home Dexter," she said with a warm smile.

"Okay but it's not the best decision you've made today."

She closed the door. Dexter heard a small laugh from her as she closed the door.

*Yeah, that's all I need is million lines that make her smile.*

Then he could swear he heard a voice in his head whisper.

"I wouldn't bet on it."

Dexter grimaced a little, got in his car and drove away. Reality never goes away.

# 103

The motel room alarm was set to a music station. The Radio programmed to do so, came on loudly. It bellowed a commercial. A man was screaming "__for our once a year Mountainous Sale at Burfords Chevy Olds."

The voice and volume slammed into the alcohol-infested brain of Titus Lockwood. He sat up fast; his upper body looked like a bobble-head dog on the back dash of a car. His head rocked forward and back. The motion upset his stomach and the alarm shrieked like a banshee in his head. Titus was disoriented.

"__come on down for the best deals in the Ozarks."

The nasal southern drawl pierced his eardrums like a lancing needle. Titus took his hands from his ears and reached for the light. His fumbling fingers groped up and down the lamp trying to find the switch. He found a knob; he turned, pulled and pushed the button until the light came on. He struggled through blinking eyes to find the off button on the radio. Nothing he touched was silencing Lyle Burford's relentless and commercial.

"My wife says I'm crazy. She says I'm losing money on every car. But who's crazier, me for pricing them so cheap or you for not buying them."

Titus heard a man in the room next door yell and bang on the wall.

"Turn that goddamn thing off before I come over there and use it to beat you senseless."

Titus followed the cord to the wall and yanked the plug from the socket. Lyle Burford disappeared and so did the threats from beyond the wall.

Titus went to the bathroom and ran the cold-water faucet. He reached in and splashed water on his face. Handful after handful of water trickled down his face and fell back into the sink; he hoped each drop would haul away the dizziness and pain, instead he felt a convulsion in his gut.

He changed porcelains just in time. The rusty ring around the toilet bowl vanished as the vomit changed the nearly clear water to rusty brown and green. Titus started to straighten up when he realized this was not going to be a one-and-done campaign. Titus Lockwood heaved five good efforts into the bowl. He flushed and stood up; the water faucet was still flowing. He splashed more water on his face.

He pulled the towel from the rack and dabbed his face somewhat dry. The man in the mirror stared at him. Titus pressed the towel back to his face to make the man go away. He held it there like protection from the image until he realized his own breath would soon upset his stomach again. Titus did not want another embrace with the toilet. He flushed the toilet again, hoping to be more successful this time. He took some water into his mouth, gargled and spit.

He left the bathroom; the mirror was more truth than Titus wanted to face at this moment. He sat on the edge of the bed with his elbows on his knees and head in his hands. He took a few deep breaths then looked around the room.

The Jim Beam bottle was lying on the floor; a wet stain lay underneath it. He had passed out before he could finish it. An empty pizza box was tangled in the bedspread. That would account for the anchovies that were circling the drain a few minutes ago. The ashtray was overrun with cigarette butts.

"Fuck, no wonder my breath stinks like a sewer," he mumbled.

Titus walked over to the window and peeked outside; it was dark and quiet. He went to the dresser and looked at his watch. The little hand was on five. He strapped it on his wrist. As he was buckling it up, he remembered, Laura gave him the watch. She gave it to him as a reward for his first twenty win season. He had the watch but someone else had Laura.

Twelve hours ago, he began drowning Laura right out of his memory pool. He had a plan: get out of town and get drunk. He now realized he should have planned further out. Titus was not sure what he wanted to do now. His first thought was to go back to sleep, wake up later when the liquor stores are open, and start all over again.

*Could it be that simple; no counter attack, no revenge, just accept defeat?*

He walked back to the window and stared out at the road. A few minutes went by and a pickup truck drove past. Titus turned left to watch it ramble down the road. The taillights vanished over a hill. Just like that, it was somewhere else. He turned to look down the road to the right. Nothing was coming. A right hand turn would take him back to the life he lived. He had a basketball game to coach tonight. A third consecutive twenty win season was within his reach. All he had to do was get in the truck, make a right hand turn, and make sure twelve college boys play the way they have been drilled.

Titus was certain his Rams could win tonight and wrap up the conference championship. The odds makers disagreed. They posted a line of Rams plus five. They believed Dwight Timmons was more than the boys from the Ozarks could handle. Timmons was capable of scoring thirty every night he suited up but Titus was confident his matchup zone defense would frustrate him. He did not need the five points, Titus believed they would beat the Patriots straight up but he also believed he and Laura would always be together.

*If I can't manage one woman, how can I lead twelve young men?*

He walked back to the bed and sat down. He turned off the light and stared into the darkness. His eyes began to adjust. The light from the parking lot sneaked in from the edges of the curtains. Soon, Titus could see every object in the room. Nothing seemed rigid; the television swayed like a small tree surprised by a gust of wind. The disorientation had a beat to it, like the pulse in his throbbing head. His empty and unsettled stomach sent warnings to stop the swaying. Titus closed his eyes. The blackness was better.

"What am I gonna' do?' He muttered aloud.

He knew, he should get in the car and go back to town. He wanted to go home and prepare for the game. He also wanted to go home and find Laura still there, still in love with him. But through the stabbing pain in his head, he pictured Laura thrusting a knife into his heart. The knife was the greater pain and it was much too vivid. He snapped his eyes open. The wallowing was over.

He sat up and screamed, "I am not a loser! I will put you behind me and I will succeed. Your loss, Laura, not mine!"

The deep voice from the thin wall to next door came alive again.

"I've had it. I'm coming over there to__,"

Titus did not hear the rest. He leapt out of the bed, ran to the door, and went outside. He walked next door and banged on it.

"Get out here bad-ass. You're through threatening me. Get out here now," Titus yelled loud enough to be heard at any door in the low rent motel.

He slammed his fist against the door three more times.

"What are you waiting for loud mouth? Come out here and shut me up!" Titus said and wiped spittle away from his mouth.

Lights went on in several rooms but not the one next to Titus. He could not hear a sound from the man with the short temper and brave threats. He waited with clenched fists.

Through the heavy breathing, spittle, and throbbing headache, reality swept over him.

*Someone will recognize me. Someone will call the police.*

Satisfied he had scared the man, Titus walked back into his room and locked the door. The phone rang; he picked it up.

"This is the manager. What's going on over there?" He asked in an abrupt tone.

"My neighbor and I had a disagreement but it's over. It's fine now. No one is hurt. Nothing is broken. We are all going back to sleep. Goodnight," Titus said and hung up without waiting for a response.

He hoped it was over. Titus lay down and tried to formulate a plan but despite his tough words, he still felt directionless. He turned the light on and took his wallet from his back pocket. He pulled a photo of Laura from the plastic holder and rubbed his thumb across her face. Titus could not hold back the tears; they flowed down his face as his mouth twisted and struggled against the need to sob. He was out of control and at the mercy of a tired, aching, and inebriated body. Titus fell asleep with Laura's photo clutched in his hand.

# 104

Harmon lifted the phone to his ear.

"Hello." His voice answered in a sleepy whisper.

"Harmon."

It was Helen. Harmon blinked his eyes, looked at the clock, and took a deep breath.

"Harmon, why didn't you talk to me before going to see Jimmy?" She asked.

"Let's not do this over the phone. Couldn't we talk about this over breakfast? Give me a little while to clean up and I will come over," Harmon responded.

"Paula is still upset. Jimmy drove off somewhere and he's still not home," She added.

"I asked one question. They can't just pretend it didn't happen. They have to deal with this. Do you really think I'm the problem?" Harmon asked her.

Helen answered immediately, "No. I know they need to face it and get past it. But Harmon, I'm disappointed that you didn't talk to me. She's my sister and you are the love of my life. You're both very important to me. Don't you want me to be your sounding board? Don't you want me to be with you in troubling times?"

"You are the most important person in my life and I love you unconditionally but I'm not the person who should be called on the carpet. Yell at Paula for babying that boy. Yell at Jimmy for being an idiot. Hell, find Eddie Dreyer and yell at him for tempting your nephew. But Honey, don't yell at me. I am not the problem and I don't want any of these people to come between us," Harmon said.

"No one is coming between us. I don't mean to yell at you. I'm frustrated because my baby sister is hurting and I want to help. Let's skip breakfast. I think I'm going to drive to Orangeburg and help Paula find Jimmy." Helen said calmly but with a sense of dread in her voice.

"Do you really think that is necessary? He's probably just driving around thinking about what an idiot he has been." Harmon said.

"Harmon, stop calling him an idiot. Jimmy is a good kid and I'm sure he feels bad. I just don't want him to do something else stupid."

"Stupid? Like what?" Harmon asked and listened to the buzzing vacuum of the telephone line. He could sense that Helen was thinking about Jimmy being despondent and hurting himself. Harmon wanted to make her feel better.

"Helen, he'll be fine. He is a smart kid. He's not going to kill himself over something like this. He's out, talking tough to the windshield. He'll get it out of his system and come home. You go see Paula. I'm sure she needs your company."

"You're probably right. I'll go. I'll call you later."

"Yes, You do that. I worry when you are on the road. I want you safe," Harmon commanded.

"I love you, sweetie," she whispered.

"I love you more than my car," he said without laughing.

Harmon heard her say "Bye."

He laid the phone on the nightstand and got out of bed, shaved and showered. He left the house and drove to Bluebeards. As he drove, he pictured a frustrated Jimmy Gerald. Harmon was not worried that the boy would kill himself but he wondered if Jimmy thought he could make things right by confronting Eddie and returning the money. Jimmy would have no way of knowing how to find Eddie. Harmon was not certain he knew how to find Eddie. It seemed unlikely that Jimmy could locate him. That might not keep Jimmy from trying.

The Galaxy 500 rumbled to a stop at Bluebeards. Harmon walked to the door, looked around for the morning newspaper, and realized it was too early for delivery. He unlocked the door and paused before entering. He re-locked the door and went back to the car. Harmon drove to the central business district. He suspected this was a useless trip but he had plenty of time on his hands and too much curiosity in his brain. Harmon remembered a silver Jetta parked in the driveway at Paula's house. If Jimmy were in town trying to find Eddie, he would be in the Jetta.

Harmon drove toward downtown. He had no idea what Eddie was driving, so he passed time by searching the central business district for a silver Jetta.

Suddenly, Harmon remembered that Dexter said a budding journalist was trying to tail Eddie. Maybe he would get lucky and spot the guy. Harmon imagined a Clark Kent type sitting in a car with a pair of binoculars press to his eyes.

*How hard could it be to spot that?*

Harmon was not expecting to get lucky; he expected to be frying eggs at Bluebeard's in less than thirty minutes. Harmon slowed and began looking at each parked car. He could not have known that Eddie drove away an hour earlier and Clark Kent was right behind him.

# 105

April was surprised to see Dexter sitting on the curb. He was hunched over, sipping coffee. She tapped him on the head as she walked past.

"Let's go boy. If you're going to follow me around, you're going to have to keep up," April said and kept walking.

She peeked over her shoulder at him.

"Chop-chop," She said and clapped her hands together.

She and Dexter reached the bus stop, just as the bus was rounding the corner. They boarded and sat in the front seats. Dexter continued to sip his coffee.

"It's too early for clever banter. So, I'll be direct. Give me some of that coffee," April demanded.

She shaped her fingers in the classic gun look. She pointed the weapon at him.

"Well, since you asked so nice," he said handing her the cup.

"Where's your car? If you were going to force your way into my plan, the least you could have done is save me the fifty cents for the bus ride," April said.

"Yeah, Maybelline wasn't feeling well this morning," Dexter replied.

"Maybelline? Your car's name, I assume," April said.

"From a Chuck Berry song. Maybelline, why can't you be true?" Dexter sang.

"Undependable?" she asked.

"Moody is a better description," he answered.

"Not in the right mood this morning?" April guessed.

"Nope," Dexter answered. "I think it was PMS but a mechanic would say dead battery."

April nodded her head in sympathy and continued to drink the coffee. She held the cup as though Dexter had relinquished ownership of the remaining liquid. After several sips, Dexter reached for the cup. April growled like a dog over the food bowl, showing her snarling teeth. Dexter withdrew his hand. April noticed the bus driver peeked into the rear view mirror.

"It's probably getting cold any way," Dexter said.

"Just kidding, buddy. Here you go." She thrust the cup in front of him.

"No, go ahead; I really don't like it when it cools," he said.

"Okay, because I don't care, right now. I just want to mainline the caffeine," April explained.

The bus driver saw April reach up to pull the stop cord and began slowing for the next stop. Dexter and April got up and exited the bus. April tossed the empty cup into a trash container and motioned Dexter to follow her around the corner. They walked a block and turned right.

"You haven't heard from Darren, have you?" Dexter asked.

"Of course not. He believes that I will screw up his investigation by losing my cool and doing something stupid," April explained.

"Well, you are kind of hot headed," he said with unease.

"Who asked you?" April said, as she turned left at the next block.

"Yeah, my mistake. I__," Dexter was saying when April interrupted.

"Son-of-a-bitch," she said as she stamped her foot to the sidewalk. "He's gone. Eddie must have left and Darren followed him."

April reached in her purse and pulled out the cell phone. She called Darren. She kept walking toward the hotel as she waited. She clicked the end button and shoved the phone back in the purse. Dexter hurried to keep up with her fast pace.

"He has his phone turned off, right?" Dexter asked.

"Of course."

"Now what?" Dexter asked as he watched April turn three hundred and sixty degrees.

A car pulled alongside them and honked. April stopped turning; they both looked over to see Harmon Evans reaching across the seat to roll down the window.

"Where are ya'll going?" Harmon asked. Harmon looked at the hotel and then back at the two of them. "Maybe I'm being a little too nosy."

"Hello, Mr. Evans. We came down here on the bus. We were hoping to find a friend of ours but it looks like he has already left," she said ignoring the insinuation.

"Hey Harm. What are you doing down here? Isn't it time for that heart attack egg dish of yours?" Dexter asked as he knelt by the car window.

"I came looking for Helen's nephew. He took his mother's car and hasn't come home yet. I thought he might come looking for Eddie," Harmon answered.

"How would he know where to start looking?" April asked.

"I went to Orangeburg last night. His mother and I were talking. I think I said something about him being a regular at Bluebeard's. I don't know; he could have been listening. I know it's a long shot but I had to satisfy my curiosity," Harmon said.

"Well, if he is wandering around down here, he won't find Eddie because Eddie is gone. Darren and I saw him go in there," April said while pointing to the hotel. "He was driving a new blue Chevy. I just looked in the garage; it's gone."

"Maybe he's leaving this part of the country for good," Harmon suggested.

"Maybe," Dexter said crossing his fingers.

"I don't think so," April argued. "A challenge really pumps this guy up."

Harmon asked, "Ya'll want a ride back to the campus?"

"Sure," Dexter replied.

"You two go ahead. I could use the exercise," April said.

"Are you sure?" Harmon asked.

Dexter answered for her. "She's sure. If walking and running were the preferred methods of transportation, April would drive. She has to be different. She doesn't believe in the easy way."

"April?" Harmon asked again.

"I'll walk, but thanks," she answered.

The car pulled away. April shot Dexter the finger when he looked back.

April stuffed her hands in her jacket pockets and walked. She was tired of people labeling her as some kind of freak. Two days, two friends, and both consider her possessed by a contrarian's nature. She considered their assertions as she walked her way back. Suddenly she stopped.

"So, what if I am different?" She said out loud. "They can't make me feel ashamed of the way I honestly feel."

April walked with long strides as she manufactured arguments in her defense.

401

# 106

Eddie set the cruise control and relaxed. He scanned the radio frequencies searching for a sports talk station. He found a station broadcasting out of Charlotte; he locked it in. The major news story revolved around a rare Duke loss. He listened but his attention wandered west; Eddie was designing his confrontation with Powers Meade.

Revenge monopolized Eddie's desire but he knew it would be impossible to expose Meade without opening himself to possible prosecution. He could scare the professor into giving up the money. He might be able to hit Meade, once or twice without him registering a complaint.

*What will that feel like?*

Other than a few shoving matches on the court, Eddie had never been in a fight; his size kept most people at bay. He wondered if hitting Meade in the face would hurt his hand. However, a shot to the stomach might provide some joy for Eddie and pain for the Puppet Master.

Eddie began to imagine the lifestyle Meade was living. How much money could he have made over the last eighteen months? If Eddie had accrued over three hundred thousand, Powers could have tripled that because he was merely in it for the money. Eddie wanted to make money but it was not his driving motivation. He craved the competition. He needed an opponent, the preparation, and the drama of the outcome. Eddie needed to see who would pay the price and who would not.

*Meade is just a blood-sucking leech. He's a thief.*

Eddie smacked the steering wheel.

He watched a sign go by; he was approaching the Smoky Mountains. Soon he would be in Tennessee. He was devoting so much time to thoughts of revenge that the miles were passing unnoticed. Returning to reality, he noticed the electronic static of the faded radio station. He punched the scan button and tightened his grip on the steering wheel. The curving mountain roads demanded his full attention. The radio stopped on a bluegrass station. Eddie left it there; he thought it was appropriate for the travel into Tennessee.

*Or is it Kentucky.*

He decided it did not matter.

At about two in the afternoon; the road signs were announcing exits to Knoxville. He was hungry. He pulled off the highway to grab some food and refuel his vehicle. He picked chicken strips and fries; they were much easier to eat than sandwiches. Eddie situated the food and drink, buckled up, and was back on the highway in less than fifteen minutes. He snacked on his chicken. He reviewed his plan. He would spend the night in Nashville and reach Clarksville in time to deliver his envelope.

He set the cruise control and shoved the last of a chicken strip into his mouth. He took a drink of the cola to clear his throat.

His mind immediately began to broil about Powers Meade. Out loud he said, "It's just a question of how much you are going to suffer, professor."

# 107

Darren parked the Pathfinder. He was uncertain of what to do. Darren was not prepared for this trip. He did not put enough thought into tailing Eddie Dreyer. He did not expect to end his day in Nashville. Darren had a pair of Dockers, a polo shirt, and running shoes in his gym bag. He watched as Eddie pulled a bag from the back seat and walk toward the hotel. Darren wanted to check into the hotel and get some rest.

*Can I?' Eddie might leave while I sleep.*

Darren leaned his seat back and tried to relax. He was tired; he slept in the truck last night and he was not excited about another night in a car seat. He rubbed his eyes and when he opened them, he saw someone standing in front of Eddie. Darren snapped forward to get a better look. This could be Eddie's next target.

Darren got out of the truck and took a circle path toward the two men. He was not concerned with being recognized; he was sure neither of them knew him. Darren was within twenty feet of the two when he stopped and pretended to re-tie his shoe. The discussion he overheard was not civil. Darren could see that the shorter man was young; he looked to be of college age.

He heard the boy say, "I know who you are. Now, what are you going to do?"

"Calm down, let's talk about this," he heard Eddie say.

"I am calm and I am also mad," the stranger said.

"How about I buy you a beer; there's a bar in the hotel," Eddie said.

"I don't want to drink with you," the boy said loudly.

"Well, what do you want?" Eddie asked.

"I want my life back," the stranger's voice was louder.

"I can't help you," Eddie replied.

"Why not? You screwed it up," he screamed.

"No; you screwed it up. Look, if all you want to do is yell, I'm walking. We're through; do you understand?" Eddie's tone was deathly cold.

Darren stood up. He could not tie his shoe forever. He reached into his back pocket and pulled out his wallet. He retrieved an old receipt and pretended it was instructions. Darren took a few more steps and turned his back to them. He looked around as though he were acclimating himself. Darren examined the piece of paper and strained to listen for additional conversation between Eddie and the stranger.

"You know I was expelled from school. My mom cries all the time and I feel like a loser. None of it would have happened if I had not met you," the boy said.

Darren thought the boy was about to cry. His voice was on the verge of cracking.

"I'm going to be honest with you; you made a bad choice. Now, you have to live with that choice. But today is a new day. You have new opportunities. All you have to do is make better choices. Listen I have to go," Eddie said as he patted the boy on the arm and started to walk past him.

"Are you fucking kidding me?" The boy said. "You think I followed you all the way here to hear advice from a psycho."

The stranger grabbed Eddie's shoulder bag and yanked it to the ground. Eddie spun around quickly and stood towering over the smaller boy. Darren could hear mumbling conversation but it was too soft and muffled to understand. When Eddie was through speaking, he stood with his hand extended. The smaller boy picked up the bag and put the strap in Eddie's hand. Whatever Eddie said made an impact on the stranger. Eddie shouldered the bag, turned and walked right past Darren on his way into the hotel.

Darren looked at the boy; he was frozen to the same spot. Darren walked over to him.

"Hey, you look a little dazed from that collision; are you okay?" Darren asked.

"I'm fine. I'm just thinking about some things," he replied.

"Cool, I just thought I'd ask," Darren said.

"Yeah, alright, thanks," he replied.

"Hey, I'm not from around here." Darren said trying to keep the conversation alive. "Do you know where I can find some good Bar-B-Q?"

"Nah, sorry, I'm not from around here either," he answered and turned to leave.

"Really? Where ya' from?" Darren asked.

"Dude, I'm straight, alright. Hit on somebody else. I gotta' go," he said over his shoulder.

Darren thought he heard the boy mumble "Damn queer."

Darren walked back to his Pathfinder but kept his eye on the boy. He started the truck and drove slowly; he wanted to get a description of the boy's vehicle and the license number. Darren saw the boy get into a silver Volkswagen Jetta with South Carolina plates. The stranger drove away. Darren wrote the information in his pad and drove back to his previous location.

"I do not look gay," he said out loud.

Darren refocused and began to wonder if he handled the encounter adequately. It was the first time he had ever tried to gather information from a stranger. All of Darren's previous journalistic efforts were done with willing interviewees.

*Should I have identified myself as a reporter? Would that have been more effective? How would the boy have reacted if I had mentioned Eddie Dreyer by name?*

He decided to scribble each question onto his notepad. He also wrote, "Master's Thesis: Reluctant Informant Relationships."

*Cheesy title but I can clean it up later.*

Darren began to re-focus on Eddie. Eddie had driven twelve hours to get here and was checking into the hotel because he needed a place to sleep. Darren decided to get a room and get back to the truck before Eddie came back out the next morning.

He went in the hotel and checked in. He went up to the room and pulled all the curtains. Darren set the alarm for four in the morning. He went back downstairs and on the way out the door, he asked the desk clerk for a wakeup call at four. He did not want to oversleep.

Darren walked around the parking lot until he spotted Eddie's car. When he was satisfied Eddie was still in the hotel, Darren walked across the street and bought a chicken sandwich. He walked back to his vehicle and settled into the seat. He ate his sandwich while craning his neck to see both Eddie's car and the front door of the hotel. At nine o'clock, he was satisfied that Eddie would not leave for the evening. Darren went back to his room, laid down. He took one last look at the alarm, and then fell asleep fully dressed.

# 108

With the sketchpad tucked up under her arm, April walked slowly. She was analyzing the lean of a second story balcony when the cell phone rang.

"Hey April, it's Dex," the voice said.

"Hey. What's up?" She responded.

"Where are you?" Dex asked.

"Downtown. Near Battery Park, why?"

"Just wondering. I had a hunch you'd be out drawing today," Dexter said.

"So you called to confirm your hunch?"

"Yes, but I have a second reason." he said. "Are you mad at me?"

"Why should I be mad? You mean, because you made fun of me in front of your boss?" April said recalling their last conversation.

"Yeah, but you know I was doing it in fun, right?" Dexter defended.

"Forget about it Dexter," April said as she walked. "So what if you think I'm some kind of whack-job because I prefer to run opposite the herd," April added, borrowing Darren's assertion.

"I don't think you're a whack job," Dexter responded.

"Because I don't think of it as a slam; I do run opposite the herd. I am different. I like being different," April said with delight.

"It's the main reason I like you so much," Dexter replied. "I'm a fan."

April let seconds pass by as she thought about what he said. Dexter started talking before she could respond.

"Let me tell you what I think. I think you are a chooser. Everything in life is about choosing, right? That includes relationships. You don't want to be chosen. You want to choose. Because I approached you, because I was immediately attracted to you, I, practically had no shot. The reason I called was to say I'm sorry for the cheap shot yesterday. And the second thing I want to say is that I want to be chosen," Dexter said.

"You want to be chosen?" April repeated as she stopped walking and sat on a bench in the park. She watched a sailboat tack against the wind.

"Yup. I'm going to work harder to be less main-stream, just so you will choose me," Dexter said.

"Dexter, you can't change who you are." She was consoling and considerate with a tone so sympathetic she could not believe she felt it.

"Sure I can. I'm only twenty-one. What I've been doing has little bearing on what I will become. I like the way you challenge fate. I want to be more like that," he said.

"You're a trip, Dexter. I don't know what to say. I've told you that I am not attracted to you. What do you want me to say?"

"I want you to pretend we never met. I want you to turn around and say, "I am willing to do that, Dex," he said.

April stared at the bay and felt a shiver. She was not sure if it was from the cool breeze or his sincerity? She pressed the phone hard against her ear as she tried to think of the right thing to say. Then she heard him say it again.

"I am willing to pretend that we never met. Can you say it?"

But the voice she heard was not in her ear, it was nearby. She spun around to see Dexter standing behind the bench.

"Damn it. You scared me. Why didn't you tell me you were nearby?" April asked as she clicked her cell phone off.

"Because I had more important things to tell you," he said.

He held out his hand and said, "Hi, my name is Dexter Dalton."

April sat motionless for several seconds; Dexter's hand remained extended. Finally, she reached out and shook it gently.

"I don't think I've seen you here before, Dexter," she said although she was not sure she could continue the charade.

"I'm sure you haven't. I've never been here before today. What do you like best about this spot__; I didn't catch your name," he said as he walked around the bench.

"I'm April," she played along. "Dexter, why don't you tell me your first impression of this spot?"

"I look at the water and I think, what kind of people decided to get on a ship and travel across an unknown ocean. I mean it's so huge; it's deep and it had swallowed countless numbers of people and yet still, they sailed. I guess the dream of a fresh start can be stronger than the fear of death," Dexter responded as he stared at the choppy bay waters.

April watched as he turned his head to look into her eyes.

"And you? What is your first impression, April?"

"I think about the architecture and its historical significance. These houses have stood the test of time. Their designers were forward thinkers. These buildings are constructed to withstand the coastal storms and salt water and the march of time but I can't say I ever thought about it the way you did," April answered.

April watched Dexter standing there and she believed what he said. She invited him to sit on the bench. He gave her as much space as he could. They talked about the people who came to this coast hundreds of years ago. He talked about their dreams and she talked about their creativity. Night fell around them and they began to walk home.

Dexter never mentioned sports, classes, or parties. He asked questions and April answered them without punishing him for ignorance. The walk passed quickly. They came to intersecting roads.

"My apartment is that way, Dexter said and pointed. "Which way do you go?"

"I'm this way," April said pointing oppositely.

Dexter stayed in character. He did not invite her for a drink or to his apartment nor did he offer to walk with her to her apartment.

"Well, I have really enjoyed talking with you," he said with a large warm smile.

"I enjoyed it also," she said.

Dexter turned and walked down the road to the right.

April stood for a moment watching him fade into the dark distance. She expected him to turn around but he did not. She walked home.

*I did enjoy that. I really did.*

# 109

The air was cold. It bashed into the ceiling, where the icy breeze was re-directed. Eddie Dreyer's nose was taking the brunt of the chill. He was tired of the AC noise and irritated by the freezing air. He pulled the covers back, walked to the air conditioning unit, and adjusted the thermostat. The clock read three ten. Eddie had intended to wake up at four thirty and be on the road by five. He went back to bed. He pulled the covers up; he wanted them higher; he yanked on the three layers covering his body. He felt the covers pull loose from the bottom of the bed. The sheet and bedspread comfortably covered his chin and nose but his feet were now exposed to the chilly air. Shorter athletes never think of the disadvantages of height.

Eddie rolled onto his side, bent his knees to accommodate the covers, and stared at the small green light on the smoke detector. He wanted total darkness. Eddie had slept in hundreds of hotel rooms; none of them were dark. Light crept through the curtains, LED lights pierced through the room like lasers, and the light from the hallway always peered into the room from the large gap at the bottom of the door. Hotel rooms suit the intoxicated, the sexually active and the blind. The restless, the worried, and the tormented have too much time; they find the flaws.

The AC kicked in again and within moments the cold breeze settled on Eddie's face like an invisible army of ants. He threw the covers back and turned on the light. He turned the AC unit off and went to the bathroom. Eddie was through with sleep for the evening; the effort was making him tired. He clipped a new blade in his razor and shaved close. His shower was hot but he finished the rinse with cold water. He was wide-awake as he dressed for the day.

Eddie looked around the room; everything was packed. He went directly to his car and threw his bag in the backseat; he looked at his watch. In five minutes it would be four. He had plenty of time. Eddie went back in the hotel for a cup of coffee for the road. The lobby was quiet. The desk clerk smiled at Eddie as he walked toward the coffee urn. Eddie took a large Styrofoam cup and waited as the man in the wrinkled polo shirt finished filling his cup. The man finished and turned absentmindedly and nearly spilled his cup of coffee on Eddie. Eddie stepped back quickly to avoid the overflow.

"Whoa, I'm sorry. I didn't know anyone was behind me," the young man said and stared into Eddie's face.

"It's alright. No harm, no foul," Eddie replied.

The man nodded and hurried away. Eddie filled his cup, added two packets of sugar, put a lid on it and went back to his car. He placed it in the holder and drove to the highway. He settled into his seat and began to sip the coffee and watch the dark sky slowly surrender to the rising sun. Eddie passed a truck and caught a glimpse of the highway distance sign. He was two hundred miles from Memphis. He would reach mid-Arkansas by early afternoon. Everything was going according to plan.

# 110

Darren drummed on the wall with his fingers as he waited for the elevator doors to open. He could not believe he was standing face to face with Eddie Dreyer. He tossed the coffee in the waste can as the doors opened. The ride up gobbled valuable seconds.

*I should have spilled the coffee on him. That would have forced him to clean up and would have slowed his departure.*

He stared into the mirrored wall and tried to hand press some of the wrinkles from his shirt.

"Hurry up!" Darren yelled as the doors opened.

Darren sprinted down the hall to his room. He shoved the plastic passkey into the slot; a green light, a beep and he was inside his room. He grabbed his keys and ran back into the hall. Darren did not have time to wait on the elevator. He ran for the stairs and bound down them, taking several steps at a time.

He burst into the early morning air and raced toward his vehicle. He stepped inside, started the engine and began scanning the parking lot. The parking space Eddie's car had occupied was empty. Darren stepped out onto the running board of his truck and looked in every direction. He did not see any moving vehicles nearby. He slammed the roof of the Pathfinder.

"Damn it!" He stepped off the running board. "Of all the fucking luck."

He fell into the seat and pounded his steering wheel a few times. Suddenly, he raised his head, reached into the back floorboard, and grabbed a pair of shoes. He got out of the vehicle and ran back in the hotel. He rushed toward the clerk.

"That guy that just drove off, he sat his running shoes on his roof and forgot about them," Darren said as he held up the shoes. "I might be able to catch him. Did he mention where he was going next?"

"No, he sure didn't," she said.

"Oh well, thanks anyway," Darren replied as he started out the door.

"You can leave the shoes here. He will probably contact us and make arrangements to collect them," she suggested.

Darren tried to formulate a story for keeping the shoes. He decided it was not worth the effort.

"They are my shoes. I was lying. I was just trying to find out where the guy went," he explained. "I apologize for lying."

He did not wait for her to respond. He walked back to his vehicle, sat inside, and reached for his cell phone.

# 111

Dexter sat up, swung his legs over the side of the bed, and reached for the ringing cell phone.

"Don't hang up; I'll be right back," he said into the phone and then dropped it onto the bed. He hurried to the bathroom. He had to pee; the sleep-intruder would have to wait. He flushed and went back to sitting on the edge of the bed.

"Okay, hello." Dexter said.

"Where the hell did you go?" April asked.

"To relieve myself."

"What if this had been a matter of life or death?" She asked.

"Are you dying?" Dexter asked.

"Never mind. Darren just called me. He lost Eddie," April said.

"That's unfortunate."

"Unfortunate? That's all you have to say?" April asked.

"Listen April. That's the way I feel. Yesterday was about starting over. I am starting over. That includes erasing the page titled Eddie Dreyer," Dexter responded.

"Dexter, I don't want to play your stupid little game right now."

Dexter heard her and paused without responding. He hated the words that reached his ears. His affection for April was unusually strong but he was not capable of withstanding her fury. He knew April summoned words like Thor drawing lightning from the sky. She brought her entire arsenal to every battle. April always leveled the playing field. Nothing had changed. She hurt Dexter where it mattered most to him. She made fun of his best effort to show his fondness for her.

"That too, is unfortunate." Dexter whispered into the phone as he hung the receiver up.

He stared at the telephone for a moment. He thought she might call back and apologize.

*No, she won't.*

He knew she would never admit to being wrong. April's frustration with Eddie Dreyer was more important than Dexter's feelings.

*How many lessons must I learn?*

Dexter sprawled out on the sofa, elevated his head on the arm of the couch, and waited for sleep to take him back to anywhere before April.

# 112

For three consecutive days, Powers Meade had sat at his computer composing thoughts into text. Two pages of composition were all he had to show for his efforts. The last entry read, "*Yawn*." He recognized his topic as mundane, his analysis as unprofessional, and his motivation as pathetic. Powers considered a better topic to be a comparative analysis of overachievers and underachievers. However, he was rather uncomfortable as a model for the underachiever, despite the fit.

As he had done countless times in the last three days, he rose from the chair found something that had to be done rather than work on the Article. This time he went to the kitchen and filled a glass with orange juice.

Powers paused at the window to view the pool. It was nearing two in the afternoon, curvy blonde Meghan was picking up her towel and leaving the pool. She deals black jack at Binions; her shift began at three. Powers watched her muscular lean legs stride across the pool deck to her condo. Within minutes she would be showering her tan body and getting ready for work. He broke his gaze and imaginings to scan the rest of the poolside condos.

It seemed that everyone he had met worked with a hotel or casino in some capacity. It was an eclectic mix of educations, specialties, and backgrounds. The diversity and anonymity allowed Powers to introduce himself as a gambler. He expected the title to be more acceptable than psychology professor and it was closer to the truth. Although he knew the names and profiles of a couple of dozen people, no one went out of their way to establish friendships.

Powers was an intelligent man; he knew these people socialized in existing relationships and he did not expect them to be dazzled by his personality. However, he expected reciprocation. He expected a friendlier environment. He was beginning to suspect that people resented him because he was not required to be at a job on a daily basis. His analysis of their attitude toward him was much more detailed than the Article he was attempting to write.

Meghan closed the door to her condo; the noise and echo broke his train of thought about establishing friendships. He adjusted his sunglasses and turned his attention to his yellow pad. He walked back to the computer and rested his fingers on the keys. This Article would be the key to his next venture. Once the opinion paper was written, then he could arrange an interview with the university. A position with UNLV could change the future. He would have a secure income and stability. Powers would be back in a familiar environment.

Powers would build new relationships with his fellow academics. He would be the picture of normalcy. Maybe, hustling off to punch a clock would make him more palatable to his neighbors. Maybe, then, they would warm up to him. His entire adult life had been spent with other psychology professionals, partly because most people think psychologists are always working. No one wants to be under constant scrutiny. Powers considered the assessment to be unfair but to discover why people feel that way is analysis. Some psychologists are passionate about their craft, just as some business professionals cannot turn it off, or artists cannot stop framing a shot. The essence of passion is pursuit. Powers was not that passionate.

He began typing his speculations about Eddie Dreyer's obsession with winning but the very thought of Eddie caused his concentration to stray.

*What about the three hundred thousand dollars?*

Powers remained baffled that Eddie had not requested the money. Powers considered it impossible that Eddie was not livid and consumed with vengeance.

*Is it possible that Eddie had not figured it out? Is it possible Eddie, in frustration, being manipulated by an inferior man, was suppressing the truth?*

Yes, he decided. The opportunist closed the laptop. Powers liked this line of thinking. The Article, the university, and the psychologist were all being shoved aside by the opportune gambler. Powers was feeling lucky. A gambler bets something will or will not happen. Powers was ready to wager Eddie Dreyer would never seek the money.

*I will leave it untouched for a little longer, just in case he comes and I need to buy my safety from his anger.*

# 113

The car rolled to a stop at two-fifteen. Eddie had made great time. He grabbed the sealed envelope from the front seat, stepped out of the car and pulled a garment bag from the hanging rack in the back seat. Eddie slung the garment bag over his shoulder and walked into the athletic building. He walked to the end of the hall and found the men's room. Once inside he slipped into a stall and removed his jeans and t-shirt. Eddie donned the crisp white shirt and tied a Windsor knot into the red and blue tie. He reached in the bottom of the bag and retrieved the black leather belt and matching black shoes. He tossed his casual clothes into the bag. Eddie stepped out of the stall and took a quick glance around. He was alone. Eddie closed the door, reached over the top and locked the stall from the inside. He slipped the navy blue jacket on as he stood in front of the mirror. He reached into the inside pocket and put a pair of rimless eyeglasses onto his face. Eddie looked in the mirror and gave the tie one last wiggle. The transformation was complete. He looked older and professional. He was ready.

He walked down the hall and looked at a directory board. He found the number for Coach Titus Lockwood and started up the stairs. The office was the first door. He entered and found a female student sitting behind a desk; she was sipping on a can of Slim Fast through a striped straw.

"Hi. I'm sorry to disturb your lunch," Eddie said as he flashed a broad grin.

"If I was drinking this," she said as she held up the can, "to wash down a plate of Shrimp Alfredo that would be lunch. This is a ritual I go through to remind me of how much I hate thin people."

"I know what you mean; I hate dieting," Eddie said as he laughed at her response.

"Like you have to diet," she said as though they had been friends for years. "You look like a poster for Abs Of Steel," she sat her can down noisily.

"Well, thank you but this suit hides a lot. Listen, I have some information for Coach Lockwood," Eddie said.

"He's not here. Did you have an appointment?" She asked.

"No but it's not necessary that I talk to him. I can leave this. It will explain everything," Eddie said as he thrust the envelope toward the girl.

She reached out and took it. *"Malone Danbridge"* Is that your name?" She asked looking up from the envelope.

"No," Eddie answered.

"Is this about tonight's game?" She continued to quiz.

"It's a private matter," Eddie responded.

"Are you like some kind of spy dude, out there gathering dirt for the Coach?"

Eddie smiled. The girl was fun. He wished he had more time to talk with her. It was good to laugh. But he did not. He reached up to do an exaggerated tie adjustment and said, "The name's Bond, James Bond."

"Cute. But you need to work on your accent."

"Yes, ma'am." he responded.

"Hey, I ain't your mama. Call me, Roxie."

"Okay, Roxie."

He stood there watching Roxie tap the large envelope.

"Is Coach Lockwood expecting this information? Do I need to find him and let him know it is here?"

"That depends. I do want him to read it soon?" Eddie said.

"He'll be here before tonight's game. All his stuff is here," she said as she continued to fidget with the envelope.

Eddie could see the intrigue was eating at her more than her weight problem.

"That will be soon enough," he replied.

"Okay. I'll see that he gets it. Do you want to leave your name?" She asked.

"No, everything he wants to know is inside. Thank you."

He picked up a business card from the desk. "Do you mind if I take one of these?"

"Nope. That's what they're for. Anything else I can do for you?" She asked.

Eddie knew the question was meant to be suggestive but he did not pursue it.

He shook his head and said, "Nope, not today." He turned to leave the office.

"It was nice talking to you Mr. Bond," she said as he opened the door.

"It was nice meeting you, Roxie."

"Hey," he heard and looked back over his shoulder.

"I know I'm a little younger than you but do you ever date fat chicks?" She asked with a smile.

"Never, but if I were available I'd date you in a heartbeat," he said as he returned her smile and closed the door behind him.

Eddie hurried down the stairs. He expected her to follow. He heard the office door open as he reached the bottom of the stairs.

She did not see Eddie quietly slip into the men's room. He unlocked the stall door and changed back into his road clothes. Eddie threw the garment bag over his shoulder, covered his eyes with the sunglasses. He left the building and climbed back into the car.

"Alright Coach, let's see how smart you really are," Eddie said as he drove to the student union building.

He went in the bookstore and purchased a white sweatshirt with the Rams mascot emblazoned on the front. He walked to a nearby coffee shop, sat, and opened his iPad.

He clicked on one of the new wagering sites from his Favorites menu. He logged in and scanned through the games until he found the contest between the Rams and the Patriots. He pressed the button to wager five thousand dollars on the Rams straight up. He opened another gambling site and posted another five thousand on the Rams. Eddie pecked on the keyboard until another five thousand dollars was wagered on the Rams. Eddie visited six sites total; he had thirty grand riding on the game.

Eddie finished his coffee and left for his car. He pulled back into the highway traffic. He relaxed and settled in for a short drive. Eddie would reach Ft. Smith before he called it a day. With Coach Lockwood checked off the to-do list he re-focused on Powers Meade.

# 114

A blaring horn sounded and Titus Lockwood snapped to a sitting position. The nightmare rushed adrenalin to his veins. It was a horn he had heard hundreds of times; it was an air-horn trumpeting the end of a basketball game. No time left.

This time there were no fans to absorb the blaring echoes, no cheering for the victors, and no players celebrating. Titus was alone at center court listening to the deafening sound. The game was over, the scoreboard was empty, and Titus Lockwood had missed the game.

The nightmare was over. He rubbed at his eyes and shook his head. He had two priorities: check the time and take something for his headache. He looked around for the clock. It was on the floor, unplugged, just where he had flung it hours ago. He rushed to the window and opened the curtains. Sunlight tortured his eyes. He squinted and studied his wristwatch. It was just after two in the afternoon. He was not late but he would have to hurry. Titus looked around the room. He saw his car keys on the dresser. He walked over to pick them up. As he passed the bed, he saw the crumpled picture of Laura. He stuffed it in his shirt pocket and walked out the door.

Titus went to the motel office to tell them he was checking out. He had paid for the weekend but he wanted to tell them he had made a mess of the place. He gave the old man a twenty-dollar bill.

Titus told him, "This is my apology to whoever has to clean up. I've been a little sick."

A thick pane of glass separated the man from the outside world. He reached into the metal tray took the money.

He said, "I'll see that Marla gets it."

Titus suspected Marla would never see the money but his intent was enough to clear his conscience. He began to jog to the truck but his headache insisted he stop; walking would have to do. He started the Wagoneer, buckled up and pulled up to the highway. Hours ago he stared at the highway, trying to believe freedom was to the left and responsibility to the right. He made the right hand turn without hesitation. It was not a responsibility; it was his life. Twelve young men wanted to play a basketball game and Titus Lockwood wanted to coach them.

The Wagoneer took a little time to get up to highway speed. It was a present from his father. His father came to the campus on Titus's birthday, gave him the keys and they went hunting for the weekend. Those three days ranked as one of the best times of his life. If forced to admit it, he might say, it was better than the state championship game in high school and better than the day he married Laura.

The vehicle was old but Titus loved it. His players kidded with him about his "ride" and Titus used it as a threat. Players who missed shots during drills were forced to ride in the Wagoneer around the school. Dad's present was a fortress; Titus was invulnerable from life's miseries when he rode in the Wagoneer.

He reached for the handle, rolled down the window, and pushed the vent window out. The air was blowing forcefully into his face. It was not fresh; it carried road film, highway fumes, and diesel soot from the truck ahead of him but it was fresher than the air in his lungs. He took deep breaths. He pulled the air in so far his lungs ached from the pressure. He continued to suck the air in time after time. With every breath exhaled, he reminded himself that only idiots and morons could have been as stupid as he had been in the last twenty-four hours. With every breath inhaled, he considered how lucky he had been. No one knew where he was and no one had recognized him at the motel. In a drunken stupor, he screamed in public and tried to start a fight and yet, no one called the police or recognized him. Titus was lucky indeed. He sucked in another lung full of highway air and watched the landscape change from lost to familiar.

# 115

Eddie passed an old farm truck on a hill. The aging farmer nodded his head as Eddie's blue Monte Carlo powered past. Eddie returned the head nod and eased the car back into the right hand lane. He set his cruise control to fifty-five and reached across the seat to unlatch his laptop. After a short wait and a few keystrokes, the machine was ready for use. Eddie opened his journal; he wanted to add a few notes as he drove. Eddie checked his rear view mirror; the truck was fading in the distance and he could not see any traffic in front of him. Eddie took another quick look at the road. A car was pulling into the left hand lane to pass him. Eddie grabbed the steering wheel with both hands as the Lincoln neared. It passed.

He looked back at the laptop; the journal was loaded. Eddie was trying to lock the laptop into the special holding device on the dashboard, when his cell phone rang. The noise caught him off guard. He was unaccustomed to receiving calls. Only three people knew the number. He answered it.

"Where are you Eddie?" The voice demanded.

"Who is this?" Eddie asked; his irritation was apparent.

"It's Harmon Evans and I know what you have been doing."

"I guess Dex told his tale, huh?" Eddie said as he maneuvered to pass a diesel truck struggling to climb the hill.

"Does it matter? What matters is the number of people who know. It's at seven and growing. Eddie someone is going to turn you in and some smart DA is going to convict you. Do you really want to go to jail?" Harmon asked sincerely.

"Harm, I'm not going to jail. I'm quitting, okay?" Eddie said and pulled the car back into the lane for slower moving traffic.

"What makes you think I believe that?" Harmon asked.

"Harm, you know me. Do you think I am stupid? Why did you call me? Is it to tell me you were going to turn me in? Have you found anyone willing to undergo the public humiliation to testify against me? Is it to tempt me back to righteousness? Are you hoping I will turn myself in? Tell me Harm, what is the purpose of your call?" Eddie asked.

"I know you're not stupid, Eddie. And you're right; I have no idea what I hoped to accomplish. I just want you to stop. Beyond that, what else is there? No one can undo what you have done," Harmon said. "Whatever you've done."

"So, I've tested the character of a few people. Harm, this doesn't concern you," Eddie replied.

"Yes it does, Eddie. Jimmy Gerald is my girlfriend's nephew and he has stolen his mother's car and has been missing for a couple of days," Harmon explained.

"Damn, it's a small world," Eddie responded. "I saw Jimmy yesterday. He was following me. He was mad. I have no idea what he thought he could accomplish. I finally threatened him and he left. I expect he tucked tail and ran. He's not very strong."

"Well, that makes everything peachy, doesn't it Eddie?" Harmon said.

"Harm, I'm just trying to tell you to stop worr__," Eddie heard silence "Harm? Hello."

There was no response. The phone was dead. Eddie looked at the face of the phone. His battery was charged and the signal was strong. Harmon ended the conversation by hanging up. Eddie looked at the phone for a few seconds. He thought about calling him back but Eddie knew he could not make things better. Eddie tossed the phone in the passenger seat and checked his rear view mirror. Another car was traveling fast and preparing to pass. Eddie returned his attention to the traffic.

Eddie liked and respected Harmon Evans. They met at a booster function when Eddie was a freshman. Harmon was a former ball player and understood the game. They used to talk frequently about the art of scoring and defending. They even played a little one on one, once. Eddie smiled as he remembered the game.

*Not bad for an old guy.*

It bothered Eddie that Harmon was disappointed but Harmon was right; the past could not be undone.

The passing car was nearly even with the Monte Carlo. Eddie glanced to his left as the small car crept by. Something registered in his brain. He recognized the driver.

# 116

Harmon pulled the cell phone away from his ear, punched the end button, and tossed the phone to Dexter. Dexter fumbled it around a couple of times before trapping it against his body. He glared at Harmon in disbelief.

"Hey. If I had dropped this, you would owe me for the cost of a new phone," Dexter complained.

"Well, you didn't so quit complaining," Harmon grumbled.

"What did I miss? What did Eddie say?" Dexter asked.

"He said he was giving it up. He said he was going to quit bribing people," Harmon said as he poured himself a drink.

"Do you believe him?" Dexter asked as he shoved the phone in his pocket.

"I don't know. I want to but it is hard to believe," Harmon said. "What would he do for competition?"

Harmon twirled the empty glass by the top while contemplating another shot of whisky.

He looked up at Dexter and said, "Eddie Dreyer has spent the last twelve years perfecting the science of outwitting people. It's who he is; hell, it's what he is."

Harmon poured another drink.

"Did Eddie ask how you knew his cell phone number or where you got it?" Dexter asked and began to nibble at his fingernails.

"Dex, keep your fingers out of your mouth." Harmon reached over to knock his hand away but Dexter moved first. "Are you still worried Eddie will come down here and kick your ass?"

"Shouldn't I be? He's not sane," Dexter answered.

"Eddie's not crazy. He's smart. Whatever Eddie is doing, he has a strategy to win at it. And you and I are not going to out-think him."

"We know he went to Nashville; maybe he is going to California. No one knows him there. He could start all over," Dexter said. "You said he was smart. Smart people learn from mistakes. As far as we know, one locked door is the only mistake he ever made. I think all the basketball players on the west coast should start worrying."

"Dex. If you are going to theorize, couldn't you speculate on something positive? Dream up a scenario where he quits; let him find Jesus, or concoct a medical miracle that repairs his shoulder and makes his hand good as new?"

Harmon wrapped his large hand around the glass of whisky and peered into the contents like a mystic seeking answers from a crystal ball.

"Paint a picture of a fluid tall guard leading his team to victory. That's what I want to see. I don't want hear tales of shattered dreams. I don't want to hear Helen worrying about her nephew. And I don't want to think about Eddie Dreyer hurting someone else's nephew or son," Harmon lectured as he pulled the cork from the whisky bottle and carefully poured the golden nectar in his glass back inside the bottle.

"I'm sorry Harm. I was just trying to be funny. Bad timing, I apologize. What about Jimmy? I heard you mention his name to Eddie. Did you get any response about that?" Dexter asked.

"He said Jimmy had followed him. Evidently, Jimmy confronted Eddie in Nashville. That was a mismatch," Harmon said.

He shook his head as he imagined little mop headed Jimmy being pummeled by a fearless warrior like Eddie.

"Oh shit; did he hurt him?" Dexter asked.

"Eddie said he scared him. He believes Jimmy put his tail between his legs and headed home. I've met the boy; he's not looking to get hurt," Harmon said.

"Well, we're back to square one. Darren lost him. No one knows where he is headed and no one believes they can stop him," Dexter said.

"What about your girlfriend? Doesn't she have any more bright ideas?" Harmon asked.

"She's not my girlfriend, Harm. Right now, she's not even a friend. She's alone, I guess and liking it."

"If you were half as committed to stopping Eddie Dreyer as you are to making that girl like you, Eddie's scheming days would be over," Harmon said as he walked past Dexter, toward the office.

Harmon expected a snappy come back or an adamant denial; he heard neither and he was relieved. Dexter's love life angst was low on the list of problems to resolve.

426

# 117

In reality, Jimmy's hand was waving a gun in a slow figure eight. A cartoon like grin tortured his face and his eyes almost leapt from the sockets. But in his mind, Jimmy perceived himself to be a calm defender of justice. He was presiding over a court of evidence that had already convicted Eddie Dreyer.

Reality tagged Jimmy as a Judas when he took the bribe. Reality labeled him a loser when he was expelled from school and again when he had to watch his mother cry. Reality exposed him as a coward when Eddie Dreyer threatened him in Nashville. Images and sound bites flickered though his mind like a strobe light on a slow setting.

"You'll make two thousand dollars and everyone will think, it's hilarious", the unknown briber said.

"Oh my God, Jimmy. You've been expelled and everyone is laughing at us", his mother sobbed.

"Jimmy, I can't believe you did this to your mother", Aunt Helen said.

"You're soft, son. I'm going to keep striking your ass with this belt until you cry like a little girl. And when you've had enough, you'll tell me what I want to know," Harmon Evans promised and delivered.

"Boy, your own mama won't recognize you. I will beat you black, blue and bloody. Now, pick up my bag and get the fuck outta' here," Eddie Dreyer threatened in the Nashville Marriott parking lot.

In reality, Jimmy Gerald was too weak for reality.

Jimmy left reality when he walked into the pawnshop in Nashville that night. Jimmy needed an equalizer. He figured a handgun would make Eddie Dreyer tremble with fear. He was not planning to shoot Eddie but he had not planned to be a Judas-loser-coward either. Jimmy wanted to go back to life before Eddie Dreyer. Jimmy was not sure how the handgun would get him there but somehow it would. Things have a way of working out, when reality is not part of the equation.

The owner of the pawnshop wanted three hundred dollars for the old Walther 9mm handgun. One, two, three, Jimmy put the money on the counter. The man asked Jimmy to fill out several forms.

"No forms," Jimmy said calmly.

Four, five, six, the pile totaled six hundred dollars on the counter.

"No forms, no gun," the man said as he looked at the money. Seven, eight, nine, ten, Jimmy placed a thousand dollars on the counter.

"Why do you want this gun so bad," he asked as his fingers tapped the counter.

"Do you want the thousand dollars or not?" Jimmy asked.

The man picked up the money.

"That should cover a box of bullets," Jimmy said.

The man tossed a box on the counter. Jimmy left and went back to the parking lot of the hotel and waited for Eddie. He saw Eddie come out; Jimmy raised the gun but he could not pull the trigger.

Jimmy followed him. When he saw Eddie go into the Athletic Building on the Rams campus, he knew what Eddie was doing. He knew someone was going to feel the pain of Eddie's sick game. Jimmy wanted to go in and expose him; make him admit to his crimes. He was feeling like Dirty Harry. Jimmy could see himself pistol-whipping Eddie but again fear paralyzed him. Eddie got back in his car and began to drive out of town: Jimmy followed again.

Now, on this highway, driving seventy miles an hour, Jimmy was leaning across the car seat. Sweaty palms were in control of a gun and a steering wheel. He could see surprise in Eddie's face; but he wanted to see terror.

He accelerated and yelled. "Hey big boy, call me a loser now."

It made Jimmy feel tough to yell but Eddie did not hear it; his car windows were up. Jimmy was elated to see Eddie ducking down.

*Now, he's afraid.*

Jimmy laughed with his mouth wide open and his tongue hanging as far as he could stretch it out.

Eddie sped up but Jimmy accelerated and kept Eddie Dreyer framed in the passenger window of the Jetta. The highway air swirled through the car scattering his mop like hair. Strands lashed at his face as he bellowed insults, "You scum. You Bastard. Piece of shit. Has been."

Eddie sped up.

Jimmy kept yelling, "Yeah! Run like a little girl."

Jimmy pushed the accelerator to the floorboard.

428

"Are you scared, Slick? You still feeling like you run the show, now?"

The clear road was not an advantage for Jimmy. He looked at the speedometer; he was doing ninety but the Monte Carlo was beginning to pull away. Eddie took advantage of the gap to pull in front of the Jetta. Jimmy slammed the dash with his pistol hand and pointed the revolver forward. Both cars streaked past a slower moving vehicle.

Jimmy could see traffic ahead blocking both lanes. Eddie would be forced to slow down but Jimmy would still be stuck behind Eddie. Jimmy drove the Jetta directly behind Eddie's Monte Carlo. The big tortured grin returned to Jimmy's face as he took the only path available. He pulled on the steering wheel and took the Jetta across the solid white line. With no on-coming traffic in sight, Jimmy could pull up next to the Monte Carlo; Eddie would be blocked.

"Gotcha, you sonofabitch!" Jimmy screamed out the passenger-side window as he pulled even with the Monte Carlo.

Jimmy's victory was short lived. The minivan in the left lane was signaling. Soon it would be in the right hand lane and Eddie would be free to use his V8 powered car to race away.

"No. No. No," Jimmy screamed as his pistol filled right hand pounded on the steering wheel. He whipped the Jetta back behind the Monte Carlo to avoid a red vehicle coming head on.

The minivan began to move into the right hand lane but a truck took its place. Eddie was blocked again. Jimmy stomped on his accelerator. The Jetta dropped to lower gear, the engine groaned as the rpm needle climbed up the gauge. Just as he was about to hit Eddie's bumper, Jimmy checked the oncoming traffic and crossed the center line again. The Jetta pulled even with Eddie's window. He leveled the gun on Eddie's window. The truck signaled to return to the right hand lane. The Jetta pulled even. The lane opened; Jimmy heard the big V8 rumble.

"Not this time, Hotshot." Jimmy screamed as he pulled the trigger. "Buy your way out of this!"

The automatic ripped off three shots before Jimmy realized he had fired. He pulled the trigger again; another burst of bullets sprayed the blue Monte Carlo. He saw glass shatter on the driver side window.

Jimmy reached up to pull the mop hair from his eyes as he roared with laughter. He turned to look at the road; two vehicles were in front of him and the Monte Carlo blocked his right. He had nowhere to go.

Horns blared; tires squealed. The laughter stopped, the smile disappeared, and the gun fell to the floorboard. He whipped the wheel to the right. The Jetta hit the Monte Carlo and careened back into the path of the oncoming cars. He tried to turn the car back to the right. In his frightened confusion, he stomped on the brakes. The tires dug into the pavement but inertia would not be denied. His Jetta was air born; it rolled three times before an oncoming car hit it. The second vehicle skidded into the ditch. Screeching tires filled the air, cars swerved and skidded, but there were no other collisions in the westbound lane. The Monte Carlo crawled to the shoulder and stopped. Car doors slammed as drivers emerged from their vehicles to approach the wreckage. Instantly, several drivers were talking into their cell phones. A state trooper siren blared onto the scene ten minutes later.

# 118

Titus Lockwood felt blood running down his face. He wiped at it; his fingers glowed red. He opened the glove box it was stuffed with napkins from every fast food restaurant a highway offered. Recruiting required a lot of road travel. Titus saved time by eating as he drove. He grabbed several napkins and blotted at this right eye. It was not a bad cut; it was just in a bad place.

Titus got out of the Wagoneer and rushed toward the car that until a few moments ago was driving next to him. The front end of the Volvo was smashed all the way back to the dash and the roof of a silver Jetta was wrapped around it. Several people were pulling the woman from the Volvo. She seemed shaken but capable of walking and she was not bleeding. Titus examined the wreckage and walked around to the torn and twisted metal of the Volkswagen. A heavyset man gently pushed his stout hairy forearm into Titus's chest.

"You can't help him; he's gone," the man said.

"Are you sure? Shouldn't we get him out?" Titus said as he checked his napkin blotter. The wound was clotting.

"Mister his head is facing backwards. That neck is snapped.

If you just want to see what it looks like, go ahead satisfy your curiosity. But just remember I warned you," the burly man said.

Under normal circumstances, Titus would have resented the man's bossy attitude but he glanced at the highway beneath the two cars and watched as fluids flowed in tiny streams atop the concrete. He saw a bright red among the browns and greens. He pictured the victim's head twistable like a Ken doll. Titus turned his back on the scene and walked away. He did not want to see the actual distortion.

He heard the sirens of a second state trooper squad car and saw the officer jump out and start setting off flares and directing traffic. He saw another asking questions and recording answers. He heard the ambulance pull up to the scene. Two paramedics were rushing to a blue Monte Carlo. Titus walked toward the car. It was not damaged except for shattered glass and strange holes in the metal on the driver side. As he neared the westbound Monte Carlo, a State Trooper stepped into his path.

He asked Titus if he had seen how the accident happened. Titus gave him his name and told him what he saw. The trooper told Titus to stay clear of the glass-shattered Monte Carlo. Titus watched as the paramedics pulled a very tall man from the car. He was covered in blood. Another couple reached the area where Titus and the trooper stood. The state trooper asked for their explanation of what happened. Titus listened as he watched the paramedics tend to the bloody man.

"It was wild, like something from a movie. Both of these cars passed me miles ago but I could see that it was a chase. I thought maybe it was just a coupla' stupid kids until I saw the gun. The guy in the silver car pulled right up next to that fella' there and began firing shots out the passenger side window. He was swerving all over the road."

"You saw him fire a weapon?" The trooper asked.

"I saw him waving a gun. I saw that big fella' trying to duck and I saw glass hitting the highway," the man said. "Plus that big boy is bleeding. That's two plus two stuff. Somebody fired something. And that cat over yonder was the only one with a gun," the loud witness pointed across the highway to the mangled Jetta.

"Thank you," the trooper said and walked back to the Monte Carlo.

"Hey," Titus heard the witness yell.

The trooper and Titus turned to see why the man was yelling. The balding man with a Razorbacks baseball cap cocked back on his head, waved off the trooper and pointed to Titus.

"Hey," he said again as he moved closer. "You're Titus Lockwood. Am I right?"

Suddenly Titus was reminded of his circumstances. The twenty-four hour pity party had left him dirty, unshaven, wrinkled, and ashamed but he had no choice but to answer the man.

"Yes I am. Have we met?" Titus asked.

"No, no but I recognize you. You've been doing great things for that basketball program. But I gotta' tell you; you look like hell; are you okay?" He asked.

"I'm fine. I've been up in a cabin battling a fever. I didn't want the team to catch anything from me," Titus lied. "I'm feeling much better. In fact, I have to get going. I need to get cleaned up."

Titus hoped the little lie satisfied the man. He turned to walk away.

"Yes you do. That's a huge game for the Rams this evening," the balding witness said.

"Yes it is," Titus echoed as he watched the trooper walking back toward them.

"Mr. Lockwood, may I have a word with you, please?" The trooper asked.

Titus walked slowly toward him. He could feel his heart begin to race. Fear was pumping juice into his veins. He was not worried that the trooper would involve him in this accident. He was scared of being exposed.

*Did he smell alcohol on my breath? Did the motel attendant report his conduct?*

He took a deep breath.

"Mr. Lockwood, would you mind taking a look at the man in the blue Monte Carlo?"

"Why?" Titus asked as he leaned to look in direction of the body.

"Mr. Lockwood, while searching the victim's car__,' Titus interrupted the trooper.

"Victim? You mean he's dead."

"Yes sir. The bullet went straight through the neck ripping through carotid arteries," the trooper said.

Titus could see the trooper's eyes cut over his shoulder. Titus turned to see the man in the red Razorback cap had walked up behind them.

"Are you kidding me?" He said loudly. "Man that had to be one lucky shot. I mean, the guy in Jetta' was out of control; he was just firing in the general direction of the Monte Carlo."

"A man is dead. I don't think luck is an appropriate word and if you don't mind, I'm talking with Mr. Lockwood," the trooper said.

"That's Coach Lockwood. He's coach Titus Lockwood, head coach of the Rams," the man said.

"Thank you. Now, could you excuse us?" The trooper said to the man.

The red-capped witness seemed hurt that he could not be included in the conversation but he moved away.

"Are you Coach Titus O. Lockwood? " The trooper asked.

"Yes." Titus said. His paranoia felt like a python squeezing the last gasp of air from his chest. His mind was scrambling for a reasonable explanation for his disheveled appearance when the trooper continued.

"Your business card was found in the victim's car. The name on his driver's license is Edward Douglas Dreyer. Do you know him?" The trooper asked as he extended the business card as proof.

Titus reached for the card and seemed to freeze in mid-exchange.

"Edward Dreyer? I know an Eddie Dreyer. He was a freshman basketball player during my first Assistant Coach job. It could be just a coincidence," Titus said as he looked past the trooper to examine the face too far away to recognize.

"It would be helpful if you could confirm his identity. Would you mind?" The trooper asked.

"I'll take a look," Titus said and followed the trooper to the blue car.

The paramedics stood aside; Titus saw the face but his eyes studied the pool of blood soaking into the patchy grass and brown clay. He blinked and focused on the face of the tall man.

"It's Eddie Dreyer," Titus said and turned away.

Eddie's eyes were open and Titus's stomach was still on the mend.

"Are you certain, Mr. Lockwood?" He asked.

"Positive," Titus said.

The memory of Eddie Dreyer swaggered into Titus's mind like John Wayne crashing through the doors of a Wild West saloon. It was the last game of the season. With two and a half minutes to play, Coach Barkley had just been ejected from the game. Titus took over as coach. With forty seconds remaining, Titus and the Cougars held a three-point lead. A time out was called.

Titus yelled into the huddle, "Listen up guys. Danbridge is killing us. They will try to get the ball to him again. Stay in the zone and double him as soon as he gets the ball. Force him to pass. Someone else will have to beat us but it will not be Danbridge."

As the Coach Titus paused a voice cut through the huddle.

"He won't pass," the eighteen-year-old Eddie Dreyer, said resolutely as they all stood in the huddle. "He'll back up and shoot over the zone. A three ties this thing up. Let me take him. He can't shoot over me. I can force him to take a two-point shot."

Titus was stunned. He had seen glimpses of Eddie's impertinence and arrogance in practices but he had never seen him question Coach Barkley's instructions during a game. He was unsure how to handle the dissenting opinion but he chose an aggressive approach.

"Eddie, do you want to coach or play?" Titus asked training his eyes directly into Eddie's.

"Play," Eddie answered without hesitation or emotion.

The Cougars broke from the huddle and set up in the zone. Two seconds after the whistle blew a crisp pass fed the ball to Malone Danbridge. Eddie broke from the wing at a full sprint and crowded Danbridge. Titus remembered yelling, "Get back! Stay in the zone!"

Eddie continued to stick to Malone Danbridge like a shadow. Eight players and a couple of coaches looked confused but the cocky freshman and the all-conference senior knew exactly what was happening. Titus watched as the clock wound down. Danbridge was dribbling with flamboyance but Eddie stuck. With twelve seconds on the clock, Eddie over extended while reaching for the ball. Danbridge was able to move forward and take advantage of Eddie's poor positioning. Malone Danbridge strode forward with his eyes wide. He was open for the jumper. He pulled up and fired a shot. It was textbook. It was nothing but net.

But Eddie had been right. He had been able to draw Danbridge inside the three point arc. It was only two points. Seven seconds, six seconds.

Titus wanted a time out but could not get the attention of Colton Gavin as he grabbed the ball for the in-bounds play. Colton spotted Eddie streaking toward the Cougars basket. He hurled the ball down the length of the court. Eddie caught and held the ball under the goal as the clock clicked. With two seconds left, Eddie was airborne and jammed the ball through the rim.

Time had expired. The crowd had shaken the building with excitement. Everyone was happy except Coach Titus Lockwood. He raced out on the court. He was furious with Eddie Dreyer. The victory was unimportant to Titus Lockwood at that moment. His explicit orders had been disobeyed. He tried to yell but fans and teammates were swarming around Eddie Dreyer. A reporter was already thrusting a microphone in Eddie's face.

Later, Titus had relayed his account of the events to Coach Barkley. Coach Barkley consoled Titus and said he would discipline Eddie. But Eddie was never disciplined and Titus felt any respect he might have earned was gone. It was one of his strongest motivations for moving on to a new job.

The trooper interrupted the nightmare and asked again, "Are you sure?"

"Yes, absolutely positive," Titus said to the trooper.

435

The trooper seemed satisfied with the response. , and then he turned a laptop computer around so that Titus could see the screen.

"Take a look at this Mr. Lockwood," the trooper said. "This thing is running on a battery. It looks like he might the last thing he might have been doing was researching your game. This note says $5000 Rams straight up," the trooper said.

Titus examined the screen. His brain was filling with questions much faster than his imagination could create answers.

"I had no idea he gambled but I would say he's picked a winner," Titus said.

"He didn't even take the points. Me, I would have taken the five points," the trooper said as he took the laptop back into his custody.

"Eddie Dreyer seemed to always know what he was doing," Titus said and then added, "Can I go? I need to get cleaned up for a game."

"Yes sir. If we need you, we know where to find you."

Titus walked back to the Wagoneer. He walked around to inspect the vehicle. The right front bumper was wearing a large dirt clod and a patch of weeds but it was not damaged. Titus crawled inside, started the engine, and backed out of the ditch. He waited for the trooper controlling traffic to signal. The trooper waved Titus onto the highway. He drove over a hill and then looked in the large side mirror. The motel, the accident, and two deaths were all behind him now. Evidence of a bazaar incident was gone, as though it never happened. He wished he could say the same for Laura.

# 119

Titus tugged on his seat belt; to be double certain it was secure. He took a quick glance in the rear view mirror to see the cut; he dabbed at it with another napkin. It was dry.

He shook his head and said, "Laura won't believe this."

He instantly remembered, she would not be there to tell. Titus softened his grip on the steering wheel. He swiveled his neck to release some stiffness. A green highway sign caught his eye; in ten minutes, he would reach the campus. Again Titus looked at his face in the rear view mirror and instantly decided; he was tired of being Titus Lockwood, the victim. As if he had just watched a player give a halfhearted effort, Coach Titus Lockwood gave himself a half-time tongue-lashing.

"Loser! Do you really want to be a loser? A quitter? Is that what you want to be? You've got about five minutes to straighten your act up Coach Lockwood. In five minutes you better have it totally together or just keep on driving," he screamed.

He listened to his heavy breathing briefly.

"Those young men don't need a loser. They need a confident man, a man with a plan. They want a leader and a winner. A winner knows how to work through pain. How can you expect them to do it if you can't?"

The coach continued to preach to the congregation of one.

"Laura left. Does that mean these twelve players do not deserve the opportunity to win the biggest game of their lives? Yeah, you saw a scary accident. Yeah, two men died. But you would not have seen it if you had not been drunk in a motel."

He paused and glimpsed at himself in the mirror. He wanted that one to sink in.

"Does that mean you should drop out of life? People are depending on you. Are you just going to live in a pity party and let everyone down? You want to feel like this for the rest of your life?" He asked as he looked in the mirror again.

Titus could see spittle dribbling through the bristles on his face. He wiped his chin on his shoulder. Titus had run out of highway and time. He pulled into his parking space at the Athletic building.

He took one really deep breath and said, "Do it well or not at all."

It was the one command his father left him and Titus always pledged it before every game. When the words sailed through the air, Titus could feel his father watching him.

"Dad, I hope you took the last day off,' Titus mumbled with embarrassment.

Titus had spent a lifetime making his father proud. He might let himself down but he would never let his father down. He got out of the car and entered the building through the side door. He had to check in with Roxie. Titus knew there would be calls. It was highly unusual for a coach to be missing the day before a big game. He started up the stairs. He could hear someone fumbling with keys. He peeked around the corner and saw Roxie locking the office.

"Whoa, where do think you are going?" Titus asked.

"I gave up on you. I'm going home," she said.

Titus continued to walk out of the stairwell and toward the door.

"Hey, I'm still the boss. Unlock that door."

"Yeah you're the boss but you can't hire anyone else to put up with your crap," Roxie said as she stood there defying his orders.

Titus stood next to her.

"Holy shit! What happened to you?" She asked.

"Unlock the office and let me in and I will tell you," Titus replied.

Roxie re-opened the door and stepped inside; Titus followed her in and then walked toward his office. She closed the door.

"So, how many messages do I have?" He asked.

"No. It ain't going to be like that. You can have information after I get some answers. And the first thing I want to know is- Damn, you smell awful," Roxie said.

"That's not a question," the coach responded as he thumbed through the mail.

He looked to see Roxie standing with her eyebrows raised and arms folded across her chest.

"I went out of town to get away from everybody and everything. I haven't showered. As I was coming back to town, I was involved in an accident on the highway."

438

"Are you serious? You haven't showered?" She said.

"I am serious. Two men are dead out there," Titus said.

"Oh my God. I'm sorry Coach. I thought you were kidding around."

"It is hard to believe. One man fired a gun while traveling at high speeds. The bullet ripped through the other man's neck. The shooter was driving on the wrong side of the road. He was hit by another car and the crash snapped his neck."

"So, that's how you got that cut," she said getting a closer look. "It looks pretty bad."

"It will be alright. I need to grab my messages, get home and clean up. I can put a butterfly bandage on it. So about those messages?" Titus said.

"Kelly called about his knee wrap."

"That's one superstitious kid," the Coach replied.

"Coach Olson wants to know if you can hold an extra seat for him. Something about bringing in a hotshot quarterback," Roxie said with an eye roll.

"Okay. What else?" He asked.

"Oh yeah, Thurston called." She smothered the name with nose-up arrogance. "He called four times wanting to know why you missed the media event."

"Roxie, please refer to him as Dean Rayburn. He's just doing his job," Titus said.

"Coach, he used the word 'dreadful' a dozen times," Roxie complained.

"Is that all?"

Titus was feeling better. There were no crises. If the Rams could win this evening, Dean Rayburn would be forced to soften his reprimand for screwing up his media event.

"Well, there is this," she said and handed him the envelope reading "Malone Danbridge."

"Where did this come from? And what's it supposed to mean?"

"It's from Adonis," she answered and paused to let his memory wash over her. "He said it was an inside joke and that you'd understand."

"Adonis?" Titus said. "Meaning a great looking guy?"

"Oh my God. He was gorgeous," she squealed.

"What was Adonis's real name?" Titus inquired.

"He wouldn't leave it. I think it was because he was afraid I would track him down and make him my love slave," she said.

"Okay that's more than I need to know. Is he coming back or what?" Titus asked as he began to open the envelope.

"Don't know. He just took a business card and disappeared," Roxie said.

Titus stopped. He walked a little closer to Roxie.

He asked, "He took a card? Roxie was this guy tall with unusually blue eyes?"

"Yeah, real tall and real dreamy eyes. Why? I know you two know each other. What's his name? How available is he?" Roxie asked with hopeful interest.

Titus was overwhelmed by the potential coincidence. He did not have enough time to explain the Eddie Dreyer relationship and he certainly did not want to tell her that Adonis was dead.

"We'll talk about it later. I gotta' run," he said.

"I know you are running out of time but please don't forget that shower," Roxie begged.

"Lock up, will you?" Titus asked as he walked toward the door with the unopened envelope.

"Again?" she said as Titus walked out the door. "I'm putting in for overtime pay, damn it," Roxie yelled to the closed door.

Titus took two steps at a time as he hurried down the stairs and out to his truck. He tossed the half open envelope into the passenger seat, buckled his seat belt, and started the engine. He wanted to know what was inside the envelope but he had to get ready for the game. His drive home took eight minutes.

He shaved and showered. He brushed his teeth twice and gargled with Listerine, full strength. Physical evidence of his trip out of town was erased except the cut above his eye. He patted it dry after the hydrogen peroxide stopped bubbling and pulled the gap tight with a butterfly bandage. He put gel in his hair and combed it into place.

Titus had never intended to make a fashion statement but he wore the same combination of clothes to every game. He took his bright green shirt off the hanger, tied the snow white tie into a knot, and slipped on the black jacket. He was making a statement that he was proud of the school colors. Dean Rayburn had suggested that his clothing seemed "a bit garish"; the criticism stopped after the first twenty-win season.

Titus was ready for work. He strapped on the watch and checked the time. He jumped into the Wagoneer and began a slow drive to the campus. There was no need to hurry; he had thirty-five minutes. Everything was going to be fine. He parked in his space and

440

looked at the envelope in the passenger seat. Titus grabbed it and took it with him into the gymnasium. As he entered the small office for the coaches, he saw Perry and Deon.

"Hey, Coach," Perry said.

"Hey guys," Titus countered.

"What's with the bandage?" Deon asked.

"I'll tell you later," Titus responded. "Any problems?"

"No. Everything's on schedule but I think a green bandage would have gone better with the ensemble," Deon quipped.

"Cute. I need a few minutes alone. Loosen the guys up. Alright?" Titus said.

"Sure," Deon said.

"No problem," Perry added.

The two assistant coaches left the office. Titus sat in the chair behind the desk. He pulled three pages from the large envelope.

The first page said, "You are going to let Dwight Timmons beat you."

It leapt off the page in large letters. Resentment raged as Titus stared at the bold headline. Eddie Dreyer was dead yet he was still trying to tell Titus how to coach.

"Fifty-nine wins in three years; I think I'm doing something right, Eddie!" Titus said to the ghost.

He turned the page and read page two.

"Timmons shot over the top of your zone in January and scored thirty three. He will do it again. He's a shooter. Pressure him. Make him work, and then give him the two point shot. The rest of the team will stand around as he tries to be macho and score. The pressure is a challenge, he cannot resist. He'll score twenty; you'll win the game."

"With all the shit on my plate, he wants me to think about Malone Danbridge all over again." Titus mumbled. "I can't wait for page three."

The third page was a short letter.

"Coach, I've been following the Rams since you arrived. It is a program turned around by one man. That man is you. Have you been lucky in recruiting? Yes. Have you won a few you shouldn't? Who hasn't? But the one common denominator is your passion for the game. You give it all. You want to win. It shows. I admire that. If you had been the head coach for the Cougars, when I disobeyed orders, you would have benched me. Barkley wanted my offense more than my respect.

441

The reason I have contacted you is because I want a job as your assistant. My bet is that Deon Haynes is moving this year. He wants his own gig. Perry Parker is a career assistant. He'll still be there when you move up.

My passion is dead. Somewhere along a path that included heavy drinking, gambling, and a whole bunch of things that seem dreamlike now, I killed it. I need it back. I am rededicating my life to the sport I love. I don't know what a normal life is but I can't live without basketball. It's not all I know; it's all I want to know.

I'm ready to start over. I have a lot to offer. Coach, I can help a talented kid be smart. I can make an average player better. I know how to create offense.

I'm making one last bet today. I'm betting the Rams straight up; which I believe will happen, if you hold Timmons to twenty points. If I lose, I'm broke and I am really going to need a job. If I win, then I will know I have judged you correctly, as a man who does what it takes to win and that's who I want to work for."

Titus did not need to read the letter twice. He pushed the pages back in the envelope, stood up, and paced the room. He checked his wristwatch. Coach Lockwood knew he should be on the court watching the pre-game warm-ups. Instead, he walked into the locker room, rolled a blackboard out, and began making his pre-game notes. As he wrote, a new thought came to him; he erased every word and line of chalk.

Moments later, the Rams filed into the locker room and began taking seats on the three benches. Coaches Haynes and Parker asked everyone to "Listen up." Anxious breathing and buzzing neon lights replaced the nervous murmuring and shuffling rubber shoes.

Coach Lockwood sat on the corner of a desk at the front of the room. His hands were resting on his thighs, his head was hanging, and his eyes were riveted to the floor. Everyone was waiting for him to speak. Ten seconds of silence was forever to twelve players waiting to start a championship ballgame. He made them wait thirty. Titus did not look up when he finally spoke.

"How many points did Dwight Timmons score on us last time? Anybody?" Titus asked as he stood and turned his back on the players to face an empty blackboard.

"Thirty-three," came a voice from his left.

"That's right. Thirty-three." Coach Lockwood wrote it on the board. Then he wrote the name *Eddie Dreyer* on the board and turned around.

"Eddie Dreyer," the coach said as he turned to face the team. "One of the smoothest college players, I've ever seen. Has anyone ever heard of him?"

No one spoke as Titus scanned the room slowly. He saw Coach Parker beginning to raise his hand.

"Coach Parker. Anyone else?" Titus asked; still no one spoke.

"He had a sweet shot, didn't he, Coach?" Titus asked Parker.

"The boy could drill 'em like bombs on Baghdad," Coach Parker said.

"Yeah, my dad said he was a lot like Pistol Pete, only stronger. Titus looked at Perry; Perry nodded back. "Eddie led the Southern conference in scoring three consecutive years but he doesn't play anymore. An injury made him mortal. Eddie finished without a championship," Titus said.

He turned and wrote "No Ring" to his blackboard list.

"There are two reasons why Eddie Dreyer never won a championship. One: Eddie believed he should control games at crucial moments. He talked team, team, team, until it was really tight, then it was Eddie, Eddie, Eddie. The second reason: his coach allowed him to play that way," Coach Lockwood explained.

He walked to the desk, picked up the envelope, and held it up. Every set of eyes looked at the coach as he held it up like an attorney brandishing Exhibit A.

"This is a letter from Eddie Dreyer. He asked me to hire him as an assistant coach," Coach Lockwood said.

"Eddie thought he could help me create better offensive players. Eddie wanted to find the best candidate among our crop and cultivate him into an end-of-the-game-take-charge guy."

Titus paused to let the words sink in. He purposely avoided eye contact with coaches Parker and Haynes as he continued to wave Exhibit A.

"Gentlemen, I would never hire a guy like Eddie Dreyer." Titus tossed the envelope back on the desk.

"I do this job for the same reason you play. You love to play and I love to see it played by teams. I'm not impressed with the Michael Jordan clear out strategy. I'm impressed when motion is achieved, screens get set, defenders get lost, and the open man gets the ball with a good look at the basket. To me, anything less than that, is just playground theatrics. Do it in the park; it doesn't belong on a hardwood floor." Titus raised his voice because he believed it, not because volume incites a team.

He paused and walked closer to his players, "But you guys, you're a team; that's what you are."

"Damn right," Titus heard someone say.

"I coach because I love the David and Goliath thing. Last year we lost the championship because a Goliath named Reilly wore us out while dropping thirty-five on us." Titus turned and walked back to the blackboard.

"And this year, we're David again. You know why the oddsmakers have made us the underdog? It's because we don't have a Goliath like Derrick Reilly, Dwight Timmons, or an Eddie Dreyer to take over at the end of the game."

Titus wrote "Timmons" on the board.

He turned to look at his players.

"We don't need one," he said and then repeated it with spacing between every word. "We do not need one."

With both hands, Titus pointed toward his chest and continued.

"I made a mistake; I thought we had to make these guys shoot below their average. I exhausted you in a piss-poor strategy," Titus said as he surveyed the room.

"I apologize. We are going to run the same defense but with a different strategy. I'll tell you why. When Timmons hits his average, their team averages sixty-eight points per game. We average seventy-five points per game." He went to the board and did the math. He circled the seven.

"Why should we create a game plan to stop Timmons? Right down the hall, their coach is telling them Team. Team. Team. But when they fall behind, it will be Timmons, Timmons, Timmons, and it is a flawed plan. As great as he is, he only hits forty-five percent of his shots and thirty percent of his three-pointers," Coach Lockwood said.

He walked over to the board and erased everything except the word "Ring." He turned to look at every player, one at a time.

"Coach Haynes, who's our leading scorer?" Titus asked without looking at him.

"The Open Man, Coach," Deon Haynes said without hesitation.

"Gentlemen, our leading scorer has a forty-eight percent shooting average. Get the ball to our leading scorer and the Ring is ours. All we have to do is take it," Titus said as he moved closer to the players.

"Are you ready to show Goliath what happens when team mates trust each other?" The coach asked in a control whisper.

The group jumped to their feet and growled a variety of responses. The players were ready to play. Coach Haynes ordered them to the court; they left the locker room like Rams butting their way through the door. Coach Parker walked out with Coach Lockwood.

"Coach, is that Eddie Dreyer stuff for real?" Perry asked.

"Eddie asked for a job but I didn't get the chance to turn him down. He was shot and killed on the highway this afternoon," Titus responded as they walked toward the court.

"Holy shit. Shot? With a gun?" Perry said.

"Let's talk later, Perry," Titus said as he remembered the pool of blood beneath Eddie's neck.

"Sure. Sure. We got a championship to win." Perry said as he slapped Titus on the back and took his place on the court.

Titus walked. He watched as Perry hustled to the bench. He watched the players standing around Coach Haynes, listening to his last minute reminders. He reached the scorers' table where he met Paul Glenn, the opposing coach. He extended his hand.

"How are you doing Paul?" Titus asked.

"Great, just great." Paul Glenn leaned closer to Titus." Have you heard? The local news is reporting that Eddie Dreyer was shot just outside of town today. Wasn't Dreyer with the Cougars, when you were there?" He asked.

"Yeah he was there. Great player." Titus said.

"I wonder what he was mixed up in."

"Beats me. I gotta' get over to the team. Good luck to you, Paul," Titus said.

"Yeah, same to you, Titus," Glenn responded as they shook hands.

Titus went to the huddled group waiting for him. He stuck his hand in the middle. Coach Haynes led a quick prayer, the players all yelled, "Rams."

The Patriots controlled the tip-off. Dwight Timmons gathered the ball and calmly drilled a long two-pointer. The rowdy hometown crowd yelled "Lucky shot" in unison. The orchestrated cheers lost favor when the Rams fell behind by eight.

# 120

Helen and her sister wept into drenched white handkerchiefs. It was a small somber and respectful group assembled for the funeral but the two sisters were the only ones shedding tears. Harmon held Helen's hand as she cried. The man in the black suit was preaching. He touched on short lives, the mystery of God's ways, and a heaven of no pain and suffering. He spoke of Jimmy's participation in Sunday School, the Choir, and his baptism as a young teen. He consoled the weeping sisters by saying Jimmy had gone home to the Lord. As the preacher finished with a prayer to the group of bowed heads; Harmon studied the casket and wondered who would fare better in paradise, Eddie Dreyer the manipulator or Jimmy Gerald the murderer.

The service ended and everyone mingled about, hugging and shaking hands and mumbling condolences. One by one, people drifted away from the gravesite. Car motors rumbled in the mid-morning sun and the attendees drove away. As Paula Gerald and Helen talked with a few close friends, Harmon watched as the casket was lowered into the hole. The sisters heard the whirl of the hoist and new tears crowded the strained handkerchiefs.

Harmon remained next to the entwined sisters because he wanted to be by Helen's side. He wanted her to know he would always be there for her. But his mind was on Eddie Dreyer. He felt sad for Helen and Paula but he could not muster any genuine emotion for Jimmy Gerald. Jimmy was a boy who snapped under a small amount of pressure. He was weak; the doomed are decidedly unlucky. But Eddie had the power to impact. The loss of Eddie Dreyer saddened Harmon. Helen spoke and broke his trance.

"Honey, I'm ready to go."

"You want to go back to Paula's for a while?" He asked.

"No. She wants to be alone."

"Are you sure? The house is going to be a painful place for her," he said even though the last thing he wanted to do was watch and listen to Paula mourn and potentially blame Harmon for Jimmy's confrontation with Eddie. A mother's first choice is blame anyone other than her baby.

"Yes, it will be awful for her but she wants to do it alone. Let's go."

Harmon and Helen strapped themselves into the Galaxy 500 and left the cemetery. They rode in an unsettling silence. Harmon wondered how soon it would be before Helen would talk about Jimmy snatched away in his youth or Paula dealing with the pain of a lost son or the avalanche of pain caused by Eddie Dreyer. Harmon preferred the silence but he expected it to end. He drove; he waited; he thought.

He watched the roadside blur by at seventy miles per hour and thought about Helen. For weeks, Harmon's thoughts had been on marriage and he had reached a decision. He wanted to marry her. Would she say yes? Every man wants to know the answer in advance. Helen was independent, skeptical, and set in her ways. Harmon figured his chances of getting a "yes" response to be fifty-fifty. A coin flip is flimsy protection for the ego.

"Thirty miles to Charleston," the sign read.

Harmon had played through so many proposal scenarios, he had forgotten most. He concluded that asking her in a public place under special circumstances would not pressure her into saying "yes." However, a spontaneous "Hey, let's get married" would be a messenger fated to die on the spot. Harmon was tired of thinking about it. He just wanted to get it over with. He propped his elbow onto the window ledge and leaned his head onto his open hand as though the weight of the decision was too much to bear. Helen saw the movement. It prompted her to break the silence.

"Deep in thought honey?"

"Yeah. There's a lot to think about," Harmon responded.

"I know what you mean," she moaned.

Harmon took his elbow off the window ledge and grabbed the wheel to free his right hand. He put his hand on her shoulder and gave her a gentle massage and smiled. He was sure they were not thinking similar thoughts.

"Life and death and destiny, how are we supposed to understand it all?" She asked.

"We can't." He answered.

He knew his response was simplistic. He wanted her to know he was listening but he did not want to talk about the mysteries of life and death.

"Maybe we can but we're too afraid to put it in perspective," Helen said.

"Maybe," Harmon said as he saw another distance sign.

*Man, I wish the next eighteen miles would fly by.*

"I mean, take destiny. Why are some people destined to die needlessly? Jimmy was not an abnormal boy. But he got caught up in Eddie's plan and now he's gone," she said.

Helen's words tapered into hopelessness. Harmon was willing to let them go.

"Do you think he was destined to die young?" Helen asked.

"No." Harmon said.

"Harmon, do you believe in destiny?"

Harmon did not answer. He stared down the highway hoping, that if he waited, she would move on. Hoping, she did not really expect an answer to the question.

"Harmon, did you hear me?" She asked.

"Yeah, darling. I heard you." Harmon answered. "No. No, I do not believe in destiny."

Harmon kept his eyes trained straight ahead.

"Really?"

"Really." He tried to sound uninterested.

"So there's no plan?" Helen asked as she turned in her seat. "If there's no plan, there's no planner. Are you telling me, that God has no plan?"

*Geez, I don't want to talk about this.*

Helen had discovered a distraction for her mourning.

"Honey, let's talk about this kind of stuff at another time." Harmon suggested.

"I just watched them put my only nephew in the ground. Death is on my mind right now. This seems like a perfect time to discuss the meaning of life. I'll go first. I believe there is a God and an afterlife. How about you?" Helen said.

Harmon could not avoid this discussion; Helen would persist until she got the truth.

"No God, no afterlife," Harmon said.

"I had no idea you felt that way. It's hard to believe that you haven't mentioned it in all the years we've known each other."

Harmon sat like a sphinx.

"Harmon, you've been to church with me dozens of times. If you don't believe, why do you go?" She asked.

"Because you asked me to go. Because it's not a big deal. Because I like being with you, in case you haven't noticed," Harmon answered.

"It's not a big deal?" Helen questioned.

Her shock sent a jolt through his body.

*Is this going to be the deal breaker?*

Harmon wondered if his fifty-fifty chance had shifted. He wanted to look into her eyes and give her his full attention. He could not navigate traffic and read Helen's face. He exited from the highway and pulled to a stop at a gas station.

"Don't make much of that, the point is, I don't see it as a waste of my time. The more I understand about what you believe, the more I can understand you." Harmon said.

"Wow. I always thought we would have a church wedding. I pictured us at the altar praying to the Lord to protect us and keep us together," she said.

"I promise," Harmon responded.

"You promise? Harmon, I will stand in the church and swear to God that I will honor the vows of marriage. Who are you going to swear to, yourself?" She asked.

Harmon looked into her eyes. She was not angry; she was sincerely confused by how a ceremony could be sanctioned, if only one believed in the sanctifier.

"Helen, honey, I will swear to you. You are the most important person in my life. My life has been narrowed to forty or fifty years. You are the foundation of that time. I want to share that time with you. Nothing can be more important to me," Harmon said as he reached across for her hand.

"Harmon, I love you but life is not a crapshoot. God brought us together," she told him.

*And God let Eddie abuse people and let Jimmy kill people.*

He pulled the curtain on the thoughts flashing through his mind.

"Maybe crap shoot is the wrong phrase. But all I know is that you're the first "Seven" life ever rolled for me. From where I stand, it feels like a lucky roll of the dice," Harmon said.

"You don't believe in God or Jesus but you do believe in luck?" She asked.

"Absolutely. And I'm on a lucky streak," Harmon said.

"How do you figure that?" Helen asked.

"You just asked me to marry you and I said yes," Harmon answered.

"Harmon, I did not ask you to marry me," Helen said as she straightened up.

"Sure you did. You swore to the Lord and everything," Harmon said as he turned the key in the ignition. The Galaxy 500 rumbled alive.

"You turn that engine off right now. You aren't driving off until this is settled. If I'm going to marry you, there are some rules that need to be clarified," she said.

Harmon shut the car down, took a deep breath, and turned in his seat to face her.

*I can't believe she still wants me.*

Harmon felt the pull of her brown eyes, eyes that would have shamed a puppy in a cute contest.

"Okay. Do I need to write this down?" He asked.

"No," she said. "Be assured; I'll remember them and I will remind you regularly."

*I know you will.*

He smiled and started the engine again.

# 121

Darren closed the door and sat down opposite the man with thick long gray hair. The Puka shells around his neck, a dagger tattoo on his forearm, and a t-shirt so threadbare, Columbia Lacrosse was barely visible. Carl Trenton pushed the lines of acceptability for newspaper editors much the way hitters kick away the chalk of a batter's box.

The man pulled the bifocals from his nose and tossed them on a pile of papers. There was no danger of the glasses breaking against something hard; the desk was covered with piles of papers, newspapers, and mail.

"Darren I cut it up so bad, I know you are going to hate it," Carl said.

"You mean you were unhappy with my style of reporting?" Darren asked.

"No. I mean, I cut it down to a small three inch column," he explained.

"Why? This is feature material," Darren claimed.

"It's interesting. It's well written. But it's also conjecture," Carl said.

"Conjecture? Eddie Dreyer bribed Jimmy Gerald. That's a fact. Jimmy Gerald shot Eddie. That's a fact. Dexter Dalton can testify that Eddie Dreyer set up Michael Pendleton. There must have been others." Darren ranted.

"Darren, read the column," Carl said as he tossed a sheet of paper to him.

Darren picked it up. He scanned the sentences.

"No, read it aloud," Carl instructed. "I want to hear it."

"Former Cougar basketball star, Eddie Dreyer died yesterday. The twenty three year old son of Pauline and David Dreyer of Greensboro, North Carolina was shot and killed on a highway in Arkansas. The shooter was Jimmy Gerald of Orangeburg, South Carolina.

451

The authorities have no explanation for the shooting. There is no evidence the two young men knew each other. Jimmy was emotionally distraught about being expelled from school for an incident during a Grizzlies basketball game.

"Jimmy told everyone, he regretted his actions during the basketball game. But obviously, something snapped. I had no idea his anger and embarrassment would cause harm to another human being and cost him his own life. My heart is broken and I cannot convey the sincerity of my apology to Mr. & Mrs. Dreyer," said Jimmy's mother, Paula Gerald."

"Where did this quote come from?" Darren asked.

"I got it from her. I called and told her we were writing a story about the death of Eddie Dreyer. I asked her if she had any idea why Jimmy would shoot Eddie. "No," was the answer. No matter how I phrased the question, she kept saying "No." That quote was the only thing she gave me permission to print," the editor said.

Darren leaned in and said, "According to my friend April Pyle, Harmon Evans managed to get Jimmy to confess that Eddie Dreyer had bribed Jimmy."

"Harmon Evans told me he had no knowledge of Jimmy's reasoning. He said he only met Jimmy a couple of times," Carl countered.

"Goddammit!" Darren said. "Harmon Evans is lying. This is a great story, Carl."

Carl did not react as Darren nearly screamed his plea. A ranting reporter was not uncommon in his office.

"I believe it is a great fuckin' story. But we need more than we have to print your version. The authorities have a solved crime. Why it happened is of no interest to them. If Michael Pendleton would confess to being bribed, then this story could be revived."

He watched Darren sulk and said, "Face it Darren. Neither of us is Perry Mason. He's not going to break down. He wants to stay in school and he knows Eddie is dead. The hooker might leak a little something for some cash. But we have no idea who she is," Carl lectured.

"This sucks," Darren said.

"It won't be the last time," Carl volleyed back.

"Great," Darren said as he stood to leave.

"Maybe you should turn this into a novel. It sure sounds like fiction," Carl said as he stood to follow Darren out the door.

"Maybe I should," Darren mumbled as he left the office.

# 122

Dexter rubbed the bar with the towel. It was not wet, but it kept his hands busy as he talked.

"Evidently, Darren is trying to write a story about Eddie. He named Harmon as a source. Harmon said the editor called and wanted to confirm information about Jimmy and Eddie's relationship."

"I assume Harmon admitted nothing," April said.

"Harmon told me there is no reason to investigate this any further. He said "Only a callous bastard would want to drag these kids through the mud just to create a headline," Dexter responded. "I agree."

"I guess so, but it seems a shame that Eddie wasn't punished," she remarked.

"Wasn't punished? He was shot through the neck and died at the hands of one of his victims," Dexter said while glaring at her in disbelief.

A patron from the middle of the bar yelled, "Hey Dex, two more Coronas, okay, and no lime."

"Excuse me. I'll be right back," Dexter said to April.

April spun around on her stool and looked around the room. Considering how many people are strapped down by jobs, classes, and marriages, Bluebeards was crowded for three o'clock in the afternoon. April spotted a foursome throwing darts. She watched as a thrower launched his dart with his eyes closed. He hit the center of the board.

"You lucky shit," one of the group screamed.

"Skill. It's pure skill. I'm blessed with radar," gloated the thrower.

"You're full of bullshit, that's for sure," said another.

"Let's go, pay up," the thrower said as he held out his hand.

April turned back toward the bar because the bell was ringing. Harmon was pushing money into the chest and the dart throwers were not the only patrons laughing. Dexter returned to April's position at the end of the bar.

"He really enjoys embarrassing people, doesn't he?" April asked.

"He enjoys taking money from assholes," Dexter replied.

"Harmon can give it but he doesn't like to take it," April said and sipped beer.

"What the hell are you talking about?" Dexter said.

"He likes to ride people and throw little insults at them but when they say something back, he gets mad and tries to embarrass them."

"That's not true. Harm likes funny people. It's the arrogant, snotty, know-it-alls and drunks who get rung up." Dexter said.

"Rung up? It's so queer that you guys have to create your own macho lingo to communicate." She giggled and shook her head.

"It's so hard to believe that you are single and devoid of prospects," Dexter said.

"I am single by choice, Dexter, by choice." April explained. "You said so yourself. I've looked around and I haven't seen anyone that I want to spend time on. And don't go getting mad because I said anyone," April said.

"No sweat April. I'm way over you. As a matter of fact, you don't deserve me," Dexter said.

He turned and listened as Lauren ordered four shots of Jose Cuervo and four beers. He filled the order quickly. Lauren walked away and Dexter watched. Reality vanished every time Lauren sashayed across the room.

The spell broke and Dexter turned back to the bar and saw April talking with two girls. His eyes were locked on the girl with short red hair and a tight red beaded necklace. She wore it halfway up her milky white neck. The second girl was stocky and wearing a navy colored polo shirt. Her arms were athletic and tanned.

Dexter walked past them to unload the dishwasher. The steam cleared and he placed the glasses in overhead hangers and the mugs on the shelf. He peeked through the steam at the girl with the red hair. He walked back toward April and the two girls. He hoped for an introduction; he got it.

"Dexter, this is Ursula and this is Jill. They live in the apartment across from me," April said.

"Hi. Can I get y'all something to drink?" Dexter asked.

Jill ordered a tap beer, Ursula asked for sweet tea, and April decided on a refill. Dexter watched as the girls talked and laughed. He delivered the drinks and collected money from Jill. She insisted on buying the round. He laid the change on the bar in front of Jill.

"Why do you look so familiar?" Dexter asked Jill.

"I don't know," she said.

Ursula cleared up the mystery. "She's the best golfer on the Cougar's team. Maybe you've seen her picture in the newspaper."

"Yeah, that's it. Holy crap you shot a sixty-eight at Mossbridge," Dexter said.

"I was putting well, that day," Jill said.

April reached for the new mug of beer. "So a sixty-eight is good?" She asked.

"No, a sixty-eight is great," Dexter answered.

Dexter walked away. Customers at the far end of the bar were summoning him. He mixed a rum-and-coke and a vodka tonic but Ursula divided his attention. He watched as she squeezed the lemon into her tea and stirred it in. He finished with the two customers, wiped down a section of the bar and worked his way back toward the girls.

He watched as the golfer put her finger on Ursula's beaded necklace. Dexter began to wonder about the relationship between Ursula and Jill. April said they live together. Ursula pushed the finger away just as Dexter reached the end of the bar.

"Dexter is loaded with opinions. Let's ask him," April said.

"Ask Dexter what?" He said.

"Does Ursula need to get out in the sun more?" Jill asked.

"Who thinks she should?" Dexter asked.

"I love her to death but I'm tired of looking at her pale naked body every day," Jill said.

April sat silent and Ursula looked annoyed. Dexter had no idea what to say. Ursula broke the silence.

"Dexter, don't pay any attention to her. She likes me just the way I am. If she didn't she wouldn't check me out so long, when I'm naked," Ursula replied.

Dexter was real confused. His biggest issue was trying to act cool while picturing Ursula naked. His second biggest concern was his bad luck.

*Ursula is gay; move on.*

He did not like the thought. Dexter looked at Ursula. He had to discover whether she was straight or gay. He re-joined the conversation.

"I suspect Ursula's tan does not deter her admirers. I bet her dating life is quite active," Dexter said fishing for clues.

He saw April snap her head up and stare at him. But Dexter kept his attention focused on Jill and Ursula.

"Really? Anything you want to tell me, Ursula?" Jill asked. "A sister has a right to know."

"This is why I don't go out with you. Your favorite activity is teasing me," Ursula said.

She stood up and moved two stools away in protest. April and Jill laughed.

"You and Jill are sisters?" Dexter said as he moved in front of Ursula.

"Unfortunately," she replied.

"Not for me," Dexter said with a huge smile.

"Dexter!" April squealed. "I'm surprised at you. On the make so soon after we split up."

"We were never together," Dexter said quickly as he stole a glance at Ursula to gauge her reaction.

"I'm Dex and I can't believe you have been on this campus all along and I haven't seen you. I'm not normally this forward but would you like to go see a movie this weekend?"

"The way you raved about my sister's golf score, I thought you were interested in her," Ursula said.

"Nope. I've been thinking about you from the minute you sat down. My first worry was that you were gay," Dexter said.

"Really? I look like a lesbian?" She asked.

"Not to me but the way you two were carrying on, I thought it was a possibility. And that would be about par for my luck. Get swept off my feet by a girl and find out she's gay."

"That's funny. You were half right; Jill is gay and she's got the hots for April," Ursula said in a very soft voice.

"Now that is funny," Dexter said.

"You think she has a shot? You think April might like girls?" Ursula asked.

"I'm not sure she likes anybody but avoid sports talk; she hates sports," Dexter advised.

"I'll clue her in," Ursula answered.

Dexter slung his bar towel over his shoulder, leaned across the bar, sat his elbow down and rested his chin on his fist.

"You know this seems like the classic subject change. By directing the conversation toward April and Jill, you don't have to answer my question," Dexter said.

"You mean the question about whether or not I would go out with someone I just met five minutes ago," Ursula asked.

"Yeah, that's the one."

"You bet; I'll go out with you, Dex," Ursula said.

She used a small smile to seal the deal.

"Finally a lucky day," Dexter exclaimed. "The losing streak is over."

"You've been asking girls out and all of them say, 'No?' Ursula asked.

"No. I mean unlucky karma is all around me," he said.

"Oh, kinda' like the way Chipper Jones feels when he and Sheff are hitting but the Braves are losing?" Ursula said.

Dexter stood with his mouth open. His eyes blinked as he stared at her. He could not believe what he had just heard. He was prepared to make numerous comments but all of them seem inappropriate to describe the way he felt.

"That's it exactly. A Braves fan? You put the sweet spot on the ball. This is so my lucky day."

Dexter walked down to the end of the bar. He reached across like he wanted to whisper something to April. She leaned over. He grabbed her by the back of the head and planted a kiss on her lips.

She gave him a huge smile and said, "What's the matter with you?"

"Absolutely nothing. I want to thank you, April. If I hadn't hung in there trying to win you over, I might never have met Ursula. This may drain my pot of luck but I know a good bet when I see one," Dexter said and walked back to the stool Ursula occupied.

April sat there stunned. She initially wore a smile but it faded. Jill reached over and touched her hand.

"April, are you okay?" She asked.

She looked at Jill's tanned strong hand sitting atop hers.

"I'm fine but Dexter is an odd boy."

"Aren't they all?" Jill said with a smile.

# 123

The clink of silverware against plates played like a symphony, a little joy that continued to enliven the moment for Powers Meade. A city inside an air-conditioned building, the Paris Hotel and Casino was his favorite spot for breakfast. Outdoor seating in an indoor environment permitted him to be separate from the throngs seeking the pot at the end of the rainbow. He could enjoy "three-minute eggs" and watch the ants scurry about as he read the morning newspaper.

Powers sat his knife across his fork in an X alignment. He dabbed at his face with his napkin, folded it and placed it atop the plate. The server arrived and removed the dishes. He respectfully wished Powers "a good day" and left the check on the table. Powers reached into his pocket and dropped a twenty on the bill and left.

As Powers strolled the floor, a single betting chip rotated cross his fingers like an amateur magician might practice dexterity. It was a one hundred dollar chip. It slipped out of his hand; he bent over to pick it up.

Last night, Powers played blackjack at the one thousand dollar table. He lost ninety thousand dollars. The single chip was all he had left from the blackjack table. His cushion was exhausted. He was near broke. There was less than eight hundred dollars in his bank account and Eddie's money. He knew not to touch Eddie's money. He knew Eddie would come for the money; it was just a question of when.

Yet it never occurred to Powers to panic. He would not be thrown on the street; the last wise thing he did was pay cash for the condo. He had no outstanding bills. He had mailed his paper and resume to the university.

*A job will come.*

In the meantime, he would ration his expenditures. He continued to fidget the chip in his hand.

Amongst a backdrop of dreamers, Powers strode toward the cashiers cage. He tossed his single chip onto the counter. The woman whisked it away with the same cold stroke employed by the dealer at the blackjack table; she replaced it with five twenty-dollar bills. Powers folded the money in half and pushed it into his pants pocket.

He heard the mechanical chant "Wheel Of Fortune." He turned to see the woman smack the Spin Wheel. It spun around and stopped on one hundred. The woman screamed and the machine began spitting coins into the metal bin. Powers wondered if the slot machines could change his luck.

He walked into the High Stakes Slots room and spied a Wheel Of Fortune game. He unfolded the twenties and fed them all into the machine. Ten dollars per pull but the Bonus Wheel was active only with a maximum bet. Maximum it shall be. He hit the button and watched his thirty dollars stop on an orange, a lime and a lemon. He hit the button again. He got a different crop but the same results. Sixty dollars had disappeared. Powers hit the button again. He did not hear the mechanical voice of jubilation and he would not hear coins clanging loudly in the metal bin. Powers stared at the machine; he had ten dollars left in the machine. A single ten-dollar pull would not multiply his wealth but it seemed insincere to cash out.

Powers felt the vibration in his pocket before he heard the ringing. He reached into his pocket to answer his cell phone.

"This is Powers Meade."

"Powers, it's Jim."

"Hi Jim. Can you give me five seconds?" Powers said as he returned his gaze upon the machine.

"Sure," Jim answered.

Powers reached over, pulled the handle and then returned the phone to his ears.

"Okay. Sorry, Jim. How are you?" He said as he watched the machine spin. A cherry stopped in the first box.

"I'm doing great. I'm starting to think about how to spend the summer?" Jim said as Powers watched the second box fill with a cherry.

"Wondering if you and the little lady can come visit me?" Powers said as a bright yellow Lemon laughed at Powers from box three.

"No, but thanks for offering," Jim responded.

Powers was not really listening.

"It's just not my day," Powers mumbled.

"What? Are you talking to me?" Jim asked.

"No, I apologize. I was talking to a slot machine."

"It's early on a Wednesday morning, Powers!"

459

"So, you called to verify time and date?" Powers asked.

"No. I called to tell you Eddie Dreyer is dead."

"What? What did you say?" Powers stood from his stool and pressed the phone tighter to his ear.

"I read about it in the newspaper. Some distraught kid shot him. He was driving on a highway in Arkansas and this kid fired several bullets into his window. The shooter had a fatal crash as well," Jim said.

"How very, very bizarre," Powers responded.

"I thought you would want to know."

"Absolutely. Thanks Jim but I do not know what to say or think, for that matter," Powers explained.

"Listen, I will call you after exams. We can catch up then," Jim said.

"Yeah, sounds good. Bye Jim." Powers said as he closed his phone.

He walked out of the High Stakes room and back among the din of dreams. Powers was filled with one single thought. Eddie Dreyer will not be coming for his money.

*I'm no longer broke.*

Powers walked to the nearest ATM and withdrew five hundred dollars. The machine spit out five one hundred dollar bills. Powers walked back to the High Stakes room and sat back down at his Wheel Of Fortune game. He fed the five hundred dollars into the machine and hit the maximum bet wheel; the spin was a loser. He hit it again and lost again. He hit it a third time and this time the Special Spin Wheel stopped in box three. "Wheel of Fortune" the machine screamed.

Powers did not notice the other people turn their heads to watch his free spin. He hit the extra spin wheel and tilted his head up to watch it turn. It came to rest on a thousand; the highest number on the wheel. The machine began to ring and a red light began to flash overhead. An attendant walked over and stopped the noise. He pushed a few buttons and handed Powers a receipt for his winnings. He took the paper to the cashier's cage. He won ten thousand dollars on a ninety-dollar investment. Powers was pleased.

Powers decided to stroll home and get some rest. As he walked, he thought about Eddie Dreyer. Professionally, Powers had concluded that Eddie would never be happy because he could not trust anyone. He was driven to be in control. Yet, his skill, intelligence, ambition, and cold-blooded soul were not enough to maintain control. Even with ruthlessness as a weapon, Eddie could not control every unfolding event.

*If Eddie could not control life. It cannot be done.*

It had been a while since Powers spent time in deep philosophical thought. Powers never agreed that 'the meek shall inherit the earth' and it seemed that the ruthless lacked the correct formula as well. To Powers, it now seemed there would be no inheritance; there would be a repetitive struggle. The rise and fall would continue throughout time. The line would be crossed and someone or some empire would fall.

Powers remembered hours of discussions with his collegiate cohorts about the ultimate plight and evolution of man. Powers had always faked interest. At last, he knew why; it bored him and it was a waste of time. Now, more than ever, Powers was convinced life is a crapshoot. Life is the dice bouncing past the chips, praying hands and gaping eyes. The dice roll will be a winner for someone; it will be less arousing for others.

Powers quickened his pace. He wanted to get to his laptop and record some of these thoughts to be expanded later. Why does philosophy ostracize luck? Why is it good and evil or right and wrong? Why do human traits carry so much weight?

Talent is not bulletproof. Intelligence is not immune to runaway ego. Strength bows to balance. Dedication elevates some from mediocrity to the debt-laden middle class. No matter how good you are, or how hard you work, there is somebody better or somebody working harder. And there is always somebody luckier.

He expanded that one out loud, "Lucky exists and you cannot game plan for it. Good and bad, it exists."

Powers wanted to engage his former colleagues in discussion. His head was crowded with topics. He wanted to hear their arguments; Powers wanted to hear them dispel good luck.

He opened the door to the condo and went straight to his desk. He typed all of the ideas he could recall from the walk.

Powers rose from the chair and opened the liquor cabinet. He poured a generous portion of Whisky. He held it high.

"Here's to you Eddie. You are gone but the money is still here. You put your trust in yourself. I will put my trust in good luck."

Powers drank to his toast. He stood holding the empty glass high in the air. He felt a slight grin slink back onto his face.

Powers said, "Eddie, if there is an afterlife, it is only logical that I should expect a settling of scores. Maybe that's where I will experience an equal share of bad luck and maybe pain. Maybe. Well I have chosen. And I can live with that. Because, right now, in this life, bad luck died in Arkansas and left me three hundred and sixty three thousand dollars with no one to dispute my claim. Morbid as it may sound today, that is a clear picture of good luck."

Powers knew the eulogy was disrespectful but he could not assemble words for an apology. It was after all how he actually felt.

He drank the last swallow and said, "So be it."

He sat his glass in the sink and went to bed.

# 124

"Your Uncle David said Eddie wanted you to have it."

Ben Dreyer opened the laptop and stared at the screen. His mother reached over his shoulder and hit the Power button. She kissed the top of his head and walked out of the room. It looked like any other laptop computer except this one had been riding in the car where his cousin Eddie had died. Ben had been told it was the top of the line and should not be wasted. Ben took it because it was super fast. Ben watched as the machine quickly ran through the power-up sequences but he viewed it as though the ghost of Eddie was watching him. Ben was not short on imagination.

Ben was not close to his cousin Eddie. Eddie was six years older and an athletic legend. Ben did not possess the athletic gene. Ben's sole passion in life was comic books. He created characters, drew them, and wrote stories about them. Art and English were the only subjects in which he excelled. Although he had not given his parents the full story, Ben intended to camp at the doorstep of Marvel Comics until they gave him a job. He did not care what kind of job. He just knew he wanted to be part of that world. His parents, both college graduates, were very displeased that Ben had no intention of going to college in the fall. They knew his grades would limit his choices but still they felt he should try.

The log-in screen appeared and the sound of a crowd roaring filled the bedroom. Basketball sound effects. Ben pressed the key to bypass the password-protected box. A referee whistle sound meant Ben could not bypass the screen.

"Those sounds will be the first thing I change," he said.

His uncle had told him the passwords might be a problem. Ben had a plan to remedy that problem as well. Ben's friend Hugh was on his way over. Hugh would be entering MIT in the fall and he thought he could set up a software program to work on guessing the password. Hugh promised to not explain what he was doing and Ben promised to not tell him about his latest superhero. The two boys got along well because Ben was the only person who could beat Hugh at chess. Hugh's blood pressure went off the charts every time he lost.

"There is no logical explanation for how you continue to beat me. I'm the Chess Club President, for Christ's sake," he would complain.

Ben heard his mom say, "Ben, Hugh's here."

"Ok," he answered.

He met Hugh on the stairs; they went to his room. Hugh loaded a CD into the drive. He asked a few questions about Eddie; Ben answered to the best of his knowledge. The two boys left the program to run and went downstairs for a snack. Ben's mom baked daily. The smell of chocolate was in the air. They had pie and talked about graduation activities. They cleaned up their dishes and went back to Ben's room. The program had quit running. Hugh looked at the details; it had only run for four minutes. It had found the password, "EddieD22."

"Wow; that was amazingly easy. Jocks can be so un-complex," Hugh said.

"I can't believe it. First name, last initial, and his jersey number. I guess no one tried very hard to get in," Ben said as he typed in the password and clicked OK.

The sound of a roaring crowd and the swish of a basketball net filled the silence.

"Basketball sound effects? That's lame," Hugh said.

"I know, right? I'm disabling those right now." Ben replied.

"Yeah, but the sad thing is you'll replace them with "Zap, Pow, and Holy Joker Batman," Hugh responded with the roll of his eyes and a shaking of his head.

"Listen Geek, you have only have one friend as it is; don't push your luck," Ben went on the offensive.

"Soon I will be surrounded by people just like me," Hugh said with a smug smile.

"Yeah, they should put a fence around the place," Ben said.

"Whatever, Bat Boy," Hugh countered. "I gotta' go. You want me to leave the program, in case you run into some other protected files?"

"Yeah. Thanks," Ben answered.

Hugh showed Ben how to start the program and left. Ben disabled the sound effects and began deleting stuff that he did not need in the computer. While exploring, Ben found much more than he ever imagined. He used the program to uncover "ego" as a password to six

Internet Betting Sites. Each of the sites had a positive balance. Ben put the numbers in a calculator and the total was three hundred and sixty three thousand dollars. He just stared at the number. It was as though the number would not sink into his mind.

He spoke the number out loud, "$363,000."

Ben heard his mother call for dinner. He went down and quickly ate the chicken meal. His parents carried on a conversation about the weather and something about traffic. As always, they quizzed Ben to assess his awareness of current events. His answers seem to pass muster even though what he really wanted to discuss was Eddie's computer. But he finished his dinner without any conversation about his new treasure.

His urge was to rush up the stairs but he kept his demeanor in check. Ben did not want them to come up and check out his new laptop. Once inside he closed and locked his door. A wiggle of the mouse and he was exploring again. His next discovery was a journal.

Ben blinked his eyes and scrolled back to the top. He was stunned; his cousin was blackmailing people. He began re-reading the journal. Eddie did not name anyone. The journal chronicled how he had pressured, hurt, browbeat, bribed and abused people to affect the outcomes of basketball games. Eddie described in detail the psychological pressure he put on his victims. He exalted some who did not buckle and criticized those that did. His words were cold. It was clear to Ben that Eddie believed his actions were acceptable.

*No one should believe this is acceptable.*

Ben also discovered a file labeled Shrink. Inside the file were assertions and questions about a professor named Powers Meade. Eddie asserted that during hypnosis, the doctor planted suggestions that made Eddie place bets at a specific website. Eddie alleged the doctor mirrored those bets and made a lot of money.

Eddie wrote, "I estimate he could have made over a half a million dollars off of my bets. I can't prove he used me and I don't know if any of the money is left but I will find out."

He read where Eddie had recorded an address in Las Vegas, Nevada for the shrink.

Ben read where Eddie had vowed to stop gambling and start Coaching. He hoped to convince a Coach in Arkansas to give him a chance. His name and address at the University was in the journal.

Lastly Eddie wrote his concerns with finding Powers Meade. He worried that the shrink might have moved and left no trace of his whereabouts. Eddie had only a limited time to find him if he was going to truly commit to a change. He could not spend a lifetime hunting Powers Meade. He recorded the name Colt Gavin. A former teammate who was in FBI training the last Eddie heard from him. Eddie thought he might be able to help find Powers Meade as a last resort.

"Can he help without prosecuting me?" He had written.

At the funeral, Ben's parents and other relatives and friends were discussing the details of Eddie's death and they wondered what Eddie was doing in Arkansas. It was obvious to Ben that Eddie was there to meet this Coach who might give him a job and then he would go to Las Vegas to find the shrink, Powers Meade.

It was after midnight, and Ben had reached overload. He exited the programs and closed the lid on the laptop. He turned off the light and lay down on his bed. Ben closed his eyes but he was still in disbelief with all he had discovered. His legendary cousin was a gambler, involved with a shrink, and blackmailed people for a living. It played in his mind like a scrolling New Alert on television. Yet Ben could not ignore that a large sum of money was being held by some shrink in Las Vegas. Money that should not belong to him.

*The shrink does not deserve it.*

He opened his eyes. The moonlight filtered through the open blinds casting shadows like jail cell bars on the wall. He was tiring but his imagination was stirring in the background. Ben's brain could not stop thinking about Eddie trying to turn his life around and the shrink spending Eddie's winnings.

"Why shouldn't I collect Eddie's money?" Ben said to the moonlit ceiling. That money would help me out a lot."

Ben struggled to remain calm as his brain seemed to throb. The throbbing was so loud he was afraid it could be heard outside his room. His thoughts were besieged with imagination, curiosity, providence, and greed.

Ben said, "No one knows about this except me. I could have the money and expose the shrink who thinks he gets to walk around scot free."

Ben began to imagine a new Marvel character based on Eddie and a villain based on the shrink. He pictured pages of frames with the two adversaries confronting each other. Eddie making amends for the wrongs he had inflicted. While the shrink constantly crossed the line and erased it behind him.

"Powers of the mind versus Powers of the heart," he themed.

Ben was fading in and out. Sleep would eventually control the darkness but at dawn, all bets would be off.

# 125

FBI agent, Colton Gavin put on his rubber gloves and opened the large envelope and allowed the contents to fall to his desk. He looked at the rough pages stapled together. He snapped his head up and looked around the room. Dozens of Agents were doing their jobs and no one was sneaking a peek at him. As a new agent, he had been on high alert for months. He was certain at some point a prank would take place at his expense. There had always been hazing during his twelve years of competitive athletics. He expected no less here.

He picked up the colorful document. It was a comic book. Not a finished and published comic book. It was hand drawn and hand written. He picked up the envelope and peeked inside for a note. There was nothing inside, nothing to explain why this book had been sent to his desk.

He began to read the introduction. "A star basketball player is seduced by the evils of gambling. He becomes a blackmailer who fixes games and profits from the fix. He is discovered, shot and killed."

Colton paused; a slight shudder ran through his blood.

*Could this be about Eddie Dreyer?*

Colton had received an email from Eddie weeks ago. All it said was, "You owe me, right? Let Ben be. I'll consider it debt paid." He knew the debt Eddie was referring to but Ben was an unknown to Colton.

Agent Gavin was convinced this story book had something to do with Eddie Dreyer. The coincidence was too strong. He continued reading the colorful document.

"In the afterlife, the player is given the opportunity to go back to Earth and atone for his sins. He is told there is an evil man masquerading as a Psychologist preying on people and taking their money. This offender is named Powers Meade. Find him, capture him and bring him to this place and your salvation will be granted."

Colton took his personal iPad from his briefcase and googled Eddie Dreyer. He found the story. He read where the killer was identified and that it was a closed case. There was no record of motivation or motive. Nor was there any initiative to examine motive. It seemed a little odd to Colton but not reason for investigation.

He returned his attention to the Story Book. He read the panes and examined the drawings of the former basketball star confronting and battling the Psychologist. He finished. He was convinced it was not a prank. The drawings were too intricate. This had to be the efforts of someone talented and someone who wanted the FBI to investigate Powers Meade. That seemed obvious to Colton.

He swiveled his chair in front of his keyboard and typed Powers Meade.

*Okay, shrink; what's your connection to EddieD?*

The last known address appeared as Las Vegas, Nevada. No known employer. Recent Tax Returns show income from Gambling. Colton made a few more notes and returned to the computer. Several more keystrokes and he located Benjamin Alan Dreyer. Cousin to Eddie and his last known address in Greensboro. He recorded the information. And went back to Powers Meade.

"Let's dig a little deeper, Mr. Lucky and see what we can find."

# 126

Powers took the cell phone from his ear and exited the taxi. He stood on the sidewalk and looked at the house. He had hoped there would be a rush of memories to gladden his heart. There was not. He had returned to Charleston to the only possessions he still owned. His house was here but the incubator, the protective womb was missing. It was just the next property he would lose.

He opened the door and stood in the doorway; it had changed. The students who had lived here had left their mark. Holes in the walls from posters. Spills had stained the floors. Walls had been painted garish colors. Powers was disappointed but not brokenhearted. A broken heart can only occur when genuine affection and connection are felt. Powers could not recall ever experiencing an affection deep enough to leave a permanent scar.

The sound of a car snapped his thoughts. He turned and saw a woman getting out of her car and walking up the sidewalk. She had a big smile on her face and her hand was extended for introductions.

"Patty Wager", she said and handed him a business card.

Powers shook the hand while looking at the business card.

"You can bet on me?" He said reading from the card.

"You sure can. I've sold 5 houses on this street," she said still brandishing the big smile.

"Well, come on in and take a look around. Students have been renting the place. It doesn't look as good as it once did," Powers said.

She went in and began dictating notes into her iPad and snapping pictures. They talked after her tour and agreed to terms. The house would be listed the next morning. Powers walked into the backyard still searching for the fond memories to wash over him.

Instead his mind was stuck on the carousel of events that lead to this backyard today. It was three weeks ago that he received the envelope with the crude comic book. The comic came with a not so funny note.

"Send the $363,000 to this address within 5 days or I send the whole story to the FBI. Including the part where you ran an illegal gambling site."

Powers went into full blown panic. Someone knew the story. He wrote a check for $320,000 and sent it to the address given with a note that said, "This is all there is. Now, please leave me alone!"

He called the best known Realtor in Las Vegas and listed the Condo for $90,000, less than half what he paid for it. The market was bad and he wanted to cash out as fast as he could. It sold for $80,000. He had to be out in 2 weeks. Just before he left, he received another envelope from the anonymous thief who took Eddie's money. The note inside said, "I sent the comic book to the FBI anyway. It's time you dealt with a little bad luck."

Powers remembers screaming, "Fuck!" as loud as his voice could yell.

He took his money, left no forwarding address, arranged to meet the Charleston Realtor and get whatever he could for his house. She seemed to think pricing it at $275,000 should get him $250,000. He would pay off the bank and realtor and net $35,000. Powers would disappear with about $115,000. The details beyond now were non-existent. He would consider options as soon as he had time.

The rental company truck pulled into the driveway. Fifteen minutes later he had a bed and a chair. The delivery truck drove away. Powers looked at the bargain priced accommodations and hoped the sell would go quickly.

Powers went for a walk. He headed toward the campus instinctively. And forty five minutes later he strolled across the grounds. He walked past students and familiar landmarks. Some sentimental feelings tiptoed across his mind, not many. Powers spied a landmark which brought a smile, Bluebeards.

He walked across the street and through the door. He stood momentarily, removed his Ray-Ban sunglasses, and walked to the far end of the bar. He ordered a tap beer and pulled his cell phone from his pocket to check email. Junk, junk, and 4 more rejections.

Four days before he had received the demands of the thief who took Eddie's money, Powers sent resumes to seventy five universities. He had received forty eight rejections counting these four. Getting a job without the recommendation of his former employer was proving to be a difficult task. Not that it mattered anymore.

Powers was certain that the FBI was poking into his whereabouts in Las Vegas.

*Surely the FBI will find me with their vast resources.*

He briefly flirted with the hope that the thief who took Eddie's money was bluffing. How could this person expose Powers with exposing himself? However, it was not a gamble he was willing to take.

Powers laid the phone on the bar and tilted the beer glass to his mouth. He noticed Harmon Evans at the other end of the bar. Harmon eventually noticed Powers and walked his way.

"Professor, I haven't seen you in quite some time. How are you?" Harmon asked forgoing the handshake formality.

"I am well and how about you?" Powers said feeling an unusual amount of sincerity in his response.

"Doing great. Business is great," he replied.

"Are you back for good?" Harmon asked.

"No. I just came to town to sell my house," Powers explained.

"Really. Where you headed?" Harmon asked.

"Not sure," he answered. He could see the puzzled look on Harmon's face. "I know it sounds unlikely but I really have not decided where I want to go."

"Must be nice to have that luxury," Harmon replied.

Powers gave a little shrug of his shoulders without answering. He had no desire to try and detail the shortcomings of his so called luxury.

Harmon asked, "Where's the house?"

"Small house couple of miles from here on Montagu." Powers told him.

"Really? How much you want for it?" Powers asked.

"Do you know someone in the market for a house?"

"Maybe. I'm getting married this fall and I would like to have something close to here but not on top of Bluebeards. Montagu would be good for me." Harmon explained.

"Well, it will be listed tomorrow morning for $275,000." Powers said confidently while trying to read Harmon's face for a reaction.

"Let's go look at it," Harmon said.

"Are you serious?" Powers asked. "Right now?"

Harmon said, "Are you serious about selling?"

"Alright but you'll have to drive. I walked over here." Powers answered and finished his beer.

Harmon yelled at someone named Dexter and told him to watch the bar. They slid into Harmon's car and drove by Helen's house. Powers stayed in the car.

471

"Nice car; I do miss my Thunderbird," he lamented.

Powers watched as Harmon talked to Helen. It was clear to him that this was not something Helen and Harmon had discussed previously.

After five minutes of pointing, hands on hipping, and head shaking, they came walking toward the car. Powers opened the door to offer the front seat to her.

"Stay seated, professor. I'll hop in the back," she said and did.

They drove to the house and everyone got out of the car. Powers rushed ahead to open the door. As he did, he turned to tell them that it had been rented to a few students for a while and could use a little sprucing up. They went in.

Powers began to explain the layout when Helen raised her hand in a stop sign fashion. Powers shut up. He decided to sit on the front porch. Ten minutes later they came back to the front porch together.

"We will give you $240 for it," Helen said.

"That's very generous," Powers told her as he stood.

"However, my realtor assures me I will get $250."

"Cut the real estate commission out of the equation and $240 is a better deal than that," Helen said. "$240 and we will Close whenever you want."

Powers could not resist the immediacy of the deal and accepted the offer. They drove to Harmon's Attorney's office to get the deal started. They scheduled a date to close in fourteen days. Helen and Harmon dropped Powers at the house and joked with him about not tearing it up in the next two weeks. They drove away.

Powers called Patty Wager and said he would not need the listing and explained what happened. He hung up and thought how well all the details were proceeding. Condo sold. Thunderbird Sold. Bank Account emptied. And Now House Sold. It was time to decide; what would he do now? His phone rang. It was Jim.

"Powers, I just got off the phone with the FBI. They called me looking for you. They are coming over to my house tomorrow morning to ask me some questions. What have you done, Powers?"

"Jim I am sorry they have bothered you but I need to go. Bye," Powers uttered and ended the call.

"The thief that took Eddie's money was not bluffing," Eddie said as he paced the room.

Powers Meade was terrified. He knew Jim would tell them everything. He cannot lie to the FBI.

472

"The FBI could be on the way here right now," he said while looking at the window.

Powers called a taxi. He had decided it was time to leave. The driver arrived 15 minutes later.

"Bluebeard's Bar," Powers told him and slid into the back seat.

He dialed Harmon and explained that he had to leave and wanted a check from Harmon for the house. After a brief explanation. It was clear he would not get the money this quickly. He redirected the Taxi driver.

"Take me it the airport," Powers said.

Twenty minutes later, Powers exited the taxi and paid the driver. He walked into the terminal and began looking at the departing flights.

# 127

Agent Colton Gavin got out of the blue Dodge that had been following the Taxi and walked toward the Airport Terminal. Two Agents followed him. They spotted Meade reading the Flight Schedule. They walked to his side and Agent Gavin identified himself and the other Agents. They told Powers Meade he was under arrest and read a list of charges. One of the Agents put handcuffs on the suspect.

The agents watched as Meade stared at the handcuffs and did not speak. He did not answer questions posed to him. He just kept looking at the handcuffs. It appeared as though Meade could not comprehend what was happening. Colton did not want to mess this one up. Agent Colton Gavin repeated the Miranda to be sure Meade heard the words. They led Meade back to the blue Dodge. An Agent started the engine and began the drive to the district office.

Suddenly, Powers Meade spoke, "Eddie always said, Betting against him was gambling. The sonofabitch was right. I should have listened. Even from his grave he had a plan for me. A comic book; hilarious."

Colton turned to look at him. Their eyes met.

Meade raised his voice and said, "Powers of the mind versus Powers of the heart. I loved that one."

He was shaking his head from side to side and then he stopped and looked at directly at Colton.

"What do you think? Did I win or did Powers of the heart win," Meade said to him. "Keep in mind, Powers of the heart is dead."

He began shaking his head with a subtle left to right swing.

Meade said, "A comic book."

He continued, "Not even a good comic book. I mean, no one had super powers. Come on."

Agent Gavin turned back to face the front windshield. He was processing the mental stability of Powers Meade. He wondered if it was truly like what he had just witnessed. One minute a man is rationally trying to find a flight and then, snap, he is a babbling loon.

*Has this dude lost it? Has he crossed the line or is this a strategy to seem nuts?*

Deep inside Colton knew it was not a strategy. Based on the investigation Colton had conducted, Powers Meade never bothered to develop a strategy. It appeared he just bounced along the path before him. Why would he suddenly think he could create a strategy on the fly?

No. Colton was looking at a man who was facing reality. It was a new reality to Powers Meade. A reality without alternatives. Powers Meade had just learned that bad luck is just as real as good luck.

Colton decided he would answer the question posed to him from Meade. He turned to face him.

"Mr. Meade," he said.

Colton waited on Meade to face him.

"Powers of the heart won. Yes, Eddie Dreyer is dead but you're going to jail. Eddie arranged that. His strategy was successful." Colton paused, and then asked, "What is your strategy, Mr. Meade. Are you still planning on good luck to set you free?"

Agent Colton Gavin grinned and fixed an icy stare into the eyes of Powers Meade until the man buckled and turned his head to look out the side window.

Silence once again from Meade. He continued to stare out the side window. Agent Colton Gavin turned to face the windshield.

He lifted the cover to his iPad and opened the file for Benjamin Alan Dreyer. He stared at the photo taken of the young man carrying his portfolio into the Marvel Corporate headquarters. He studied the photo and Ben's file without actually thinking about anything. He just stared. Colton shifted his eyes to a second photo of the "known associate," Hugh Sheffield as he walked across the campus of MIT.

He changed the screen to look at Ben and thought he could see a slight resemblance to Eddie. Colton looked out his side window and remembered his playing days with Eddie. Basketball scenes were screening through his mind at lightning speed.

A noise from the back seat brought him back into the blue Dodge. Colton snuck a peek at Meade. He was still staring out the side window. Still silent and still beaten.

Colton returned his attention to the file. He opened the menu over the boys file and without hesitation he deleted it. The file disappeared.

*Betting against EddieD is gambling.*

Colton closed the iPad cover and stared at the road ahead.

19102282R20262

Printed in Great Britain
by Amazon